BLURB

Returning to Cedar Cove, Maine, wasn't on my bingo card for this year or, well, any year. This town is less "quaint seaside charm" and more "where all my worst memories live." But my grams took a bad fall, so here I am back where my parents and my first love were murdered a decade ago. A real Hallmark homecoming.

I barely unpack before another murder rocks the town, on the exact anniversary of the one that wrecked my life. I'd say I'm here to help, but honestly? It's my journalist instincts that won't let me walk away. Cedar Cove's new sheriff, Jack Mercer, thinks I'm in over my head. He's infuriatingly good-looking, disarmingly nice, and doesn't seem half as grumpy around me as he does around everyone else. Annoying.

Then there's Reed. He's tall, dark, and unsettlingly similar to Rhett - the type of guy I should be avoiding at all costs. Now I've got two men in my life: One who's paid to keep the town safe, and another who's setting off every alarm in my head. Both of them are hiding something, and if history is any indication, trusting the wrong person here could be lethal.

In Cedar Cove, love can be murder. And if I'm not careful, I might be next.

Cover Design by Haya

Edited and Formatted by Represent Publishing

TELL Me SOMETHING

Charli Cotner

RP Represent Publishing

DEDICATION

For the women who can't resist a bad boy with a dark side . . . or a charming gentleman who knows all the right moves. Welcome to Cedar Cove, where love is a game, war is inevitable, and murder? Well, that's just an unfortunate plot twist.

CONTENT WARNINGS

Murder

Gun violence

Explicit sexual content (18+)

Themes of loss and grief

WELCOME TO
CEDAR
Cove
FISHER'S BOOKSHOP
PINE HARBOR
CEDAR COVE
POLICE STATION
LENNON'S HOUSE
CALLAHAN'S HOUSE
SHORELINE SIPS
SAM'S GROCERY
CEDAR COVE DINER
BIRCH HAVEN WOODS
JACK'S HOUSE

CHAPTER 1

Lennon

Whoever coined *"Don't be such a worrywart"* clearly never met Lillian Harrington. My grams didn't just worry—she *mastered* it. Anxiety wasn't her shadow; it was her lifelong partner, spinning her through sleepless nights and turning overthinking into an art form.

Maggie, my best friend, isn't far behind. Same relentless worry, just with more glitter.

"Promise me you'll text the second you get there, okay?" Her plea lingers in the cab like thick summer air—heavy and inescapable.

"I will." I try for conviction, for authority, but the slight tremor in my voice betrays me, selling me out faster than a Nordstrom clearance rack.

"Good." She softens, but concern still laces her words. "Because I know you, Lennon. You're stubborn—impossibly so. And sometimes, that stubbornness stops you from asking for help when you need it most."

She's not wrong. Stubbornness and I go way back. It's the

Jimmy Choo of my personality: impractical, uncomfortable, but undeniably mine.

"You say that like it's a bad thing," I mutter, more bitter than amused.

"It *is* a bad thing," she deadpans.

Maggie's right. She usually is. She's been there since the unraveling began, catching the pieces—especially after *the* call. You know the one; expected, yet still a gut punch.

Two weeks later came the inevitable encore—another fall. Not a harmless stumble Grams could brush off with a joke about being "spry as a mountain goat". This one was catastrophic. Nearly fatal. When I pressed the doctor for details, he said she'd been outside, fixing the backyard fence. Apparently, the fence wasn't the only thing that gave way. *Classic Grams.*

And no, she's not the warm, cookie-baking, afghan-knitting kind of grandmother. She's been my parents, my anchor, my accomplice. Every ounce of good in me traces back to her.

By 27, I thought I'd built something stable—Columbia degree, respectable journalism job at *The Walla Walla Watch*, a life that felt, if not perfect, at least solid. But life has a way of yanking the ground out just when you start to trust it.

Maggie exhales, the kind of sigh that only comes from years of friendship. "Lennon, I'm serious." Her voice is velvet-soft yet iron-willed. "I know things are hard right now, but please . . . don't shut me out."

"I won't."

The silence lingers a beat too long, so I add, "Anyway, I'll be there in about an hour." I can picture her nodding, probably gnawing her bottom lip—Maggie's tell when she's worried but pretending she's not. That's her in a nutshell: All nerves and heart wrapped in relentless loyalty.

Funny how I never knew I needed someone like her until I

left Cedar Cove. I'd spent a few years in Grams' house, in a tiny Maine town where gossip spread faster than weather reports. Then, on my first day at the paper, Maggie strutted into my doorless cubicle in heels that could double as weapons, her lipstick as red as a warning sign.

"We're going to be best friends," she announced, eyeing me like a questionable purchase she might return.

She wasn't wrong. By day two, we were bonding over horror movies and our mutual obsession with unsolved mysteries. That was all it took. We clicked, as if the universe had been biding its time, waiting for us to meet.

"Okay, Mags, I'm hanging up now." I steer the conversation toward an exit. "I'll call once I'm settled."

In the background, a door creaks open, followed by a soft thud. No mystery there—she's heading to Paxton's room. Another journalist. Another complication. Best filed under *things we don't discuss.*

"Alright, love you, girl," Maggie whispers.

I shake my head, though she can't see me. "Be careful." The warning carries more weight than just sneaking into Paxton's place. We both know it.

"Always," she promises, her grin practically audible. Then the line clicks dead.

I toss the phone onto the passenger seat and exhale, shifting into drive.

The hour crawls by; the scenery blurring into streaks of pine, winding roads, and mist clinging stubbornly to the earth. I've driven this route a dozen times—usually with Grams waiting at the end, a mug of tea in hand, gossip at the ready. Sometimes we'd meet halfway, other times we'd chase the peculiar charm of Maine's back roads together—wood-carved moose, haunted inns, the oddities only small towns can conjure.

Today, as the weathered *Welcome to Cedar Cove* sign rises on the horizon—its paint chipped, its edges bleached by salt and time—something feels . . . off. A quiet unease coils in my stomach, as if the town has shifted slightly in my absence.

Cedar Cove takes its name from the inlet behind Grams' house, a crescent of coastline where the Atlantic creeps in like a shadow that refuses to retreat. On the farthest cliffs, a derelict lighthouse leans precariously, exhausted from standing for so long. Some swear its beam still cuts through the fog on certain nights.

I roll down the window, and the September air rushes in—briny and sharp, laced with pine and seaweed. The scent stings my lungs but feels like home. Wind whips my hair across my face, and I reach out, letting it curl through my fingers.

Cedar Cove hasn't changed. Not really. Same old charm, just a few new cracks. The Cedar Cove Diner still clings to its spot on Main Street, though its red-and-white awning has faded to a weary pink-and-gray. I slow as I pass, glancing at the corner booth by the window. It's empty now, but in my mind, Grams is still there—hands in motion, mid-story, blueberry pie crumbs scattered across the table. I can almost hear the clink of forks. Her laughter—bright and boundless—lingers in the air.

Deeper into town, I drive through layers of my own history. Sam's Grocery still flickers its half-lit neon sign, and Fisher's Bookshop clings to life—stubborn against Amazon and e-readers. I spent countless summers there, lost in novels, while Grams and Mr. Fisher reminisced about *the good old days*—though they never agreed on which decade that was.

A small smile tugs at my lips as the road curves along the cliffside. Below, the Atlantic churns, a restless smear of blue-gray. Dad used to say the ocean was a metaphor for life's endless flow. He was a sucker for metaphors. I wish I'd inherited his optimism instead of just his nose.

The farther I drive, the deeper the houses settle into the landscape—some fresh with new paint, others wearing their chipped exteriors like battle scars from too many Maine winters. A pack of kids shriek through a front yard, all grass stains and tangled limbs. For half a second, I'm back in my own barefoot summers, when my biggest worry was making it home before the streetlights buzzed to life.

And then—*SCREEEEECH.*

My tires shriek, snapping me out of my thoughts as my hand flies from the open window to the wheel. Adrenaline surges through me as I slam the brakes, stopping just shy of turning Cedar Cove's Main Street into a crime scene.

Breathe, Lennon. You're fine.

Well, I am. The guy in front of my car? Questionable. He stares—equal parts annoyed, surprised, and . . . something else I refuse to dissect.

Also, he's fine. Warning-label fine. The kind of fine that makes you wonder where he was when you were growing out tragic bangs.

Ignoring the fact that my car is now an impromptu roadblock, I kill the engine and exhale. Main Street will survive the delay. This is Cedar Cove—where a stalled golf cart gets more sympathy than a city slicker in a rush.

Stepping out, I slam the door harder than intended. My pulse is still erratic, but curiosity—and mortification—keep me moving. He's tall, easily 6'3", with tousled brown hair, electric blue eyes, and a beard that says *rugged but approachable.* And because the universe has a sense of humor, there's a dimple—one that deepens as he half-smiles, the kind that could short-circuit basic speech.

Then, just as quickly, his expression hardens—the same look he had when I nearly mowed him down. Honestly, who just stands in the middle of the busiest street in town? If I had clipped him, it would've been Darwinism at work.

"Are you planning to apologize?" His tone is flat, expectant.

I fold my arms, matching his energy. "For what? You're the one loitering in traffic."

One perfect eyebrow lifts. Annoying. "Actually, you're mistaken." He gestures downward.

I follow his hand. His feet are planted firmly—in the bike lane.

Damn it.

When I lift my eyes to his, amusement flickers there. My jaw tightens. I don't have time for this. I need to get to Grams, fix the sink, deal with her stairs—maybe even convince her that installing a basement handrail isn't a government ploy. She'd lose it if she knew I left work for this, but someone has to look out for her. Her home nurse sure isn't.

I wave him off, eager to end this standoff, but he chuckles again—low, warm, and laced with that damn dimple.

"Fine," I mutter, turning back to my car. "Sorry."

Footsteps crunch behind me, unhurried. He's not done. I whirl, ready to shut this down, but my shoe catches on a crack in the pavement.

I stumble—straight into his chest.

His very solid, unfairly broad chest.

For a beat, neither of us moves. Something unspoken hums between us, but I don't have the bandwidth to process it.

He clears his throat and steps back, his nose scrunching slightly. Oh god—do I smell? Panic bubbles, but before I spiral, he extends a hand, the other still clad in a worn work glove.

I hesitate, suspicious.

When I don't take it, he lowers it, looking almost sheepish. "Look, I'm sorry too. I wasn't trying to be in the way." A small, tentative smile tugs at his lips. "Truce?"

"A truce?" I echo, skepticism bleeding through my tone.

He shrugs, the movement tugging his henley taut over arms that clearly belong to someone who worships the gym. Of course. The guy who nearly got himself flattened has biceps like that.

"Maybe we both could've paid more attention," he concedes, unexpectedly humble. He tilts his head, almost apologetic, though the confidence in his stance suggests otherwise.

I let the silence linger, unsure if I'm irritated or—something else. Finally, with a sigh, I extend my hand in reluctant surrender. "Okay . . . " I draw out the word, waiting for him to explain why this exchange feels so bizarrely significant.

"Jack," he blurts, then clears his throat as if catching himself mid-misstep. A faint flush creeps up his neck. "Jack Mercer."

"Solid recovery," I remark, one brow lifting.

He smirks, eyes burning with challenge. "You know, asking for my number would've been easier. More mysterious, too."

"Where's the fun in that, Jack?" His name rolls off my tongue too easily, as if it's been there longer than the five minutes we've known each other.

His expression shifts, the mischief dimming into something quieter, heavier. A look I recognize too well—the kind that lingers in mirrors when thoughts turn unwelcome.

I clear my throat, swallowing against the sudden tightness there. "Lennon."

He repeats it, testing the sound. His gaze doesn't waver. "So . . . a truce?" This time, when he offers his hand, there's no teasing, just sincerity—disarming in its honesty.

Before I can second-guess it, my palm meets his. Rough. Calloused. A stark contrast to my own. And then—just for a moment—a spark, fleeting but unmistakable, skims up my arm. It anchors me in the present, making me hyper aware of the space between us, of the strange gravity of this moment.

"Truce," I concede, the word settling like an unspoken promise neither of us quite understands.

CHAPTER 2

Lennon

"Grams!" Her name ricochets off the faded wallpaper as I shove the stubborn front door open. It groans in protest—long, dramatic—like I've personally offended it. Another thing on the to-do list that never gets done. Fixing it was supposed to be my first project. Then life happened.

This house has always been on the verge of collapse. Peeling paint clings to the walls like it's trying to escape; floorboards complain with every step. Growing up, money was as reliable as the plumbing—barely functional. Grams worked two, sometimes three jobs, picking up shifts wherever she could. We got by, mostly by pretending the cracks weren't getting wider.

And now I'm back. Older, allegedly wiser, and "successful" in that vague way people who leave this town love to brag about.

"Grams, where are you?" Louder this time. The house swallows my voice and exhales silence. A prickle of something—unease, irritation—crawls up my spine. Her ancient Buick is still out front, keys dangling from the ignition, a silent rebellion against doctor's orders. Not that I'm surprised. Listening has never been her strong suit.

Inside, the silence feels wrong. Just the hum of the fridge, the steady tick of the grandfather clock—calm, predictable sounds. The kind that signals disaster before it strikes.

My hands are slick, a faint tremor at the edges. Old panic stirs—uninvited, but familiar. Years of late-night calls trained me for this. Neighbors, friends, home nurses—each one a prelude to bad news. But every time, Grams defied it. Stubbornness always outweighed frailty in her book. She swore she was fine, insisted I keep moving forward, never looking back too long, never letting her burdens clip my wings. She was ground control while I chased the horizon.

And now, I'm back. Grounded. Swearing I'd only return in memories.

I flip the light switch. The bulbs flicker, undecided, before settling into a dim, half-hearted glow. My gaze drifts to the staircase, its curve as familiar as breath. Once, this house was everything—mattress races down the stairs, treehouse wars, first friend, first kiss, first heartbreak.

But it holds its ghosts too. The cries, the fights, the grief that took root and never let go. I shut my eyes, willing them to stay buried. They don't. They never do.

This isn't real. It can't be. I force a breath, lungs tightening around the lie. *Get it together, Len. That was then. This is now.*

A groan from upstairs snaps me back. Adrenaline spikes.

"Grams?" I call, already taking the stairs two at a time, heart hammering. The noise leads me to the guest bathroom —the usual epicenter of catastrophe. Another groan, low and irritated.

I shove the door open, bracing for disaster—and come face-to-face with far too much Grams. Stark naked, clinging to the shower curtain like a lifeline, her pale backside on full display. The fabric strains under her grip, sagging but somehow still holding. Honestly, I'm impressed.

"Grams, what the hell?" I lunge to steady her. She swats me away, dignity apparently stronger than balance.

"Out!" she barks.

"Not happening," I shoot back, planting my feet. Same standoff, different roles. More nudity than I'd prefer.

For a moment, it's a battle of wills—her defiance against mine. Then the sheer absurdity of it all shatters our resolve. Laughter erupts, sharp and unrestrained, careening off the bathroom tiles. It's ridiculous. It's a release. And for once, we're too breathless to bicker.

As the laughter ebbs, I reach for her again—gentler this time. She doesn't recoil, though her grip on my arm is vise-like, fingers trembling just enough to betray the strain.

"Grams, which part of 'no solo showers' sounded option-al?" My tone mellows, balanced between affection and exasper-ation. She's always been this way—convinced that sheer willpower trumps physics or, more importantly, brittle bones.

She levels me with a look: *I had help.* Right. Probably the home nurse—nowhere in sight, likely scared off by Grams' signature charm.

Carefully, she steps out of the tub, her slight limp more pronounced as she clings to the shower curtain. The sudden modesty almost makes me laugh—like I haven't seen it all before. I lost count years ago, back when I was a teenager helping her bathe in this very spot.

Back then, I braced myself every time, convinced one wrong step would be the beginning of the end. But at least we weren't alone. There was a whole village—neighbors, friends, a steady stream of well-meaning intrusions. Someone was always there to catch her.

That ended the night we lost my parents. And Rhett. After that, people stopped coming. Stopped calling.

Now it's just me. Well, me and Gus, the handyman, who installed grab bars and a shower chair downstairs after Grams' last stunt. The plan was unanimous—doctor's orders, my insistence, even her begrudging agreement. And yet, here she is, staging her rebellion in this upstairs tub, gripping it like the last scrap of her independence.

I almost respect it. Mostly, it makes me want to scream.

"What're ya thinkin', walkin' in here while I'm showerin'?" Grams chides, her Maine accent cutting through the steam. It's more teasing than scolding—a reminder that, even naked and off balanced, she's still calling the shots.

"Don't just stand there gawkin'. Hand your Grams a towel, will ya?"

I shake my head, a grin creeping in. Grabbing a towel from the linen closet—one of her favorites, still laced with the scent of saltwater—I catch a whiff and suddenly, I'm sixteen again.

When I moved in after the accident, Grams overhauled the house, swapping Victorian clutter for breezy coastal charm. She thought a fresh look might help me forget. What she didn't understand was that memories don't cling to furniture. My parents are in the bones of this house, as permanent as the foundation.

"Off you go now." Grams waves a damp hand, her mouth twitching toward a smile—a quiet insistence that she's still unbreakable. Some of the tightness in my chest eases as she steadies herself, reclaiming a sliver of dignity.

I turn to the door, fingers brushing the cool metal handle. "Wild Blueberry Tea?" I ask, layering normalcy over the moment.

"Ayuh." Her eyes crinkle with approval. "Ain't nothin' else worth drinkin'."

I smirk. "Hey, Grams! Great to see you too."

"Can't say the same, Lenny," she fires back, never missing a beat.

I huff a quiet snort. Classic Grams—tough as a lobster trap and just as quick to snap. If she had her way—and for too long, she did—I wouldn't be here at all. But stubbornness is the family legacy, and we both inherited it in full.

At last, I reach my old bedroom, the door I once slammed in defiance and later closed in quiet grief. My fingers drift over the familiar grooves in the wood, smoothed by restless hands and time. Sunlight filters through the tiny window, painting a golden streak across the floor—an open invitation to the past.

Stepping inside, nostalgia slams into me, swift and unforgiving. The room is a shrine to the early 2000s, frozen under a thin veil of dust. Green Day and Avril Lavigne still sneer from faded posters, their edges curling like old memories. It's strange—how the things you leave behind stay untouched, yet the things you carry warp beyond recognition.

The little window overlooking the water hasn't changed. It remains a silent witness to everything lost and left behind. I used to sit there for hours, cross-legged on the bed, watching the waves and wishing life had a rewind button. Back when Mom and Dad were still alive. Back when laughter came easy, and smiles weren't something you had to force.

The old twin bed still hugs the wall, its faded pink comforter sprawled out like it's been waiting for my grand return. The stuffed animals, once my loyal army, have been exiled to a corner, their fur dulled by dust.

I grab Mr. Piggie, the lumpy stuffed pig Dad won for me at the Cedar Cove fair, back when life was simpler and winning prizes for your kid was a matter of honor. His legendary stubbornness—second only to Grams'—is the reason I have it. One summer, some girl named Shalia, brimming with overconfidence and questionable life advice, strutted past with a fresh prize and a snide remark. Dad didn't take the bait—he took the challenge.

With his jaw set in that "time for war" way of his, he

stepped up to the line. First throw: Two pins down. Second throw: Three. No words, no hesitation—just Dad vs. the milk bottles, a silent act of vengeance. Then, without ceremony, he turned and pressed the plush pig into my hands. *"Lenny girl,"* he said, dead serious, *"let no one else decide what you're worth."*

Clutching Mr. Piggie, I catch the faintest trace of Dad's aftershave—spiced warmth, a mix of cinnamon, cloves, and too much Old Spice. Nostalgia tugs at me, but movement in the window next door snaps me back.

My heart stutters. I set Mr. Piggie down and push the window open, inhaling salt, pine, and the ghosts of everything I've been avoiding. But my gaze stays fixed on *his* window— the one that once meant everything.

That room was our refuge, where homework blurred into gaming marathons and late-night conversations tried to unravel the universe. His space was my escape hatch, my lifeline, when the world felt too tight.

Time collapses, memories surging like the tide—insistent, inescapable. And just like that, I'm back there, drowning in the past.

"Don't be a baby, Len," Rhett goaded that night as I clung to the rickety trellis, my sneakers slipping like they had a personal vendetta. The wood groaned beneath me, each creak a reminder that one wrong move could mean a hospital bill Grams and I couldn't afford. And yet, dangling three feet above certain humiliation, I wouldn't have been anywhere else.

Rhett's grip was steady. So was his grin. "You got this, Rocky," he said, smug enough to make me roll my eyes—if I weren't so focused on staying alive. The nickname was new. I hadn't decided if I hated it.

At first, I thought it was a dig at my scrawny frame or my sneakers slapping the pavement like bad theme music. But

Rhett, in that rare, unexpected way of his, just shrugged. "Because you're solid," he said, like it was obvious. "Like the cliffs. No matter how hard the ocean slams against them, they don't move."

It was corny. It was also the nicest thing anyone had ever said to me.

At that moment, I knew—Rhett wasn't just my best friend. He was my person. My Roo.

The sudden roar of a vacuum jolts me back. I blink hard, swallowing the sting in my eyes. *Get it together, Len.* My gaze snaps to the window just in time to catch movement—not Mrs. Callahan, but a woman in a maid's uniform. She vacuums, dusts, wipes the glass in slow, practiced strokes, her motions methodical, almost robotic. She's done this a hundred times before.

But why *his* room?

"She comes every week," Grams admits, breaking the silence. She shuffles closer, leaning on the new walker—the one I'm sure sparked a full-scale war at the doctor's office—until she's beside me. Her wiry frame wobbles, gray-white hair a wild tangle she refuses to brush when I'm around. I grab my old hairbrush, working through the knots, my eyes never leaving Rhett's window.

"Why so often?" From here, the room looks untouched. Preserved. Like time sealed it off.

"They wanna keep it the same."

Her words settle like a weight in my chest, tangled with something colder—grief, maybe, or just the raw ache of uncertainty.

"They're still grievin', ya know." Her voice is thick with sorrow, years-deep and unmoving.

Yeah, I know. We all are. Still circling the same question.

What really happened that night?

What happened to you, Roo?

My nose burns, my throat tightens, but I swallow the tears before they surface. *Not here. Not now.*

"All done."

I set the brush on the vanity as Grams turns to me, her tough-as-nails expression softening—just barely. Vulnerability isn't her style; she's always been more *suck it up* than *let it out.* But now, she pulls me into a hug, and the moment her arms wrap around me, steady and warm, I realize how much I needed it.

I exhale, shaky and slow.

"Ya shouldn't have come back," she breathes, something close to regret. "Ain't nothin' good gonna come from diggin' up the past. Some nights . . . are best left buried."

But let's be honest—the past doesn't need digging up when it's already clawed its way back.

Grams doesn't get that. To her, memories are jagged things, sharp enough to cut you if you're not careful. And maybe she's right. But she doesn't see the whole picture. She *can't.*

She's my grams—my anchor, the only person left in this world who feels like home. When everything crumbled, she held me together, even when there wasn't much left to hold.

Now it's my turn. Whether she likes it or not.

She studies me like a puzzle she's determined to solve— gentle, but unyielding. Whatever she's searching for, she won't find it. I buried that part of myself long ago.

Just as I open my mouth to ask what's on her mind, she turns, gesturing for me to follow.

We walk in silence, her arm looped through mine, the floorboards groaning beneath us. She doesn't stop in the kitchen but heads straight for the sunroom.

It's exactly as I remember—walls of windows, a mismatched collection of furniture, and a view that makes it feel like the ocean is breathing beside you. The backyard stretches toward the water, calm and contained, holding the chaos of the world at bay.

Grams hands me a mug of tea, the warmth seeping into my fingers. The scent of wild berries curls from the steam—sweet, earthy, and so evocative it pulls me straight into the past.

Summers with Rhett.

Laughter. Sunlight. Berry-stained fingers and food fights.

For the first time since I got here, my shoulders loosen. The tension melts like frost in the morning light. It's not quite home—but for now, it's close enough to pretend.

CHAPTER 3

"Lennon Harrington? That really you?" Gus' words hang with cautious curiosity, rough and disbelieving. His squint lingers, as if expecting me to vanish. Then, slowly, his face splits into a grin.

"Hi, Gus." The smile comes unbidden, like it's been waiting for this exact moment. "Long time."

His laughter rattles through the store, loud and familiar. I remember that sound filling these aisles when I was a teenager, fumbling with wrenches and grief, trying to make sense of both.

"Ayuh, been a while," he drawls. Pine Harbor Hardware still smells like sawdust, motor oil, and too much nostalgia. Walking in feels like cracking open a time capsule no one meant to seal.

"What brings ya back?" His brows do most of the talking. The way he says it, I know he figured I'd stay gone—and wouldn't have blamed me.

"Grams." I glance down the aisle where the usual suspects —light bulbs, duct tape, misplaced ambition—still hold their ground. "She's still convinced she's the Queen of Home Improvement. You know how it is."

Gus chuckles, shaking his head. "What's she banned you from fixing this time?" His tone carries the kind of teasing reserved for those who've witnessed my worst DIY disasters firsthand.

"Front door's been creaking like a budget horror flick," I admit. "Grams told me to hire a professional, but it's just hinges and elbow grease. I've got it covered."

"Ayuh, you always was handy," Gus muses, amusement threading through his words—though we both know *handy* is generous.

We walk down the aisle I could navigate blindfolded, past bins of mismatched screws and paint cans old enough to have seen multiple presidencies. I grab the essentials: hinges, a screwdriver, wood glue. There's something grounding about these small, practical things—they don't argue, break down, or need a Wi-Fi signal to work.

We head to the checkout, where a few unfamiliar faces shuffle through the line. Good. I'm not in the mood for Cedar Cove's unofficial welcome committee. My boss already torched my morning with a *friendly* reminder that PTO apparently stands for *Prepare To Overwork*. Remote access is the only reason I'm here helping Grams instead of drowning in emails from my Washington office, so I'll call it a win.

"How long you sticking around?" Gus leans an elbow on the counter, giving me the look of a man who's heard *not long* too many times.

"Not sure. Long enough to make sure Grams is okay."

He nods, slow and knowing. "She given any thought to Coastal Breeze Residences?"

I bark out a laugh. "Grams? In a senior center?" I peek at him—he's already grinning.

"As if," he quips, his tone laced with irony, dabbing at an invisible tear.

"Yeah, she's too stubborn for that," I murmur, an exasperated sort of fondness settling in. That same stubbornness raised me—and bullied me back into school, work, and life after everything fell apart.

"It's good to see you back, Lennon," Gus says, his words softening to something almost paternal as I set my supplies on the counter. "Stop by again before you head out?"

"Yeah." I offer a small smile. "I will." And I mean it. Gus was there when I needed someone—just like Grams.

He nods and shuffles toward the back, floorboards groaning beneath his familiar gait. I step outside, the damp air pressing in as rain looms on the horizon—Cedar Cove's constant promise. The scent of wet earth lingers as I cross the lot toward my SUV.

Then, two things hit me at once: The creeping bite of cold worming through my jacket and the quiet presence beside me. The faint chime of the shop's doorbell drifts into the air, but my focus sharpens on the man striding toward it.

His head tilts just enough for the brim of his hat to cast a deliberate shadow, obscuring his face. But the sheriff's uniform is unmistakable—crisp, authoritative, unfairly tailored to broad shoulders built to bear every small-town burden. Dark brown hair escapes from beneath the hat's edge, tousled with the kind of nonchalance that suggests either a grueling day or a habit of running his fingers through it. Either way, it's maddeningly perfect.

Then, with measured ease, he lifts his head, eyes locking onto mine—dark, piercing, and intense enough to make me wonder if he moonlights as the brooding hero of some romance novel.

Time slows as an unwelcome flush creeps up my neck. I knew I'd run into him eventually—Cedar Cove isn't exactly vast—but not here. And definitely not with that damn uniform making him look less like the man I argued with and more like the cover model for *Small-Town Sheriff Monthly.*

Wait—*he's* the sheriff? Of course he is. Because the universe wasn't content with Grams vetoing my renovation plans; it had to throw *him* into a badge and uniform, too. Fantastic.

His lips curve into a half-smile—equal parts mischief and invitation.

Definitely trouble.

"Lennon." My name rolls off his tongue in a low, gravelly drawl that snakes through me, settling somewhere *way* too warm. It's like a shot of whiskey—fiery, unexpected, and impossible to ignore.

Jack. The man I nearly ran over when I screeched into town two days ago. Now, apparently, the law in Cedar Cove.

His stare doesn't waver. Neither does mine. Silence stretches between us, tight as a drawn bowstring, daring one of us to break it. Then his smirk unfurls into a full grin—easy, assured, and entirely too devastating. Damn it.

He should come with a warning: *May induce reckless heart palpitations and an uncontrollable impulse to flirt.*

I force myself to speak. "Jack."

He dips his head, eyes gleaming with mischief. "So we meet again." Not a greeting—a challenge, tossed like a gauntlet at my feet.

And just like that, I'm ten years old again, caught midheist, fingers inches from a stolen slice of Thanksgiving pie. Guilt and defiance twist in my chest, locking me in place.

I reach for indifference, but my body betrays me. My heart pounds like a drum solo, my legs threaten collapse, and— fantastic—my hormones have chosen this moment for an unsanctioned encore.

I summon a smile, feigning composure while my nerves

riot. Outside, the sky broods in shades of gray, the kind of weather I usually find soothing—steady, predictable, comfortably bleak. But even the misty gloom is no match for Jack, standing there, maddeningly composed.

His brow lifts when he catches me—traitorously—giving him a once-over.

Get it together, Lennon.

"No harm done," he remarks, as if I've spent the past minute fretting over his well-being. He gestures to his immaculate uniform, the very picture of unshaken composure.

It takes me a beat to catch up—oh. *That.* He's talking about how I nearly ran him over the other day.

I shove him, my hand colliding with his starched shoulder. Solid as a brick wall. The impact jolts through me, and before I can steady myself, I'm the one tipping backward.

"Oh, shit," I blurt, heat crawling up my neck. "I mean—shoot." *Smooth. Real smooth.* Because why stop at ogling him? "Why not *shove* the officer while I'm at it? Maybe throw in a felony for good measure."

"Sheriff," he corrects with an easy drawl, each syllable steeped in quiet authority.

I meet his gaze, and something in it has shifted—darker, unreadable. Not anger. No, this is something far more dangerous. My stomach flips as a slow smirk tugs at his lips.

"Didn't mind it, honestly," he muses, like getting shoved by a panicked woman is just another Tuesday.

Then he winks.

My stomach plummets.

Is he flirting with me?

Nope. Not going there. This is just small-town charm—polite, professional, entirely harmless. He's a sheriff, not some guy leaning against a dive bar. And I'm Lennon Harrington—a walking disaster, barely clinging to my dignity.

"I had no idea you were a . . . " The words slip through my fingers.

"Sheriff?" he offers, one brow lifting like it's the most obvious thing in the world.

I nod, swallowing hard. Sure, I can handle a sheriff—probably. But standing here in Cedar Cove, caught in the pull of his too-knowing gaze, old memories stir, pressing against the mental junk drawer where I've crammed them for years.

"How long have you been around?" I ask, too chipper, the kind of forced cheer usually reserved for awkward small talk at a funeral.

"Here in Cedars?" he repeats, gaze still locked on mine.

I nod again, composure unraveling, thread by thread.

"A few years now," he explains. "Came here on a case."

Case. That one word trips something in my chest before settling into a rhythm I don't entirely appreciate. I avert my gaze, feigning interest in a group of locals drifting into the store. Outwardly poised. Inwardly? A tangle of questions I won't ask.

Jack watches me, studying, assessing.

Good luck with that.

But then, his expression softens. No cocky grin, no sly smirk. Just a slow, effortless smile, like sunlight cutting through morning fog. Irritatingly . . . genuine. Probably his best feature, though those ridiculously blue eyes might argue otherwise—too clear, too deep, like the water by the cove.

He nods toward the supplies clutched in my hands, then tips his hat in one fluid motion—practiced and devastatingly smooth.

"Miss. Harrington."

A step toward the door. A pause, just long enough to feel intentional.

"Oh, and Lennon?"

I still, caught between curiosity and the instinct to run.

"Yeah?"

"Watch out for the locals," he teases. "They've got a knack for drifting into the bike lane at the worst moments."

I snort. Loud. Unintended. The kind that ricochets off the walls and turns heads. Heat surges up my neck, setting my ears —undoubtedly—ablaze.

I manage a stiff wave, the picture of grace. "I'll, uh, keep that in mind," I mumble, then make a beeline for my SUV like it's a lifeboat and I'm sinking fast.

CHAPTER 4

Lennon

"Lenny, if ya don't quit that racket, I'll hire a handyman myself!" Grams barks from her rocking chair, wielding a wooden spoon like a general's baton.

"Almost done, I swear," I lie, wobbling atop a ladder as unreliable as my word. The hinge resists, and I'm two missteps from making Grams' afternoon with an ER visit.

Time moves strangely here—slow as molasses, quick as a blink. A week has slipped by in that small-town haze, equal parts tranquil and stifling. Grams, of course, has filled the gaps with her usual commentary: No, she doesn't need a new home nurse (she does), and yes, she requires a full briefing on the cases I left behind in Washington.

She's always had a way of bending time. An hour with her can stretch into an eternity or disappear in an instant, depending on whether she's unspooling family lore or cross-examining me. As a kid, I watched her do the same with my parents—perched between them, eyes gleaming, prying into Dad's latest case while Mom spun crime scenes into polite parlor talk. They never fooled her. She just enjoyed the sport of it.

I think that's where the journalism bug first bit me—listening to Dad's clipped summaries and Mom's grimly cheerful evasions. But the real fire didn't catch until everything fell apart. Two nights. Years apart. A decade ago. The kind of nights that etch themselves into your mind whether you want them there or not.

Flashing blue lights. Shouting. Blood on pavement. It all unraveled in seconds—my parents, Rhett. The loss was brutal, but the silence after was worse. No leads. No motives. Just questions left to decay.

Even now, the lack of answers gnaws at me, a dull, familiar ache. And then there's Jack. What brought him here? The same shadows that swallowed my parents' case? Rhett's?

Grams has a theory for everything, including this: *Murders don't just vanish.* Not when she's around. To her, mysteries are unpaid debts, and she's been charging interest since the '70s. If Jack's case connects to theirs, someone missed something. And Grams always says the truth can hide, but it can't outrun a stubborn mind. It's out there—buried under dirt, denial, and bad police work—just waiting for someone reckless enough to dig it up.

I used to think I'd be the one to piece it all together—to write the ending and finally close the book. But between Grams' nagging, my therapist's warnings, and my own survival instincts, I've learned one thing: Some ghosts are better left undisturbed. Peace of mind is hard to come by when you're the one digging up the past.

"Grams, hand me that." I nod toward the screwdriver tip beside her.

Just as my fingers graze the hinge, it slips from my grasp, clattering to the floor with all the subtlety of a cymbal crash at a funeral.

"Oh, for crying out loud," I mutter, scowling at the wayward piece of metal now splayed across the floorboards like it's making a scene.

Grams doesn't bother stifling her laughter. It's a full-bodied, unapologetic cackle. I level her with my best unimpressed stare, but she's already on the move.

With a swift shove of her walker, she drops to her knees like she's auditioning for *Mission: Impossible.*

"Grams, seriously. Let me get it," I demand, already resigned to how this ends.

She swats at the air like my concern is nothing more than a pesky fly. "I can damn well do it. Ain't my first rodeo," she snaps, her tone so commanding you'd think the hinge was a matter of national security. "My physical therapist says this is good for me."

Right. Because crawling on hardwood is *definitely* what he meant. But arguing is pointless—her eyes have that familiar, unshakable glint. This isn't about the hinge. It's about proving, one reckless stunt at a time, that she's still as stubbornly independent as ever.

Her faded nightdress brushes the floor as she scoops up the hinge with a triumphant flourish. For three whole seconds, she basks in victory—until two steady hands appear behind her, lightly bracing her back.

It takes me a beat to process. When I peek over my shoulder, there he is. Jack. Because *of course* he's here. The man has a supernatural talent for showing up at the worst moments.

He stands behind Grams, silent and steady, his expression hovering between quiet concern and unreadable intensity. My grip tightens on the chair as I shift, one hand catching the doorframe for balance. My gaze flicks to his hands, then back to those piercing blue eyes—eyes that, without fail, short-circuit my brain.

My stomach revolts—twisting, buzzing, like a jar of

furious bees knocked askew. Perfect. Just the humiliation I needed to cap off my afternoon.

Jack moves with unexpected softness, brushing a stray curl from my cheek. The tenderness is disarming, and before I can stop myself, I'm smiling—an involuntary betrayal, both irritating and oddly reassuring.

His other hand stays secure on Grams' back, supporting her with effortless ease, as if he belongs in this space.

His fingers linger a fraction too long as he tucks the curl behind my ear, and for a moment, the world narrows to just us. The creaky chair, the fallen hinge, Grams muttering about stubborn screws—gone. All that remains is the warmth of his touch and the unwavering heat in his eyes, stripping me bare in a way that feels both unsettling and inescapable.

This man. Either he's trouble wrapped in an infuriatingly attractive package, or there's an undeniable, absurd chemistry crackling between us. Probably both. My nerves are on high alert, and my body—traitorous as ever—chooses now to remind me I'm alive in the worst possible way.

Grams clears her throat—loud enough to wake the dead—shattering the moment. "Well, don't just stand there gawkin', Lenny. We've got work t' do," she declares, leaning into Jack's arm like he's her personal walking stick.

I blink, reality snapping back into focus.

Then her gaze hones in. "Better yet, why don't you lend a hand, Officer Mercer?" She gives Jack the kind of once-over usually reserved for blue-ribbon pies at the Cedar Cove Fall Festival.

Oh no. Whether she's enlisting him for manual labor or playing matchmaker, one thing's certain: It's both.

Jack's grin unfolds—slow, easy, maddeningly smug, yet somehow charming enough to get away with it. The look of a man who's been caught in Grams' web before. "Lillian, how many times do I have to ask you to call me Jack?"

And heaven help us all—Grams blushes. She flicks her wrist in dismissal, but the soft pink creeping across her cheeks betrays her. "Nonsense," she mutters, though there's warmth in her tone. "It's just nice to see a real officer in this town."

A real officer.

The words hit heavier than they should, stirring memories that refuse to stay buried. I know exactly what she means. The others had been little more than placeholders, enduring Grams' demands for justice—justice that never came. Not for my parents. Not for Rhett. Just years lost to indifference.

But Jack . . . Jack doesn't seem like the others. Or maybe that's another lie I'm feeding myself.

"Always at your service, Lillian." Jack winks shamelessly, and Grams feigns disinterest. But I catch the faint twitch at the corner of her mouth before she turns away. Her steps are quiet but sure as she retreats to the kitchen, and Jack's laugh follows her—low, rich, rolling like distant thunder.

I really wish my body hadn't noticed that laugh. But here we are.

I inhale, steadying myself. *Stay in control.* He's just a stranger. Nothing more.

But when Jack turns back and takes my hand, my mind loses all authority over my body. With a simple pull, he lifts me from the chair, his strength so seamless it feels as if the ground shifted, not me.

We're suddenly close. *Too* close. The air crackles, charged with something undeniable. His heat radiates, drawing me in, making me wonder—would it scorch me or ensnare me? The space between us narrows to a dangerous inch. One reckless step, one lapse in judgment, and I'd fall. I'd taste the promise in his gaze. I'd lose myself.

But I came here for Grams, not to unravel for a man who probably collects broken hearts like souvenirs.

His eyes flicker to my lips, lingering just long enough to

send a pulse of want through me—uninvited, undeniable. His mouth looks soft. Tempting. *Trouble.* A kiss I'd regret—just not right away. And he knows it.

A loud clatter from the kitchen shatters my daze. Distance. That's what I need. I step back, seizing the excuse. Jack's grin falters—just enough to tell me he notices—but then it shifts, softening into something less cocky. Less dangerous.

The space helps. Not as much as I'd like, but enough to even out my breathing. To remind me that he's still him.

Not the scowling man from Main Street, dust-covered and brooding. Not the polished officer, all rules and restraint. No—this Jack is something else entirely. *Inconveniently* disarming. A white T-shirt that fits too well. A Carhartt jacket slung over his shoulder. Dark jeans that should be illegal. And that damn baseball cap—*Coach* printed across the front—worn soft by time, sun, and sweat.

He catches me staring, and for a second, something bashful drifts through his gaze. But then, that smile returns. The kind that could charm nuns and buckle knees.

Did mine just wobble? Maybe. Probably. Honestly, I wouldn't bet against it. I'd wager half my paycheck he's got at least half the women in Cedar Cove eating out of his hand—including the infamous Wives of Cedar Cove.

Rhett's mom was one of them—maybe still is. Pearls, passive-aggressive charm, manipulation masked as hospitality. She had it down to an art. Grams always warned Mom to keep her distance, not that it stopped the Wives from luring her in with wine nights disguised as "community meetings." Mom never took the bait. She had a sixth sense for saccharine deception. It repelled her then, just as it repels me now.

"Seems like I'm always uncovering something new about you."

Jack's mouth twitches, a barely there smirk. "Since you're learning so much, why don't you tell me something,

Lennon?" His question is casual, but there's an undertow—he's probing, fishing for whatever lurks beneath the surface.

So that's the game we're playing now.

Grams' rule number one: Never offer more than necessary.

I arch a brow. "Like what?"

He shrugs with ease. "Anything—how you take your lobster, favorite kind of pie, best spot to watch the . . ."

I cross my arms, tapping my chin as if in deep contemplation. His dimple flashes—because of course it does. That stupid, unfairly disarming dent in his cheek. How does one small divot wield so much power?

I let the silence linger—just long enough to turn awkward—before dropping the most absurd fact I can summon. "Believe it or not, I once won a blueberry pie-eating contest."

Jack's laughter erupts, rich and unrestrained, but then he stops short, blinking as if I've just claimed intergalactic origins. "Wait—hold on. You're serious?"

"Dead serious." A flicker of smug satisfaction warms me. "Somewhere, there's a photo of me, face smeared in blueberries, looking like I barely survived a food fight."

He shakes his head. "How was that not in your town bio?"

I cross my arms. "Didn't quite make the résumé. But yeah, I can demolish a pie faster than anyone I know. The trick's in the crust—keep it flaky so it doesn't slow you down."

His blue eyes spark with something between amusement and admiration. "I have to admit, I didn't see that coming. You don't exactly scream 'competitive eater'."

"Don't judge a book by its cover," I tease. "It's not just eating—it's strategy."

"Strategy, huh?" Jack chuckles, his tone laced like he's already figured me out.

Grams squints between us, as if piecing together a mystery. "You two have met before?"

Jack and I exchange a glance—one of those magnetic looks

that feels like muscle memory. There's an undeniable familiarity between us, a pull I can't decide is reassuring or reckless.

With a decisive clap, Grams snaps the moment back into
focus. "Well, if you're here, might as well make yourself
useful."

Jack grins as he takes the hammer from her—easy, effortless, annoyingly charming.

What a shameless flirt.

The afternoon drifts by in a blur of sawdust, small talk, and
unexpected laughter—rusty at first, like I've forgotten how it
sounds in my own voice. By the time the sun sinks low,
bathing everything in gold, Grams exhales, satisfied. "Now
that's a good day's wuhk."

Jack steps off the porch, the light catching his features just
right—turning him into something of a golden god. I hadn't
expected to enjoy having him around, but now . . . well,
watching him leave feels oddly disappointing. Ridiculous,
really. We barely know each other. Still, there's an itch, a quiet
pull to unravel the stories behind his eyes. Maybe it's the journalist in me, always chasing the truth. Or maybe it's something else entirely.

"Well, I bettah let ya go, Officer Mercah," Grams teases,
her accent thicker than usual, laid on for effect.

Jack groans dramatically, rolling his eyes in that easy, good-
natured way, and Grams laughs. Before heading inside, she
throws me a sly, knowing look. I do my best to ignore it.

Now it's just us, silence settling like a held breath. Jack
stuffs his hands into his pockets, his usual confidence fraying
at the edges. There's a hesitance in the way he shifts his weight,
his gaze flitting over the water, the trees, the chipped railing—

searching for the right words, as if they might be hiding in the scenery.

"So . . ." he begins, voice tentative, like a pebble tossed into still water.

"So . . . ?" I echo, one brow arched. We hover in the moment, poised like teenagers anticipating a kiss that won't come.

"Go out with me?"

My pulse spikes. I freeze, caught between laughter and flight.

Jack exhales, half amused, half mortified. He tugs off his cap, raking a hand through his hair with a self-conscious chuckle. "Huh. That sounded smoother in my head."

A snort escapes me—loud, graceless, utterly ill-timed. Perfect. He winces, certain he's ruined everything.

"Is this really happening?" I murmur, half expecting the universe to deliver some sarcastic reply. It doesn't.

"Why not?" He shrugs, then immediately backtracks, panic flaring in his eyes. "Unless . . . you're spoken for?"

Spoken for. The words linger, quaint and almost laughable.

It's ridiculous. We've had maybe five real conversations, yet here he stands in the fading sunlight, hair tousled, impossibly endearing after a day spent helping Grams and me. And now, this—a curveball I never saw coming.

The worst part? A small, treacherous part of me wants to say yes.

My lips twitch upward. "No, I'm not."

"Then what's the problem?" There's an easy coaxing in his words, as if the answer should be obvious.

It's not.

I bite my lip, sifting through the reasons I can't—or won't —say aloud. Because I'm only here temporarily. Because things could get messy, complicated—chaos I've spent years outrunning. I came back for Grams, not to fall into something, into someone like this. A sheriff.

And Jack? Jack is anything but simple.

He's the kind of man who unravels you without trying, who shifts the energy in a room just by walking in. He draws every glance effortlessly. And when he looks at you? The world softens at the seams. He leans in at the right moment, says the right words, like he's been reading your mind long before you've made sense of it yourself. He's dangerous that way. He could make you believe in things you swore you'd buried—hope, desire, connection.

I open my mouth, ready to throw out some flimsy excuse, something logical enough to mask the fear beneath.

But then I see it.

A shadow flickers through the fading light. My breath snags, muscles tightening.

A stranger.

But not just any stranger. These eyes are different—too deep, too knowing. They skim my skin like a whisper, raising goosebumps in their wake. There's something unsettlingly familiar about them, an intimacy that shouldn't exist. As if they've watched me unravel at 2:00 a.m., mascara-smudged and hollow-eyed, and never once looked away.

I can't move. Can't look away. These eyes don't just see me; they recognize me. And that's what terrifies me most.

"*Roo?*" The name escapes me, barely a breath. It doesn't even sound like mine. The world lurches, the porch tilting beneath me like a breaking tide.

Then hands—solid, reassuring, undeniably real—close around mine, anchoring me. Jack's hands. Keeping me from shattering, from digging my nails into my palms.

The edges of everything blur. A raw, aching weight lodges in my chest, something I haven't felt in years. It's a trick of the mind. It has to be. Because it can't be Roo. It can't be Rhett. Rhett is gone. Has been for years.

"Lennon." My name, spoken softly, pulls me back. I blink, refocusing on Jack. His face is tight with concern, brows knit like he's willing me to stay whole.

His hand grazes my forehead, light and searching, like he's hoping for a fever—some easy explanation for the way I'm unraveling in front of him.

The touch is careful, almost cautious, as if I might break. It's been so long since anyone has really seen me and not flinched when things got messy.

A carousel of hollow, fleeting encounters spins through my mind. Three months here, two weeks there. Mutual. Doomed. Forgettable. Nothing ever lasted, and I told myself that was fine.

But this? This is different. And different is terrifying.

I take his hand, guiding it to my jaw. "Yes," I whisper.

His eyes widen, clouded with confusion. It's almost endearing—like watching a dog try to understand algebra. A quiet smile sneaks onto my lips.

"Uh . . . um, yeah," he stammers, his grin widening. "So . . . yes?"

I nod, giving his hand a quick squeeze. A laugh slips out—breathless, uneven. Even the gravity of this moment can't override the absurdity of *us*.

Jack releases my hand, and for a second, I think he's leaving. And he does. At first.

Halfway to his truck, he stops. I expect him to turn back for something—a tool, maybe. Or his dignity. Instead, he pivots, boots crunching over gravel, moving with a quiet, deliberate energy.

Before I can react, he leans in, lips brushing my temple—so light, so fleeting, it's almost imagined.

Five stars. My inner monologue all but applauds. Most

guys these days treat romance like a race, sprinting past *hello* straight to second base. But Jack? He moves with the unhurried charm of handwritten letters and actually waits three days to call. Not that this is a date or anything. But still. Manners.

As he turns back toward his truck, something tugs—deep, insistent, unwelcome. Like an elastic band snapping tight. The force of it catches me off guard.

"Jack, wait!" The words spill out, instinct overriding logic, pride be damned.

He hesitates, one hand on the open truck door, scanning me.

"Tell me something."

Jack exhales, a half-smile on his lips—wry, edged with something softer. "My roots are in Cedar Cove."

CHAPTER 5

Jack

"What's with the getup?" Sawyer pops open another cheap beer, the hiss ricocheting off the high ceilings—a sharp reminder that this isn't a home, just an echo chamber in townhouse form.

I steal a final glance in the mirror by the door. Collar? Straight. Jacket? Sharp. Confidence? Present, though in need of reinforcement.

Sawyer watches me like I'm some cryptid dragged into the light. The townhouse may be mine, but he inhabits it with the entitlement of a frat house despot. A stray cat that never left— if stray cats drank Keystone Light and ignored the concept of cleaning.

But tonight, for once, his tone is more curious than mocking. I can't blame him.

I have a date.

I snatch my keys from the entry table, their weight an easy excuse to avoid eye contact. "Going on a date," I say, as if announcing I'm off to meet Bigfoot. My boots strike the hardwood with deliberate ease as I turn for the door, feigning indifference. Sawyer lifts an eyebrow—his version of astonishment. High praise.

Dating in Cedar Cove has never been my forte. The choices are slim unless you have a thing for PTA presidents or the self-appointed Wives of Cedar Cove. Well-meaning, sure, but their matchmaking is relentless. Dodge one ambush in the cereal aisle, and suddenly, you're "aloof" or "too picky." I've learned to navigate these waters with the same finesse I use in my actual job: polite deflection and a well-timed escape.

But this? This is different. This is Lennon. The woman who nearly ran me down the day we met. She's not another blind leap into small-town dating theatrics—she's something else entirely. Something I never saw coming.

When I told Lennon I was from Cedar Cove, it wasn't exactly a lie. Technically, I was born here. The rest? Complicated. My biological parents are a question mark, a mystery that's shadowed me my whole life. So five years ago, fresh out of the academy, when a cold case in Cedar Cove opened up, I didn't hesitate. The department needed someone to learn the town's winding roads and even more tangled rumors. I needed something else—a chance to unravel the past. Maybe solve the case. Maybe figure out where I actually come from. Either way, I'm not leaving without answers.

"Who's the poor soul brave enough to take a chance on you?" Sawyer deadpans from the couch, flipping on the TV. The roar of a stadium crowd fills the room—the unofficial kickoff to another NFL game. Football season turns our town-house into a part-time sports bar, complete with flat screens, nachos, and a beer pyramid that multiplies weekly. But tonight, I'm not sticking around for the usual chaos. And, for once, I don't mind.

"Lennon." I let her name hang between us like a challenge. Sawyer doesn't look away from the screen, but I catch the barely perceptible twitch of his eyebrow. He has a knack for reading me—like he's tuned into my thoughts, skimming the highlights.

We've been like this for years. Since the academy, really—bonded by too many late-night stakeouts and gallows humor only cops seem to master. When I landed the sheriff's job in Cedar Cove, Sawyer somehow wound up next door, like fate had a terrible sense of humor. Or maybe it just didn't know when to quit. Either way, he's been stuck in my life ever since, offering a constant supply of sarcasm and unsolicited opinions.

"You sure about that?" he asks, still staring at the TV. "Sounds like trouble."

"She's not trouble."

"Hmm." He pauses, grabbing a handful of chips.

"She's new in town." Like that explains everything.

Sawyer's brows inch together, his curiosity officially piqued. "How new?"

"Couple of weeks." Two, if we're being precise.

A smirk pulls at my mouth before I can stop it.

The whole thing kicked off this past Wednesday when her grandmother had declared war at the DMV. Poor clerk never stood a chance when Grams bulldozed her way through a failed eye test, insisting she deserved her license because, apparently, vision was optional. She had carried on like she was exposing government corruption. Stubbornness clearly runs in the family—though, somehow, she had still walked out victorious, license in hand.

That same day, Grams had decided to moonlight as a matchmaker. She insisted I ask Lennon out in person because, in her words, *"Texting isn't how we did things back in the day."* Translation: A not-so-subtle attempt to set her granddaughter up with me. I hadn't argued—any excuse to see Lennon again was a good one.

When I showed up at Grams' house to ask her out, she was

in mid-DIY disaster. A paint tray had claimed her as its latest victim, streaking her jeans, cheek, even knotting into her hair. The bathroom walls got a fresh coat, but so did she. It should've been ridiculous. Maybe it was. But then she smiled —soft, self-conscious, unbearably sweet—and suddenly, it was worth the trip.

"Little early, don't you think?" Sawyer's dull monotone snaps me back to reality.

I shrug, draining the last of my beer like I hadn't just been lost in my own personal rom-com. "Probably."

Who even decides when something counts as a date? A day? A week? Is there a committee? The empty bottle hits the trash with a hollow thunk, and I shake off the thought as I head for the door.

My townhouse sits on the edge of the forest, quiet except for kids squabbling over kickball rules and who cheated at tag. If you squint near the front steps, you can spot the lighthouse blinking through the trees, a patient but unimpressed observer. That little flash of light—and the lack of nosy neighbors—is what sold me on the place.

At first, I was worried about living around so many families. I figured it meant forced small talk, wary parents watching me like I'd start handing out speeding tickets. But reality proved different.

Now, I'm used to the kids. Half of them recognize me from town, pedaling up on their bikes, eyes wide. *Caught any bad guys lately?* they ask. I always say yes. No need to tell them most of my "bad guys" are more Walmart shoplifters than criminal masterminds.

Ten minutes later, I pull into Grams' driveway, the Explorer kicking a few stray pebbles into the dark. I round the hood, open the passenger door, and find Lennon watching me —head tilted, expression teetering between curiosity and judgment.

"So . . . is this your usual date etiquette?" she muses, her smirk betraying just how much she enjoys making me squirm.

My lips twitch. "Oh, so it's a date now? Glad we cleared that up."

A flush creeps across her cheeks—unexpected, disarming. I want to see it again.

She ducks her head instead of answering, sinking into her seat. I ease us back onto the road, darkness stretching ahead. I steal a glance at her, but her face gives nothing away.

"That's how it should be. No other way," I say, mostly to the void between us. Then, because I can't help myself: "Ever heard of something called manners?" A habit drilled into me early—one of the few things my adoptive parents insisted on.

She just looks at me, lips curling at the corners before she reins it in.

When I finally pull into the gravel lot by the docks, the glow of the overhead lights spills across the car. Lennon's profile catches in the haze, soft and almost unreal.

I steal another glance. This time, she catches me. Her expression shifts—then comes the smile, wide and unguarded; it halts me mid-breath. Just like that, the tension fractures, replaced by something warmer.

God, she's beautiful. Not in a way that demands attention, but in a way that quietly dismantles your defenses before you realize you've surrendered.

"Dock & Diana's?" she asks.

I nod. Her gaze drifts back to the dock, lips curving slightly. The planks creak beneath the weight of history— secrets, whispers, and probably tetanus.

"You know this place?" The question escapes before I can stop it. Obvious. Pointless. This is her hometown.

I hop out of the truck and round to her side, reaching the door just before she does. I pull it open, hand extended—

maybe too eagerly. She takes it anyway, her fingers warm against mine.

Then it happens. A jolt skimming down my spine.

"Yes." The word unfurls slowly. She steps down, hair spilling over her shoulders, catching the breeze, the moonlight.

For a moment, I just watch. She moves with an easy gravity, drawing me in without trying.

"You coming?" She peeks back, teeth grazing her bottom lip. My pulse stumbles. I nod, mutter something useless, and jog to catch up.

When I reach her, I take her hand hesitantly. She doesn't pull away. Her fingers settle into mine like they belong there.

The next hour drifts by. She orders a vodka tonic; I go for a Sea Dog Blueberry Wheat. When it's time for food, she scans the menu briefly before deciding.

"Lobster-Stuffed Mushrooms to start," she says with a grin. "Then the Pan-Seared Scallops with Wild Blueberry Reduction."

I don't bother looking at the menu. "I'll have the same." Maybe it's cliché, but I don't care. Tonight, I want to see what she sees, taste what she tastes.

While we wait, her attention drifts toward the water. A September gust ripples the surface, scattering gold as the sun sinks lower.

"What does this place mean to you?" I ask, breaking the easy silence.

She turns slowly, eyes meeting mine with a trace of hesitation. Whether it's the question or the memories it stirs, I can't tell.

Looking down, she twists the tiny straw in her drink, fingers moving absently. "My parents and I used to come here," she admits. A pause. A breath. Then, a sip—like the drink might dilute whatever's rising to the surface.

"Every weekend."

I watch her closely as she grips her glass, her gaze unfocused, lost in thought. She takes another sip—not from thirst, but to steady herself. I don't ask, but the question lingers: What happened to them? I've only ever seen her with her grams. Never anyone else.

"It was nice . . . a family tradition, I guess."

Without thinking, I reach across the table and cover her hand with mine. It's instinctive, maybe too forward. Her eyes flick to the touch, her fingers hesitating before relaxing beneath my own. When she looks up again, something in her expression softens—a quiet, wordless gratitude that tightens my chest.

For a moment, we sit like this, her warmth beneath my palm, the rest of the world fading away.

"Is this . . . weird?"

At first, I don't follow. Weird? Then I see where she's looking—our joined hands, my thumb tracing slow, idle circles against her skin. My breath catches.

Subtle, Jack. Real subtle.

My hand jerks back as if burned. "I—I'm sorry," I stammer, heat rising up my neck. "Guess I'm just . . . used to it." The words land clumsily, wrong the moment they leave my mouth.

Lennon watches me, unreadable. "As Sheriff, I spend a lot of time consoling people. Comes with the job." A weak excuse. My attempt at a smile barely holds.

A shadow skims across her face—brief, unreadable. Then she looks away, and I feel it: A thread snapping, a distance settling between us. Did I just ruin this?

The server arrives with our appetizers, and I seize the distraction. "Thanks," I mutter, ordering a refill I don't need. Lennon picks at her food, silent, lost in thoughts I can't reach. The knot in my stomach tightens.

After a few tense, silent bites, an idea sparks—half-formed, maybe reckless, but better than sitting in this thickening quiet. I take a slow sip of beer, set the glass down, and push my chair back.

Her head snaps up, brows lifting.

"Miss Harrington," I say, aiming for confidence—or at least something steadier than flight. "May I have the honor of a dance?"

For a beat, she studies me as if I've spoken in another language. My chest clenches, but before I can retreat, she smiles.

Not just any smile—the kind that knocks the breath from my lungs.

Her hand slips into mine, delicate but sure, leaving a trail of goosebumps in its wake. She's close now, close enough for me to catch the faint mix of citrus, lavender, and vanilla clinging to her skin. It's dangerous how familiar it feels.

"Miss Harrington, is it?" she teases. "Haven't heard that since college."

I let out a quiet, uneven chuckle as a strand of her dark hair falls across her face. Without thinking, I tuck it back, fingers grazing her jaw. Warm. Impossibly soft. My hand lingers a second too long.

Her pupils dilate, her breath falters. I lean in—closer than I should. "Better get used to it," I murmur.

I pull back just enough to meet those impossibly blue eyes, daring me to go further. I smirk. "My mom always said, 'Manners don't cost a thing, but they're worth a lot.'"

She laughs, light and effortless, pressing a palm to my chest. The sound warms me, sharp and sudden, almost embarrassing in its intensity. Hand in hand, we drift to the dock's edge, where an old record player waits, its needle hovering over the vinyl.

I drop the needle, and *Real Love Baby* by Father John Misty spills into the cool night, twining with the hush of water lapping below. Overhead, strings of golden lights sway, their glow catching in her smile, making it somehow brighter.

We sway, tentative at first, our rhythm unsure. But soon, the music finds us, and we fall into it like muscle memory, our movements instinctive. The last of her tension unspools, and for a while, the world softens, dissolving into rhythm and light.

"Tell me something, Lennon."

She turns, her back brushing my chest. I slip an arm around her waist as she leans into me, her warmth seeping through the fabric of my shirt, her hair a whisper against my jaw.

"Growing up, I only had one best friend," she murmurs, a soft ache woven through her words.

Just one best friend? The way she says it—without self-pity, yet weighted with quiet restraint—pulls me in.

I twirl her out slowly and when I pull her back, her smile lingers, and she leans in, just the slightest bit closer.

"Tell me something, Jack."

My hands find her hips, instinctive. For a moment, we stand there, bodies aligned, watching moonlight ripple across the water.

"I'm adopted." The words escape before I've fully chosen them.

She stills. So subtle most wouldn't notice, but I do. No judgment, just quiet curiosity, maybe caution. It urges me forward.

"It's fine," I add quickly, easing the weight I've placed between us. "I don't mind talking about it. My parents—they're amazing. They adopted me right away, so I never dealt with foster homes or anything like that. I got lucky. Some of my friends . . . their stories weren't so easy."

She stays quiet, giving me space to find my own rhythm. Somehow, that makes it easier.

"My parents told me what they could, but there's still so many . . . I don't know. Loose threads." I glance at the water, its surface stretching endlessly into the dark. "That's part of why I'm here in Cedar Cove—trying to piece it all together."

She softens, tension ebbing as she leans in, tilting her head back until our eyes meet. Something in her gaze holds me there, the world shrinking to just her and the quiet pull between us.

God, the urge to kiss her—it's unbearable. The thought of those impossibly soft, naturally pink lips against mine sends a slow, aching heat through me. What would it feel like to lose myself in that kiss, to taste something I've only dared to imagine?

Only one way to find out.

My hand drifts to the back of her head, fingers threading through her hair, drawing her closer. Her eyes flick to my lips —a silent invitation. My pulse pounds as I lean in, caught in the gravity of her, everything else fading.

Then, just as our lips are about to meet, a rough hand clamps down on my shoulder.

Instinct takes over. I pivot sharply, grabbing the intruder's wrist and twisting it in one clean motion. Years of training kick in, and in a blink, I've got him pinned—his back pressed to me, his arm locked in a chokehold.

"Jesus, Mercer! It's just me," a familiar voice grunts.

I freeze. My brain catches up with my body, and I realize it's Benson. *My deputy.* Eleven years older than me, with streaks of gray in his hair, now wide-eyed and struggling against my hold.

Jules, his wife, stands a few feet away, hands clapped over her mouth in shock as she watches me untangle myself from her husband. I release him with a muttered curse, a flush of heat climbing up my neck.

"Damn, sorry, man." I clap Benson on the back, hoping

it's more "we're good, right?" than "I just nearly choked you out."

Benson shakes out his wrist with a wry grin, brushing off the moment. "No worries, I get it. Trust me."

He would. After years in the field, he knows how intuition guides him. There's no time to think when danger looms—you react, hands up, ready to protect, ready to defend. If you're lucky, you don't end up accidentally taking down one of your own.

Our server catches my eye, signaling that our food's ready. On a whim, I invite Benson and Jules to join us. Maybe their company will help smooth out the awkwardness still clinging to the air—and keep me from jumping out of my skin again.

Jules doesn't need much convincing. Ever the social butterfly, she slides into a chair with a warm smile, instantly easing the tension. "So, Lennon," she starts, her tone friendly, almost too polite, like we didn't all just witness me almost strangle her husband. "I heard you're helping out your grandma? How much longer are you planning to stay in town?"

Lennon pauses, her fork hovering midair. She hesitates, her fork dropping to her plate. "I haven't decided," she admits. "I guess it depends on my grams. I want to make sure she's all set before I leave."

That last word—*leave*—hangs in the air.

I try not to react, but it hits me—a dull, heavy ache right in my chest. Of course, she's not here to stay. Why would she be?

Jules, oblivious, keeps the conversation moving. "That's so sweet of you. Not everyone would uproot their life to help family like that."

Lennon smiles politely but doesn't look up. I can tell she's trying not to let the weight of the question show, but it's there, lingering in the quiet spaces.

I grab my beer, hoping the bitterness will wash away the thought creeping in: *What am I doing?*

Benson bulldozes the moment. "Lillian's granddaughter, right?"

Lennon nods as she cuts her food with precision, her movements neat and deliberate, leaving me to follow suit. I spear a scallop and take a bite. Sweet, buttery, perfectly seared —it's a world apart from my usual grease-bomb burgers. For a second, it feels like an escape.

Benson and Jules order another round of drinks, but Benson keeps stealing glances at Lennon, like she's a riddle he's determined to solve. Finally, he clears his throat.

"That's what I thought," he mutters to himself. Then, louder: "So that would make Samuel your father, right?"

The question lands hard. Lennon's face shutters, fast and final. She dabs her napkin against her lips, as if it's the only thing anchoring her in the moment.

Benson, either oblivious or indifferent, presses on. "Must've been tough, huh? Losing them like that. Poof, gone. And then the Callahans' only son, years later." He clicks his tongue. "Interesting cases, if you ask me."

Jules shoots him a warning look that should have shut him up on the spot. It doesn't. Benson just leans back, plucks a cold mushroom off the plate, and pops it into his mouth like he's talking about the weather.

"Oh, and did you know Jacky-boy over here is working on Rhett Callahan's case?" Benson jerks his thumb my way, grinning like he's letting her in on some private joke. "Well . . . trying to work it."

The bastard winks.

I level him with a withering look, the kind that should make it painfully clear: *What the hell is wrong with you?* Benson's been a thorn in my side since he got hired as my deputy, but in a town of 5,000, the hiring pool isn't exactly deep.

Across the table, Lennon stiffens. Her piercing gaze locks with mine, but beneath the anger in her eyes, there's something quieter—resignation, maybe. She's bracing herself; daring me to come clean or forcing her hand to dig out the truth herself.

This was supposed to be a date. Good food, small talk, maybe some harmless banter. Not . . . this. Murder cases from the past don't belong at a table with cloth napkins and overpriced drinks. But Benson? Benson's about as subtle as a lit match in a firework factory.

Lennon hasn't said a word since his latest bomb dropped. She's pale now, a shade that suggests she's holding her breath or bracing for impact. I glance at her again, and something about the way she looks jolts me, as if she's seen a ghost. Or maybe worse, she's recognized it.

Rhett Callahan. That name has haunted this town for years, hanging in the air like smoke that refuses to clear. An unsolved murder so raw people still whisper when they mention it. He was Lennon's age back then. *Seventeen.* A high school senior.

I try not to piece it together, but the fragments connect anyway.

"Did you know him?" Benson's question, far too casual to be innocent. "He grew up here."

Lennon's breath hitches—barely noticeable, but I catch it. Her shoulders tense, her whole frame radiating unease.

This is the moment I should step in. Shut Benson down. Crack a joke, change the subject—anything to steer us away from the edge.

But then Lennon confesses, "He was my best friend."

Fuck.

My brain stumbles, tripping over itself to catch up, to

make sense of what I should've seen sooner. The best friend she'd mentioned before—was it Rhett? I don't need the universe to confirm it; the truth's already twisting its way into my chest, biting and unforgiving.

Benson doesn't seem to notice, chewing lazily on the last of the appetizers. Across the table, Lennon sits frozen.

Rhett. Samuel. Hannah. One after another, stolen from this town. Brutal, senseless. I've spent sleepless nights combing through their files, haunted by what's buried between the lines. And now Lennon—sitting here in front of me, like she's been living in the middle of it all this time, caught in a nightmare that started long before I ever stepped into it.

"I'm so sorry, Lennon." Jules leans across the table to embrace her in a soft, protective hug. Lennon offers a faint, brittle smile, but it's strained; her gaze locked somewhere far away—and definitely not on me.

Jules shoots Benson an unmistakable *we're done here* glare. For once, he doesn't need it spelled out.

Benson fidgets, clearing his throat as he leans across the table to give Lennon's hand an awkward squeeze. "Looking forward to seeing you around Cedar Cove, Lennon," he mumbles, his usual bravado peeling back just enough to sound almost sincere.

Lennon waves weakly as he leaves, and then it's just us. The silence that follows is heavy. The server swoops in to clear the plates, looking like she regrets every life choice that brought her over at this moment.

After an eternity, Lennon speaks, her words hushed, fragile against the clink of silverware. "Why didn't you tell me?"

Her hands tremble, tracing invisible shapes on the table. Then, slowly, she curls them into fists; her knuckles bone-white, like she's holding herself together by force.

Do something, Mercer.

However, before I'm able to, she pushes her chair back with a grating scrape of wood on tile. "Sorry. This was a mistake." She snatches her purse and heads for the parking lot. Her movements are quick, almost jagged.

It takes me a second to snap out of it, adrenaline spiking as I follow her outside. She stops suddenly, spinning to face me. Her expression is wiped clean except for the hard, unrelenting line of her mouth.

"I'm ready to go home."

I nod, stepping closer and taking her hands. They're trembling, ice cold. I hold on tight, hoping she can feel what I can't seem to say—that I didn't know about Rhett, that I'd have told her if I did.

Her entire body stiffens. Her fingers lock around mine, tight as a vise.

Her eyes flick past me, wide and dark, locking on something—or someone—behind me.

"Jack," she whispers, her breath trembling. "We need to leave. Now."

CHAPTER 6

"I can't exactly say, 'Hey, I think I saw my best friend and first love'," I mutter, rubbing my temples. "'Oh, and, by the way, he's also the guy in the case you're working on.'" The words barely leave my mouth before I realize how completely ridiculous they sound.

Maggie's face on the screen stays unreadable—her version of a poker face, except with more judgment. "I mean, you *could* . . . " she says, dragging the words out like they're walking through mud. The hesitation says it all.

I narrow my eyes. "And sound completely unhinged?"

Her mouth twitches into a grin as she lifts her mug—pumpkin spice latte, naturally. I don't even need to smell it to know it's brimming with cinnamon, nutmeg, and smug autumn superiority. It's obnoxiously perfect for her, just like everything else. And fine, maybe I'd want one too—if it weren't forbidden territory here, where Grams' herbal tea empire reigns supreme. October doesn't make that easier. October *wants* me to cave.

Maggie chuckles, low and knowing. "Yeah, you'd sound crazy. Not that you don't already."

I groan, tossing another pair of socks onto the chaotic pile of half-unpacked clothes on the bed. When I packed for Grams', I figured I'd be back in a week, tops. Now, it's three weeks later, and I've been living out of the same five shirts and a revolving door of Grams' vintage cardigans. She says I'm rocking the "classic librarian" vibe. She's too polite to add, "and possibly homeless."

At least my boss doesn't care that I'm working remotely now that my PTO has officially run out. He called this morning to remind me—like I might have forgotten—that the Washington case is still mine. "Don't lose focus," he said. I didn't bother telling him this case has been living rent-free in my head for weeks.

Fifteen years ago, a family of three vanished from their suburban home. No struggle. No break-in. No nothing. Then, out of nowhere, the mother's wedding ring turns up in a pawnshop 300 miles away. No big deal, right? Just one of the weirdest leads I've seen in years. Lucky me—I get to unravel it.

I groan as I sift through my clothes, more out of frustration than anything else. It's not the case that's bothering me. I'm good at this part. Too good, honestly. But cases like these —missing families, long-dead mysteries—they have a way of stirring up things I'd rather leave alone. Things like my parents. The last time I stayed in this room for more than a week, I was learning how to live without them.

"Lenny, we both know you didn't see Rhett."

I freeze, fingers curled around the sleeve of an old sweater. "I don't know, Mags . . . "

The silence stretches, heavy and expectant, until she sighs. "Lennon," she says, softer this time, like she's afraid of pushing too hard. "You know it's not possible."

She wants me to say she's right. That it wasn't him. That

my mind's just dredging up ghosts from being back here. But I can't. Because there's a small part of me—desperate and foolish—that isn't so sure. I can still see his dark eyes, always brimming with secrets and jokes meant just for me. That boyish charm, like he was on the verge of saying something important, but never quite did. Every part of me wants to believe it wasn't just a trick of the mind. It *was* him.

I curse myself, for the hundredth time, for buying into the fantasy. The memory of him sprawled on the pavement barges in uninvited—blood pooling, bruises blooming like some horrific garden, fingers twisted at impossible angles. It clings to me, vivid and stubborn, but the tears never come. They never do.

Maybe Maggie's right. Maybe Grams is, too. When I told her what I'd seen, she just shook her head. "Told ya you shouldn't have come back. Nothin' good's gonna come of it."

She's probably right. But I'm here now. Leaving isn't an option. Not anymore.

I dig through the heap of clothes on my bed until I find my brown sweater dress. Cozy, but with enough structure to double as armor. Pair it with tall boots—the ones with just enough heel—and maybe, with a little mascara and a few curls, I'll pass for someone who hasn't completely unraveled. At least to strangers.

"I've always loved that dress," Maggie comments wistfully, her words a lifeline to my sinking mood.

I force a thin smile and smooth my hands over the fabric, pretending it's enough to anchor me. I grab my phone, exhale slowly, but my eyes slide to the window. They always do. The late afternoon breeze carries a hint of salt from the ocean, wrapping around me like an almost-comfort. Almost.

"You're still going to the festival, right?"

I nod absently, but my attention stays on the window. The same woman is in Rhett's room again, moving like she's locked in some eternal contract to clean up his ghost. The question gnaws at me as it has every day this week: Why? What's left to clean in there, over and over again?

But today, something's different. She's not carrying her usual bucket and rags. No, today it's black garbage bags—big ones. Several of them. I lean forward, squinting. There's writing on the bags, but it's so small it might as well be hieroglyphics. My heart starts to thud.

"Len, you there?" Maggie's voice pushes in, but I'm already drifting toward the window. I drop to my knees, pressing my nose against the glass. Subtlety has officially left the building.

"Lennon, what the hell are you doing?" I press a finger to my lips, the universal sign for *mind your business*, and she huffs, crossing her arms. But for once, she doesn't argue. Small miracles.

The woman reappears, dragging another garbage bag. This time, she steps into a patch of light, and I catch part of what's printed on the side. Faint, but unmistakable: *RC*.

Rhett Callahan.

My stomach flips. Those are his things. His *stuff*. And they're being tossed into garbage bags like leftovers from a bad garage sale. My mind goes straight to panic mode: Why? Who gave her the right? Rhett would've wanted his things donated to someone who needed them, not dumped in a landfill like a stack of expired coupons.

Maggie clears her throat, clearly unimpressed. "So, are you planning to keep spying, or are you going to clue me in before you sprain something?"

I slump against the wall, letting out a breath that's about 80% existential dread. "I just . . . " The words choke somewhere on their way out. I peek at her, and for once, she's not scowling. She's just waiting, arms still crossed, but her gaze softening.

I drop my face into my hands and rub my eyelids like I'm trying to erase a smudge on my brain. "This is insane," I admit finally. "The dreams, the memories, this . . . feeling."

Maggie tilts her head. "What are you saying?"

I shake my head. Honestly? No clue. But I know one thing for sure: *Everything happens for a reason.* Mom used to say that all the time, and somewhere along the way, it became gospel. Those words carried me through my parents' deaths, through Rhett's, and now . . . well, now I'm back in Cedar Cove, staring down ghosts I didn't even know were still haunting me.

"I don't know." A defeated sigh escapes me.

"This is why I told you to keep me in the loop," she states, equal parts exasperated and fond. "I knew this would be hard on you, Lenny. I can see it. The weight of it clings to you, twisting you up in ways you can't shake loose."

I sigh. No point in arguing. She's annoyingly observant.

"I know," I whisper. "I guess I just thought . . . after being away for so long . . . coming back wouldn't feel so—"

"So what?" Maggie prods.

"Hard. Messy. Sad. Like someone dumped a pile of ghosts on my chest," I half-wince at the words.

"Sweetie, you knew this wasn't going to be easy. But you're stronger than you give yourself credit for. You're a badass journalist, one of the smartest detectives I know—your instincts are keen enough to catch anything. And even though this isn't about solving a case, you'll get through it. You've got this, Lenny."

I look at her, skeptical.

Maggie smirks, completely undeterred. "Spend time with Grams. Don't overthink everything for once in your life. Maybe even have fun. I know, *fun* is a radical suggestion, but humor me."

Her words hang there like an open door, but one phrase

sticks: You're not here to solve anything. Then why does it feel like I am? Why did I run into Jack the second I got back? And why is he wrapped up in the case that took Rhett and left me stuck in its orbit, tangled with memories of my parents and every other thing I can't seem to let go?

"Speaking of fun . . . " Maggie's voice jolts me back. She takes an unhurried sip of coffee, her eyes gleaming with mischief over the rim.

"Not happening," I declare, already standing. I grab the dress off my bed and hold it up, catching my reflection in the mirror. The fabric drapes over my figure in a way that actually looks . . . kind of decent. One of those rare outfits that reminds me I do, in fact, have a shape under all the existential dread.

I roll my eyes. "Fantastic."

"Oh, come on, Lennon. It's just a festival. It doesn't have to mean anything." She doesn't say Jack's name, but she doesn't have to. This entire conversation is wearing a neon sign that says *Jack*, and I hate it.

Maggie keeps going. "When was the last time you even let yourself have fun?" she asks, as I slip the sweater dress on.

I'm opening my mouth to throw out some kind of deflection when the door creaks. We both turn as Grams steps into the room, looking between us suspiciously. Her eyes narrow with a no-nonsense look that could make a criminal confess on the spot.

"Ready t'head to the festival?" she asks, her gaze missing nothing.

Am I ready? Not remotely. It's not just *a* festival; it's *the* festival. The one day of the year that sticks to me like gum on the bottom of a shoe. My usual strategy for surviving it involves burying myself in work, inhaling an unhealthy amount of takeout with Maggie, and pretending it doesn't exist. Maggie, to her credit, hasn't brought it up. Yet.

"Hi, Grams!" Maggie chirps, waving through the tension like it's invisible.

Grams looks me over, her lips quirking with faint amusement. "Lennon, you look like you heading to a root canal, not a festival. Try to remember, it's a celebration, not a court summons."

Her attention shifts to my phone. "Maggie! How's life treatin' ya?"

Maggie grins, already slipping into her usual charm. "Can't complain. Just trying to keep this one from overthinking herself into early retirement." She jerks her head toward me, her eyes sparkling as she mouths, *Told you so.*

I roll my eyes, pretending not to notice, though a flicker of warmth tugs at me. Watching the two of them fall into their easy banter, like old friends who've known each other forever, reminds me of the first time I introduced Maggie to Grams. They hit it off immediately—Grams' boundless energy matched with Maggie's quick wit was a recipe for chaos I'd somehow survived.

"Please tell Lennon to let herself have some fun," Maggie remarks.

"Not happening." My response is practically on autopilot at this point.

"What's not happenin'?" Grams' curiosity perks up.

"Jack," Maggie answers, blunt as a hammer.

Grams' eyebrows arch, her mouth forming a small "O" before curling into something that screams, *Oh, this is going to be fun.* "Ahh . . . Jack, is it?" Her chuckle has enough mischief in it to make me regret all of my life choices. She shoots me a sidelong glance, her grin too pleased. "Well, don't you worry yourself none 'bout that, Lenny."

I shake my head, grabbing my phone like it's a lifeline. "Like I said, not happening, Mags. Love you. Tell everyone I say hi." Before she can lob another verbal missile, I jab the end call button a little too hard, my heart thumping like I just sprinted up a hill.

Grams gives me a look so flat it could level a city block. "That was awfully rude, Lenny."

I shrug, aiming for indifferent but probably landing somewhere in the neighborhood of guilty. "She'll live." Then, without waiting for further judgment, I take her hand and help her down the creaky stairs, the wood groaning louder than my conscience.

Outside, the cool autumn air slaps me across the face—a seasonal memo that I forgot my gloves. I open the car door for Grams, and she slides in with a sigh so deep it could fuel a power grid. Before heading to the festival, I make an essential pit stop at the coffee shop. If I'm going to survive Cedar Cove's annual trifecta of pumpkin crafts, repressed grief over my parents and Rhett, and the usual small-town theatrics, a pumpkin spice latte is non-negotiable.

"How you feelin', Lenny girl?" Grams asks as we navigate the crowded tents of the fall festival. Around here, this isn't just an event; it's a spectator sport with a side of everything. Everyone shows up, not for the apple cider or handmade soap, but to confirm that nobody's moved, improved, or escaped.

I glance at her. We're both thinking the same thing, because we always are. My parents—her son and daughter-in-law—are gone. This festival has a knack for stirring that up, like grief has a standing invitation. It's also the anniversary of when I lost my best friend and first love. Cedar Cove doesn't forget, and neither do I.

But that's not happening now. And I don't feel like wrestling with ghosts today.

"I'm good."

Grams raises one of her eyebrows. "Good, huh?"

"Better than good." I muster some fake-it-til-you-make-it enthusiasm. "I'm fantastic. Practically glowing."

She snorts, clearly unconvinced, but lets it go. "That's more like it."

The surprising thing is, I might actually mean it. When Maggie guilted me into coming to this festival a few hours ago, I wasn't so sure. This used to be the family event—Dad sneaking extra funnel cakes, Mom laughing at corny scarecrow contests, Grams herding us like the unpaid CEO of Holiday Cheer, Inc. Coming here should sting. And it does, but this year it feels . . . softer, like grief with the edges sanded down.

We wander into a jewelry tent, and my stomach does a weird jump when I see the setup. It's that tent—the one where they permanently clasp a delicate chain on your wrist. I've wanted one of these for years, but always chickened out. Too impractical. Too permanent. Too . . . much.

But today, there's this flicker of something—call it rebellion or stupidity—nudging me forward. Maggie's voice lingers in my mind: *Do something fun, something just for you.*

This counts as fun, right?

I eye my wrist, nerves kicking in. Back in Washington, where my days were all deadlines and deliverables, this would've felt pointless. Maybe even silly. But now? Today? It feels strangely important.

It's not just jewelry, it's a tiny, shiny reminder to stop sprinting through my life like it's a to-do list.

I grab Grams' hand, grinning. "We're doing this together."

Her eyes light up like I've just told her we won the lottery. "Oh, honey, I thought you'd never ask."

We sit down in folding chairs as two women with pliers approach us like jewelers-slash-surgeons. Grams and I exchange a conspiratorial glance and say in perfect unison, "Gold link, with an H."

For Harrington.

When the clasps snap shut, I raise my wrist, letting the delicate chain glint in the autumn sunlight. It's perfect.

Grams holds up her own wrist beside mine, and we exchange a look that doesn't need words. I snap a photo of our matching bracelets and send it to Maggie.

LENNON

Having fun

MAGGIE

That's not what I meant, but now I want one too!

I nudge Grams. "Looks like we just started a trend."

She pats my hand with a straight face. "Brace yourself, darlin'. By Christmas, everyone's going to be copying us."

I chuckle, slipping my phone into my wristlet, still smiling as we step out of the tent—only to walk straight into something solid.

Not something. Someone.

Jack.

His hands catch my forearms, steadying me, and even through my sweater dress, his touch feels unreasonably warm. We both freeze. His eyes latch onto mine, and suddenly, my heart is sprinting.

"Lennon . . ." My name low and husky on his lips.

"Jack," I respond, attempting for casual and landing somewhere between a gasp and a whisper.

And, of course, I observe him. Henley shirt—salmon pink, somehow just ironic enough to work—white Carhartt jacket, dark jeans, boots. Hair a little messy, like he ran a hand through it on the way over.

My stomach churns, and for half a second, I wonder if someone else messed up his hair.

Before I can follow the thought too far, he flashes a grin—

equal parts charm and trouble. "You okay? Didn't mean to bowl you over."

"I'm fine," I manage, attempting to sound nonchalant as my cheeks betray me by turning red. "Just wasn't paying attention."

His eyebrow quirks, amusement flickering in his eyes. "Not exactly a new habit, is it?"

And I know exactly what he's thinking about—the time I nearly ran him over with my SUV. One time. That happened *one time.*

I open my mouth, ready to fire back, but Grams clears her throat behind me. Jack drops his hands from my arms so fast it's like he's been caught doing something far more scandalous.

I step back, trying to shake the swirl of emotions twisting inside me, but it's no use. Because Jack's still standing there, smiling like he knows *exactly* what kind of trouble he is.

Grams and Jack slip into conversation with the ease of old friends. Watching them, a pang of guilt hits me—not sharp, just a dull ache I've been carrying around all week. I'd kept myself busy with an endless list of pointless tasks—fixing faucets, patching porch steps, scrubbing grout like it was a competitive sport. But it wasn't just me. I'd dragged Grams into it too, keeping us locked in the house as if staying busy together could undo what happened at the dock.

"Oh, I almost forgot!" Grams announces, her voice a little too chipper. She turns to me with a smile so bright it's practically suspicious. "I need to swing by Betty's booth. Promised I'd pick up some of her jams and that herbal tea."

I frown, catching the overly casual tone. "Grams, I can go with—"

She cuts me off with a dismissive wave. "No need, Lenny girl. You stay here and catch up with Jack." Her eyes dart between us like she's matchmaking two stubborn mules.

It hits me: She knew. She *planned* this. The sudden, almost gleeful lack of concern she had back home? This was why. This was her plan all along.

Before I can fully grasp the betrayal, she's already melted into the crowd, her cane in hand, the walker she stubbornly left behind today vanishing with the practiced stealth of someone who's mastered the art of disappearing.

And just like that, I'm standing there with Jack. Alone.

Around us, the festival buzzes with laughter, the clink of cider glasses, the faint smell of caramel apples. Neither of us speaks right away. The silence feels thick, heavy with things neither of us seems ready to say.

When I finally lift my eyes, I find him already watching me.

CHAPTER 7

Jack

Her eyes flit everywhere—the game booths, the distant Ferris wheel, even the ground—as if anything else might hold her attention more than this moment.

How exactly do you strike up a conversation with someone who scrambles your nerves *and* ties you to the worst chapter of their life? Best friend, first love, unsolved murder—it's a trauma buffet, and I'm the guy asking for seconds.

I jam my hands in my pockets, every muscle in my body screaming *bail.* But no, running won't fix anything. I've waited for this. Haven't I? The chance to see her, to finally set the record straight.

I glance at the carnival games, honing in on the baseball toss. "Wanna give it a try?" I ask, aiming for casual, though my heart's pounding loud enough to qualify as background music.

She follows me over, but her gaze is miles away, her face softening in a way that makes my chest tighten. Is she thinking about Rhett? The thought lands bitter, but I push it aside.

Jealous of a memory? Get over yourself.

I pay for three tries, the carnie behind the counter looking like he'd rather be anywhere else. The first baseball feels solid in my hand, grounding me. I offer it to her.

She shakes her head. Her faint and bittersweet smile is somehow sad and lovely at the same time. Something shifts. My chest goes from tightening to aching, and before I know it, I squeeze her hand—quick, gentle, gone—then turn and throw the ball.

"I'm glad I ran into you," I confess.

She pauses, then smiles for real this time, letting it reach her eyes. "Me too."

Fueled by a surge of adrenaline, I land the winning throw on my last attempt and earn a ludicrously oversized stuffed animal that I have zero intention of keeping. Grinning, I hold it out to her, fully expecting an eye-roll or a sarcastic "thanks". But Lennon laughs, shakes her head, and asks the carnie for a caramel-brown trucker hat instead—one with *Cedar Cove* stitched across the front. She pops it on, tilts the brim, and shoots me a look so playful and flirtatious it makes breathing seem optional.

The next hour slips by in a haze of carnival lights. We eat our way through donuts coated in cinnamon sugar, steaming clam chowder, and cider that's nearly hot enough to scorch my tongue. When I joke about finding something pumpkin-flavored, she scrunches her nose and says she's hit her limit after an earlier latte—a drink her grams didn't approve of. I laugh, and for some reason, I add "Pumpkin Spice Latte" to the mental list of things I suddenly want to try.

For a while, it feels weirdly normal. Just two people at a fall festival, with no trauma weighing them down.

As we near the Ferris wheel, I catch a trace of excitement on Lennon's face. She tries to mask it, stoic as always, but I know some of her tells by now. I nod toward the ride, and she doesn't argue. I hand over our tickets and watch a couple of kids climb into the seats ahead of us before it's our turn.

The narrow four-seater is colder than it looks, the metal pressing against my back as the operator pulls the gate down with a decisive *click*. It feels unnecessarily final.

No backing out now.

The Ferris wheel lurches to life, lifting us into the crisp autumn air. For a moment, we just sit there, silent, as Cedar Cove stretches out below—a moody postcard of cloudy skies and muted light. The cove itself is dark and glassy, licking at the rocky shore. The lighthouse stands off in the distance, perfectly stoic, like it's judging the rest of us for falling apart.

Lennon breaks the silence, just a breath of sound. "I'm sorry."

I blink, caught off guard. "What?"

She turns to face me, her knee bumping mine in the cramped gondola. The casual contact is enough to short-circuit my brain. Suddenly, I'm hyper-aware of everything: her perfume, the tight space, and the fact that there's literally nowhere else to look but at her. On autopilot, I grab her fidgeting hands, holding them still in mine.

"For what?" I ask, though my heart is beating so loudly it's amazing she can't hear it.

She exhales, "Honestly? Everything." She lets out a small laugh, one that falls flat before it even leaves her lips. "For messing up our date—or, I guess, not-date. Whatever that was."

"Date," I blurt out before my brain catches up to my mouth.

Her eyes flick up, a smile tugging at the corners of her mouth. "Fine, date," she says, lighter now. But then her attention drops back to our hands, her smile fading. "And for how I left things before. I know I shouldn't have let it . . . get to me so much, but . . . " she trails off, clearly struggling to find the right words.

"It does," I finish for her.

Her eyes snap to mine, startled, then softening with a kind of quiet gratitude. It's the look of someone who didn't know they needed their feelings spelled out until they heard it.

Funny how this was supposed to be my big moment—the perfect chance to explain everything. Instead, all I want to do is stay right here, in this tiny bubble where the world doesn't matter, where apologies and confessions can wait, and all that exists is her hands in mine and the slow spin of the wheel below.

But life doesn't work like that. Sooner or later, the wheel comes down.

She nods, swallowing hard, clearly wrestling with whatever's struggling to surface. "Being back home . . . it's stirred up a lot of memories. Not all of them good." Her voice trembles. "There are good ones too, of course. But then Benson started digging into everything, and I just . . . "

I lean in, letting go of one of her hands to press my palm against her cheek. My thumb brushes lightly over her skin. "You don't have to explain. I get it."

And I do, or at least enough to recognize the shape of the storm she's in. Some questions don't just sit quietly in the back of your mind; they pitch a tent, throw wild parties, and refuse to leave.

Lennon drops her gaze, shoulders shifting as if she's bracing for an impact or deciding whether to jump ship. After a moment, she takes a breath and finally asks, "Is it okay if I ask you something?"

She bites her lip, glancing up at me through her lashes like she's waiting for me to say no. I tilt my head slightly, giving her the go-ahead.

"How long have you been . . . working on his case?"

Rhett's case.

I glance toward the ocean, where the waves roll in the same way they did the night Mason called with the job offer. For a rookie, it was an opportunity most people wait years for. But it wasn't just the job that hooked me—it was what the job might lead to. Maybe, just maybe, it'd connect me to a piece of my own story, one I'd stopped pretending I didn't care about a long time ago.

"A couple of years."

She exhales, a shaky sigh that probably carries more weight than she realizes. "Sorry. I shouldn't be asking you about this."

I give her hand a quick squeeze, steadying her, or maybe myself. "You can ask me anything," I say.

She studies me, her expression caught between doubt and something harder to pin down. "Anything, huh?"

"Open book."

Her brow lifts, and the corner of her mouth twitches. "Oh really? An open book?"

We stare at each other just long enough for the tension to feel ridiculous. Then it snaps. She laughs first, and I follow, the sound cutting through the heaviness.

I shrug. "Okay, fine. Open book, selectively edited. But for a certain brown-haired, beautiful woman, I might throw in a bonus chapter or two." I tap the brim of her hat with a smirk, earning one of those soft, sideways smiles she's so good at.

The Ferris wheel groans as it hauls us higher, its slow, rhythmic lurch pulling us closer with every turn. By the time we're at the top again, we're leaning into each other, bodies pressed together, gazing out at the dark water below.

"God, it's beautiful," she breathes.

My eyes drift to her instead of the view. The carnival lights are painting her face in warm golds and pinks, like the night is trying to show off.

"Absolutely breathtaking," I whisper.

She shifts slightly, and in the confined space, our faces end up inches apart. Her eyes flick to my mouth, and mine do the same. Then she wets her lips—a quick, unconscious swipe of her tongue—and that tiny movement is all it takes to light the match.

We move simultaneously, meeting in a hesitant kiss. It's tentative; we're testing something fragile, but there's a spark that's impossible to ignore. She shifts, straddling my lap with an ease that makes it feel like this was inevitable.

A rush of lust kicks up a path through my veins the second her body presses against mine, filling every empty inch between us. My back meets the bars of the cage with a metallic clang, and my hands instinctively find her hips. Her curves feel like they were engineered for my hands. My fingers roam on autopilot: The dip of her waist, the arch of her back. I commit it all to memory because, let's face it, I don't know if I'll ever get this lucky again.

Her eyes hook mine—darker now under the shifting carnival lights. They're a swirl of indigo and something reckless, daring; she knows exactly what she's doing to me. Her mouth crashes into mine again, and all hesitation burns away. My grip on her hips tightens as I kiss her back, deeper this time, savoring the warmth, the softness, the perfect rhythm that's already making me forget where we are.

She tastes like something I can't quite name—sweet, familiar, maddeningly addictive. Then she moans, and it's like someone flipped the breaker in my brain. Her hat tumbles from her head, landing at our feet with a faint thud. That brief interruption pulls a breathless laugh out of both of us, though it barely lasts before we're colliding again.

Her hands knot in my hair, tugging just hard enough to drag her name out of me in a rasped, "Lennon," before I can swallow it. She catches my bottom lip between her teeth and gives it a teasing pull before letting it go, a move so devastatingly perfect I almost want to applaud her. When she starts to move against me—slow, deliberate—I forget how to breathe.

This shouldn't be happening. But stopping? That's not just hard—it's borderline illegal.

Her hands skim the hem of my shirt, fingers grazing my skin. Hot. Electric. Dangerous. "Fuck, Lennon," I manage, already drowning in her. I'm on the brink of losing myself entirely when the night splits open with a scream.

A raw, blood-curdling sound rips through the air, yanking us both back to reality with brutal force.

Her fingers clamp around my arm as a scream tears through the festival grounds, loud enough to slice through the cotton-candy haze. Below us, chaos spreads—parents yanking their kids close, vendors ditching their stalls mid-sale. For a moment, we're frozen, caught between the lingering heat of our kiss and the gut-punch of whatever just shattered the night.

Lennon slides off me, her expression shifting to grim determination as she scans the scene below. The Ferris wheel creaks beneath us, moving down in fits and starts, each jolt slower than the last. Whatever romantic moment we were wrapped up in has been unceremoniously evicted, replaced by adrenaline and muscle memory. This part, we know how to do.

The second our feet hit the ground, we're moving. The scream rises above the chaos of the carnival, clearer this time, enough to make you flinch. We push through the panicked crowd, shoulder to shoulder.

Then I see it, and everything stops.

A body lies sprawled in the dirt, limbs arranged like a puppet whose strings have been violently snipped. It's a woman—middle-aged, maybe late forties. Her maid's uniform is absurdly clean, pressed to perfection, like she dressed for work this morning and forgot to account for being murdered. Whoever did this was meticulous, an artist who insists you admire their work.

She might almost look peaceful if you ignored the wide, glassy stare or the slack mouth caught mid-scream. Bruises blossom across her face in sickly purples and blues, the type of marks that come from rage—or maybe just practice. Dried blood streaks from her nose to her chin, painting her lips a grotesque, almost purposeful red.

It's a signature. I know it too well. Rhett's case all over again—the broken bodies, the surgical precision, the way it haunted my sleep for weeks. Whoever did this wants us to notice. Wants *me* to notice.

Her hands make my stomach turn, bile clawing its way up my throat. Her pinky and thumb are snapped at the joints, bent at grotesque angles, like whoever did this had a twisted sense of geometry. Just like Rhett. I can almost see the killer stepping back to admire their work, tilting their head to make sure the symmetry was perfect. The other fingers curl inward, as if trying to protect themselves too late, while a delicate ring on her left hand catches the light in a tragic, mocking glint.

Beside me, the blood drains from Lennon's face. She swallows hard, once, twice, and then bolts. No warning, no words. She just turns and makes a beeline for the nearest bush.

I don't move. I can't. I just watch her bend over, retching so hard it sounds like it tears something inside her. It's unguarded—raw, painfully human. The moment when the body stops pretending.

For a moment, I consider going after her, maybe saying something comforting, or at least something vaguely useful. But before I'm able to shift, my boss and half the squad swarm in, a chaotic tangle of voices closing in—accusations, questions, demands. It's like they're shouting underwater.

But my mind's still stuck on Lennon. On the look in her eyes just before she ran.

It wasn't shock. Or horror.

It was something else. Something deeper. Almost as if . . .

Almost as if Lennon knew this woman.

CHAPTER 8

Lennon

"Lenny! What in God's name ya doin' up there so long?" Grams yells through the attic's stillness, loud enough to make the cobwebs consider unionizing. "There's things down here needin' handlin', ya know!"

I can picture her perfectly: Hands on hips, one sneaker tapping out a rhythm of pure exasperation. And sure enough, a second later comes the huff—Grams' trademark storm front of a sigh. It rattles the floorboards under me, carrying the not-so-subtle threat of blowing me down the stairs if I don't come voluntarily. "And don't forget about that damn toilet seat!"

I bite back a grin. The infamous toilet seat incident: A tale for the ages. The other day she'd hollered with a similar intensity to the day I came back to Cedar Cove, which sent me sprinting up the stairs in a full-blown panic. Broken hip? Stroke? Nope. Just Grams, wedged in the toilet like some tragicomic game of Twister gone wrong. Her face was the color of a fire hydrant; the toilet seat dangled at a defeated angle. She muttered something about "these cheap modern fixtures," but we both knew better. One job, Grams. Just one.

"Lennon!" My name floats up again, softer now. Bribery mode engaged. "Come on down. I made us some tea."

The scent of blueberry tea snakes its way up the drafty stairwell, sweet and earthy, doing its best to lure me down. But I'm not ready to leave just yet.

The beams above me look like the ribs of a forgotten giant, warped and dark with age, crisscrossing in uneven lines. Cobwebs sway from the rafters, shimmering with dust and dim light, and the space is thick with the smell of wood, mildew, and nostalgia. A smell that has snuck into my brain and started unpacking memories I wasn't sure I still had.

Downstairs, Grams probably thinks I'm up here sulking. Honestly? I just needed a minute. Maybe two. But at this rate, the toilet seat might still win the battle for my attention.

My eyes skim the cluttered towers of boxes—monuments to forgotten projects, holidays, and fragments of life someone thought worth saving. Then I see them: Two black-and-yellow storage tubes leaning against the wall, their marker labels as clear as if they'd been written yesterday.

Hannah. Samuel.

Their names strike like a clenched fist. The ache coils tighter, a sharp, familiar sting. Will it ever soften? Will there be a day I can see their names and breathe normally, without that dull, suffocating squeeze in my chest?

I've tried to grieve. God knows I've tried. But grief without answers is like trying to mop up an ocean. There's no sense to it, no logic that makes the whole thing bearable. It's just there, gnawing away, refusing to fade.

As if on cue, the memory barrels in again. It's been doing that all week, but this time, I'm awake. No escape in the attic, not from the dust, not from the ghosts.

The screams come first. High-pitched, frantic, desperate. Then the chaos: people shouting, shoving, and finally the red and blue strobes cutting through the dark. And then . . . the body.

The Callahans' maid. A crumpled heap on the ground, limbs bent at wrong angles, her face a terrible mosaic of bruises and fractures. I wanted to look away, but I couldn't. The sight of her made my stomach lurch—a mirror image of every other loss. Mom, Dad, Rhett. The same broken fingers. The same purple bruises, painted in the same places. Like some cruel, invisible hand had reached across years and miles to leave its signature.

And, of course, my brain did what it always does: It grabbed onto the first theory it could find and refused to let go. The Callahans. Could they have done it? Killed my parents? Killed their own son? It was absurd, a conspiracy even a half-baked detective novel would reject. And yet, once the idea rooted itself, it wouldn't let go.

It still doesn't. It curls up in the back of my head, sharp and nagging, whispering the same question over and over. *They wouldn't . . . would they?*

With a sigh, I slap my thighs, roll my neck, and try to shake myself out of this self-imposed paralysis. Just go downstairs. Go for a walk. Maybe even breathe. Groundbreaking ideas.

Before I can move, my phone vibrates. I pull it out and glance at the screen.

JACK

How are you?

How am I? Let's see . . . I'm fantastic. Just casually wading through the wreckage of my past, trying not to drown. Or better yet, I'm fifteen again, stumbling through a haunted house full of memories that claw at my ankles and drag me under. But hey, thanks for asking.

I almost laugh, but it gets stuck somewhere between my chest and throat. Of course, I don't text any of that back.

Jack doesn't need the full tour of my personal horror show. Besides, he probably already knows. He's been over at Grams' house a few times this week. Grams waves him off with a quick excuse—"She's busy" or "Not feeling well"— which is about as accurate as I'm willing to let anyone get right now.

He means well. He's sweet in that persistent, overly earnest way that should be endearing, but at the moment, it's one more thing I don't have the bandwidth for.

LENNON

I'm fine. Thanks for checking in.

Absolute lies, but it's polite, right? I turn off the phone and shove it back in my pocket like that'll contain the mess of my life.

The bins aren't going to unpack themselves, so I kneel and get to work, peeling back layers of dust and years. Inside each bin is a fragment of their lives, these scattered pieces of my parents. Every object is both alien and painfully well-known, like I've stepped into a museum I helped curate and then tried to forget existed.

My fingers graze Mom's old hairpiece—a barrette with blue diamonds and pearls, the sort of delicate crown she wore to make mundane Tuesdays feel like coronations. I grab it, cross the attic, and stop at the warped mirror propped up against the wall. It's so dusty I can barely see my reflection, but I still slide the barrette into my hair, clumsy like she used to be when fastening it. For a smudged, fleeting second, I almost see her.

"Hold still now, Lenny. Won't take but a second."

Her voice slices through memory, a beam of light—soft, yet brimming with that no-nonsense, resistance-is-futile mom tone. Her hands, focused and sure, had brushed back my hair like she was sketching a masterpiece.

"Maaawm, why do you even care about this thing? It's like . . . gaudy princess cosplay from the 80s," I groaned and rolled my eyes.

She didn't answer at first, just fastened the barrette with the precision of a jeweler placing the final gem. Then her hands settled on my shoulders, and she caught my stare in the mirror.

"There's my girl," she said, barely above a whisper.

"Oh no. Are you crying?" I deadpanned, as if the very idea was offensive.

"Don't sass me," she sniffed, laughing through her tears. Then she squeezed my shoulders. "It's just . . . you're growing up so fast."

"Kinda the point," I replied, already an expert in sarcasm.

"Maybe." She chuckled, brushing my hair one last time. "But not too fast, okay?"

I shrugged and hugged her anyway, her heartbeat thudding steadily under my cheek.

The sound of home. That moment felt timeless then, her soap scent, the faint sea-salt in her sweater, the warmth of her arms. It was one of those rare times when you think maybe you can hold on to something forever.

Spoiler: You can't.

Because that's what time does best—it slips. One day, they were here. The next . . . they weren't. Life stopped being something to savor and turned into something to endure. One foot in front of the other. I stopped worrying about growing up too fast and started focusing on getting out—as far away from Cedar Cove as humanly possible.

Now, I'm back, rooting through boxes in the attic, my throat tight as I sift through years of forgotten objects. There are a few things I'll take back to Washington. Little fragments, tokens. Stuff that fits in a suitcase. But the more I sift, the less I find. Each box heavier than the last, until I'm kneeling there, completely drained, the weight of it all pressing me into the floorboards.

"How 'bout takin' my advice for once, hmm? Maybe a break'd do you some good."

I nearly jump out of my skin. I didn't hear her come up the stairs. Grams is leaning in the doorway, framed by the afternoon light streaming through the attic window. She's holding two mugs of tea, steam curling up in lazy spirals. She nods toward the old chairs by the window—the one I'd cracked open earlier to air the place out.

I give her a half-smile, because that's all I've got, and haul myself to my feet.

Grams shuffles over, no walker or cane in sight, because of course not. The limp's still there, but her doctor and physical therapist insist it's good for her to put weight on it once in a while. She lowers herself into her old rocking chair with a wince that she pretends isn't happening.

I take the chair across from her, wrapping my hands around the chipped mug she offers. The tea is too hot—it scalds my tongue—but the warmth doesn't reach the knot in my chest. For a while, we just sit. The only sounds are the creak of her chair and the distant rumble of waves somewhere beyond the fogged-up window.

After a few minutes, Grams breaks the silence, gentle but unrelenting. "You gonna tell me why you've been up here all week?"

I take another sip, letting the tea burn my throat, as if the heat might cauterize whatever's churning inside me. It doesn't.

I exhale slowly and stare out the window, watching blurry outlines of trees and houses swimming in the mist.

"Honestly, Grams? I don't know." The words feel hollow, even to me.

I glance over, expecting her to nod and let it go. But she's watching me with that steady look of hers, patient as an old tree weathering a storm.

"Ayuh, ya do."

And just like that, I'm sixteen again, buried under a mountain of "I'm fines" I used to stack like sandbags, hoping they'd hide the flood of everything I didn't want anyone to see. Grams, naturally, always knew the truth. Like now, staring me down as if she's got X-ray vision.

Her eyebrow lifts, her expression softening, though the worry in her storm-gray eyes sticks. She reaches up and taps the spot between my eyebrows, right where the faint birthmark heats.

"See this ol' thing right here?" Her finger is still firmly planted on my forehead. "Ain't just a mark. It's a damn barometer for every emotion you've got stuffed in that head of yours—anger, sadness, overthinkin'. Doctor said it'd fade when you got older, but nope, still here. Bright as ever. Just like all the junk we carry, whether or not we want to."

She leans in closer, narrowing her eyes; sizing me up for an interrogation. "When ya was little, I'd see this mark flarin' red as a firetruck in the mirror and know you were hidin' somethin'. Ya'd shuffle in all quiet, actin' like I wouldn't notice. But this ol' mark?" She gives it another tap. "Always tattled on ya."

She straightens, her gaze cutting right through me. "It's tellin' me now, same as it always has—ya got somethin' bottled up, and it's eatin' ya alive, Lenny girl."

The attic suddenly feels like it's running out of air. The tea in my hands is practically boiling my palms, but I cling to it, a fragile tether to the present. I take a shallow breath, trying not to crack, but Grams' words cut deep. She's too good at this—peeling me open just enough to leave me raw. She always sees too much, even when I'd rather she didn't.

She seems to sense it; her face softening. "Is it about yer folks?"

The question hits like stepping on a rake. My shoulders tense, my mouth goes dry, and all I can muster after a long pause is a half-hearted shrug. "Maybe. Maybe not. I don't know." I release a slow breath, words scraping their way out. "All I know is . . . after what happened at the fall festival, I just want answers. To everything."

I pause, swallowing hard. "Mom and Dad. Rhett." His name lodges in my throat like a splinter, but I push through. "I thought I was over it, Grams. Thought I could just . . . move on. But—"

"But ya can't," she finishes, matter-of-fact. There's not an ounce of judgment in her voice, which somehow makes it worse.

I nod, my words crumbling to ash before they can leave my mouth.

She sighs, "I get it, Lenny." Her eyes are distant but piercing. "Some days, I can't even look at some o' those cops."

I know exactly who she's talking about. The ones who still stroll around town like they own the place, badges gleaming like they're spotless, as if people haven't forgotten or forgiven. The ones Jack probably calls his coworkers.

"Every time I see 'em, it all comes rushin' back. The things they missed, the things they ignored." Her words catch for a moment. "And Rhett . . . " She doesn't finish, but the impact of his name hangs there, anyway. When she looks at me again, her eyes are wide open, no defenses left. "Christ, Lenny. You think I don't understand, but I do."

Her stare nails me to the spot, unflinching. "Sometimes the past don't let ya go 'til ya figure out what it's been hidin'."

The words hang heavy, suspended in mid-air. Then she snorts, breaking the tension with a brittle, half-amused laugh. "But I stopped lettin' it eat me alive a long time ago. Life's too damn short for that crap." She shrugs, one that says she's wrestled with this ghost and decided it wasn't worth the fight.

She stops, her expression drifting to some distant place. "Do I think your folks and Rhett deserve justice?" I open my mouth, but she waves me off, lips quirking in a faint smirk. "Absolutelyfuckinlutely."

A laugh sneaks out of me. Her smile fades almost as fast as it came, replaced by that pragmatic, seen-it-all look. "Thing is, Lenny, there ain't nothin' more we can do. I fought for years. Wore me down to the bone. And now? Every damn morning, I wake up creakin' like an old floorboard." She let out another snort. "And what do I got to show for it? Not a damn thing."

Her attention slides past me to the window, her eyes glazing over, like she's watching a memory she'd rather fast-forward through. "But when I saw that . . . " she trails off, snagging on that one word. Finally, she lets it out: "Body."

She shakes her head, blinking hard, brushing away tears she won't admit to. When she speaks again, her tone softens. "I get it. You comin' up here, searchin' for somethin'. Tryin' to make sense of it all." She sighs, one that's been building for years. "But there's nothin' here, Lenny."

Her eyes meet mine, steady and sure, and for a second, I almost believe her. *Almost.* She must've forgotten I'm a journalist—skepticism comes with the paycheck.

I stand, cradling the empty teacup, and lean down to press a kiss to her forehead. "I believe you, Grams," I say quietly, "but . . . I just want to go through this last tub." I shrug, aiming for casual, as if I haven't been quietly obsessing over it all week. "Maybe I'll find something 'worth keeping'."

She scans my face until landing on the hairpiece in my hair, and a faint smile pulls at her lips. She doesn't argue.

Doesn't say a word, really, just gives me a small, knowing nod before slipping out of the room, leaving me alone with the tub.

I kneel beside it, fingers digging under the brittle plastic lid until it pops off with a crack. Grams' words echo faintly in my head: *There's nothing here.* She's probably right. Most of this junk hasn't seen daylight in decades—old sweaters with that lavender-drawer smell, half-crushed birthday cards, ribbons from every "participant" trophy my childhood could cough up.

Nothing important. Nothing new.

Still, I keep digging, pulling aside layers of fabric and fading memories. My fingertips bump into something solid beneath the clutter, and I freeze. Heart skips. What now? I shove the scarves aside and try to pry it free, but it's wedged tight, like it doesn't want to be found.

Fine. Be stubborn.

I flip the tub upside down, sending everything tumbling into a pile on the floor. At the bottom, half-buried in dust and shadows, is a shard of plastic. Jagged. Small. Completely out of place. Something about it rubs me the wrong way.

I reach for it, cautious, and—*shit.* A sharp sting slices through my thumb, blood welling up instantly. I stick it in my mouth, the taste of copper steadying me. Stupid thing. Probably just a piece of broken junk.

And yet, I pick it up again, more carefully this time.

That's when I notice it's not just some random shard of plastic. It's a key. Tarnished gold. Small. Heavy in my hand, as though it's been sitting there, waiting for someone to dig it up. My chest tightens as I turn it over. What could this unlock?

My eyes flick to the corner of the room, to the first tub I'd practically shoved aside without a second glance. The wooden box.

The key presses into my palm as I cross the room, each

step heavier than it should be. The box looked so unimportant the first time—probably just some wedding relic from my parents, filled with dried-out flowers or crumbling love notes. But now, standing over it, the atmosphere feels different.

I fit the key into the lock. It turns.

The lid creaks open, and . . . disappointment hits. No secret compartments. No treasure map. Just a small, neat stack of folded papers at the bottom. I let out a breath I didn't realize I was holding and reach for the top page; my hand unsteady.

The date jumps out first:

March 3, 2014

Months before my parents died. A chill snakes up my spine, but I shove it aside and start reading.

It's a spreadsheet. Names, addresses, cryptic scrawls in the margins—notes that are messy but definitely not casual. I flip to the next page. Then the next. The same thing. Names, notes, more tension coiling in my gut with every sheet. There's a pattern here, I can feel it. But whatever it is, it's playing hard to get.

And then I spot it.

Stamped faintly at the top of one page is the Cedar Cove police department logo.

I stop cold.

This isn't some random pile of paperwork. Someone was keeping tabs. On these people. On why these names mattered.

My hands decide they've had enough and let the pages slip. They scatter across the floor, and I scramble to scoop them up, my pulse hammering like it's trying to stage an escape. And that's when I see it—something even worse.

My mother's handwriting.

It's her, all right. Messy, impatient, like she was trying to tattoo her thoughts onto the paper. Her words crawl through the margins, jagged and rushed:

Callahan—connection?

Wives of Cedar Cove?

Hospital visits

Records erased—why?

Maple Harbor

The notes wrap around me, an awkward hug I can't escape, squeezing the air from my lungs. My mother's obsession stares back at me from the page—raw, relentless. She wasn't dabbling in idle curiosity. This a deep dive that eats you alive if you're not careful.

I scan the scattered papers again. Names, dates, addresses. All arranged with unnerving precision, but not enough to spill the entire story. Whatever this is, it wasn't meant to see the light of day.

And then Grams' voice slips into my thoughts, smug and infuriatingly accurate: *"Sometimes the past doesn't let you go until you find out what it's hiding."*

The past doesn't let go. Not until you break it open. Piece by piece. Name by name. Lie by lie.

Looks like I'll be digging.

CHAPTER 9

Jack

The papers smack down onto the coffee table with a thud. Lennon stands across from me, arms crossed, daring me to start something. *Just try it,* her glare says. I glance at the stack —edges curling from the impact—then back at her. Still defi-ant. Still fiery. Still maddeningly stubborn.

God, she is cute when she is mad.

It has been, what, a week since I've seen her? Not that my brain—or any other part of me, for that matter—has stopped replaying the memory of her lips on mine. It lingers like smoke, faint but everywhere, a spirit in the air I can't shake. And now here she is, burning like a bonfire in front of me, ready to torch whatever is left of my peace of mind.

"What *is this*?" she demands, though her fingers tremble as they hover over the papers. That tremble almost softens the dare in her eyes. *Almost.* A smarter man might have chosen his next move carefully. Me? I lean back in my chair and drag out a sip of coffee like I have all the time in the world.

"Nice to see you too, Lennon," I say, setting my mug down with a slow grin specifically engineered to drive her up the wall. Before she has the chance to unload whatever verbal grenade she is about to throw, I catch something else—a trace of frustration that slips through her armor. A crack in the ice.

Carolyn, our server, barely makes it to the table before Lennon cuts her off. "Black coffee, oat milk, sugar-free vanilla, sugar-free raspberry," Lennon rattles off without breaking her death stare at me.

"That's . . . one hell of an order," I joke, tossing it out there like it might dispel the tension. It doesn't. Her shrug is cold enough to flash-freeze my good intentions, her jaw tight as she locks her stare on me again, daring me to push her further. Right. Humor is off the menu today.

Since then, I've been knee-deep in meetings with my boss, dissecting every second of what happened at the festival. None of it adds up. Why had Benson suddenly decided to drag Lennon's parents into the conversation? And where did Rhett fit into any of it? Every question I ask just leads to more questions.

Then came the moment I couldn't unsee, the thing that turned all my vague unease into a full-blown migraine: The parallels. Lennon's parents, Rhett's parents—killed in almost the exact same way. And then the festival. That poor woman.

A maid.

Not just any maid. The Callahans' maid.

It's the one thread tying any of this together, but it doesn't fit. It's like finding a piece from another puzzle shoved into the wrong box. Why a maid? What could she possibly have to do with two families being butchered years apart? Was she a victim, a witness, or something else entirely? Was she hiding someone? Or worse, hiding *something*? Did the Callahans silence her to cover it up?

I've run every angle, pored over every scrap of evidence, and it all keeps circling back to her. A maid. Just a maid—if the official story is to be believed. But it doesn't add up. None of it does.

But today . . . today, I finally got a break. An opening to talk with the Callahans. I need answers.

Right on cue, Carolyn leaned in just a little too close, giving me her best *come hither* look while twirling a strand of hair around her finger. Her tray is balanced on one hip in a pose so practiced it should've come with stage directions. "Any update, Sheriff, on the Callahan maid case?" Her eyes scan the papers scattered across the table, then back to me, hitting me with the full force of her unfiltered interest.

From the corner of my eye, I catch Lennon's reaction. A swift, irritated eye-roll. Then, the tightening of her arms as she crosses them, the exact way she had that day on Main Street. Jealousy. Clear as day, simmering under the surface. She'd never admit it, of course, and I'm not dumb enough to point it out, but it is there—a stubborn fire she doesn't want me, or apparently Carolyn, to notice.

Normally, I wouldn't humor Carolyn. But I've been Sheriff of Cedar Cove long enough to know it is better to keep things friendly with the locals. And if I'm being honest, Carolyn is harmless. Sure, she's been dropping hints since the day I rolled into town, but it is more endearing than anything else. Cute in a Pippi Longstocking kind of way—sunny, upbeat, and immune to awkwardness. But my focus isn't on Carolyn. Hell, my focus has been nowhere *but* Lennon. And at this rate, I'm not sure it is ever going anywhere else.

I give Carolyn a polite smile. "Not much . . . yet. You know how these things go."

Her face lights up like I'd just proposed marriage. "Oh, but we all *know* you'll get it solved. You're the best sheriff we've ever had in Cedar Cove." Her lashes bat so hard I think I might feel a breeze, and before I can blink, her hand lands on mine. "Just like the Wallace case last year! Took some time, but you got it done. *You always do.*" She gives my hand a squeeze, throws in a wink for good measure, and then saunters off to tend to the other customers, her hips putting in some overtime.

From the other side of the table, Lennon lets out a huff. Her heel starts tapping against the floor in a restless rhythm. The funny part? Her jealousy, as prickly as it is, is the closest we've come to acknowledging whatever this . . . *thing* between us actually is. Not that I am in any rush to slap a label on it. I'm not stupid enough to spook her, and I'm not about to let her spook herself, either. But if she told me to lock it down right then, I would've hit one knee before she finished her sentence.

Because Lennon? She isn't just a woman you keep watching; she is a woman you keep hoping might look back and decide you were worth keeping, too.

Carolyn returns and sets the drink in front of Lennon, who doesn't so much as glance her way. Instead, she wraps her hands around the cup and takes a slow sip. Her lashes flutter, like she's savoring the nectar of the gods, and there's this soft sound—half sigh, half moan—that immediately has me shifting in my seat.

When her eyes open, they wander around the café. Sunlight bounces off the blue-and-white checkered floor, and the seashell-themed art on the walls gives it that easygoing, small-town feel. Shoreline Sips never disappoints.

Lennon's gaze slides back to me, her eyebrow arching at my cup like it's personally offended her. A slow, crooked smile tugs at her lips. That look could be patented as a weapon.

I offer my best nonchalant smirk. "Thought I'd try it out."

"And?" she teases, tapping her fingers against the ceramic.

"It's . . . alright," I lie. It's not *just* alright, but admitting that to her would only give her more ammunition.

She chuckles softly, a sound tailored to make my pulse

misbehave. "Mmhmm," she murmurs, eyes glinting with a teasing lilt. "Pumpkin spice. Classic. You can't go wrong with it—coffee, pies, scented candles. It's a lifestyle."

Her smile falters. As if someone flipped a switch, and suddenly she's looking at the pile of papers in front of her like they're a personal betrayal. The mood shifts, the lightness between us sinking fast.

I nod toward the papers. "What's all that?"

She stiffens, like the question jabbed a nerve she didn't even know existed. "Kinda hoping you'd tell me," she adds quietly. Her lips press together, and for the first time, her calm mask slips. A faint crease settles between her brows—tiny, but there. The untouchable Lennon, suddenly human.

The sight knocks me off balance. I set my coffee down a little too carefully, blaming the caffeine instead of the uncomfortable churn in my gut.

I take the stack of papers; her gaze boring into me like she's trying to beam the answers straight into my brain. The first page is a disaster: blue ink everywhere, underlines so aggressive they've nearly torn the paper. Names, dates, scattered fragments—like someone dumped out a puzzle and gave up halfway through sorting it. But then my eyes land on a line about halfway down:

Callahan—connection?

Wives of Cedar Cove?

Hospital Visits

Records erased—why?

Maple Harbor

My chest tightens. What the hell?

I flip to the next page, but it's just more of the same: scribbled notes, dead ends, breadcrumbs leading nowhere. Whoever wrote this wasn't just digging, they were practically tunneling.

"Where'd you find this?" I ask, managing to keep my words steadier than I feel.

"In my attic," she confides, fiddling with the edge of a bandage on her thumb.

"Your attic?"

"Yeah." Her tone is distant, her eyes fixed somewhere over my shoulder. "Buried in one of my parents' old storage tubs." She hesitates, tugging harder at the bandage. "I've been up there all week. First few days, I couldn't even open a box. It felt like . . . I don't know, walking into a tomb. Everything exactly where they left it, like they'd just gone out for milk and never came back."

I stay silent.

"But yesterday . . . something shifted." Her voice wavers, but she pushes through. "I started going through their stuff. Grams always said it was pointless, that nothing up there mattered." She lets out a bitter laugh. "Guess she was wrong. Found this, though." She waves at the papers, then raises her thumb, the bandage peeling up at the corner. "And, uh, this. Collateral damage."

"You hurt yourself?" The words fly out of my mouth. "How bad?"

She shrugs. "Just a scratch. Paper cut, really." She tries for a breezy delivery, but the way her lips press together betrays her. For someone who pretends to have it all together, she isn't as unreadable as she thinks.

Still, I reach for her hand. The bandage barely covers whatever microscopic injury she'd managed to inflict on herself, but I kiss it anyway. Her cheeks flush pink, and the corner of my mouth twitches. A spark of something warm, human, in all this chaos.

I let her hand drop and lean back, letting my attention drift to the folder. "So, you found this in your parents' stuff?"

She nods, her face tight.

Flipping to another page doesn't help. Dates. Scribbles. The same fragmented mess as before—until I see it:

March 3, 2014

That date. Seeing it written on paper—not in a police report—sends a chill prickling the skin at the base of my skull.

"That's the year your parents were killed."

Her silence confirms it.

I exhale, working to keep my thoughts from tangling into knots. "And you're sure this is your mom's handwriting?"

"It's hers," she remarks confidently. "No question."

And suddenly, the weight of the papers double in my hands.

"And what exactly was she looking for?"

Her mouth presses into a thin line. For once, she looks unsure. "I don't know," she admits. "Not for sure. But whatever it was, she thought it was big. Big enough that someone tried to bury it."

"Bury it how?"

"Records erased. You saw the note." She gestures at the crumpled page on the table, her tone gaining an edge. "Someone went to a lot of trouble to cover their tracks, Jack. My mom must've found something she wasn't supposed to."

I glance at the scribbled names and dates, something nagging at the back of my mind—familiar, but just out of reach. "Do you recognize any of these names? The Wives of Cedar Cove?"

Her expression shifts, a flash of . . . something gone before I can name it. "Some, most of them, lived here back then. But a few . . . " Her focus drops to the list. "I don't know. They don't ring any bells." Her eyes narrow, as if glaring at the names might shake loose their secrets. "Not yet, anyway."

Not yet. There's something in the way she says it, the type of determination that says she'll drag these names kicking and screaming into the light.

She shifts her weight, arms crossed, her attention drifting somewhere distant. "Both my parents were journalists. Big cases. Stuff they couldn't always talk about." She bites her lower lip, almost like she's holding back the next words. "That's what eavesdropping was for."

I can't help but chuckle. The image of a tiny, wide-eyed Lennon snooping from behind doorways pops into my head.

"What's so funny?" she asks, her eyes sparking with mischief.

"Just picturing you as a kid," I say, grinning. "Let me guess —that's how you ended up in journalism? Early career training?"

Her smile comes and goes, replaced by something heavier. "Yeah," she whispers. "Their work inspired me, sure. But their deaths . . . their deaths made me want to make sure no one else had a mystery like that hanging over them."

The air shifts, weighted now, but she doesn't stop. "They'd been arguing a lot before it happened," she mentions, slower now, each word chosen carefully. "I remember this one night . . . I was in the living room. They were in the kitchen. It was late—way past my bedtime—but the house was small." Her lips tug upward, a hollow quirk of a smile. "Thin walls, you know? I could hear everything."

She pauses. "My dad—he always spoke in this low, intense way. He was talking about their cases. Murders, affairs, secrets . . . dangerous things. Even as a kid, I could tell they were onto something."

She leans in slightly. "Or . . . onto someone. Maybe two people. Working together."

"How do you know?"

Her fingers twitch against the edges of the papers. "It was the way they talked. The back-and-forth, the names, the way they tossed around ideas—like they were circling something but couldn't quite land on it." She hesitates. "Most of it went over my head, but the arguments didn't stop."

Her breath pulls tight, barely there. "Not until they did."

She stops, shoulders stiffening, her fingers pressing harder against the paper as she looks away.

On impulse, I reach across the table, brushing her hand. For a moment, her fingers linger against mine—warm and real —before she pulls away. The connection breaks, clean and abrupt, leaving a sting in its place.

Her hand returns to the stack of papers, her eyes fixed on the jumble of words and dates. "When Grams told me there was nothing in those tubs, I believed her," she says quietly. "I really did. But I had to check. After the festival . . . after seeing her . . . "

Her words falter.

"Josie?" I murmur.

The sound of her name startles her. She jerks back, her eyes narrowing, guarded. "Josie?" she repeats, like the name doesn't quite fit in her mouth.

I nod. "The woman at the festival."

Her expression tightens, shutters slamming down. "The maid," she mutters, her face suddenly blank, controlled.

"Yeah. Did you . . . know her?"

She shakes her head, her brows knitting together. "Know her? No. But I've seen her. Every day since I got back. She cleaned Rhett's room like it was some sort of ritual.

The hairs on the back of my neck prickle. Who cleans one

room that often? And how does someone like that—a maid, invisible by design—end up dead?

"I don't get it," Lennon mutters, "but I need to."

I rub my neck, scanning the notes again, the names and dates blurring together. "Lennon," I say carefully, "you realize what you're saying, right? If your parents really uncovered something . . . if this is connected to what happened to them—"

Our eyes lock. For a moment, the tension feels taut enough to snap. Then she breaks the silence. "I need to know," she pleads. The vulnerability from before is gone, replaced by the familiar fire in her gaze. "I've spent years, years, Jack, not knowing."

Her words hang there—a dare.

"I want to help," she adds.

I raise a brow. "Help?"

She rolls her eyes. "Before you say no—"

"No."

She doesn't even blink. Instead, I get a look so pointed it could peel paint, followed by a sigh. She stands, gripping the back of her chair as if it's the only thing stopping her from strangling me. For a second, I expect her to start yelling, but no—she leans in with a brand of determination that makes you check for exits.

"Think about it," she states. "I'm here. I'm a journalist. This is what I do."

Great. Fantastic. As if I needed the reminder. The word *journalist* lands harder than it should, dredging up memories of all the nights I've spent reading her work. She's good. Too good. But this? This isn't some puff piece or investigative scoop.

"This is too personal," I comment. It comes out more of a bark than a reasoned argument. It's a defense mechanism, I know that. But letting her help would mean handing her a backstage pass to the disaster she's been expertly ignoring for years.

The mark between her brows flares, but she doesn't back down. Stubbornness might as well be her middle name. "I get it," she starts, her eyes fastening onto mine, searching for even a hairline crack in my resolve. "But I need this." The words come out softer now, like she's convincing herself. "I can help you more than anyone."

The conversation is slipping out of my hands, which is both infuriating and completely predictable. When her stare hooks mine again, it's piercing, unrelenting, and honest. God, she's beautiful—so beautiful it should come with a warning: Caution—may impair judgment. But I can't let that matter. I won't.

The lines between us are already blurry enough. Crossing them? Yeah, that'd go about as well as a tightrope walk in a hurricane.

"Not a good idea, Lennon," I say, my tone flat. "And anyway, who knows how long you're even sticking around Cedar Cove."

She doesn't speak. Instead, her expression hardens in a way I recognize. It's the look she gets right before doubling down —defiant, unshakable.

"Then let me help while I'm here."

There's no mistaking what she's asking. It's not just about the job, and we both know it.

"Please." The quiet imploring in her words unsettles me, cutting through my defenses too easily.

"I believe everything happens for a reason," she declares, her eyes momentarily drifting somewhere far away before coming back to mine. "I came here for Grams, yeah, but there's more to it than that. I feel like I'm supposed to be part of this."

"Please, Jack."

It's the way she says my name that does it. Quiet, stripped bare, no armor left. It's not a demand or a threat—it's just her.

I stand there, completely out of moves, on the brink of giving in.

"Fine," I cave, though it's more a sigh than a decision. "But it's on my terms."

Her nod comes quick—too quick. Then a smile. Half-victory, half-chaos. It's dangerous, that smile.

I shift, stepping closer, and suddenly, we're close enough that I feel her warmth. Her breath hitches, and for a second, it's like the universe yanks me backward in time—to that Ferris wheel, her hands gripping me like I was the only thing keeping her tethered, her lips urgent, the night swallowing every gasp. I shove the memory down, hard, but she catches it. Of course, she does.

Before I can think of something—anything—to say, she tosses a couple of bills on the table and strides toward the door. Meanwhile, I'm left standing there, wondering when exactly I got drafted into a game I didn't know we were play-ing. She glances back over her shoulder, and I tip my hat like some poor attempt at nonchalance.

But Lennon Harrington? She doesn't do "leave well enough alone." Her indigo eyes drag over me, a challenge in every sweep.

Something in me snaps.

Three steps, and I'm before her, so close she has to tilt her head to meet my eyes. She doesn't flinch. Doesn't blink. My hands find her waist, pulling her gently against the brick wall outside the coffee shop. Her breath grazes my lips, her perfume weaving through the small space between us.

"I don't think this would look too good to the citizens of Cedar Cove," she murmurs.

I shrug, aiming for casual, though my pulse is doing anything but. "They can handle it."

The words sound smoother than I expect, and judging by the way her teeth catch her bottom lip, they're good enough.

Her fingers find the brim of my hat, angling it to cast a shadow over her face, like she's carving out a private little corner of Cedar Cove where only we exist.

And then she smiles—not her usual guarded one, but something unbearably soft. Quiet in a way that steals the air from my lungs.

It's brutal. A direct hit.

Whatever scraps of composure I have left? Gone.

Yeah. That's it. I'm toast.

For one reckless second, I imagine waking up to that smile every day. Living in it. Drowning in it. Burning everything else to ash just to keep it close.

Her fingers brush my jaw, feather light, before slipping to my nape. Her nails graze the hair there, purposeful enough to make even a saint forget how stoplights work. A green light you don't think twice about. So, I don't. I lean in, the space between us vanishing, her breath warm against mine.

And then it happens. A throat clears. Loud. Obnoxious. The sound smacks the romance clean out of the moment.

"Sheriff."

I stop cold; the heat between us draining so fast I might as well have stepped into a freezer. Jaw tight, I glance over, already knowing who's behind this masterful piece of timing.

Benson. Of course. His comment follows, "Shame about that maid, huh? What was her name again? Josie?"

Lennon's hand jerks back like I've gone radioactive. Her eyes meet mine, and whatever fire was there a second ago is gone.

"Nice to see you, Lennon," Benson adds, with a smugness of someone discussing the weather while tossing grenades.

"You too, Benson," Lennon replies. Her shoulders are stiff, her poise unshakable—barely. Two hits in one night, and she's holding herself together on sheer spite and willpower.

The sun ducks behind a cloud as she turns, raising a hand to shield her face. Her fingers tremble, just the faintest quiver. Enough to twist something deep in my chest.

Benson grins, all toothy charm with enough bite to make my skin crawl, and claps a hand on my shoulder. Heavy. Over-familiar. "You run into the Callahans yet?" he asks. There's weight in the words. A reminder. A threat, coiled under all that false nonchalance, one that sticks to your ribs and stays there.

I'm the sheriff, though. He reports to me. Not that you'd guess it from moments like this—Benson never passes up a chance to needle me about "stealing" the title. Says it's a joke, but the punchline always ends in the same spot: My last nerve.

And right now? He's swinging for it.

I place a hand on his shoulder, sufficient to make a point. "Not yet, Benson." I keep my response light enough to skirt the brink of dismissiveness. "I was headed that way."

For a split second, his grin falters. A hint of irritation. Then it vanishes, replaced by a curt nod reeking of forced politeness. A challenge, met and shut down. I drop my hand, turning back to Lennon. She's watching the whole exchange, her expression unreadable.

"Let me know how that goes," Benson says, his tone brisk. Then his eyes go to his watch. He doesn't have to say it—the clock is ticking. I already know.

I nod. "Of course."

He lingers only long enough to make the air sour, then saunters off toward the coffee shop. Lennon tracks his departure, her frown deepening.

"You're going to see the Callahans?" she asks.

I nod.

"When?" The question punches out, quick and forceful.

Instead of answering, I start walking toward my Explorer, each step winding the knot in my chest a little tighter. I stop at the hood, inhale slowly, and finally answer. "Now."

She doesn't flinch. "Can I come with you?"

My grip tightens on the black paint, knuckles ghostly. She's watching me—waiting, prodding.

"I don't think you should." Short. Final. My back stays turned.

"What happened to the terms? Or did those vanish along with your better judgment?"

She's got me there. I glance sideways, catching an elderly couple waddling down the sidewalk, utterly oblivious to the silent battle of wills happening two feet away. Every rational part of me is yelling to shut her out, to slam the door on her and her infuriating persistence.

But then there's the other part. The reckless, stubborn part that always wins.

I sigh, meeting her stare. "Fine. On my terms."

Her grin is instantaneous. It would've been adorable if it weren't so insufferably smug. She strides toward the passenger side of my Explorer, fingers brushing the door handle like she already owns the thing.

"Hold it," I snap.

She freezes, turning to throw me a side-eye. Her hands settle on her hips, one brow arching.

"We haven't even discussed my terms," I say, deadpan.

"By all means." She waves a hand, motioning for me to continue.

"First, this isn't a buddy cop movie," I begin. "You're not officially part of the investigation, so there will be no 'good cop, bad cop' antics."

She tilts her head, mulling it over with exaggerated patience, then gives a measured nod.

"Second, you follow my lead. That means no running off, no chasing suspects, and absolutely no interrogating people behind my back."

Her lips twitch—like I've just challenged her to break every one of those rules in record time.

"And third," I add sharply, cutting her off before the smug smile can fully form, "no withholding evidence. If you find something, you tell me immediately. I'm not playing games here."

She lifts her brow even higher, the silent equivalent of, *Are you done yet?*

I exhale. "Yeah. That's it."

Before the last word is out of my mouth, she yanks open the door like she's boarding the victory bus.

"Not so fast," I call, leaning casually against the hood. "No passenger princesses allowed in this ride. Only criminals or coworkers."

She freezes, then turns to me, arms crossed, eyes narrowing in mock defiance. "Passenger princess?"

"Yeah, you know, the kind who sits back, takes selfies, and demands to stop for iced coffee. That's not the vibe."

She stares me down for a beat before her mouth curves into a sly smirk. "Come on, Mercer," she purrs, all sugar and silk. Her baby blues flick over me, lingering. "You know I don't sit back and watch. I like being in control . . . right where *it* counts."

And just like that, she winks, slips into the passenger seat, and shuts the door without another word. And me? I stand there like an idiot, pretending I'm not thinking about her taking *control*, guiding me exactly where she wants.

CHAPTER 10

My fingers uncurl, one by one, releasing fists I hadn't even realized I'd clenched. When I open my eyes, Jack is already watching me, his look inscrutable except for the *You sure you want to do this?* lingering in his gaze. Subtle, but impossible to miss.

"You coming?" he asks.

I nod, swallowing the knot in my throat and pushing down the tangle of nerves clawing their way to the surface. Falling apart isn't an option—not now, not with Jack putting so much on the line for me. I can tell he's still holding back, not saying everything, but right now, something about him feels different. There's a softness to him. Vulnerability, maybe.

It's strange, seeing it in someone like Jack—someone who wears his badge like it's armor. But here we are, and for once, he's letting me see past the barricades. Not all the way, of course. Just enough to keep me guessing.

We reach the doorstep. Jack takes my hand, threading his fingers through mine as if it were the most natural thing in the world. "You sure about this?" He gives my hand a gentle squeeze.

I nod again. His hand is steady, an anchor in the middle of all this chaos. Without warning, he lifts our joined hands and presses a kiss to my knuckles. It's gentle, sweet, and so unapologetically, Jack.

Then he does it again—slower this time. I arch an eyebrow, a faint smile tugging at the corners of my mouth despite my better judgment. So much for Mr. Stone-Faced Sheriff.

He chuckles. "Just for good luck," he adds, quietly but with enough edge to imply we'll need more than luck.

Before he can turn back, I do the reckless thing. I lift his hand and press my lips to his knuckles. The skin is rough, calloused—real.

Jack blinks, momentarily thrown off. For a moment, the atmosphere shifts into something quiet and loaded, the silence that says too much.

And then the door swings open.

Standing there is Mrs. Callahan, staring at us with the expression of someone catching teenagers sneaking out past curfew. Her green eyes are as piercing as I remember—predatory, almost—and just as unyielding. She's a picture of Cedar Cove perfection, every hair in place, not a wrinkle in sight. Her skin has that eerie, porcelain-smooth look the local elite swear is natural (it isn't). Around here, the term "aging gracefully" is basically a slur; looking vacuum-sealed is the standard.

Mrs. Callahan hasn't changed at all.

Beside me, Jack clears his throat and lets go of my hand. The warmth vanishes, and my fingers fidget before I shove them into my pocket. This isn't a social call, and it sure isn't a high school reunion. It's an investigation.

Mrs. Callahan's stare flits between the two of us, like she's already solving some silent equation. Then, out of nowhere, her expression softens, and she does the last thing I expect: She hugs me.

Not the polite, distant kind of hug Cedar Cove's elite might dole out when forced into human contact. This is a real one—fierce, crushing, and startlingly maternal. I freeze, unsure what to do with my limbs as the overpowering floral perfume clinging to her washes over me. It's the same scent I'd nearly forgotten: heady and sweet.

The hug drags me back, whether or not I like it. Fifteen years old. Grieving. Lost. And there she was, sweeping in—a one-woman emotional SWAT team, braced to hold together what clearly couldn't be held.

She doesn't let go right away. Her arms stay firm, like she's personally ensuring structural integrity. When she finally pulls back, she doesn't step away completely. Instead, she holds me at arm's length, her hands heavy on my shoulders as she scans my face.

"Lennon," she whispers.

"Hi, Mrs. Callahan," I manage, though the words barely make it past my throat.

Her smile tilts up, tender and disarmingly familiar, before she reaches out and pinches my cheek. The same old gesture, like no time has passed since I was a kid tearing through this house with Rhett. My cheeks flushed from the sun and whatever trouble we'd gotten into. She used to call me her "second daughter," a title I'd worn proudly, a badge pinned right to my chest.

"There's my girl." The words are so tender they tighten something in my chest. "Come in, come in."

She ushers us inside, shutting the door with a thud that lands louder than it should, echoing through the too-quiet house.

"What brings you here?" she asks, though her gaze shoots past me to Jack. Her smile shifts—still polite, but tighter. Not unfriendly, exactly. Just . . . careful. Like she's weighing whether to give him the warm welcome or the diplomatic version.

Jack steps forward, all professional charm, and delivers the official explanation of why we're here. I hang back, letting him take the lead.

While they talk, I let my eyes wander. The foyer unfolds like déjà vu gone wrong—recognizable but misaligned; the details shifted just enough to unsettle. I'd expected it to look different, to feel different. Maybe a little lighter. But the Victorian bones are still here, holding their ground even under Mrs. Callahan's efforts to modernize.

Her heels click out a metronome against the glossy floors, leading us toward the kitchen. Jack fills the space with Cedar Cove gossip, breezing through the usual greatest hits—the scream that sent the whole town into hysterics, the rumors that cropped up before the echoes even could fade. He's careful, though, keeping the juicier details firmly off the table. Like where we were that night. Or, more importantly, that I was there at all.

Mrs. Callahan nods along, her hostess smile flawless. Years ago, I thought I'd be a permanent fixture in this house, back when I was young and optimistic, to the extent of believing in things like easy futures and unbroken plans. Now, the whole idea feels like something I'd read in an outdated self-help book: *How to Manifest a Life Without Any Major Plot Twists.*

Jack throws me a look over his shoulder. His expression soaked in just the right amount of concern—too much for casual, but not enough to call it out. For a guy who's never quite nailed the small-town-hero vibe, he works at it like it's a full-time job.

Their conversation drifts on, a polite background hum, as my attention slides to the hallway. The floating shelves remain untouched, not a single frame out of place. Rows of family portraits, all stiff collars and perfectly rehearsed smiles—a catalog of moments too polished to be real. No cracks, no chaos—just the sort of flawless presentation you curate for strangers.

The hallway opens into the kitchen, where tall windows command an unreasonably gorgeous view of the ocean. I falter, my breath catching in my chest. I'd almost forgotten how stunning this place is. The way golden sunlight streams through those windows, turning the waves into molten silver spilling toward the horizon.

A view that demands your attention, like it knows it's better than you. And for a moment, it's easy to see why this house always felt somewhat enchanted, back when life had more room for that kind of thinking.

At some point, she drifted closer, her hand landing gently on my shoulder. When I turn, her demeanor is so unguarded it feels intrusive.

"He would've loved to see you like this," she admits, her words slipping into the space between us.

Neither of us moves. We both just stand there, staring out at the waves beyond the salt-streaked windows. Golden sunlight dances across the water in blinding arcs, so free and careless it's almost cruel.

"So successful," Mrs. Callahan murmurs softly, precisely tucking a stray strand of my hair behind my ear. "So put together . . . so beautiful."

I swallow hard, a small, reflexive motion. Her words slip past my defenses, leaving behind a mix of gratitude and emptiness. Some small, bruised part of me aches for Rhett to see me now, to know who I've become—as if that would change anything. As if one more minute with him could fix the jagged edges he left behind.

"Mrs. Callahan," Jack's tone slices through, pointed

enough to shatter the fragile stillness. "We're not here to talk about Rhett."

Her hand drops from my shoulder. I glance at Jack, his face carefully neutral, but his furrowed brow gives him away. Our eyes meet, and I manage a slight nod. I'm okay. Or at least, I'll fake it for now.

Jack shifts his weight and flips open his notepad with a meticulous focus that screams he'd rather be anywhere else. "I know we've been over Rhett before, but today's about Josie."

The softness drains from Mrs. Callahan's face, her features solidifying into something unreadable. She pivots to the kettle, her movements brisk, each clink of mugs and hiss of boiling water precise enough to signal she's done indulging this conversation.

"Where were you the night of the festival?" Jack asks.

Mrs. Callahan doesn't blink. "At an event for the Wives of Cedar Cove."

"And where was this event?"

"Maple Harbor," she replies crisply, folding her arms. "About an hour from here, closer to the city."

That stops me cold. *Maple Harbor*. The name I'd seen on Mom's notes, scribbled in the margins like it mattered.

"Maple Harbor?" I echo, trying to sound casual. "Why not here? Cedar Cove's a lot closer—you'd get more locals to these events, wouldn't you?"

Mrs. Callahan's eyes dart to me, keen as a tack. "I suppose so," she muses, tilting her head as if the thought had never crossed her mind. "But it's good to mix things up, keep the women interested." She flicks an imaginary crumb off the counter with a practiced hand. "And Maple Harbor's such a charming, quaint little town," she adds with a shrug. "Why not?"

Jack shoots me a look, and it's clear we're on the same page: *There's something about that town she's not saying.* He shifts his attention back to her. "And what exactly do you do at these so-called events?"

Mrs. Callahan's lips press into a narrow line, the faintest crack in her otherwise flawless composure. "We take our circle of women *very* seriously, Sheriff," her words clipped. "But if you *must* know, we're working on a project."

"And this *project* is . . . within the group's discussions, I assume?"

"Precisely," she snaps, the word too quick, too pointed.

The kettle interrupts with an obnoxious whistle, and Mrs. Callahan seizes the excuse, turning to pour her tea with the exactness of someone who's decided the conversation is officially over, even if the rest of us haven't.

Jack doesn't let it slide. "What time did you arrive at this event, and when did you get home?"

The kettle pauses mid-pour, her hand hovering for just a beat too long. "I can't say for certain . . . but I believe it was around 10:30 p.m. when I got home."

She didn't say when she got *there*.

Jack tilts his head ever so slightly, but enough to make his skepticism palpable. "10:30? Bit late for a housewives' gathering, isn't it?"

Mrs. Callahan straightens as if he just insulted the Queen. Her spine goes ramrod stiff, and one eyebrow arches high enough to challenge the structural integrity of the ceiling. "I'll have you know, Jack—"

"Sheriff Mercer," he snaps, voice clipped. The badge speaks for itself.

The room tightens. The kitchen clock ticks louder than a drumline, and steam curls lazily from the kettle like it's enjoying the show. Mrs. Callahan has reduced entire PTA committees to rubble with that stare of hers, but Jack? Jack doesn't so much as blink. And God help me, there's something infuriatingly attractive about his refusal to back down.

Mrs. Callahan's expression doesn't crack, but her tone shifts gears, sliding into a saccharine sweetness. "*Sheriff Mercer,*" she coos, "it was a fundraiser. For the betterment of this town. We take that responsibility seriously."

The kettle drops on the countertop with a clank that underlines the point. Then, slowly, she smiles—a razor-thin curve of lips. "Last year, our so-called *little group* raised over a million dollars. Do you know what we did with that money?"

She doesn't wait for an answer, already advancing, an army general with a five-step plan. "We renovated the high school. We brought in new businesses. One of them, a charming little bed-and-breakfast. Tourists love it. It's vital to the local economy. Surely, you'd agree?"

Jack doesn't respond, but his notepad stays open, pen poised just above the page, but it's clearly decorative at this point. He's not writing; he's watching. Waiting.

Mrs. Callahan pours water into our cups, the silence pressing close, listening, waiting.

The tea sits there steaming, but nobody's in a hurry to drink it. Finally, she raises her eyes to Jack. "If you think I had anything to do with Josie's death," she remarks, "you're barking up the wrong tree."

Jack doesn't flinch. Neither do I, but there's a chill in the room now, coiled and waiting. Mrs. Callahan's voice isn't just defensive—it's unshakable, and that kind of certainty has a way of making everything feel off balance.

She slides the mugs across the counter, taking her own with a measured precision. The tea's too hot—obvious from the quick grimace that darts across her face before she forces it smooth again. She sets the cup down, movements careful.

"If you want answers about that night," she starts after a pause, "talk to my husband. He was home. Had a late meeting and couldn't come with me to Maple Harbor." She watches the steam curl up from her tea, like she's waiting for it to spell out her alibi. Then, she raises a finger. "You could also ask the other wives in our group. They'll vouch for me."

Jack nods, his pen gliding across the notepad. His tea sits untouched—naturally. Men like him don't drink tea; they let it cool into an interrogation prop.

Mrs. Callahan clears her throat. "But I'm truly sorry for her family." Her hand tightens on her teacup, knuckles white. Something raw flashes on her features—so quick you'd miss it if you weren't paying attention.

"Josie . . . she's been with us since before Rhett . . ."

Her words snag, and she swallows hard. When she finally speaks again, it's barely audible: "Since Rhett passed."

What? She has? I never saw her before? And passed?

Rhett didn't just *pass*. He was murdered—headline-worthy, blood-on-the-walls murdered. Yet here she is, tossing out *passed* like it's a euphemism for natural causes. Maybe it's how she copes, sanding the edges off the memory. Or maybe it's just easier to rewrite it this way, soft and sterile, instead of dragging old wounds into the light.

It's not Rhett that's stuck in my head—it's Josie. Ten years in this house, dusting rooms that don't feel like her own. Has she really been cleaning Rhett's room all this time? I can almost see it: the bed perfectly made, the dresser spotless, the whole place frozen in time—a quiet shrine to a boy who never got the chance to grow old.

A chill snakes into my ribs, and I cross my arms, attempting to shake it off. It lingers, stubborn and cold.

Jack gives a curt nod, his words sincere. "I'm sorry for everyone involved. I know this can't be easy."

Then her attention finds me, her smile angling just so. "Well, Lennon, my goodness, it's been ages, hasn't it?"

There's no actual question in her words, just the gleam of something polished and pointed.

"Something like that . . ."

She laughs, and her head bends a bit. She studies me as you might study a thrift-store painting, deciding whether the frame's worth salvaging. "Your hair," she notes, "it's not curly anymore, is it?"

My hand lifts to my hair before I can stop it. Just that little slip is all it takes for the past to creep in. *So unkempt, Lennon. So . . . uncontrolled.* She never said it outright, but the meaning was always there, sharp and crisp. Eventually, I'd given up—kept it tied back, sleek, out of sight. Easier than dealing with her silent critiques.

"I think it looks perfect," Jack states, matter-of-fact. He doesn't even glance at me, his eyes fixated on some invisible point beyond my shoulder. The words come quiet, sure, and entirely unexpected.

For a moment, the cold Mrs. Callahan left behind seems to lift.

My heart stutters, surprised, clumsy like it's forgotten its rhythm. Jack, usually the too-handsome sheriff, doesn't quite look like himself. For just a second, he feels . . . steady. *Familiar.* Maybe it's something in the way he said it—effortless and sure. It reminds me of my dad, maybe even Rhett. Men who would've stood between me and the world without hesitation. But Jack? He's not just standing in the way—he's standing *with* me. And somehow, that feels safer than anything I've known in a long time.

Mrs. Callahan, utterly unruffled, pivots with the grace of someone who's seen it all—and quietly judged most of it. She turns to Jack. "So, Sheriff Mercer, I suppose it's only fair to ask—what brings Lennon here today?"

Jack doesn't answer immediately, probably weighing how to spin it. When he does, his drawl falls just shy of bored. "Not that it's any of your business," he says, "but Lennon was there the night Josie was killed."

He lets the silence stretch, a skill honed by years of making people squirm, before adding, "She's as tangled in this as anyone else who was at the festival."

Mrs. Callahan doesn't blink. Her expression remains a fortress of poise. Instead, she lifts her teacup, taking a sip. "I see." Each word is as polished as the porcelain in her hand. She moves to the sink, and the clink of the cup against the metal basin echoes louder than it should in the quiet. The way she drains the last dregs down the sink feels . . . purposeful. The cup settles with a sigh that says more than she does.

Jack holds out his own teacup with a polite nod, even tipping his hat for effect. "We should probably be on our way," he mentions, his tone cordial but expertly tuned to discourage follow-up questions.

Mrs. Callahan presses her lips into a thin, surgical line.

As they move toward the foyer, Jack glances her way. "Mind if I stop by later? I'd appreciate a word with Mr. Callahan."

"That's fine," she replies, smooth as glass. "I'll let him know."

We pass through the living room, and that's when I notice a wall of framed photos, arranged with a borderline desperate accuracy, like the frames are physically holding each other up. Most are the usual suspects—family portraits, graduations, a wedding or two. A lineup of forced smiles and memories arranged so neatly it's almost suspicious.

Then one photo stops me.

Wives of Cedar Cove, it reads beneath a group shot of couples, all standing side by side in stiff poses, each face trying to sell "contentment" but mostly landing somewhere near "please end this." My eyes find Mrs. Callahan, wearing her usual polite mask. But beside her, where Mr. Callahan should be, he isn't.

Instead, his arm is draped around someone else.

She's petite, with a brown bob and a smile so carefully

stretched it almost looks painful. There's something about her —recognizable enough to itch at the brink of my memory, but vague enough to keep just out of reach. Maybe she's someone I met here years ago. Maybe she's new. Either way, the way she's pressed into him, so close they could share a bloodstream, feels wrong.

"You okay, Lennon?" Jack's voice chimes in.

I blink, shaking off the unease that's latched on like damp clothes. "Yeah," I say, though my gaze flicks back to the photo. A joke about closet swingers hovers on the tip of my tongue but dies before it forms. The wrongness sticks to me as we follow the trail back to Mrs. Callahan.

"Such an elite group of people," she notes. Before I can answer, she tugs me into another hug, snug and syrupy. "So good to see you, Lennon."

I almost tell her I missed her, too—missed all of them— but my eyes drift to the staircase. And there they are.

The bags.

A stack of black duffels sits at the base of the stairs, each scrawled with a familiar "RC". Rhett. I've seen them enough to know exactly who they belong to. They sit there, plain as day, accusations no one even tried to conceal.

My fingers twitch with the urge to unzip one and see what's inside. Why would she leave them out like this? Right in the open? What are they, decor?

As if sensing my stare, Mrs. Callahan shifts, her arm gently steering me back toward her. She follows my stare, then emits a soft, dismissive hum.

When her eyes meet mine, there's something there. It skitters over her face and vanishes before I can grab hold of it. Then she pulls me in for another hug, warm and practiced, like it's been rehearsed for moments exactly like this. It says everything she doesn't: *That's nothing. Don't worry about it.*

But her grip is tighter this time, and I can't shake the

feeling that whatever she's not saying could fill the whole damn house.

"Feel free to come by again," Mrs. Callahan says lightly as she opens the front door.

I give a small laugh—automatic, a reflex I didn't approve. "Yeah. I will. Before I leave."

Her head tilts, her smile still welded in place, but her eyes are doing the actual work now, studying me a little too closely. "When do you leave?"

I shrug. "Not sure yet. Still figuring things out with Grams."

Mrs. Callahan chuckles, that polite, knowing laugh people use when they want to sound casual but are listening to every syllable. "She's always been such a busy bee, hasn't she? Trying to do it all herself. I swear, that woman's going to outlive us all."

We all laugh at that—me, Jack, and Mrs. Callahan. Thin, hollow laughter. Jack, ever the smooth operator, tips his hat. "One thing we can all agree on."

A few more pleasantries follow—smiles, nods, and half-formed sentences that don't add up to much. As Jack and I turn to leave, Mrs. Callahan's stare lingers just a beat too long, like she's filing the moment away for later. The porch light flickers on above her, casting uneven shadows onto the street. I glance back as the door closes behind her with a deliberate click, her silhouette swallowed by the dark.

Outside, the breeze bites, and the streetlights paint the road in a dull orange haze. We walk in silence, the crunch of gravel underfoot too loud in the quiet. Ahead, Grams' house waits, its windows glowing a soft, familiar yellow.

Jack slows a few steps from the door, his brow creasing as he looks at me. "So . . . how was that?"

I think about cracking a joke, but nothing lands. Instead, I shrug, the weight of the evening sinking deep into my bones.

Jack studies me, his expression unreadable. Maybe he felt it too—that subtle wrongness Mrs. Callahan carried like an accessory. He nods slowly, then heads up the porch steps.

The boards creak under his boots, that customary sound offering a sliver of comfort. I lean on the door and let out a long exhale, tension leaking out in small doses.

Jack stops beside me, leaving enough space to avoid crowding. "I get it," he says quietly. "But . . . I still think this is too much for you. Too personal."

I meet his gaze and shake my head. "Let me be the one to decide that, okay?"

Jack's expression is hard to read, but then it happens—the dimple. That damn dimple. It's been so long I almost forgot it existed. Almost. It sneaks out, traitorous as ever, and suddenly, I forget how to breathe.

He pulls off his hat and runs a hand through his hair, which, naturally, falls into that perfect, just-rolled-out-of-bed look. A few days of stubble shadow his jaw, and I catch myself staring a little too long. Big mistake. And then there's the uniform—don't even get me started on the uniform. I've never been one to swoon over a man in uniform, but Jack? He rewrites the rulebook.

"You're about as damn stubborn as your grams, you know that?" He steps closer.

"Is that a bad thing?" I shoot back, raising a brow.

He doesn't answer right away. Instead, his hand moves—rough fingertips brushing under my chin, tilting my face up like he's testing a theory. My body, ever the traitor, leans into the touch I didn't ask for. "Not on you, it isn't," he murmurs.

This would be the perfect time to step back, say goodnight, and pretend none of this happened. But no. I simply stay there, locked in those stormy blue eyes of his. Too much. Too intense. Too *Jack.*

His eyes drop to my mouth, and I think he's actually going

to do it. Close the gap and put me out of my misery. But he hesitates.

Classic gentleman Jack.

"Oh, for crying out loud," I mutter, grabbing his uniform before he can second-guess himself into oblivion. I yank him toward me, and he doesn't resist—but he does pause, his eyes searching mine like he's giving me one last out.

I don't take it.

Our lips collide, and it's chaos in all the right ways. My hand slides to his jaw, fingers playing with his hair. His breath mixes with mine, warm and electric, and when he lets out a low groan, it vibrates all the way through me. Then his hands are on me—one at my waist, the other gripping my thigh, staking his claim.

In one smooth motion, he lifts me, and my legs wrap around him like they belong there. The rest of the world—my doubts, Mrs. Callahan's judging face—fades to nothing. It's just this: Jack, me, and the chemistry between us.

For once, neither of us overthinks it.

"*Now*, what would the good citizens of Cedar Cove say about this?" I gasp against his lips, my words shaky and breathless.

Jack grins, that dimple making another appearance. "They'd say it's one hell of a show."

A laugh escapes, my head thudding back against the door. It barely leaves my throat before his mouth is on mine again—urgent, relentless, pulling me under. His hands roam over me, gripping and sliding, fingers tangling in my hair. My whole body hums, heat building wherever he touches me.

For a second, the only thought in my head is, *God, just pull me inside already.*

And then it hits me.

A chill crawls up my spine, piercing straight through the

haze. My lips falter against his, my hands freezing mid-movement. Something's off.

My eyes snap open and meet his. He feels it too.

His grip loosens immediately, and my feet find the porch as he steps back, the heat between us evaporating in an instant. His expression hardens, his gaze darting past me.

That's when I see him.

The eyes hit me first.

Rich brown, flecked with gold, staring at me with a force that knocks the air from my lungs. They're older now, more defined, but still unmistakable. Eyes you don't forget, even if you try to.

My chest clenches, the ground tilting slightly beneath me. He's changed—broader shoulders, sun-darkened skin, years etched into every line of his face. But it's him.

The name slips from my lips before I can stop it. "Rhett."

CHAPTER 11

The October air has teeth—sharp, unkind ones that chew through whatever scraps of sleep I have left and spit me out wide awake. I am sitting on damp sand, toes digging in as if I could stake some kind of claim to reality, like the next wave wouldn't just roll in and snatch it away. Overhead, the sky is starting to stir; the sunrise stretching a lazy arm across the horizon.

In my hands, a holiday cup of coffee radiates enough heat to feel almost medicinal. It is 5:30 a.m., a time that Shoreline Sips typically treats as non-existent. But Lena, the owner, took one look at me—bedraggled, bleary-eyed, a human incarnation of lost luggage—and decided I was tragic enough to merit an early mercy pour.

I catch my reflection in the café's dark window, but it feels less of a mirror and more like someone else judging me. The raccoon-grade under-eye circles. The pajama pants I'd fished out of my suitcase in desperation.

The pajamas are something else, though. Faded to pastel oblivion, they still maintain their original absurdity: a print of press badges, notepads, and vintage microphones. Rhett had dubbed them my "Press Pass Pajamas" years ago, a name he'd delivered with a teasing smirk that could almost make me forget he was too charming for his own good.

Sitting there in those worn-out, ridiculous pants, I can almost hear his voice—low, amused, cutting through the waves, an echo that refuses to leave. Maybe that is the problem. The pajamas aren't just fabric; they are time travelers. And somewhere in their fraying seams is a version of me Rhett had once known, someone I'm not sure I still recognize but somehow can't let go of.

Last night's memories cling to me. The confrontation at Grams' house replays on a loop, gnawing at the fringes of my consciousness. Lena had called me a walking zombie, and honestly, I didn't have the energy to argue. Days without sleep will do that to a person. So will seeing someone who looks like Rhett.

Same eyes. Same build. The only difference is a thin, jagged scar below his jaw, something Rhett never had.

I noticed it the moment he stepped into the glow of Grams' porch light. How he stood, the tilt of his head; it was like watching a ghost come back to settle unfinished business. Jack, by my side, was just as frozen, staring like he'd accidentally walked onto the set of a horror movie. The air between us felt stuck, too heavy to breathe, until the guy finally cleared his throat, breaking the spell.

"Wrong person," he said, flat and matter-of-fact, as if he hadn't just set my brain on fire. Then he turned and walked off into the night, leaving me there, mouth open like I'd forgotten how oxygen worked.

Jack and I didn't move for a long beat. When I glanced over, his expression was no help—just the same wide-eyed confusion I was feeling, mirrored back at me. Eventually, he muttered something about making sure I was okay, then got into his Explorer and drove off, red and blue lights flashing as if that night could get any weirder.

Since then, Jack's been checking in like clockwork—texts every few hours, asking if I'm okay, if I need anything. Sweet, really. A little *too* sweet. Part of me almost wishes he'd stop. It'd be too easy to lean on his quiet, reliable concern. Too easy to forget I'm supposed to hate everything his uniform represents.

My phone vibrates, cutting off that particular spiral. I eye the screen.

MAGGIE

How's my Lenny?

I hesitate, fingers hovering over the keys, before settling on a classic lie.

LENNON

Meh. I'm fine.

Spoiler: I am not alright. Maggie knows it, too. I'd already spilled everything to her last night after hours of tossing and turning until my brain was mush. She hadn't believed me. Not really. Rhett was dead—had been for years. Whoever I saw couldn't be him, no matter how much he looked the part.

But logic and my heart have never exactly been on speaking terms.

Another ping pulls me back.

MAGGIE

"Fine" might be a stretch, but can you at least call me tonight? Just want to double, double check you're okay, okay?

I let out a tired sigh, but her persistence tugs a faint smile out of me. Maggie's stubborn loyalty feels like someone gently putting a hand on my shoulder, reminding me the ground's still there.

MAGGIE

Plus, Blake wants to know if you're still
working on your case over there.

I roll my eyes and type back.

LENNON

Tell him not to lose sleep.

Another lie, but a convenient one. Technically, I *am*
working on it—the case back home, the case here in Cedar
Cove. Both circling in my brain like vultures, swooping in the
second I try to sleep. Anything to keep me from thinking
about *those* hazel eyes.

Rhett's eyes.

"Must be someone special," someone murmurs behind
me, smooth and low.

My spine locks, every nerve pulled tight, a wire ready to
sing. That *voice.*

He's here.

My eyes stay glued to the phone screen. I don't dare turn
around. Every instinct is screaming at me to look, but I don't
trust myself. Out of the corner of my eye, I do a quick scan—
two people to my right talking about the weather, an older
man on my left nursing his coffee.

Good. Witnesses.

I swallow hard, my pulse thundering in my throat.

I peek over my shoulder, and the moment our eyes find
each other, I freeze—caught between fight, flight, and what-
the-hell. For a second, fear digs in, locking my muscles and
cutting my breath short. But then something strange happens:
It fades. His gaze isn't threatening. If anything, it's unsettlingly
familiar. Almost Rhett's.

Rhett, is that you? I blink hard, a wretch twisting through me. His smile is warm, maybe a little too practiced. Something about it seems like it's trying too hard to fit.

"Does everyone make you smile like that?" His tone is playful, like we've known each other long enough for teasing.

I open my mouth to reply, but all I manage is a faint croak. Great. Very impressive. Meanwhile, he drops into the sand next to me, as if he'd been invited.

Then he does it—just burrows his toes in the sand. Not his whole foot, just the toes. My stomach does a weird little flip. It's not the act itself; people around here treat sand like a second skin. It's the way he does it. That precise, fidgety habit that used to be Rhett's signature move.

My neck prickles, goosebumps rising like they've just remembered something I'd rather forget.

Maybe it's a coincidence. But then again, I gave up believing in those a long time ago. Coincidences are just convenient lies we tell ourselves to ignore things we don't want to see.

As he turns, the morning light catches his face, softening the edges and giving him a sort of easy warmth. Against my better judgment, I stare. The defined jawline, the faint stubble that somehow reads as effortlessly polished.

His hair falls into those sunlit amber eyes like he didn't try, but probably did. He's older than Rhett would be. Mid-thirties, maybe?

Handsome, sure, but not the obvious kind. He's the sort of handsome that creeps up on you, catching you off guard. The kind you don't realize is trouble until it's too late.

The dangerous kind.

CHAPTER 12

The way she looks at me now—it's how she used to look at him. Soft, focused, like I'm the only thing around, even though Cedar Cove is still very much here. It's the look that used to make Rhett feel like the sun, and now it's on me. Her pupils are wide, flickering with something between confusion and . . . recognition, maybe?

A blush creeps across her cheekbones—warm and recognizable. Because of me. I shouldn't enjoy this. I really shouldn't. But here we are.

Her gaze shifts, dragging over the scar under my jaw, the unruly hair, the lines I've earned the hard way. I'm not him. Not entirely. But there's enough of Rhett in me to make her pause, like she's seen a ghost she thought she'd laid to rest, only for it to stroll in and ruin her day.

Every instinct says to yank her back into the mess we came from. I don't, though. Instead, I focus on the water—so blue, so still. It's mocking me. The beauty of this place feels wrong, like I'm breaking some unspoken rule just by being here. Could this have been home? Maybe. In some other lifetime.

But I'm Massachusetts, born and bred: grayer skies, tougher air, and rules that make sense in their own warped way. Different streets. *Different me.*

"You stalking me or something?" Lennon interrupts the hush, her words incisive with just enough humor to let me know even she's not buying this moment as real life.

I grin—barely. It's one of those blink-and-you'll-miss-it things. My eyes stay on the water. Safer that way. If I look at her too long, I might give away more than I'm ready to.

I shake my head, slow. Not much else to add.

"Then what?" The skepticism is impossible to miss. "You here for the view?"

I finally turn to her, letting myself follow the curves of her face, the distinct shapes that time hasn't managed to blur. The sun glimmers in those pretty blues, and her hair dances in the breeze before settling back onto her shoulders.

"Something like that," I admit, my tone even. I let the tension stretch for a second, then toss in a wink for good measure.

And just like that, she smiles. Not the tight-lipped, I'm-fine-thanks kind she's mastered over the years. This one is real —unguarded. And for a second, it steals my breath.

"Cute pajamas." I nod toward the faded cotton she's wearing, clinging just enough to derail whatever coherent thought I had left. It takes actual effort not to let out a groan.

She laughs, pulling her cardigan tighter like it'll help. It doesn't. The blush creeping up her neck is impossible to miss.

"I can't tell if you're lying to make me feel better or if you've genuinely lost all taste," she teases, one brow arched to the point of making it a challenge.

I don't miss a beat. "Oh, I mean it. But let's be real—it's not the pajamas. It's you making them look good."

Her face flushes, and the shade is both ridiculous and completely adorable. I take it in, every instinct screaming at me to close the gap between us, to pull her in and confirm once and for all if she tastes as good as she looks in this soft, unguarded light. My fingers twitch at the thought.

But I don't move. Not yet.

The last thing I want is to watch that smile of hers slam shut again, her guard going back up because I pushed too far. Instead, I wait, forcing myself to zero in on the cool breeze and not on the way she looks like she belongs here, by my side, even when the rest of the world doesn't deserve her.

"Do you live here?" she asks. Her toes dig into the sand, leaving little nervous impressions.

I start to nod, then catch myself and shake my head instead.

She lets out a laugh—almost a giggle—and, damn, it's cute. A sound that could break through the darkest day and make it feel like maybe the sun's worth dealing with again. I can't remember the last time I heard a laugh like that, or felt anything close to it.

"Okay," she draws the word out as her eyes scan mine, half-curious, half-skeptical. "So . . . you do live here? Or . . . ?"

I force a chuckle, though it comes out stiff. "No. I mean . . . not really." My hand goes to my hair, tugging at the ends, like that'll help keep me grounded. Honestly, what was I thinking? That I could just show up here, stroll into her life like we were old friends or . . . something else?

She tilts her head, studying me like I'm one of those puzzles with missing pieces that might not even belong to the same box. A beat passes before she nods, though it's clear she's not buying it.

"Can I ask . . . how old are you?" Her tone is cautious, but curious enough to make me flinch.

I dither for only a second. "Thirty-seven. Just turned."

The number drops between us, a lead weight. Her lips part slightly, as if she wants to speak but can't find the words. She averts her gaze, her shoulders dipping just a fraction. Yeah, not the answer she wanted. She was hoping for twenty-seven, maybe twenty-eight. *His age.*

"So . . . are you just visiting, then?"

The questions keep coming, one after another. Can't exactly blame her—my timing was about as subtle as a bull in a china shop. That night at her grandmother's house wasn't supposed to be *the night.* But then I saw her pinned against the door, locking lips with that damn sheriff, and—well, plans changed.

My gut sours just thinking about it. I hadn't planned anything, just stood there in the shadows like some brooding cryptid, glaring to make him step back. No words necessary. Sometimes presence gets the job done.

Now, though, I've got to keep a lid on that particular brand of anger. Not the time, not the place. I grit my teeth and clamp it down before it gets out. "Yeah, I'm here for work," I finally admit.

She nods slowly, her head dipping until her cheek rests against her arm. Her eyes dart everywhere except at me, like she's trying to piece something together, but the picture isn't adding up.

Then, just like that, they snap back, finding mine, and the air shifts. I see everything—hurt, confusion, anger—laid bare in those eyes of hers.

She releases a breathy laugh. "Good God."

"I prefer Reed," I note, leaning on the smirk that usually gets me out of trouble. "But hey, if you're ready to elevate me to divine status, I won't stop you."

Her stare holds mine for a moment, unreadable, before she bursts out laughing—real, full-bodied laughter that throws her head back and bares her throat. My mouth goes dry, and all I can think about is tracing the line of her neck with my lips, feeling that laughter vibrate against me.

I cough, shifting, like it'll help. It doesn't. The ache in my chest turns into something warmer, heavier, a steady flame I can't ignore.

"So . . . Reed, huh?" She rolls the name around like she's testing it for durability. Her lips quirk into a grin that could mean anything—or absolutely nothing.

I nod. A self-satisfied expression stretches the corners of my mouth. "Yep," I say, as if that's all the explanation the universe needs.

The wind stirs, tossing a stray curl across her cheek. Before my brain can weigh in, my hand moves on impulse. I catch the wayward strand and tuck it behind her ear. My fingers graze her skin, and for a moment—one of those achingly cinematic moments—the world dims. No waves, no wind, no obnoxious seagulls squawking in the background. *Just her.*

Her eyes lock onto mine, and there's something in them— bold, curious, maybe even challenging. Or maybe I'm over- thinking it, but it's not like she's giving me a manual here. My pulse kicks up, hammering loud enough to qualify as its own soundtrack.

Her gaze drops to my mouth, then back up, and the air between us turns electric. My stomach flips, common sense stumbles. This is it. Every stolen glance, every fleeting touch, every almost-something that's been hanging between us—it's all been leading here.

I shift closer, my hand sliding to the back of her neck. She sucks in a breath, her eyes widening just slightly, as if she wasn't expecting this, but maybe doesn't hate it.

Then, her phone lights up. It vibrates among us, a smug little interruption jolting us both back to reality.

And with that, the moment crumbles. Her body stiffens, her expression sealing shut. The warmth drains from her eyes, replaced by something colder as she glances at her phone. I watch her retreat—first in spirit, then in flesh—shifting back like the extra inches between us are absolutely critical to her survival. Her fingers crush around her coffee cup, knuckles bloodless, gripping it as if letting go isn't an option. She doesn't look at me.

I stay put, legs sticky with sand. We both start putting on our shoes, movements stiff and robotic; an awkwardness usually reserved for strangers trying to figure out who's leaving first. Her phone buzzes again. And again. Every vibration is a jackhammer drilling into my chest. *Jack*. His name flashes on her screen in obnoxious all caps, like it's claiming ownership. Like he's already won.

I want to laugh. Or maybe punch something. She's right here with me, but he's the one who gets to drag her away with a single, stupid buzz. Instead, I lean toward her, bridging the distance she clearly worked so hard to create. My hand hovers near her elbow, hesitating at the last second. She stiffens, and it's subtle, but it's there. Her eyes meet mine—open, guarded, and carrying enough tension to make me feel like I've crossed a line. Fear? Doubt? Who knows. Definitely not trust.

Still, I press on, gently catching her other arm and pulling her in before she can bolt. She doesn't resist. In fact, she leans into me, softening just enough to make it feel like a victory. Her body fits against mine so easily it's unsettling—like this is something she's done before. Maybe with Jack. Maybe Rhett before him.

She pulls back, creating distance again. "It was nice meeting you, Reed," she says softly.

Nice. Meeting me. Like we haven't spent weeks orbiting each other, stealing glances, and toeing the line between "something" and "nothing." I want to keep her here, hold her until every other name in her life—Rhett, Jack, whoever's next —ceases to exist. But that's not how these things work, is it? So, instead, I nod. Cool. Detached. Like I'm not dying a little inside.

I reach for her hand, brushing my fingers against hers. Lifting it carefully, I press a kiss to her knuckles, lingering a moment too long. Her skin is warm, impossibly soft, and for that stretched-out second, I let my eyes close. Maybe I can freeze her here, lock this moment in place.

When I draw back, she bites her bottom lip. That lip. Red, soft, and criminally distracting. It makes me think about things I probably shouldn't, things that would absolutely undo me.

"It was nice meeting you . . . " I leave the words hanging, waiting for her to respond.

She stalls long enough for the breeze to feel heavy, for doubt to creep into the silence. Then, finally, her lips curve into a small, almost reluctant smile.

"Lennon," she whispers.

I repeat it under my breath, tasting the name. "Lennon." I'm tempted to say it again, just to see if she'll peek back, but she's already focused on her phone—the digital leash yanking her away.

Each step she takes knots something in my chest tighter. Questions bubble up, stupid and useless. When will I see her again? What did that sheriff want? Not like I'm getting answers. She disappears down the path, her silhouette quickly swallowed by Cedar Cove's bustling main street.

My phone vibrates in my pocket.

BENSON

Mrs. Callahan's appointment is set for next week at 10:00 a.m. sharp.

I huff a laugh. Right on schedule.

REED

Great. Did she mention anything about the house?

BENSON

Just that she wants to discuss "next steps".

Next steps. Of course. I can practically hear her saying it in that clipped, no-nonsense tone she's perfected. The same tone she used the first time she called my office, rattling off instructions like I'd begged her to grace my construction business with her presence.

REED

Awesome, thanks, man.

BENSON

Always got your back.

CHAPTER 13

Why am I nervous? This isn't a date. Jack didn't suggest, *"Let's have a romantic dinner at my place."* It was more like, *"I have an update on the case. Swing by tonight."*

Straightforward. Professional.

So why is my pulse doing its best impression of a drum solo?

Because it's Jack. Jack, who somehow turns everything into a tangled mess. Jack, who can't just stick to the case but has to be so damn . . . nice. *How are you, Lennon?* His soothing voice seems designed to lull me into some false sense of security. He never dives right in. No, he asks about me first, like he actually cares. Thoughtful. Completely unacceptable.

How dare he?

I exhale sharply and glare at my reflection. *This is about the case. This is about Josie.* I rake a hand through my hair, as if that's going to do anything about the restless nerves currently setting up camp in my chest.

And, right on cue, there's Reed. His name pops into my head like the last dying ember—one that refuses to quit smoldering no matter how much I wish it would. Reed. Rhett. So close, yet galaxies apart.

I roll my eyes and glance away, but the mirror doesn't budge. I've been pacing for what feels like hours, my nerves on edge, curiosity gnawing at me with sharp little teeth. He had insisted I come to his house if I wanted the update. His house.

I tug at the hem of my skirt, swallowing hard. One more look at the mirror, scanning over my outfit like a critical judge. The brown wool skirt: Professional, but with a hint of mischief. Knee-high stockings with little bows: Cute. The floral bodysuit? Hugs all the right (and wrong) places. And then the jacket, neatly draped over my chair, patiently awaiting me. I'm dressed for . . . well, not exactly for a "case update." Not unless we're planning to cross-examine Josie's murder while sipping wine over candlelight.

"You just gonna stand there gawkin' at yourself all night, or are you actually headin' out for this date of yours?"

Grams pipes up from the doorway, full of amusement. I catch her peeking around the corner, eyes twinkling, towel turban slightly askew. She's already smirking.

"Not a date, Grams," I comment, like repeating it might make it true.

"Uh-huh." She gives me *that* look; she's humoring me while mentally drafting a monologue for when she's proven right.

I gather my essentials: case files, notes, and what's left of my shaky dignity. Just as I head for the door, a flash of light sweeps across the room. I freeze mid-step, but Grams is already at the open window, watching like she's about to narrate the local news.

"Who's that?" I ask, trying for casual.

"Oh, just *them*," Grams replies, waving a hand like she couldn't care less—though her death grip on the window frame says otherwise.

Them. The Wives of Cedar Cove.

I move beside her and peer out. In their usual display of Stepford precision, they park in formation along the curb. Each one steps out dressed to kill for another thrilling evening of casseroles and coordinated gossip. Mrs. Callahan takes the lead, her helmet of perfectly styled hair resisting even the slightest evening breeze.

And there it is—that prickle on the back of my neck, the same one I felt at the Callahan estate with Jack. Since Josie's murder.

"Do they meet at the Callahan place often?" I ask, the hint of curiosity laced with something else—unease, maybe. Observing them now is like watching a ghost parade—same stiff smiles, same designer sedans, same unnerving aura.

Grams shrugs, still squinting at the scene like she's sizing up a stray dog with too many teeth. "They rotate their little meetin's, sure, but lately, they've taken a real hankerin' to the Callahan estate." She shudders, a ripple starting at her shoulders and traveling all the way down to her elbows. "Buncha gossipin' hens. Never trusted 'em."

I nod, though my attention is glued to the street as the final member of the flock arrives. She steps out of her car with practiced grace, then pauses near the front door, scanning her surroundings like she's expecting trouble—or checking if anyone's watching.

A reminder that beneath Cedar Cove's perfect lawns and gleaming SUVs, there's something darker lurking, something that doesn't belong on a postcard.

Just as I'm about to look away, she turns her head.

My heart stumbles, awkward and offbeat.

We stand frozen, separated by the quiet street and a gulf of tension I can't quite name. Her hazel eyes bore into me, cold and unblinking, shadows pooling around her like secrets that have no intention of staying buried. There's something unsettling about her stare; she's used to being watched, maybe even welcomes it.

Comforting? Not exactly.

Something about the way she observes me, then pointedly looks through me, makes the decision easy. She's my next interview. Whether Jack would approve is a later problem. He told me to "hang tight" and quit poking my nose into things like I'm auditioning for a true-crime podcast, but come on. This doesn't even count as poking. Just two women having a friendly chat. Harmless. Probably.

"Buncha old women with nothin' bettah to do," Grams mutters, yanking the curtains shut with a finality that says the conversation's over before it's begun. The room falls into a dim, suffocating silence, and I realize I've been holding my breath. I let it out slowly.

She shakes her head, still grumbling, more to herself now. "Nevah could figure out why ya mothah wanted to be part o' their circle."

I stop short. "Mom? Since when?"

Grams freezes, her jaw tightening. She's biting back something she's not sure I'm ready to hear. Her expression shifts, and for a moment, there's something foreign there—grief, anger, or maybe just exhaustion.

"They were always after her to join their little group," she finally admits. "Ya know, all secrets and scandals, the whole Stepford Wives act. But your mothah, with her journalist brain, saw it as a gold mine. Figured she'd join, dig up dirt, maybe expose some skeletons."

She hesitates, then adds, "But when she actually tried? They shut her out faster than a door-to-door salesman. Naturally, that only made her more determined. She knew they were hiding somethin'. So she kept pokin' around."

I swallow hard, my mind racing. Was it that particular investigation that got her killed? Were those the same people mentioned in her files? Or was it something she uncovered—something they were desperate to keep hidden from the world?

Before I can overthink myself into oblivion, Grams hiccups. Not a polite one—loud and abrupt, a sound that doesn't belong in the quiet. I glance over. No tears, but her breathing is off, shaky, something unspoken caught between inhales. My journalist instincts push me to press for answers, but for once, I don't.

"We don't have to talk about it, Grams." I reach for her hand. Her gray eyes meet mine, glassy and rimmed, but she manages a frail smile that trembles at the corners. I loop my arm through hers, giving her a gentle squeeze, and we shuffle downstairs together.

I ease her into her favorite rocking chair by the window, the perfect vantage point where she can gaze out at the sea grass swaying in the night.

We slip into the usual routine. I hand her a steaming mug of chamomile and dig the cooling eye patches out of the freezer. As always, she rolls her eyes. "Fancy people's nonsense," she mutters, even as she's pulling her hair back, waiting for me to press them in place. Last month, she called the ice roller I bought her a "gadget for people with too much free time." Now she won't go to bed without it. Each night, she glides it under her eyes like she's inspecting what time has stolen.

Stubborn old woman. God, I love her.

"Okay, Grams, I'm heading out. You good for the night?" I ask, as if I don't fuss over her like this every single day.

She nods, already halfway absorbed in the plot of her favorite soap opera. I've been trying to ease her into a routine, something that keeps her from bending or reaching too much. Just this week, I dragged her to the hardware store, and Gus and his crew came by to install lowered cabinets, pull-out shelves, even a pull-out trash can. *"It's the little things,"* Gus had said with a wink. *"What we all need these days, eh, Lennon?"*

Grams doesn't look up from the TV, just shoos me off with a wave. "Go on, Lenny. Stop hovering."

I lean down and press a kiss to the top of her head. "Love you," I say quietly, knowing full well I won't get an answer. But as I turn to leave, I catch a faint, distracted hum—her version of *me too.*

I climb into my SUV and head to Jack's place. A few miles in, the road turns to gravel, one that seems deliberately rugged, as if daring people to keep going. The crunch of stones under my tires is unnaturally loud, like the whole place is eavesdropping. Up ahead, a leaning sign finally appears, barely readable in the dim light: *Birch Haven Woods.* Innocent name, sure, but my gut tightens anyway—some mix of curiosity and the subtle alarm bell you only notice when it's already too late to turn around.

Jack gave me clear directions, but I'm certain this place doesn't show up on any map. It's hidden, tucked away as a secret. The trees on either side press closer, their branches tangling overhead, like they're conspiring. The last scraps of daylight get swallowed by the canopy, and just as I expect, my cell signal blinks out. Of course it does.

Then I spot it—a glimmer up ahead. A lantern dangles from a crooked post, swinging slightly, its weak light barely reaching the ground. Beneath it, a cluster of pumpkins sit in a chaotic heap, their carved faces warped and mismatched, like someone gave up halfway through an art class. It's almost funny. Almost. There's something oddly warm about it, though—a clumsy, awkward welcome in this otherwise tense stretch of woods.

At the roundabout, my GPS calmly tells me to take the first right, so I do, letting its robotic confidence lead me deeper in. A few more turns, and suddenly, Jack's townhouse appears —not the secluded cabin I'd imagined, but a compact, unexpectedly cheerful place. The walkway is lined with pumpkins, these a little more polished than the wild assortment at the entrance. A hand-painted sign by the door reads *Sheriff Mercer*.

And then I see it: The banner stretched across the front lawn. I stop mid-drive, one hand still gripping the gearshift. *Happy Birthday*, the bold letters proclaim, fluttering in the breeze like some cosmic punchline.

His birthday.

Jack hadn't mentioned it on the phone. Not a word, not even a hint. And here I am, empty-handed. Guilt gnaws at my insides, mingling with the hot prick of embarrassment.

For a split second, I consider throwing the car in reverse and disappearing down that gravel road before anyone spots me. But before I can move, a voice rises in the stillness, killing any shot I had at a clean getaway.

"Lennon, that you?"

I pause halfway out of my SUV, eyeing the driveway. Sure enough, there's Benson, stretched out in a chair by the fire pit, a beer dangling from his fingers like it's doing all the hard work. His green eyes glint in the firelight, and his smirk—he knows exactly how smug he looks—seems permanently etched on his face.

But he's not alone. Next to him, another man sits sprawled in his chair, watching me with the sort of intensity that suggests he's sizing me up for a job interview.

"What are you doing here?" Benson questions.

An excellent question, Benson, and one I'd love to answer if I weren't so busy trying to figure out who your sidekick is and why he's looking at me like I owe him money.

Instead, I opt for the shrug-and-pretend-I'm-casual

approach. "Jack invited me," I remark, as if the SUV in his driveway hadn't already answered that for him.

The stranger finally speaks, each syllable slow, like he's turning my name over in his mind. "So, you're Lennon."

Not a question, more a statement meant to still me. His smile lands after, but it doesn't invite. It lingers in the space between bait and challenge. *Let's see how you handle this.*

"Leave her alone, Sinn." An arm snakes around my waist, pulling me against a chest. *Jack.* The contact is both comforting and electric, and before I know it, I'm leaning into him, letting his calm settle over me.

Sinn's eyes narrow, regarding me as if he's peeling me apart, layer by layer. I half-expect him to say something biting, but no. He takes a measured sip of his beer instead, a reminder that he's still here, still judging. Like a beer-drinking gargoyle.

Benson clears his throat. "Any updates on the investigation?"

Jack sighs, his hand lingering on my waist like he's testing how long he can get away with it. "Nothing solid. Just some locals claiming they saw an older guy with a buzz cut and a runner's build."

Sinn snorts, the laugh practically dripping with disdain. "Right. Because the folks around here are *so* reliable. They'd tell you they saw Bigfoot if it got you off their doorstep."

Benson squints, his forehead creasing like he's actually considering Bigfoot. "I don't know. This seems . . . different."

Different. Right. Nothing about this is different. Josie's broken pinkies, her blank, glassy eyes—it all lines up perfectly with the nightmare I've spent a decade trying to bury.

"What do you mean?" The words slip out. All three men stare at me, as if I've grown a second head.

"It's been exactly ten years," Benson notes, his calmness unsettling. "Who waits a decade to reenact your parents' murders? And Rhett's?"

The hit slams into my chest, sharp and unrelenting. I flinch. No stopping the memories now—ripping open like an old wound, raw and stinging as ever.

Benson turns toward the street, his face twisting like he's chewing something sour. "What's bothering me is, why Josie? Why her, out of everyone in this town?"

"Because she worked for the Callahans," Sinn cuts in, drumming his fingers against his beer bottle like it's a piano and he's bored with the tune. "Never liked that family. Or their place. Or their . . . son."

Their *son*. He tosses the word out so casually, as if Rhett's life was just another item on his to-do list: Ignore. Complain about. Forget. My pulse spikes, heat rising in my chest, the old anger stirring again. Low and steady, always there, always waiting.

"Rhett," I snap, my teeth clenched. "His name was Rhett."

"Rhett, sure," Sinn echoes.

Jack's arm tightens around me—a quiet nudge to stay grounded, but it only works for a second.

"Alright, enough," Jack interjects, his tone firm, and the only thing keeping this conversation from diving headfirst into chaos. "This is my case. If you want to discuss it, do it at the station. With your badges on."

Benson rolls his eyes. "Right, because *you* get to discuss it out here. With *her.*" That last word makes my stomach tighten.

Her? What's that supposed to mean? This guy doesn't know me. I'm a stranger to him, but apparently, I should start paying attention. Jack's hands twitch against my stomach, but before he can fire back, Sinn raises his beer in a lazy toast, his smirk dripping with sarcasm. "Jack doesn't do dates."

I lock eyes with Sinn, my chin lifting. "Good thing this isn't a date, then." My smile is thin, sharp as glass—a dare more than anything. Before anyone can notice my shaking hands or hear my racing pulse, I grab Jack's hand and turn, pulling him toward the house.

Normally, I wouldn't do this—wouldn't challenge them so directly—but there's something about Sinn. It makes my blood run cold.

Maybe it's the sneer—the self-satisfied twist of his mouth —that takes me back to those days when the local cops saw everything and still managed to see nothing when it came to my parents and Rhett.

And just like that, I want something I've spent years pretending I didn't need: A place where my world didn't feel like it was teetering. Something solid. Safe.

Like Jack's arms.

That surprised me.

But not as much as what happened next.

CHAPTER 14

Lennon

The second we step through Jack's door, it slams shut behind us with enough force to rattle the hinges. I might've jumped if he hadn't already pinned me against it like a man on a mission. My keys hit the floor before his mouth crashes into mine, unapologetic and borderline feral. Words have officially been declared useless.

His hands frame my face like I might Houdini my way out of this if he lets go for even a second. Honestly, not the worst assumption. My bag slips off my shoulder and hits the floor somewhere in the background. Jack is pressed so close every nerve in my body lights up and suddenly, I realize how desperate I am for this—for him.

"God, that was so fucking hot," he mutters against my lips. He shifts, pinning my wrists above my head with one hand, and the wolfish smile he gives me should be illegal. "You, standing up to Sinn like that . . ."

His lips crash back into mine. No hesitation, just heat—tongues and teeth, borderline reckless. He kisses like he wants me to feel it tomorrow, and maybe I want that too.

He trails down my neck, his lips and tongue leaving fire in their wake, and a low sound escapes me. My thoughts are a blur of static until something starts piercing the fog.

His uniform.

Still stiff and starched under my fingertips.

I draw back just enough to catch my breath, my forehead brushing against his as we linger in the charged space between kisses. "Are you . . . on call?" I inquire, because apparently, my brain has decided now is the time for logistics.

He hesitates, then grins. "Technically"—his lips dip to my collarbone, dragging goosebumps across my skin, making it difficult to think about *anything*, let alone his work schedule —"I just got off."

For a second, my brain misfires. He just wrapped up a long shift—probably exhausted from handling every petty emergency this town could throw at him—and yet, here he is. Making time for me. Prioritizing this. Prioritizing *me*. And at this exact moment, I am fully on board with this plan: His lips on mine, his body pressing me against the door like he's been counting the minutes for this all day.

Naturally, I pull back. I have to. That's when he laughs—soft, easy, maddening. He takes a step back, giving me some space, and my hands, with absolutely no self-respect, shoot out and grab the front of his uniform.

His brows lift, the picture of amused patience. I flush and drop my hands like they caught fire, mumbling something unintelligible. Before I can retreat further into awkward oblivion, Jack catches one of my hands and presses it to his mouth.

The kiss on my knuckles lingers—both smug and stupidly intimate.

It feels . . . right. Like it belongs. Like *he* belongs. And that is the problem.

Because someone else kissed my hand just like that. Reed.

Quiet, confident Reed, who I barely know but still can't quite forget.

I shove the thought away and let Jack lead me into the kitchen. He opens the fridge, peering into its sad, nearly empty depths, while I lean against the counter, working overtime to look unbothered.

"That was one way to say hello," I quip, aiming for nonchalance.

He shoots me a slow, cocky grin. "Don't act like you didn't like it."

I shrug, trying to appear cool and failing miserably. My body is buzzing, though, because Jack is a man who can derail your entire thought process just by existing. Solid. Rough around the edges.

And, of course, my brain immediately detours into dangerous territory. What would it be like to have him in bed? The chemistry between us has been off the charts from day one. Our make-out sessions alone could void a homeowner's insurance policy. Actually taking things further? Yeah, the thought leaves me a little dizzy.

"Bud Light?" Jack interrupts, holding up a can like it is a peace offering.

I wrinkle my nose. "Pass."

"Not a beer girl, huh?" he asks, chuckling.

I shake my head and sidle up to the fridge, bumping him lightly with my hip in an attempt to look breezy. My pulse, meanwhile, is pounding like it has something to prove. He chuckles, bumps me back, his hands sliding down to my waist effortlessly . . . and absolutely intentional.

Maybe it is the heat still lingering on my lips, or maybe it is the reckless streak in me, but I bend over, leaning farther into the fridge like I am on a life-or-death mission to find something.

The groan that slips out of him is deep and unfiltered. Out

of my peripheral vision, I catch him tilting his head back, squeezing his eyes shut, like he needs a moment to collect himself. It sends a thrill straight through me.

"Okay, okay, I see you," he utters, clearing his throat. His hands slip from my waist, and I immediately miss the warmth. For a split second, I almost feel bad for teasing him. Almost.

Then I spot it: a pack of Cayman Jacks, tucked behind a pathetic six-pack of Bud Light. Jackpot. I pull one out, crack it open, and sigh.

Jack eyes me, shaking his head with a slow, disbelieving smile. "Margarita fan, huh?"

I raise the can in a mock toast and take a sip, letting the tangy lime settle on my tongue. "What can I say? I prefer a drink with some personality."

He laughs as we wander into his living room. But the second we step in it, the vibe shifts.

Papers. Laptops. Notes. Everywhere. Spilling off the coffee table, covering the couch, even creeping onto the floor. It is less "living room" and more "detective's office mid-investigation." It reminds me of my bedroom—a chaotic mess of half-finished ideas and unanswered questions, all desperately circling the same puzzle.

Because we are still searching—for something, for anything, for whatever it is we are supposed to find but haven't. Doubt creeps in, as it always does. Will we ever actually find it? Or are we just chasing our own tails, burning gas and optimism for nothing? I know the drill too well: the endless pursuit of answers that refuses to show up. Long nights with evidence that ties itself in knots, going nowhere fast. My parents' case. Rhett's case. Years of nothing. The police? Useless. The sheriff? Less than useless. They gave up before they even broke a sweat.

But Jack? Jack isn't the type to quit. Night after night, he has been chasing every half-baked lead, no matter how faint or absurd. And that stubbornness of his does something to me. It presses into the cracks of my cynicism with this dangerous little warmth, a feeling I haven't invited and definitely don't trust. The sort of feeling that, if left unchecked, might lead to hope. And hope? Well, hope has a habit of turning on you.

He must have noticed me staring because he glances up from the chaos of papers and catches my eye. Before I can think better of it, the words fall out of my mouth: "It's your birthday?"

"Yeah," he comments, like it is no big deal. "It is."

I sink into the couch, and wow—this thing is ridiculous. Like sitting on a cloud. Feathers? Memory foam? Black magic? Regardless, I am a goner. My gaze drifts around Jack's place, taking in the details. It isn't one of those sterile, minimalist magazine spreads where everything's white and you're afraid to touch the furniture. No, this place is *lived in*. Rustic, with a dash of rugged charm—like a cowboy who discovered Pinterest.

The mantel catches my eye first, lined with framed photos. Jack with his friends. Jack with who I guess are his adopted parents. Above the mantel hangs a TV big enough to double as a drive-in movie screen, and flanking it? Two mounted deer heads, staring down at me with those lifeless glass eyes that usually give me the creeps. But here? Somehow, it just fits. The whole place is so unapologetically *Jack* that I smile. This isn't just a house; it is his personality with walls.

"You saw the banner, right? The kids around here just worship me," Jack drawls, oozing sarcasm as he settles into his chair.

I smirk. Teasing him has quickly become my favorite sport. "Oh, totally. Local hero. Any day now, they'll probably rename the town after you."

From across the room, he gives me this look—half a smirk, half a challenge. But before I can continue, the moment cracks open, and we both break into laughter. It isn't forced or polite—it is real, the type that fills the room and bridges the gap between us. One laugh, one shared moment, and whatever we are building between us just got a little stronger.

"Happy Birthday, Sheriff," I tease, tossing in a wink.

Jack's cheeks turn a shade of crimson red and he raises his beer. I follow his lead, lifting my drink and taking a sip. The cool liquid slides down my throat, and I emit a quiet hum of approval.

"That good, huh?"

I cock my head, as if giving it some deep philosophical consideration. "Not bad . . . for my first time trying it."

His brow creeps up. "Wait, I thought you said you liked those?"

I pull my lips between my teeth, doing my best to stifle the laugh threatening to escape. "No, I said I liked margaritas. *This*"—I hold up the can like it is some ancient relic—"this is a whole different experience."

A hint of a smile plays on his lips, and his eyes—those unnerving blue's—spark like he knows he is winning whatever game this is. He doesn't say anything, just watches me over the rim of his glass.

He beats me to the punch. "Order some food?"

I nod, the slow warmth of alcohol loosening my limbs. He leans forward, pulling open the table's cluttered drawer, its chaotic tangle of takeout menus spilling out without rhyme or reason.

"Very professional." I gesture at the chaos.

He shrugs. "Sheriff life."

More like *bachelor life*, I think, but keep it to myself. I can imagine his schedule, constantly on call, grabbing quick meals between shifts. Probably easier than spending hours in the kitchen alone.

We sift through the takeout menus and land on pizza—

big, greasy slices from The Salty Slice. Just thinking about it makes my stomach growl, loud and unrepentant. I duck my head, cheeks warming.

Jack chuckles and before I can brush it off with a joke, he reaches out and tilts my chin up. His touch is light, brief—but enough to send a jolt through me, one that makes my brain short-circuit and my skin feel two sizes too small. He is looking at me with that soft, unreadable expression of his, making me feel seen in a way I'm not sure I want to be.

And then the doorbell rings.

I snap back like someone hit a reset button. Probably for the best.

Jack stands, but not before his fingers brush against my lower lip.

"That smells amazing," I breathe, watching as he places the pizza box on the counter.

We settle onto the barstools and eat in almost comfortable silence, where small talk fills the gaps like packing peanuts. Functional, forgettable, and mildly annoying if you overthink it. Still, curiosity itches at me like a tag on the back of my shirt. Eventually, I scratch.

"So . . . who's Sinn?" I ask, as I take a too-big bite of pizza —as if an innocent mouthful can defuse the question-shaped grenade I just lobbed.

Jack pauses long enough to notice. "My neighbor, coworker, long-time friend."

"Ah." I lift a brow. "A real multitasker."

His smirk flickers and disappears, faint as smoke. "Yeah. We go way back. Trained together at the police academy."

"Where was that?" The question is out, bringing with it the familiar pang. I don't know much about his life outside Cedar Cove.

Jack's head drops to the countertop, like it might feed him a script. "Well, I was born here," he states, picking his words carefully. "But my adoptive parents—they're from Eastpoint."

"Eastpoint . . . that's, what, an hour away?"

"Hour and a half," he corrects, taking another bite of pizza.

"So, you and Sinn . . . met there?"

His gaze slides past me, settling on some distant point over my shoulder. "Yeah." The word is quiet enough to barely land. "During training." For a second, something shadows across his face—regret, maybe? But it vanishes as he adds, "Then I got called up for . . . "

The pause stretches long enough for me to feel the invisible wall click into place, the one that always comes up when his name enters the room.

"Rhett's case," I finish for him.

"Yeah." His eyes fixated somewhere just above the table. "Anyway, that's when I came back here—wanted to dig into my birth parents' pasts. And Sinn . . . " he falters. "Well, Sawyer. Sinn's his last name."

I blink, then let out a startled laugh. "Wait—are you telling me that wasn't his actual name?"

Jack finally looks at me, his lips twitching like he is trying not to smile. "Would've suited him better, honestly," he mumbles.

"So . . . what happened? He ended up with a job here too?"

Jack nods, his shoulders easing like someone who just remembered how breathing works. "Yeah. Wild coincidence, right? Trust me, I was just as shocked. Small town like this, and his parents lived here before? I guess it tracks."

That makes me pause. Sawyer was from here? And Jack's parents used to live here, too? When? Why did they leave? Questions start multiplying in my head like over-caffeinated rabbits, but one look at Jack's expression tells me not to ask.

"Anyway," he continues, his tone shifting into something smoother, "the three of us—Sawyer, Benson, me—we're kind of a package deal. Not a lot of people our age around here, so we stick together. They weren't exactly thrilled when I ditched them on my birthday to hang out with you. Something about cheap whiskey by the fire being more important than . . . whatever we were doing."

The way he said *whatever* makes my pulse skip a beat. Is that guilt? Regret? Something else? I'm not about to test my luck by asking.

We finish the rest of the pizza in silence—the heavy, awkward kind, full of unsaid things neither of us seem brave enough to touch. Eventually, we migrate to the couch. Jack starts shuffling through a stack of papers on the coffee table, his movements precise but with enough tension to suggest the papers personally offended him.

"So," I say, struggling to keep my tone steady, "what's the latest?"

He doesn't answer right away. His fingers keep shuffling through the stack of papers until he finally pulls out a spiral-bound notepad—the one he's been scribbling in like a conspiracy theorist for weeks. My stomach clenches. This is it. The big reveal. The missing piece to possibly make sense of all this chaos.

"Well." He flips to a clean page.

My pulse kicks up a notch. I lean in. "And?"

Jack sighs—one of those long, theatrical ones. "Honestly? Not much."

My brain scrambles for context, but hope is already gone. "That's it?"

Jack's jaw tightens, frustration flashing across his features, though it isn't aimed at me. We are both stuck in the same miserable holding pattern, and we know it. "According to Mr. Callahan," he mutters, flipping through his notes again like the answers might magically appear. "He was out of town, and Josie is usually off on Saturdays."

Of course, he was "out of town." They were always out of town. Neatly packaged alibis, each more threadbare than the last. But this one feels . . . too smooth. Too rehearsed. And there is something else—something in the way Jack said it, or maybe just the sinking weight of what I already know.

Because I saw Josie that night.

"I saw her there," I blurt before my brain can catch up with my mouth.

Jack's head whips up, eyes narrowing. "Where?"

"At the Callahan house." My gut twists as the memory drags itself to the surface. The bags. The initials. That creeping, suffocating wrongness. "I saw her through the window. I was talking to Maggie, my best friend, and Josie was . . . carrying these big, black bags. Two of them."

Jack leans back slightly, his face carefully neutral. "Okay, but maybe she was running an errand? Dropping something off? Doesn't mean she was working." His tone is calm, steady —someone who hasn't spent the last week wading knee-deep in paranoia.

"Maybe," I admit. "But those bags, Jack. They had initials on them. RC. Big, bold letters. And the whole thing just felt . . . off."

"Off how?"

I rub the back of my neck. "I don't know. Just . . . wrong. And I saw them again when we interviewed Mrs. Callahan."

Jack stares at me, the gears clearly turning. "Was that what caught your attention that day on the stairs?"

I nod. He makes a low "hmm" noise, his version of the conversational ellipsis.

"So, you're saying you think the bags were Rhett's?"

"Yeah." I nod, though it's more an automatic reflex than confidence. It should make sense. I mean, it should.

"Could be something. Could be nothing. Either way, we need to think outside the box."

Jack raises a brow. "Go on."

I stall, then push forward. "We need to look at other cases. Similar ones."

Jack's stare hardens, his usual quip nowhere to be found. "Why do I feel like you've got one very specific case in mind?"

I swallow hard. This is going to be hell, but I know it is progress, especially after the little bombshell Grams dropped tonight.

"That's because I do." Then add, "My parents."

Jack's expression doesn't shift, but I can feel the incoming pushback. Before he can interject, I hold up a hand. "And before you say no, hear me out. I believe this is the next step."

"Why's that?"

"Well, Grams all but told me my mom wanted to be part of the Wives of Cedar Cove. At one point, they were open to it. Then, when she started showing a serious interest, they shut her out." I shrugged. "Grams didn't spell it out, but not getting into the group only made Mom more determined to get in. Now, we're finding these documents in the attic, and somehow . . ."

"You think that's what got her killed?"

"Yeah." I force the word out, keeping my emotions in check even as they surge beneath the surface.

Jack nods, his jaw tight as he mulls it over. "I can run it by my boss. He's iffy about reopening cold cases, but I'll see what I can do."

Heat flares in my cheeks, frustration bubbling up. "Don't you think it's a little odd you came to Cedar Cove for Rhett's case and didn't notice the parallels right away? My parents' case is practically identical, but it's just gathering dust in some filing cabinet."

Jack doesn't answer immediately, and his silence is louder

than anything he could've said. Finally, he sighs. "Yeah. I've thought about it. But back then? I was a rookie. Eager to impress. Your parents' case wasn't mine to touch. It wasn't until Josie's murder that the connection even clicked. Benson kept bringing it up, and I finally looked deeper."

I sigh, rubbing my eyes. I'm running—another murder, another case headed for a dusty shelf. But isn't this why I became a journalist? To make sure stories like this don't end with a shrug and a locked drawer?

"Have you talked to anyone besides the Callahans and a few locals?"

Jack shakes his head, then pauses. "What's going on in that beautiful head of yours?"

My heart betrays me with a flutter I don't have time for. "What if we start interviewing people who weren't at the festival?"

His brow furrows, but I am already grabbing the papers I'd pulled from the attic. I point to a cluster of names: The Wives of Cedar Cove, a few store owners. "We're not looking at the right people."

Jack frowns, leaning closer. "And you think the right people . . . are the ones nobody's paying attention to?"

"Exactly. My parents were onto something. Maybe Josie was onto the same thing—and that's what got her killed."

Jack dips his head slowly, and for the first time all day, it feels like we have traction—like we aren't just spinning our wheels. His baby blues find mine, and his dimpled smile breaks through.

"Come here," he commands, crooking a finger at me.

I lean back against the couch. "Give me one good reason why I should."

The smile widens as he sets his beer down with meticulous care. "Because it's my birthday."

I snort, "And?"

"And," he drawls, stretching the word like he had all night, "you showed up empty-handed. Least you could do is offer a little something."

His voice is hushed, teasing, and the way he says it stirs something I really don't want stirred. Damn him.

I grab my margarita and down the rest in one go, letting the burn give me something else to think about. For a moment, I stay where I am, pretending I haven't noticed the tension hanging around us. Then, I move.

I'm on all fours, crawling toward him, each movement deliberate. He scans every inch of me, a hunger flaring in their depths, raw and unapologetic. How he looks at me—*possessive, predatory*—it triggers a rush of cravings through my body, pooling between my legs, making my core clench with need.

I stop just short of him, the heat around us palpable. He reaches out, fingers brushing my cheek, trailing down to my jaw, tilting my face up to meet his stare.

Neither of us says a word. Maggie's words float into my head, uninvited: *"Don't overthink it. Have fun."*

I press my hands to his chest—solid, unfairly solid. The type of chest that should make any sensible person run the other way. And maybe, in another life, I would have.

But in this one? The risk is like gasoline on a fire I've no interest in putting out. The thought of having the Sheriff of Cedar Cove at my mercy sends a wicked thrill through me. To be the one who makes him lose control, to watch him unravel piece by piece?

Now that's a game I could play all night.

My fingers trail slow lines over his chest, feeling the way his breath hitches, his body going taut under my touch. The balance shifts, tilting in my favor, and a spark flares inside me —wild, heady, dangerous. One smooth movement, and my legs slide over his hips, wrapping around his waist. The move hikes up my skirt, exposing my skin to the cool air. If I had any sense, maybe that would make me pause. It doesn't. It just makes the heat shared by us burn hotter.

His hands settle on my waist, firm—maybe too firm—like he's barely holding himself back. His stare darkens, sharp and hungry, and for one brief, rational second, I realize how close I am to crossing a line I won't be able to walk back over.

And instead of stopping, I lean harder into it.

His gaze latches onto mine, unblinking, like I'm the only thing in the world worth seeing. The only thing he wants.

It's been a while since someone's looked at me like that—like I'm something vital. Like oxygen.

The way Rhett used to look at me.

The thought strikes without warning. Rhett's face flashes through my mind, unwelcome—his eyes, that same hungry intensity. It stirs something deep, something messy, but I shove it down before it can dig its claws in. That was then. This is now. And right now, there's a very solid, very real man looking at me like I'm the last thing standing between him and insanity.

So I let the moment pull me deeper, reckless as hell.

Because if there's one thing I want right now, it's to see how far I can push him. How far he'll let me go.

"God, Lennon, has anyone told you how insanely beautiful you are?" Jack's eyes trace the wild curls framing my face, lingering like he's committing every strand to memory. I know he likes it like this—natural, untamed, the way I used to wear it before I stopped caring. Before Rhett left.

His hand moves slowly, fingers weaving through my hair, tucking a curl behind my ear before sliding down to the curve of my jaw. He doesn't stop there. His hand settles at the nape of my neck, gentle and secure. A shiver runs through me, and I close my eyes—maybe to savor it, or maybe because looking at him would make this whole thing feel too real.

With my eyes shut, the world narrows to just him. His

breath, warm and steady, brushes against my neck, followed by the faint, almost teasing press of his lips. I don't open my eyes. I don't need to. Right now, feeling is enough.

"So," he murmurs against my skin, his lips brushing lower, unhurried. "Damn . . . " Another kiss, lingering, just enough to make me forget how to breathe. "Beautiful."

And then he stops.

My eyes snap open, ready to demand an explanation, but his mouth crashes into mine.

It's not gentle. It's desperate, like we've both been starving for this exact moment and finally broke. He lets out a growl, deep in his chest, the sound vibrating through me, and I'm not sure which of us moves first, but suddenly his hands are everywhere—gripping my hips, sliding lower, and then they find my ass.

He squeezes hard enough to pull a gasp from my throat, but instead of slowing down, he pulls me closer, like he doesn't trust the space between us to stay out of the way.

When he exhales a breathless, "Fuck," my lips twitch into a smirk. He knows. It just hit him—I'm not wearing panties. Why would I? Stockings do the job, and honestly, panties seem like overachieving at this point.

The realization snaps something in him. His grip on my waist tightens, pulling me flush against him as we kiss—harder now, faster, like we've decided oxygen is overrated. His hands roam everywhere, claiming my whole body, and the hunger between us spirals into something feral.

I want more. My fingers fumble at his uniform buttons, clumsy in their haste, desperate to strip him down. Finally, the fabric parts, revealing the white tank beneath. A hint of chest hair peeks out, and it's hotter than it has any right to be. My mouth goes dry.

No time to overthink. I lean in, my lips brushing over his chest, tasting the salt of his skin and the solid thrum of muscle underneath. His heartbeat pounds fast and uneven, matching the rhythm of mine.

I trail kisses up his neck, along his jaw, my hands skimming over the hard planes of his body, mapping him like I'm memorizing a route. But it's not enough—not even close.

"Has anyone ever told you how beautiful *you* are?" I purr, my lips brushing his.

He grins against my mouth, and my heart does something stupid, like skip a beat. "A time or two," he teases, and then—without warning—he shifts us, flipping me onto my back with a speed that makes me squeal. My spine hits the couch, and for a moment, we stare at each other, both breathless.

In seconds, we're a flurry of hands, tugging at fabric, clothes vanishing faster than I can keep track. When his fingers hook the waistband of my skirt, though, I grip his wrist, stopping him.

I waggle my finger at him, teasing, and press a hand against his chest, shoving him. He stumbles slightly and lands against the coffee table, leaning back on his palms, watching me with that smoldering stare that's somewhere between *sinister* and *I'll die if I don't touch you again.*

Time to take control.

Still in my skirt, stockings, and—thankfully—lavender bra (good call, past me), I step toward him. I tap his thigh. "Up."

His brow quirks, but he listens, standing without a word.

"Off," I demand, nodding toward his pants.

His stare stays fixated on mine as he undoes his belt, slow enough to make a show of it, before letting his pants drop to the floor. He's left standing in nothing but boxer briefs, the hard length of him pressing against the fabric, practically begging for freedom.

I don't waste time. My hand wraps around him, and even through the fabric, I feel him pulse. A few slow, deliberate strokes, and his head tips back, breath hitching.

"Lennon," he groans, thick with need.

"Sit your ass down, Mercer," I snap, full of sass. His eyes flutter shut like I've got some kind of magic over him, a smirk teasing the corner of his mouth. But he obeys, sliding back onto the table like it's his life's purpose.

I step closer, slipping between his legs, fingers hooking under the waistband of his boxers. When I finally tug them down, his cock springs free, and—wow, okay. My brain short-circuits for a second. The gods have clearly been working over-time on this one. Thick, veined, ready for worship. A bead of pre-cum glistens at the tip like it's showing off. My lips part.

Jack's thumb brushes my lower lip, and instinct takes over. I pull it into my mouth, sucking gently, and the way his gaze burns into me. I release him with a soft pop, hands sliding to grip his thighs. His muscles tense beneath my palms, like he's holding back from shattering the moment. But then my head dips forward, and my lips close around him.

Control tastes damn good.

His hands tangle in my hair, guiding my movements as his hips buck forward, needy and insistent. "Fuck, Lennon," he rasps.

He tightens his grip and mutters through the haze of lust, "Did I mention this is the best birthday gift?"

I laugh, the sound vibrating against him as my lips curve around his cock. Retreating, I raise a brow. "Oh, so *this* is a birthday gift?"

He grins, that signature charm cutting through the heat of the moment. "Best damn gift if you ask me."

I roll my eyes but can't hide my smirk. "Not quite," I murmur before diving back in, taking him deep with long, measured strokes. My mouth moves over him with practiced precision, each bob of my head slow and controlled. If he's a lollipop, I'm the kid, determined to get to the center, the taste of him only sharpening my focus. His breath stutters, a moan slipping free as his hands roam over my chest, fingers finding my nipples, toying with them, and a moan of my own escapes.

"Fuck, fuck . . ." he moans.

"Yes, Len." The nickname catches me off guard for half a second. It's been so long since anyone's called me that. The familiarity of it brushes against something tender inside me, but I don't let it trip me up. Instead, I smile against him—soft, private, just for me—and sink even deeper into the moment, determined to finish what I started.

With a few more deep pulls, his groans melt into a breathless chant of, "Yes . . . yes . . . " until he's spilling into my mouth. I swallow without hesitation, not breaking stride, and drop back onto my heels, breathless but steady. Before I can even wipe my face, he's on me—collapsing beside me and dragging me into a kiss that's downright feral, like he still needs more.

Our foreheads press together, breaths mixing in the quiet aftermath. I manage a small, smug smile. "Now it's the best gift."

He laughs, a low, rumbling sound that ripples over me. "No argument here."

He wraps his arms around my waist and hoists me to my feet like I weigh nothing. I smack his chest, more for show than anything, but he pulls me right back in. The way he holds me—strong, unrelenting—makes it impossible to protest. Not that I want to.

He eases us down onto the couch, his chest rising and falling beneath my chin as he watches me with a dark, hungry look. It doesn't ask permission. It just promises.

And then he moves. Takes control. His mouth finds mine, his hands guiding me like he's played out this scene in his head a hundred times. Each kiss, each touch, wipes my mind clean, leaving nothing but him.

Almost.

Because just as I'm about to lose myself completely, some-thing pierces the murk. A shred of memory. The notepad on the table.

The name.

Reed.

Bold, unmistakable, inked across the page.

CHAPTER 15

Tell me something. Anything. Doesn't have to be groundbreaking.

Is this your clever way of tricking me into oversharing?

If I wanted to trick you, I'd be way more subtle. Just throw me a bone.

. . .

I talked to a few people around town today.

And here I thought we agreed on terms.

It was accidental journalism. I was with Grams at physical therapy, and it kind of fell into my lap.

JACK

Sure. Just like that.

LENNON

Don't worry, Sheriff. You'll get an invite to the next interview.

JACK

Next interview? It's been a week, and you're out here operating like a one-woman news outlet on caffeine.

LENNON

Journalism, baby. It's my thing.

JACK

Then let me know the time and place for the next one. No exceptions. No loopholes. Terms are terms.

Now tell me something real. Something I don't know.

LENNON

Like what? Be specific.

JACK

Anything you feel like sharing. But since you're clearly stalling, I'll go first. Two things.

LENNON

Two things? Ambitious. Okay, I'm listening.

JACK

You sure you're ready?

LENNON

As I'll ever be.

JACK

First thing: I've got a serious thing for this girl.

LENNON

Oh, really? Go on.

JACK

She's got this fire in her. Stubborn as hell, but in a way that makes you want to root for her. And when she looks at me—game over. Most breathtaking woman I've ever seen. Totally unfair.

And her smile? Yeah, I'm done for.

LENNON

Hmm.

She sounds . . . alright, I guess. Should I be concerned?

JACK

Only if she doesn't feel the same way. That would be awkward.

LENNON

Well, I think she's VERY flattered.

Now spill—what's thing #2?

JACK

Updates on the case. But there's no way I'm texting all that.

LENNON

Oh, so you're just leaving me hanging? Bold strategy.

JACK

Hey, I gave you two things. Like I said I would. Besides, if I spill everything now, what excuse would I have to see you later?

LENNON

Ah. Playing the long game, huh?

JACK

Can't let you slip away that easily.

Tomorrow, I'll fill you in.

LENNON

Only if you promise to be as smooth in person as you are over text.

JACK

Done.

LENNON

See you tomorrow, Sheriff.

CHAPTER 16

Lennon

Just one more. *Thwack.* Damn it. Pain shoots through my thumb as the hammer tumbles from my grip, bouncing against the sun-bleached planks of the treehouse floor with a clatter. I shake my hand out like that'll help, even though the throbbing heat in my thumb pulses in perfect sync with my heartbeat. I should've pulled that rusty nail days ago—maybe weeks—but no. I just had to let it sit there, waiting to bite me. *Real genius move, Lennon.*

"What in tarnation was that? Sounded like a cat caught in a screen door!" Grams yells from the side door, hands on her hips like she's about to file a noise complaint. "You alright up there, Lenny girl?"

She stands on the porch, her eyes narrowing as she scans the yard. Finally, her gaze lands on the old treehouse—the one she built years ago smack dab between her place and the Callahans'. Strange spot for a treehouse, sure, but for Rhett and me, it was perfect. Our middle ground. Neutral territory. The site of poorly kept secrets, endless summer laughs, and one unforgettable moment when we stopped pretending we were just friends.

"Are you sure, Len?" Rhett's concern came through, quiet, softer than usual. He was the guy who could joke himself out of anything, but there was none of that now. Instead, he was all careful hands and careful words, like he was afraid I'd shatter if he moved too fast.

The bark dug into my back, anchoring me, but not as much as Rhett did. He was so close I could feel the warmth of him. His hand moved along my jaw, slow and unwavering, like he was trying to memorize the angles. There was nothing fragile about this moment, though. It was heavy and real, the kind of thing that left a mark.

I met those hazel eyes I'd known for years, gazed at me like I was the only thing in the world. In the dim light that came through the treehouse window, I noticed little flecks of gold in them, like sunlight breaking through fog. Funny how I'd never noticed that before. Or maybe I had, and I just didn't let myself think about it.

"We can stop if you want," he reassured me. His hands cradled my face like it was something precious. It should've felt awkward, being here like this—bare in every sense of the word. But it didn't. It felt like we'd been building to this moment all along.

"I-I want this. I do." The words came out barely above a whisper, but they're enough. My hand moved to his cheek, brushing over the scruff that was too patchy to call a beard, but still made him look older. More grounded. The steady I'd always needed.

And then he smiled—that boyish grin that had been messing with my head since we first met. God, I loved him. I didn't care if we're only seventeen and no one believed love could feel this certain at our age. For us, it just was. It always had been.

We were written into each other's stories from the start—ever since I had shown up in this same treehouse, spilling my guts about my parents to a boy who didn't say a word, just sat there and listened. That was Rhett. Always steady, always there.

I reached for him, pulling him closer, wanting to burn this moment into memory—the warmth of his skin, the way his touch felt like sparks running through me. This was it. Him. Always him.

"Takin' a trip down memory lane?" Grams' question pierces through the stillness, and instantly, I'm snapped out of my thoughts from the past. I glance toward the small, open window of the treehouse. There she is, standing below with that look she gets, all gentle and knowing. A look that doesn't just remind you of your pain, but insists on poking at it with a stick.

When Rhett was taken, I thought I'd manage. Cry it out, dust myself off, and march on, just like I always had. And for a while, I tricked myself into thinking I'd nailed it. Leaving Cedar Cove felt like slamming the door on the past, locking all the bad memories inside, and tossing the key into the ocean for good measure.

Turns out, healing isn't that neat. It's more like dragging a suitcase through an airport with a busted wheel. You can keep moving, sure, but it doesn't stop being heavy, and it definitely doesn't stop making that awful noise.

"It takes time, Lenny," Grams notes, her stare steady but soft. I don't argue, but my attention turns toward the waves in the distance. They look restless, like they're mocking me. She's not wrong, but that doesn't make the truth any less annoying.

Grams clears her throat. "You know, I'm right there with ya."

I peek back at her, and for a brief moment, her guard is down. I see it in her eyes—grief, raw and recognizable, one that sits in the corner of your heart and refuses to move out no matter how many eviction notices you issue.

"But I know they're still here." Her hand moves to her chest. I do the same, without even thinking, like it's some unspoken ritual we share. And for a moment, I swear I feel it too—Rhett, just out of reach, watching, probably rolling his eyes at how much time I have been sulking in this rickety old treehouse.

"*Let it go*," I can almost hear him say with his infuriating mix of half-teasing and half-serious tone.

Letting go, though? Not my strong suit. The treehouse feels like my last thread connecting me to him, and cutting it would be snapping the only lifeline I have left.

The familiar ache rolls in, uninvited as always. I blink hard, staring past Grams toward the waves again. "It's just . . . hard, ya know?"

She watches me for a moment. Finally, she tilts her head, her delivery careful but pointed. "Do you think working on the case is really helping . . . you?"

There it is. The polite-but-loaded "you" that does all the heavy lifting. She doesn't need to spell it out—I know what she's hinting at. She's worried I'm too stuck in the past, pawing through Mom and Dad's old notes like I can turn back time. Like solving Jack's case will patch up the cracks and make everything neat again.

Maybe she's right. Maybe I am clinging too tight.

But it doesn't feel that way, not to me. It feels like I'm doing something that matters. Josie's family deserves answers, and they deserve closure.

Closure. The one thing I never got.

I shrug, hoping the motion will shake off the ache in my chest. *It doesn't.*

Grams means well—I know that. She's just trying to keep me from diving headfirst into a brick wall. I get it; I do. But I've already hit pause on everything else for the last two weeks—my job, my own case, my entire life. The second Jack called with that update, I knew I wasn't walking away from this.

Blake, my boss, doesn't see it that way. How could he? Blake's never lost anything—family intact, best friend still kicking, first love probably making him pancakes every morning. He hasn't had to claw his way out of the rubble, so when I told him I wasn't coming back yet, he went ballistic. Full-on fury, spitting words like "reckless" and "unprofessional" as if he'd pulled them out of some HR manual.

Luckily, Maggie swooped in to cover for me. *"I'll handle Blake,"* she'd said, calm and convincing, the way you'd talk to someone holding a live grenade. She's my best friend, and if there's anyone who can keep him from detonating, it's her. Or at least, that's what I'm banking on.

I release a slow breath, my fingers tightening around the hammer's handle again. The cold metal feels solid in a way nothing else does. "Too late for that, Grams," I mutter.

The hammer hits home with a satisfying thunk. I barely pause before lining up the next swing.

"Need some help?"

I don't turn. I don't have to. *Reed.*

Heat rushes through me, my fingers unsteady on the hammer. How does one person's voice manage to short-circuit my brain like this? Especially after Rhett. And Jack. Jack, who I spent that *night* with. But Jack's just a friend. Obviously. Totally. Right?

A shrill, ear-splitting scream tears through the air.

Grams.

I whip around, adrenaline kicking in, and zero in on the treehouse window. There she is—clutching one of my saws like it's a weapon from her glory days. No walker, just trembling hands and a look that implies she's one ill-timed gust of wind away from catastrophe.

"Grams, put that down before you hurt yourself!" I laugh, though it comes out shaky. My pulse is still hammering as I take in the absurd sight of her looking like she's auditioning for a low-budget horror movie. Somewhere, poor Reed must be regretting his life choices.

But nope. Of course he isn't. Reed stands there, hands shoved in his jeans pockets, radiating that annoyingly casual confidence, as if the situation is perfectly normal. And then, because apparently the universe enjoys irony, he throws Grams a crooked grin. It's the type of grin that makes my breath catch. One that looks so much like Rhett's.

The past isn't just a memory; sometimes it haunts you when you least expect it.

An intense pang hits me as past and present collide. How is this even happening? The way they both look at me—smiles curling just enough to make everything else fade away—feels like being trapped in some endless loop, history stubbornly refusing to let go. Reed and Rhett feel connected somehow, like two threads pulled taut across time, knotted in ways I can't seem to undo.

"Grams, put it down," I repeat, more firmly this time. She shakes her head, gripping the saw tighter, her knuckles white with determination.

I descend the ladder quickly. Too quickly. My foot catches on a loose rung, and in a flash, I'm tilting backward. Panic shoots through me as I brace for the inevitable fall.

Then, strong hands catch me, pulling me back from the edge.

Everything blurs, but his hands—solid and certain—anchor me. My pulse races, not just from the near-miss, but from how close he is. It's as if time itself has stopped to watch us, waiting to see what happens next.

It takes every bit of restraint not to let myself lean into him, to lose myself in the sense of safety he so easily offers.

"Hi, Len," Reed whispers. His fingers brush my cheek, and the tenderness in that small gesture threatens to undo me completely.

Len.

The wind tugs at my hair, but it does nothing for the furnace raging in my cheeks. My face could probably toast a marshmallow. My heart, meanwhile, is auditioning to break out of my chest, like it's got somewhere better to be. Preferably back in time, with Rhett, when life wasn't such a mess.

"H-Hi, Reed," I squeak.

Then—Grams, loud and indignant. "Git off my granddaughter!"

Reed's hands shoot up, his expression hovers between startled and mildly entertained. He pulls me to my feet with a half-smile, and a laugh escapes me—part relief, part *"what even is my life right now?"*

"It's fine, Grams," I reassure her, reaching for the saw in her hand. "Really."

She doesn't flinch. The saw stays glued to her white-knuckled grip, her pint-sized frame radiating pure defiance.

"Ain't fine, not one bit," Grams snaps. "Someone needs to explain ta me why . . . why R-Rhett—"

Her lips are wobbly on his name, and for a split second, I swear the whole world tilts. I reach for her hand, giving it a light squeeze, trying to ground her—or maybe just myself. "That's not Rhett."

Her watery eyes dart to mine, blinking furiously, as if sheer willpower can keep the tears from falling. She points to Reed as he stands there. "But he's right there," she states, her words small, bewildered.

"It's not Rhett, Grams," I murmur, swallowing the lump in my throat.

Reed steps forward, cautiously, as if he's approaching a stray cat with claws out. He offers his hand, along with an apologetic smile. "It's Reed," he comments, gentle but firm, as if he's done this before or at least thought about how he would.

Grams hesitates. Her eyes narrow, like she's mentally running a side-by-side comparison of Reed and Rhett, probably noting every hair out of place. Finally, she sighs, releasing the tension like air leaking from a tire, and slips her hand into his. A faint, nervous laugh escapes her.

"Well . . . shit," she mutters, shaking her head. "Thought I was losin' it. Really thought . . . " she trails off, chuckling at herself.

Reed chuckles too, a quiet, warm sound, but his expression shifts. His eyes darken, carrying something heavy, something he doesn't say. "It's okay," he says quietly. "Really. I get it."

Grams wipes her tears with the back of her hand, the waterworks drying up as her grip on my arm loosens. But then her expression changes with a suspicion only years of nosiness can hone.

"Wait now . . . you from 'round here?" Her gaze sharpens. "How come I ain't never laid eyes on ya before, huh?"

Reed shrugs, unbothered, like being interrogated by an old woman in a floral apron is just another Tuesday for him. "I live a little ways out. Came here for some work."

Grams squints at him a second longer, then huffs, her scowl easing into something that might pass for polite. "Didn't mean to sound rude." Her voice slips back to normal. "Just was being—"

"Protective?" Reed finishes for her, his smile slow and disarming. There's a warmth to his tone, sure, but there's also something else—a hidden threat, a shadow stretching too far. "Don't worry, I get it. I'd do the same thing in your shoes. No need to apologize for looking after such precious cargo."

His attention moves to me. And then—he winks.

My heart trips over itself like it's forgotten how to function. This man didn't just show up looking like he'd wandered off the cover of *Wilderness Chic Monthly*—dark jeans worn just right, boots scuffed like he wrestles bears for fun, and that blue denim jacket catching the light like it signed a deal with the sun. His tousled brown hair walks a fine line between "effortless" and "strategically messy," and his hazel eyes have this glint that's equal parts playful and . . . unsettling.

Grams gives a "mhm" sound, her stare glued to Reed. "Oh, you're a charmer, aren't you?" she comments, then cuts me a look—brow raised, expression smug—as if to say, *Well? Isn't he something?*

She turns back to him. "Though," she continues, "I thought Jack was the only young man around here with that particular charm."

And there it is. Jack. His name crashes into the moment, abrupt and bracing. Reed doesn't flinch, but his jaw tightens, his easy grin just a shade too stiff. For a split second, his expression shifts—not with understanding, but with something rougher, sharper. Jealousy.

Then Reed looks at me again, holding my stare long enough for the spark to flare into something dangerous. It's stupid. It's impractical. And it's starting to feel inevitable.

No. I tear my gaze away and remind myself of Jack.

Just a few days ago, he'd admitted he liked me—*really* liked me. It wasn't supposed to get complicated. Jack and I were meant to be a passing thing, nothing serious. And yet, he'd managed to slip past my defenses like water finding cracks in stone. A sheriff, of all people—the kind of man I've sworn to avoid.

Before I can dwell on it, Reed moves. Not with words, but by extending his hand. To Grams. Again.

The thick tension hanging over us alters as Grams eyes his outstretched hand, hesitates, then finally takes it in a firm shake. Her expression softens, though her approval comes grudgingly. "Ayuh," she remarks, glancing at me. "I'll be back in a jiff with some tea. Don't y'go disappearin' now."

She shuffles off, her steps trailing into the house, and I release a breath.

"So"—Reed arches a brow, his boyish charm sliding neatly back into place—"that was your grandma?"

I nod, keeping my face neutral. His grin, unfortunately, is as disarming as warm pie on a cold day, and it's not helping.

"She's . . . protective of you," he observes.

"Understatement," I mutter, my eyes dropping to the saw in my hand like it's the most fascinating thing outside. "She's a bit much sometimes. Figured I'd cut down these branches before she decides to chase off the next poor soul who wanders too close."

Reed laughs, shaking his head. "I can see that."

"She has her reasons." I lift the saw to get to work. But before I can start, two warm hands close over mine, halting me mid-motion.

My head snaps up, and there he is—those hazel eyes pinning me in place. They're recognizable, but with just enough distance to make them unsettling.

"Why's that?" he asks, cautious but curious.

I shrug, avoiding his eyes, but the words spill out, anyway. Maybe because he feels oddly familiar, or maybe because saying it out loud makes it feel real. "Well . . . " A dry chuckle escapes me, and I pause, as if that'll make this easier. "No nice way to say it, but . . . my parents were murdered."

I shrug again, gripping the saw like it might anchor me. "Grams stepped in. She raised me. She's . . . all I've got."

For a moment, something flickers in Reed's expression—something softer, gentler. It startles me. Most people respond with pity, but not him. He looks . . . thrown, almost unsteady. Like he's not the confident, hard-edged 37-year-old in front of me, but someone younger, almost vulnerable. *Roo, is that you?*

I push the thought away.

"I'm sorry for your loss," he says quietly. He motions to the saw in my hands. "Here, let me."

He doesn't wait for permission. He takes the saw and gets to work, his movements so smooth it's like second nature. I step back, observing him, and realize just how little I actually know about this man.

The thought prompts a question. "So, you're here for work?"

"Mm-hmm," he grunts, not pausing. The rhythmic scrape of the saw fills the silence. His muscles flex with every pull, sweat starting to bead at his brow.

"Construction," he finally says.

Well, that explains the forearms.

"Here in Cedar Cove?"

November's creeping in, and soon the cold will make outdoor work miserable. But Reed keeps sawing, controlled and precise, like he's spent years perfecting it.

He pauses long enough to shrug off his jacket, and the movement catches me off guard. Now he's in a deep olive V-neck that clings just right, his muscles moving with each stroke of the saw, veins standing out like they're competing for attention.

I tell myself not to stare. Really, I do. But then there's a shiver—maybe from the cold, maybe not—and before I realize it, I've stepped closer. Too close.

"I do consulting and estimating, mostly," Reed states,

breaking the tension. His eyes settle on the space between us, a smirk forming—devilish, daring enough to make even a nun have second thoughts. He knows I moved closer. Worse, he knows I noticed him noticing.

I clear my throat, ready to retreat, when Grams reappears.

"Oh!" she exclaims, her eyes darting between us. She's holding two teacups, but her focus lands squarely on Reed. "Well, look at this," she drawls, the words soaked in meaning I don't want to decode.

My face warms under her scrutiny.

Reed doesn't miss a beat. "I've done a few projects around Cedar Cove," he casually notes. "Smaller stuff. My crew handled most of it. But this current project is different." His tone is easy, but there's just enough intrigue to draw both me and Grams in.

"And what kind of project, deah?"

Reed stops the saw with a flick of his wrist and straightens, chest rising and falling as he wipes the sweat from his brow. The sunlight catches on his skin, and my tongue's darting out to wet my lips.

Get it together. This isn't a rom-com, and you're not the flustered heroine.

Reed hesitates, eyeing me for the briefest moment before starting back in on the branch, the saw springing to life again. Each measured pull of the blade sends a subtle flex through his arms, which is distracting enough that I almost miss his next words.

"A demolition," he blurts.

"Demolition?" I echo, my stomach doing an odd little flip. What's there to tear down in Cedar Cove?

"I'm here visiting a client," he admits, eyes fixed on his work. "Same as always. I assess the property, give cost estimates, and figure out the best approach."

Grams steps forward, folding her arms. "And just what are ya blowin' up, then? Ain't nobody need more wreckin' 'round here unless you're plannin' on fixin' the town hall."

Reed lets out a chuckle—dry and strained, like he's bracing for impact. "Nothing like that."

Finally, his gaze lifts to meet mine, and the space between us shifts. For a second, I forget to breathe. I should be worrying that he's piecing together my connection to the Callahans, but instead, all I can feel is the burden of whatever he's about to say.

"The Callahan place." He jerks his chin toward the edge of the property.

The words don't hit me gradually—they barrel in as a freight train, leaving me winded. He's planning to tear it down. *Rhett's home.* The house where every creak in the floorboards carries a memory, where laughter and heartbreak have seeped into the walls like stubborn stains.

He's taking Rhett away.

I choke down the knot in my throat. "Excuse me?"

Grams makes a noise—part gasp, part croak. I rub her back without taking my focus off Reed. At the moment, he might as well be a cartoon villain twirling a mustache.

He shuts off the saw, and the last branch thuds to the ground. He wipes his hands on his jeans and steps toward us. Grams glare is so sharp it could slice drywall. I'm pretty sure my face matches hers.

With a huff, she hands him a mug of tea. Her lips pressed tight; it's a miracle the cup doesn't crack under the pressure of her disapproval. Reed accepts it as a man accepting a peace offering he doesn't deserve and guzzles it down, his Adam's apple bobbing like it's trying to escape.

He glances at the ocean, because, sure, staring at the horizon always solves uncomfortable conversations—before turning back to us. For half a second. Whatever he's hiding is practically oozing out of him, but he's not offering it up.

"It's not finalized." He sets the mug down carefully. "The Callahans . . . " he trails off, the name landing hard, as if it alone explains everything. "They reached out a few months ago. Wanted a quote."

Reed bends down to grab his jacket from the ground, and for a second, I lose my train of thought entirely. The man could sell denim for a living.

I snap out of it, my cheeks heating as I force my brain back into the present. There's no time for distractions—not with everything on the line. Reed shrugs into his jacket as if he hasn't lit a match under the foundation of my world. "So that's why I'm here—assessing the property. It's just the job."

The job. Of course, *it's just the job*. My stomach churns, but I keep my face impassive.

"And here I thought you came all this way just to track me down," I mutter. I know he doesn't deserve the jab, but some unhelpful part of me still hoped—just for a moment—that maybe his arrival in Cedar Cove wasn't all spreadsheets and demolition plans. As if this town's gossip mill wouldn't have already announced that to me with fanfare.

Grams shoots me a quick look. We don't need words to communicate the obvious: The house isn't ours, hasn't been for years. All I've ever owned are the memories etched into its walls, like carvings in soft bark—fragile, impermanent, and now at risk of being sanded away.

"Best get going, then." My tone is flat as I fold my arms. I refuse to give him the satisfaction of a scene.

Reed pauses, his eyes lingering on mine, trying to pull apart the meaning behind my words. Good. Maybe then he'll understand just how deep the roots run here, even if the deeds don't bear our names.

"Right . . . " Reed mumbles, scratching the back of his head. "It was nice seeing you, Lennon."

I nod, more to speed his departure than anything else. The damage is already done.

But then he steps closer, and his chest brushes against mine. My pulse stumbles, my breath catches—what is this? A moment? A scene?

Nope. It's a hug.

I pat his back once, mentally ejecting him from my personal space, but something in the background catches my eye. Past Reed, through the Callahans' family room window. I spot something that pulls my body into a tight knot. The black bags. A pile of them slumped together like ominous punctuation marks in the middle of the room.

First in Rhett's room, then the staircase, and now the family room? It's as if they're following me.

Grams' quick gasp pulls me back, and I glance at her just in time to see Reed—of course Reed—take her hand in his and bow slightly. Oh no.

He presses a soft kiss to her knuckles with the precision of someone who's watched *Pride and Prejudice* one too many times. Grams, to her credit, flushes the faintest shade of pink before she schools her expression into a stern glare. But I know better. She's toast.

And, damn it, so am I.

How does someone manage to look like the poster child for heartbreak *and* a home renovation disaster all at once? Rhett's house isn't just a building—it's a piece of us. And Reed, with his charm and his sawdust-stained hands, is standing here like the human embodiment of a wrecking ball.

Reed walks away and my chest aches with a strange mix of anger and something softer, something I'm not ready to name. Part of me wants to chase him down, to demand answers. Why Rhett's house? Why now? But I stay put, one arm still wrapped around Grams. She's the only thing keeping me tethered.

She shakes her head, muttering, "So much for a charmer."

I nod, lips pressed tight, but my eyes can't help sliding back to the Callahans' window. The black bags are gone now, the room beyond them nothing but empty glass.

CHAPTER 17

"What did you say Reed does again?" Jack asks, his eyes glued on the slow creep of traffic ahead.

"He's a contractor," I reply as he signals and veers into a quieter stretch of downtown Maple Harbor. This town has been on our radar since Mrs. Callahan brought it up that day, and now we finally have a reason to check it out.

Tonight's mission: My interview with Melanie, one of the Wives of Cedar Cove. Her glare through Grams' window last week—like she'd hacked into my search history—made the decision for me. Now we're heading to an event so extravagant, even Grams, the town's top-tier gossip sponge, can't stop talking about it.

"And he's working on the Callahan place? Doing demo?" Jack questions as we hit a red light.

I nod, sensing the shift in his posture. Mentioning Reed was a calculated risk—part unease, part relief. Mostly, I just wanted Jack here with me.

"And you don't think it's weird?" he presses, steering us down a narrow, brick-lined street.

"What's weird about it?"

Jack shoots me a look like I've just announced my plans to join a cult. "What's weird about it? The guy rolls into town in *November*, Lennon—not exactly tourist season—and now he's demolishing the Callahan place with his golden sledge-hammer? That doesn't strike you as . . . odd?"

I cross my arms, side-eyeing him. "What's your obsession with him?"

"I'm not obsessed," Jack mutters, jaw tightening.

"Mhm, totally. A little jealous, huh?"

The muscle in Jack's cheek twitches, and I bite back a laugh. Oh yeah, he's jealous.

"It's not about jealousy," he snaps, almost like he believes it. "It's part of the job. He's new in town, so yeah, I'm going to look into him."

I sink back into the seat, pretending to mull it over. He's not wrong, but I'm not about to hand him the satisfaction of admitting it. Instead, I let it drop. The furrowed brow and white-knuckled grip on the wheel are warnings enough.

"You're right. We agreed to interview everyone," I say, letting the words land somewhere between sincere and begrudging.

Jack exhales, tension melting as he pulls into the parking garage. When he finally parks, he peeks at me with a rare soft look, sending a quick, disobedient flutter through my stomach that I refuse to analyze. For half a second, I regret mentioning Reed. Half a second.

Jack hops out, strides around to my side, and yanks open my door. His hand finds mine, but instead of helping me out like a normal person, he grips the fabric of my dress and plants his hands on my hips.

And suddenly, I'm airborne.

I shriek, the sound ricocheting through the empty garage. "Jack! What the hell—?"

He grins up at me, completely unapologetic. "Figured you could use the assistance."

I swat his chest. "Assistance with what? Defying gravity?"

Still grinning, he sets me on my feet—only to follow it with a tap on my ass. I spin around to glare at him, but he just shrugs, completely shameless. My traitorous heart stumbles.

Taking my hand, Jack leads me toward the event. The cool November air nips at my skin, but his warmth at my side keeps the chill tolerable.

"Remember the two rules?" he asks.

"Don't overdo the margaritas and avoid Mrs. Callahan."

"Good girl," he murmurs, smirking.

Good girl? Oh, that's dangerous. My brain short-circuits, my mouth forgets its job.

Then he steps back, eyes moving over me with a slow appreciation that makes my skin hum. When he finally meets my gaze, that dimple—the one I've memorized—appears, soft and teasing.

"Pretty sure I just died and woke up in heaven," he murmurs, voice deep and reverent. "You look like a damn angel."

My first instinct is to roll my eyes or hit him with a sarcastic comeback, but I don't. Not when he's staring at me like I'm his new favorite thing. Honestly, it's been a while since I've gotten this dressed up—definitely not around Jack.

He, on the other hand, is in a suit. *A suit.* Not his usual jeans and flannel or work uniform, but something crisp, tailored, and entirely too distracting. He looks like a five-course meal I shouldn't even glance at, but suddenly, I'm starving.

I clear my throat, hoping it will scatter the warmth pooling in my core. "Well, you clean up okay too, Sheriff Mercer."

His smirk stretches wider. "Okay? Lennon, I'm *wounded.*"

Prior to my firing back, he's beside me, his hands slipping

around my waist; it's second nature. As we approach the hotel's towering front doors—currently drowning in enough holiday lights to cause a power outage—he gives my waist a quick squeeze. Smooth. Real smooth.

The whole setup is ridiculous. A bellhop holds the door open with a polished smile that says, *Yes, you belong here. Sure.* This is the sort of place where you expect to see celebrities sipping $30 martinis, not a casual meetup about "community work." When Grams mentioned the venue, I thought it was weird. Who drives an hour into Maple Harbor more than once now to talk about pothole repairs?

Jack nudges me forward, breaking my train of thought. Inside, the lobby is predictably grand—vaulted ceilings, chandeliers straight out of a period drama, and front desk staff who probably judge you based on your shoes. Jack lets go of my hand to ask about the event, leaving me to fidget. Not nervously. Just . . . curiously.

He returns, too calm, and signals toward the ballroom. My stomach twists as we walk—not in the tequila-margarita way. More like something's off. Jack must sense it, because he leans down and murmurs, "We got this." His breath brushes my ear and sends tremors straight down my back. Not the time.

His hand presses lightly against my lower back, steering me toward the ballroom doors. I peek through the windows, and my stomach drops. This isn't some casual little meeting. Inside, a sea of people in sharp suits and designer dresses mill around tables big enough to double as banquet props. In the corners, I spot a DJ, a bar, and—of all things—a packed dance floor where retirees are cutting loose like it's their last hurrah. The vibe screams "retirement gala turned rave."

I look back to find Jack watching me, his expression unreadable.

"You positive about this?"

He doesn't answer right away, just pulls me into his arms. His cologne is the same—woodsy, expensive, and faintly smug. It steadies me more than I'd like to admit. When I look up, he kisses me—quick, teasing, and perfectly calculated to leave me wanting more.

Then, on cue, he nods toward the ballroom, tips an imaginary hat, and strolls off into the crowd.

I watch him vanish, his exit annoyingly smooth, before slipping toward my destination: The far corner. Bar stool. Out of sight, out of mind. The bartender shows up, and I order a margarita on the rocks. Classic, simple, mildly distracting.

When the drink arrives, I automatically scan the room for Jack. Of course, there he is, already watching me. I raise the glass, tilt it just enough for a "cheers," and take a sip. The tequila does its job, easing the tension in slow, pleasant waves.

I relocate to an empty cocktail table in the corner. Quiet. Out of the way. I survey the room: A mix of people who wouldn't recognize Cedar Cove if it came with a name tag. They're here anyway, sipping overpriced drinks and pretending this charity event isn't just a socially sanctioned excuse to drink while feeling virtuous.

Mrs. Callahan is in fine form tonight, working the room like a seasoned diplomat or a soap opera villain. She doesn't spot me, thank God. She's busy; one manicured hand draped on some donor's chest, the other artfully gesturing like she's negotiating world peace. Or possibly swinging. Hard to say with that level of commitment.

I keep scanning the room and spot Jack again. He's cutting through the crowd with laser-focused intensity, probably hunting for interview material—wives, most likely. But every few minutes, his attention snaps back to me, followed by a maddeningly smug smile. He knows something I don't. It's infuriating. Naturally, it's also working.

At one point, he actually ducks behind a table like he's dodging sniper fire, which earns an involuntary laugh from me. Subtle, Mercer. Very subtle.

Before I can fully appreciate the fleeting absurdity, a man approaches and sits beside me. We settle into a silence that's just this side of uncomfortable before I blurt out the question I've been holding onto since Grams first mentioned this event. "Can you tell me more about this gala?"

He barely gets out a word before a feminine voice answers from behind me. "It's a fundraiser for Cedar Cove's fishing docks and local museums."

I turn, and there she is. *Melanie*.

She approaches, her eyes sweeping over me like she's sizing up the competition. "But you'd know that, wouldn't you? If you were invited."

Her delivery is a carefully veiled insult. It stings just enough to let you know she meant it. I don't shy away. I won't let some perfectly coiffed Stepford prototype rattle me. Not tonight.

I take a sip of my drink, letting the tequila do its thing. For good measure, I lick my lips—deliberately slow—just enough to make her blink. Then I smooth out my dress, dragging the moment further. If nothing else, these heels were worth it. It's hard to feel threatened by someone who barely clears five feet and looks like a knockoff Snow White.

"How do you know I wasn't invited?" I ask, keeping my tone light, almost bored.

She scoffs, tilting her head like she's addressing a slow child. "Because I coordinated this event. I know exactly who was invited."

Okay, fair. She's got me there.

"Plus," she steps closer, "I know who you are. Lillian Harrington's granddaughter. Samuel and Hannah—your parents."

My breath catches, but I don't dare move.

She takes another step, her gaze pinning me in place like she's savoring her kill. "Am I right, *Lennon*?"

The way she says my name—it's unsettling, like she's been practicing it for this very moment. How the hell does she know me? Sure, my family made the news back when everything went to hell, but she shouldn't *recognize* me. And yet, here she is, staring like I've been on her to-do list for years.

Just as I am about to respond, Jack appears out of nowhere, sliding a hand around my waist with practiced confidence.

"Oh, hi, Jack!" she chirps, her demeanor flipping so fast it's almost impressive. "What are you doing here?"

Jack greets her with a wide, unguarded smile. It's warm, easy, and just a little too familiar. Then he steps away from me and pulls her into a hug. A *hug*.

My gut twists. They embrace like old friends, as if they've been swapping holiday cards for years.

Since when does Jack know this woman? And why is he *so* friendly with her?

"You know," Jack comments smoothly as he retreats, "just checking out the local community events Cedar Cove puts together."

She narrows her eyes, her lips curving into a sly smirk. "Sure it isn't to line up one of your interviews?"

Jack lifts a brow at her, but she just laughs and swats his arm like they're in on some private joke. "Don't worry," she adds, adding a wink. "Your secret's safe with me."

His smile tightens—polite, but strained—and then, just like that, his whole presence alters. His shoulders square, his jaw firms, and the sheriff in him takes over.

And, my god, it's so hot to witness such a thing.

"Well, since you brought it up," his tone is cool and professional, "I see no harm in asking a few questions."

Her smile falters for a split second, but she recovers quickly, signaling a passing waitress with a flick of her finger. "Sure," she says lightly, almost flippantly. "Go ahead."

She takes a sip of champagne as Jack starts in, his questions measured and routine—the same ones we've asked every suspect so far. She nods here, shakes her head there, hums thoughtfully at times. Her expression stays so neutral, it's practically a work of art.

But then Jack throws out the last question.

"Where were you the night of the festival?"

Her champagne glass freezes just shy of her lips. The pause is brief—subtle enough to pass unnoticed by most. Not by me.

"I was in Maple Harbor, of course." But her eyes give her away, flitting about the room before snapping back to us like she just remembered the first rule of lying: Maintain eye contact.

Jack tilts his head, silent, giving her space to fill the void.

I step in, barely reining myself in. "Where in Maple Harbor?"

Her eyes latch onto mine, irritation flashing like a warning light. "At an event with the Wives of Cedar Cove."

"Dressed like this?" I gesture vaguely around the ballroom. She nods, neutral as ever.

The corner of my mouth twitches. "Which event?"

Her lips press into a thin line, and we're suddenly in a silent standoff—her glare versus my patience. I don't blink.

"Did there happen to be a name of *that* event?" I lean in slightly. "What about the time? When did you get there? When did you leave?"

She stiffens, her perfect composure slipping by a hair. Her gaze slides to Jack's, but he stays quiet, letting me run the show.

And damn if that doesn't make him even hotter.

"I don't see how that's relevant," she snaps, her polished veneer starting to crack.

"Oh, it's relevant," I reply, almost cheerfully. "Especially since nobody we've talked to remembers seeing you at any events in Maple Harbor that night." Joke's on her—we haven't asked anyone.

Jack shifts beside me, and I can feel the barely contained smirk radiating off him.

Her expression hardens—anger or panic, it's hard to tell. "I don't appreciate being interrogated at an event I organized. Maybe you should focus on thanking me for all I've done for Cedar Cove."

Classic deflection. I almost admire it. Almost.

"And maybe," I set my drink down with a soft clink, "you should spend less time dodging questions. When. Did. You. Leave?"

Her mouth opens. For a second, I almost think she's going to give in. But then she snaps it shut.

Jack eases into the conversation, his words smooth but carrying enough weight to shut down any argument. "We're just trying to confirm a timeline. Shouldn't be a problem if there's nothing to hide."

Her eyes scan around the room, calculating. Then, with an exaggerated sigh, she forces a smile that barely touches her lips. "I don't remember the exact time, but it was late. Sometime after midnight."

"Convenient," I mutter, loud enough to sting.

She clears her throat, brushing it off. "Are we done here? This is supposed to be a *fun* event—raising money, not suspicions." Then, as if to punctuate the performance, she leans in and presses a kiss to Jack's cheek.

And there it is—the ugly spike of jealousy.

My focus lands on Jack, arms crossed, attempting to keep my expression concealed. Did he and her . . . ?

Jack catches my look and shakes his head, already answering the question I haven't asked. He takes my hand and pulls me to a quiet corner, away from the crowd. My heart pounds as he backs me against the wall, bracing his hands above my head.

"It's not what you think."

I swallow hard, willing him to keep talking.

"She's just . . . Melanie," he explains, shrugging slightly. "I've known her since I came to Cedar Cove. She kind of took me under her wing. Showed me around. You know—*motherly vibes.* She still drops off baked goods sometimes. That's all it's ever been."

He steps closer, his breath hot against my skin, his eyes fixated on mine. "There's only one woman I'm looking at, and she's standing right in front of me."

And then his lips crash into mine, effectively short-circuiting any sarcastic remark I was about to deliver. The kiss is . . . well, thorough. Like he's finally decided to stop pretending he has self control. A shiver zips down my spine as my hands—traitorous things—tug at his suit, pulling him closer. He groans, desire thick in his throat. "Fuck, Lennon."

For a moment, I think I'm winning this unspoken game. Then his lips move to my jaw, to my neck, and I'm officially done for. His pulse is hammering beneath my fingertips, and I'm seconds away from throwing all dignity out the window when he interrupts.

"If we keep this up, I might lose all self-control," he chuckles, forehead pressed to mine. "And this is not the place for that."

Right. Not the place. Because apparently making out in semi-public doesn't scream "class." I straighten up, brushing nonexistent lint off my dress, trying to look like I didn't just have a minor existential crisis in his arms. He smirks—because of course he does—and leads me back into the ballroom like we're two reasonable adults who weren't just thinking about breaking several social norms.

The lights have dimmed. The crowd sways on the dance floor, couples lost in some slow country song dripping with nostalgia. Jack glances at them, then at me. His lips curve into that annoyingly charming, lopsided smile—the one that's basically cheating.

Oh. He's asking me to dance.

My face heats up, but I take his hand anyway, because, well . . . I'm not going to say no to that smile. He pulls me closer, and all at once I'm pressed against him, chest to chest. His heartbeat is maddeningly consistent, which feels unfair, considering mine is auditioning for a drum solo.

Jack tilts my chin up, his movements slow. His lips brush mine in a kiss so soft it feels more like a question. And just as I'm leaning in for an answer, he pulls back. Rude. I'm left breathless, leaning into him like I forgot how to stand upright.

We sway to the strains of *Gettin' Old* by Luke Combs, his arms wrapped around me like this is where I'm supposed to be. Like this isn't completely insane. And for once, it doesn't feel insane at all. Jack spins me out, then reels me back in, my back pressing to his chest.

He rests his chin near my shoulder, his breath warm against my cheek. We stand there, watching the other couples dance, but all I can think is that his hold feels like something permanent. Something I'm not sure I'm ready to let go of—even if I wanted to.

"Tell me something, Lennon," he whispers, spinning me out once more. When I twirl back, my chin ends up resting against his chest, his impossibly blue eyes boring into mine. I should probably focus on why we're even here, but with him eyeing me like that? Fat chance.

A nervous laugh escapes me, too light for the weight of the

moment. "This is, uh, only my second dance ever with a guy. Technically."

His eyebrows shoot up, surprise darting across his face. And then it happens—the shift. That look. The one where surprise melts into pity, like he just stumbled across some tragic backstory he didn't ask for.

I pull back instinctively, heat crawling up my neck. But Jack? Jack tightens his hold, his arms wrapping around me like he's daring me to run. Then, because he apparently doesn't believe in letting me off easy, he reaches up and catches a stray curl, twisting it between his fingers like it's the most fascinating thing in the world.

"Who was your first?"

The obvious move would be to laugh it off, dodge the question with something flippant. But Jack's looking at me with a quiet, insistent expression that makes lying feel like a sin.

"You," I admit softly.

For a second, something flashes in his features. It's heavier than his usual charm; unreadable. And then, without another word, he kisses me. No hesitation, no teasing. Just Jack, leaning in like he's trying to solve me one kiss at a time.

The world tilts. His hands slide to my hips, then lower, giving my ass a quick, playful squeeze that sends a startled laugh tumbling out of me.

When we finally break apart, his forehead rests against mine. He exhales, "God. How did I get so lucky?"

I blink at him, still catching my breath. "What are you talking about?"

He smirks, leaning closer as if he's about to tell me some great secret. "How often do you find someone these days who hasn't danced with a guy before?"

His tone is teasing, but there's something else there too— something softer, warmer.

I raise a brow, both embarrassed and mildly offended. "So . . . what? You're calling me pathetic?"

He grins, brushing his lips against mine as he murmurs, "Pathetic? No. Rare, sweet girl."

Sweet girl? And just like that, I'm undone. Again.

Because for the first time in forever, I feel seen. Truly seen.

And I haven't felt that way since Rhett.

CHAPTER 18

"Grams, is all this really necessary?" I set down yet another one of her delicate china plates. The table's practically groaning under the weight of all this antique dinnerware—silverware, cloth napkins, even those crystal goblets she only brings out on *very special* occasions.

Across from me, she's placing each fork and knife with meticulous care, like we're prepping for a royal banquet or, worse, one of those dinners where you introduce your boyfriend to your parents for the first time.

Let's be clear: There are no boyfriends here. And this is not that type of dinner.

She casts a look up, her eyes sparkling with mischief. "Are we talking about the china, or the fact that—"

"That you invited both Jack and Reed?" I jump in.

She chuckles, the way someone does when they know precisely what kind of chaos they've orchestrated and they're enjoying every second of it.

I sigh. Damn her. I love her, but her meddling has all the subtlety of a toddler finger-painting on a white couch. And now here we are—just the four of us. Cozy Thanksgiving dinner. Small table. Lots of silverware to clink awkwardly.

No big deal. It's just dinner.

Of course, it *is* a big deal. Jack and Reed are the problem.

Jack, with his all-American charm and that cocky grin he throws around like confetti from behind the wheel of his police SUV. He's been popping up everywhere lately, smirking like he knows exactly what kind of havoc he's wreaking on my pulse.

Next is Reed. Quiet, steady, good-with-his-hands Reed. He's been hanging around all week, "helping out." And by helping out, I mean fixing anything Grams can imagine needs fixing. We are both still very upset at him, but some things we need help with. It's infuriating how competent he is. Even more infuriating is how good he looks doing it.

But it's not just that he's here—it's where else he's been. The Callahan house. He said they're still on "talking terms," whatever that's supposed to mean. The thought makes my stomach knot up tighter than a pretzel.

The doorbell rings, slicing through my train of thought.

Then—his voice.

"Hello, Lillian."

Jack.

My pulse stumbles, then takes off at a sprint. Heat blooms under my skin, spreading like a slow, traitorous fire. My thighs press together, instinct over reason, desire over dignity.

I barely have time to breathe before Grams' warm greeting floats in from the hallway.

"Welcome, Reed."

A pause. Then another voice. Low, rasping, unshakable. "Hello, Mrs. Harrington. Good to see you again."

My stomach flips. Of course it does. Fantastic. Butterflies? Deployed. Wings? Beating like they're on a deadline.

Jack and Reed. Here. In the same space, in the same breath of time.

I grip the china plate like a lifeline, fingers trembling. Carefully—too carefully—I lower it onto the table, like one wrong move might shatter something fragile. Maybe the plate. Maybe me.

This can't be happening.

It's just two men. Two men who shouldn't feel like gravity and fire and freefall all at once.

To ground myself, I slap my thighs—because why not—and instantly regret it. The sting radiates across my bare skin, and I wince. Should've thought that one through. Or worn a longer dress.

Not that I'd trade this dress for anything. It's vintage, one of my mom's old favorites I dug out of the attic. Blue-and-white floral fabric, soft with age and just snug enough to feel like armor. To top it off, I've got her matching barrette in my hair. The whole look is sentimental and battle-ready.

I smooth out a wrinkle in the skirt, ignoring the tremble in my fingers. Just a normal dinner. I've got this. Nothing I can't handle.

And then the room goes silent. Too silent.

A throat clears.

I glance up, and there it is: Three pairs of eyes, all locked on me.

Grams, of course, is smirking—a picture of pure, unfiltered mischief. Just as I'm about to shoot her a glare, she scurries off to the kitchen, leaving me stranded with the wolves.

The air shifts, heavy and awkward. My throat goes dry. My fingers fidget with the hem of my dress, as if it holds some kind of magic answer. Spoiler: It doesn't.

And then there's *them*. Staring. Why are they *staring*?

Reed's gaze lingers, quiet and searching, like he's trying to piece together a memory that doesn't quite fit. It's unsettling, and worse, it feels . . . familiar. As if he's somehow more significant than he should be.

And then comes Jack. He's not subtle about it—his eyes drag over me intentionally until his mouth curls into that *grin*. It sends a spark zipping through my chest like static electricity.

Fantastic. Now I'm apparently the prize in some unspoken tug-of-war, and I have no idea which side I'm leaning toward. These two couldn't be more different if they tried. Jack's in his usual uniform—jeans and a flannel shacket, hair in that perfect "I definitely didn't try but also ran my hands through it fifty times" mess. And Reed? Khakis, a polo shirt, and that ever-reliable blue jacket that screams "I've got a Costco membership and I'm not afraid to use it."

It shouldn't work on me. Either of them. But here I am, stuck in the middle, trying not to think about the fact that maybe, *just maybe*, it does.

The tension finally cracks when one of us laughs—awkward and uneven, but at least it's noise. Reed, ever the boy scout, tosses me a wink and heads for the kitchen like it's his sworn duty to defuse the situation. It's harmless enough, textbook Reed charm, but it still leaves me smiling.

Just as I'm about to follow, a hand clamps around my wrist and yanks me back. Jack. He's closer than I expected, all sharp jawlines and dimly lit brooding, like he stepped straight out of a cologne ad. His other hand caresses my cheek, his thumb grazing my skin.

I go still, the rest of the room fading out. His eyes scan mine, intense, and then—there it is. That damn dimple, popping up like it's just been waiting for its cue.

"I'd be a fool not to tell you how beautiful you look tonight, baby."

Baby. My toes curl. Betrayers.

He leans in, bridging the gap between us, his lips meeting mine like it's his life's work. "Missed these lips," he sighs.

The kiss turns possessive, his hands finding my waist and tugging me closer until all else vanishes. It's just Jack, his mouth, and the vague sensation that my knees might give out. He growls, his hands sliding south to grab my ass. A territorial claim. I gasp and bite his lip—not hard, but enough to make a point.

He pulls back just enough to smirk, a husky chuckle rumbling in his chest. We're both breathless, hovering in that dangerous space between self-control and very bad decisions.

I reach up to wipe my lipstick off his mouth, but he catches my wrist midair, his grasp strong. My pulse stutters.

"Leave it," he demands. Then, because Jack's nothing if not an opportunist, he throws in a final slap on my ass for good measure before stepping back—as if letting me go is his decision, not mine.

I roll my eyes, purely for the performance, and head to the kitchen.

"Took you long enough," Grams quips. There's a faint twitch at the corners of her mouth—a near-smile that only Grams can pull off. She's always two moves ahead of everyone, and she knows it.

What I *do* notice, though, is the way Reed's jaw clenches the second we walk in. His eyes flick toward Jack, and the pressure in the room intensifies. Jack, naturally, doesn't help. His hand rests at the small of my back, light but unmistakable, like he's claiming prime real estate for everyone to see.

I smile sweetly, because that's just who I am, and peel his hand off, letting it drop. "I've got it from here, Sheriff," I tease, stepping toward Grams and away from the standoff.

The tension dips by a hair. Barely.

Grams, either blissfully oblivious or choosing to ignore it (the latter, knowing her), sets a pot of her famous lobster stew on the table. The rich, buttery aroma fills the room, warm and nostalgic, a sharp contrast to the silent territorial battle brewing behind me. She's even baked her blueberry lemon bread for dessert and started the tea. She's determined to carry on with this wholesome holiday scene, no matter how many powder kegs are waiting to go off in her kitchen.

We settle back at the dining room table, and Reed ends up beside Grams. Not that I planned it, but I can't ignore the way he pulls her chair out for her, all polite and gentlemanly. Sweet, considerate . . .

Jack and I take the seats across from them, and it doesn't take long before his leg brushes against mine under the table. It's casual enough to pass for accidental, but the pressure lingers and sends a little thrill through me. I focus hard on my spoon, attempting to keep my attention on the stew, but honestly, my brain's nowhere near food right now.

And then Jack starts. "So, you're a contractor?" he questions Reed.

Reed, unfazed, nods and calmly spoons up another bite of stew. "Yeah. I own Casco Bay Builders."

Jack settles back in his chair, cradling his beer, his posture loose but with enough swagger to make it clear he's not actually relaxed. "So, do you actually do the work yourself, or just give orders from behind a desk?"

The question comes out smooth, but the dig is unmistakable. My spoon hovers midair as I eye Reed, waiting to see how he'll handle it.

He doesn't flinch. "I do both." He wipes his mouth with a napkin. "Depends on the project. I like to stay hands-on when I can."

Jack's smile creeps up slowly; he's gearing up for a fight. "Hands-on, huh? Must be tough juggling all that."

Reed holds his stare, still unshaken. "It has its moments."

"How long have you been in contracting?"

Reed takes his time answering, like he's savoring the question—or just mildly inconvenienced by it. "Since I was eighteen."

Eighteen? At that age, I was barely mastering boxed mac and cheese and convincing myself skipping class was a form of self-care. Meanwhile, Reed was out there with a hard hat and a hammer, building an actual future . . . It's impressive.

Grams, never one to let an opportunity slide, gives him a slow, up-and-down once-over. "Well, that explains why you're so . . . *physically fit.*"

Reed turns pink. Not just a light flush—no, full-on neck-to-ears embarrassment, like he's debating if a trip to Canada might solve his problems. He fidgets until our eyes connect, and instantly, the room shrinks.

His stare holds steady, annoyingly self-assured, with a flicker of humor like he's daring me to mock him. I don't. Unfortunately, the flutter that follows settles somewhere inconvenient.

Meanwhile, Jack drapes his arm over the back of my chair, fingers grazing my shoulder in some halfhearted Morse code: possessive, protective, and—let's be honest—mildly overdramatic. Yes, Jack, we kissed. No, I didn't realize that made me your limited-edition collectible.

I shift in my seat, willing away the flush creeping up my neck, while Jack keeps staring at Reed like he's daring him to break an invisible rule. The unspoken message is clear: No trespassing.

"You're from Massachusetts?"

Reeds produces a "yep." He's relaxed, almost bored, which makes Jack's whole alpha performance look even more ridiculous.

"It's a small town, outside of Massachusetts, about an hour away from here," Reed adds, setting his glass down.

And then Jack, social savant that he is, drops this grenade: "Parents alive?"

My elbow connects with his ribs before I'm able to stop myself. My look screams, *What is actually wrong with you?* This is dinner, not an episode of *CSI: Small Town Edition.* But the damage is already done.

Reed doesn't flinch, though. "Don't know. I was adopted," he states, his tone unwavering but distant. His eyes drop to his hands, tracing the rim of his glass in slow, deliberate circles. There's a pause, not long enough to be awkward, yet enough to feel weighty.

For once, Jack seems to sense the shift. "Guess we have that in common. I am, too." The usual bravado is gone, leaving something more vulnerable in its place.

Reed lifts his eyes, but his expression doesn't soften. If anything, it tightens. Guarded. Tense.

"Best thing that ever happened to me, if you ask me," Jack adds, as if that'll smooth it all over, tie the whole moment up with a nice, tidy bow.

It doesn't.

Reed doesn't say a word. His jaw tightens as he stares at his stew. Then, without warning, he gets up and walks off. A few seconds later, the bathroom door clicks shut behind him.

Grams looks between Jack and me like she's just tuned into a soap opera mid-episode and expects subtitles. Jack takes an exaggerated sip of his beer. I don't even bother with theatrics—I'm already on my feet, heading for the bathroom.

Outside the door, there's nothing but muffled silence. After a beat, I knock softly. "Reed?"

The door opens just a crack, and my heart trips over itself. I was bracing for pissed off Reed, ready with some biting comeback or sarcastic glare. Instead, his eyes are glossy, teetering on the brink of tears he refuses to shed.

Before I can think, I'm moving. My arms wrap around him like it's reflex, and he tugs me into the bathroom without a word. The door stays half-open. Neither of us bothers to close it.

We just stand there, tangled together, until he exhales deeply, his chin resting against the top of my head.

"God, this is . . . "

I bury my face in his chest, squeezing tighter. "Don't." I know where this is going—straight to the self-deprecation station. Embarrassing. Like it's a crime to be human. It's not.

None of us know the full Reed backstory—adoption, foster care, or whatever plot twists he's keeping under wraps. Sure, maybe Jack's life was puppies and sunshine, but Reed's? Probably came with a thunderstorm or two. The thought of little Reed navigating all that mess twists something sharp in my chest.

"You're really something else, you know that?"

I laugh softly, more out of reflex than confidence. "Yeah, I'm not sold on that."

He withdraws, hands on my face, and just like that, I'm done for. Those amber-flecked eyes lock onto me, and I might as well be a deer on a well-lit highway.

"Trust me, you are." The slight break in his words knocks the air from my lungs. "You came in here. You didn't have to, but you did. You wanted to make sure I was okay."

His lips quiver at the end, and something deep inside me knots up. Has anyone *ever* done this for him? Checked in, made sure he was okay? Or has it always been just him against the world?

"That's just . . . what you do for people you care about." It comes out quiet, like I'm saying it more to myself than to him.

Reed stares at me, his throat bobs as he swallows hard, and his thumb brushes my cheek so lightly it's almost unbearable. We're stuck there for a moment, suspended in time, until—of course—a throat clears behind us.

I peek over to find Grams in the doorway, her piercing eyes

taking in the scene. "So . . . are you two planning to come back and eat, or is the bathroom the new venue for dinner?"

Reed lets out a soft laugh, his hand falling back to his side like he's just been caught stealing cookies. I can't help but grin. We nod and shuffle out after her and back to the table. Where things are . . . awkward. The sort of awkward where you can hear every clink of silverware and every overly loud swallow. Jack, naturally, decides to wade into the silence.

"I'm sorry, Reed. I know adoption can be . . . a sensitive topic."

Reed doesn't look up. Just stirs his stew, the spoon clinking against the bowl with an impressive level of apathy. "Mhm," he says, which is about as near to a full sentence as Jack's getting tonight. The conversation dies right there, its grave unmarked.

Enter Grams, wielding her uncanny ability to bulldoze uncomfortable silences like it's a family tradition. "Got any updates on that case?" she asks, her hawk-like gaze zeroing in on Jack.

"Josie?" Jack straightens up instantly.

Sheriff Mercer activated.

Grams takes a sip of her wine, looking as content as ever. I consider—briefly—reminding her that alcohol and her meds aren't exactly besties, but that ship sailed long ago, torpedoed by her insistence that Dr. Boben said, *"a little wine won't kill her."* Probably. Still, I keep an eye on her glass like the world's most reluctant babysitter.

"You talking about the Callahans' maid?" Reed asks, brow furrowed as he glances between Grams and Jack.

Jack narrows his eyes. "How did—"

"I mean," Reed cuts in with a smirk so casual it should be illegal, "I prefer to be informed. Especially when I'm working with someone on demolition and their maid just got murdered."

The room screeches to a halt. Absolute silence.

I clear my throat, shifting in my chair. "Yes . . . the maid," I mutter, because someone has to say *something.*

Reed taps a finger on the table, his tone as nonchalant as it is unnerving. "Terrible thing. Can't imagine what she could've done to deserve that."

Grams doesn't even pause. "That's what I keep saying! And I'm telling ya, those black bags? They're involved. Mark my words."

My stomach drops. She *did not* just say that. I'd told her and Jack about those bags in the strictest of confidence, and now she's tossing it out as if it were a scandalous tidbit at bingo night. But it's not her indiscretion that grabs my attention—it's Reed's reaction. His face goes just a touch pale, his eyes flickering nervously before he smooths it all over with that practiced, unflappable demeanor of his.

"She worked for them a long time, didn't she?"

"A few years," Grams answers breezily, entirely unbothered.

Reed hums, but his attention swivels to Jack. The look isn't exactly warm—more like he's poking at something hidden, waiting for it to twitch. "Does that sort of thing happen often around here?"

Reed's staring at Jack, not with anger exactly, but like he's waiting for . . . what? Reassurance? An excuse? I can't tell, but it's clear Reed's fishing.

Jack doesn't flinch. Instead, his expression sets like drying cement. "Does this happen often?" he shoots back, the words so taut you could pluck them like a banjo string. Translation: *Don't mess with me, my town, or my ability to handle this mess.*

The muscles in Reed's neck flex beneath his collar, and the strain between the two of them is thick enough to suffocate. Jack's hand slides to my thigh under the table, his grip firm— just shy of possessive. It's not painful, but it's impossible to ignore. My pulse pounds, not entirely sure whether this is some territorial display or if I'm imagining it.

"You know . . . " Reed starts, his tone quieter now. His eyes move away briefly before landing back on Jack. "You get a lot of cases like this around here?"

Jack doesn't answer right away. His spoon halts halfway to his mouth, dripping broth back into the bowl, as he turns to Reed with a look piercing enough to shatter glass.

"You mean murders?"

"Yeah. That's what I mean."

Jack sets his spoon down with a deliberate *clink*, the sound cutting through the quiet like a gavel. "Not often," he replies evenly. "But we don't let them go unsolved."

The stare-off that follows could probably blister paint. Reed leans back in his chair, arms folding. "Seems like this one might be a little more complicated than usual."

Jack's grip tightens—barely, but enough to make me notice. "What are you getting at?"

Reed shrugs, though the glint in his eyes suggests he's enjoying this just a little too much. "Just seems like a lot of people in town are talking. Josie wasn't some random employee. She was well-liked. You'd think whoever did it would've slipped up by now."

I glance between them, suddenly feeling like the referee at a wrestling match where someone forgot the rulebook.

"People talk," Jack states, unbothered. "Doesn't mean they know what they're talking about."

Reed's lips curl into a cautious, calculated smile. There's a chill to it that sinks under my skin. "Maybe. Or maybe they know more than you think."

Jack doesn't blink. "Is there something you need to say, Reed? Or maybe something you want to tell us?"

"No, nothing at all. I just find it . . . odd."

"Odd?" Jack's voice tightens.

"Yeah." Reed tilts his head to look like he's circling prey. "That you haven't found anything yet. No leads. No suspects. Have you even bothered to—"

"First off," Jack interjects, "you don't know what I've found. Or who." He leans forward, pressing his beer bottle into the table like it might crack under the weight of his frustration. "And second, I'm looking into everything I need to."

Reed raises a brow. "Even the black bags?"

The silence could drown a clock. Jack stares at him before finally shaking his head.

Reed doesn't push, but the hint of a grin lurking on his lips does all the work for him. I suppress a sigh. The bags again. I told Jack last week they should be checked—basic journalist instinct. But, of course, we can't just waltz into the Callahan house and start rummaging through their stuff. It's got to be done carefully, and Jack loves reminding me of that.

Before the stress can bubble over—or Reed can needle Jack into losing it—Grams steps in. She's been watching the whole exchange with the calm, unshakable authority of someone who's seen far worse nonsense in her day.

"Now, now, boys." Her tone is light but with just enough steel to pierce the standoff. "No need to turn dinner into a battlefield. Let's eat in peace, hmm?"

Her eyes flick to me briefly, a silent *I see you dealing with these fools.* The conversation pivots to safer ground, but the tension lingers, a faint hum just below the surface.

Dinner wraps up soon after, and Jack joins Grams in the kitchen helping with the dishes. I hover by the threshold, caught between rooms, watching them. It's . . . cute. Grams is shameless, tossing compliments at Jack like she's gunning for the lead in a rom-com. And he's eating it up, grinning as he rinses plates.

She's always had a thing for him.

Join the club, Grams.

Wait, what? I *do?*

"Have a good night?"

The question comes from behind me. Then I feel it: Fingers brushing lightly against my arm. My body short-circuits on the spot, a jolt of static zipping under my skin. When I glance back, Reed is there, standing close.

I swallow hard, trying to play it cool. Spoiler alert: I fail. Heat flares in places I'd prefer to ignore, and I mentally file a complaint against my nervous system for gross misconduct. I nod because talking isn't an option, but inside, my brain is running full-tilt into panic mode.

Seriously, Lennon? Pull it together. It's stress. Hormones. Maybe allergies. But two guys? Absolutely not.

I step back until I'm flush against the door, hoping a little space will help. It doesn't. Reed's eyes—a deep, molton brown—find mine, pinning me in place. He smiles, easy and boyish, but there's a hardness to it. My heart speeds up like it's auditioning for a new job: Chaotic mess.

My breath stutters as his hand lifts. His fingers brush a stray curl from my face, tucking it behind my ear. It's such a simple gesture, but it roots me to the spot. My eyes close for half a second—his touch is too soft, too familiar.

And then it hits me.

It's not Reed I'm seeing—it's Rhett.

My heart pounds, torn between two instincts. One half reaching toward him, the other breaking, overwhelmed by memory.

"You look . . . so much like I remember," Reed notes, his breath hovering near enough to raise goosebumps.

For a second, reality blurs. Reed? Rhett? My stomach lurches as my pulse skips ahead of me, leaving the rest of my body in a state of confusion. *He remembers?*

I part my lips to ask—demand, really—what he means by that, but then he moves closer.

"Still crossing your ankles when you get nervous, huh?"

Everything inside me freezes. My breath lodges somewhere in my chest, unwilling to budge.

What?

I stare at him as every alarm in my brain wails like it's the apocalypse. That wasn't just a random comment. That was Rhett. Rhett, who used to lean in close with that infuriatingly easy grin, brushing my hair back like it was second nature. *"You know I can always tell when you're nervous, right?"* he'd tease, as if he could see straight through me.

The memory slams into me so vividly it nearly knocks me off balance. For a dizzying second, it feels like Rhett is here instead of Reed. But Rhett isn't here. He can't be.

I blink hard, dragging myself back to reality. Reed hasn't moved. He's still too close, still watching me with a look that has my nerves doing cartwheels.

"How do you . . . ?" The question scrapes out, dry and unsteady.

Reed's lips twitch in the barest hint of a smirk as his gaze drops. My ankles. Crossed.

Oh.

Relief floods through me, leaving embarrassment right on its heels. He's guessing. Of course he is—it's just a lucky guess. I uncross my ankles, as if that will magically wipe the moment away. It doesn't. My skin still tingles, and my heart stumbles like it forgot how to do its job.

A shaky laugh slips out. "You're pretty observant."

His hand grazes my cheek again, sweeping away the anxiety I didn't realize I was clutching like a life raft. All else in the world? Gone. It's just us now; the universe hit the pause button for this very scene.

"And I've noticed how stunning you look tonight," he adds.

A traitorous smile sneaks its way onto my lips, and

warmth rushes through me like I've accidentally stood too close to a bonfire. He steps closer, and the space between us seems laughably irrelevant. My heart's off to the races again, but it's not the panicked kind of sprint—it's something warmer, something I have no intention of stopping.

His eyes lock on mine, then flicker down to my lips. Instinct kicks in before common sense, and I lick them. His gaze sharpens, the heat in it so blatant it's practically indecent. He leans in, slow and purposeful, his lips hovering just a whisper away from mine—

And that's when the universe slaps the play button with an evil grin.

Laughter booms from the hallway, loud and jarring. A cheerful clap, followed by the unmistakable voices of Grams and Jack, blissfully unaware that they've just murdered the moment in cold blood.

I freeze like I've been caught committing a felony. Reed pulls back immediately, the air between us cooling so fast I almost shiver.

Grams and Jack round the corner, all smiles and unearned joy. I straighten up like I'm auditioning for "Posture Queen of the Year", hoping it'll disguise the unresolved tension hanging in the air like neon signage.

Jack's eyes meet mine, and he smiles—soft, easy, devastating. Somehow, it lands like a sucker punch.

My stomach plummets.

I almost kissed another man.

The same night Jack kissed me.

Not that Jack and I are, you know, *a thing*. But still— doesn't exactly scream "stellar decision-making."

"It was nice having you boys over for Thanksgiving," Grams announces as we shuffle toward the porch. Jack and Reed lean in for hugs, but Jack, being Jack, kisses her cheek, earning a swat and a laugh. Grams blushes. So do I.

Because of course *he'd* get her to blush. The man could flirt with a brick wall and make it question its priorities.

And yet, the thought lingers like an annoying pop-up ad: *Why is Jack spending so much time with me?* He's the one who keeps showing up. The one asking me out. The one kissing me. Sure, most of his feelings arrive in text form, but they're there. So what's the endgame here? We both know this thing between us is a limited-time offer. A complicated, messy, beautifully temporary train wreck. So why act like it's something else?

The porch suddenly feels too crowded for three people and is far too loud with all the words none of us are brave enough to say.

Reed steps in first, pulling me into a hug that feels like saying goodbye to something you never quite had.

"I had a great time tonight, Lennon. Thanks for inviting me."

(*Technically Grams did, but okay.*)

He retreats and presses his lips to my forehead. It lingers —gentle, but weighted, leaving behind more than just warmth.

Behind me, Jack practically sizzles with irritation. The anger radiates off him.

A guttural growl escapes him, sharp enough to cut through the night. I don't need to turn around to confirm it— he's glaring. Hard. Probably imagining Reed spontaneously combusting.

Reed, of course, chooses this moment to gracefully exit, sliding into his car and disappearing into the night, along with any excuses I might've clung to. And suddenly, it's me and Jack. Him, scowling like I've personally wronged him. Me, crushed by whatever just happened.

I spin around and slap my palm against his chest. "Seriously, Jack?"

He flinches, hand flying up like I've mortally wounded him. "Ow! What was *that* for?"

I narrow my eyes. "Oh, don't play innocent. You've been acting territorial all night."

He shrugs, annoyingly casual, like I've just accused him of forgetting to put the toilet seat down. "Can you blame a guy? That dude was practically drooling over you."

I cross my arms, my breath coming out in an exasperated huff. "And so what? It's not like we're *dating*, Jack. You don't get to go full jealous boyfriend just because—"

He cuts me off with a sigh; the fight drains out of him all at once. His shoulders sag, his scowl softening into something that looks suspiciously like guilt. "Yeah. You're right. I'm sorry."

For a second, I think that's it—an awkward apology, maybe a halfhearted high five to close out this weird chapter. But no. Of course not. Jack steps closer, right into my personal space, until he's all I can see. His hands cradle my face, warm and disarmingly gentle, as if he thinks I might shatter if he holds me wrong.

"I don't know how to explain it," he murmurs, carrying a vulnerability I've never heard before. "When it comes to you, I just . . . I feel things. Things I don't know what to do with. And it's messing with me."

It's not exactly Shakespeare, but the raw honesty of it hits harder than I'd like to admit. My chest tightens. Guilt nudges at the edges of my mind—because, yeah, I lashed out earlier—but guilt has never been my strong suit. So instead of apologizing, I close my eyes and lean forward until our foreheads touch. His breath mingles with mine, and for a moment, everything else just fades.

Then it happens. His lips brush mine—hesitant—like he's bracing for me to slap him. The kiss is awkward but layered, tangled up in a mess of unspoken things: tension, jealousy, confusion. But the moment I grip the front of his jacket, all of it unravels.

For a single, breathless second, I let go. I fall—into him, into this. Holding onto him is both a lifeline and a terrible idea.

And then, without warning, he pulls back. His lips leave mine, though the warmth of them lingers, stubborn and traitorous. Before I'm able to even register it, he leans in again—not for another kiss, but to press one to my cheek. It's not sweet, not possessive. Just . . . apologetic.

"Thanks for tonight, Len," he says softly, almost too softly for someone like Jack. "I . . . had fun."

I laugh, short and awkward, because the alternative is yanking him back by the collar and doing something reckless. He turns, tossing a wave over his shoulder—no doubt at Grams—and then he's gone. Just like that. Walking away and leaving me standing here with a racing heart and lips that don't feel like mine anymore.

Behind me, Grams clears her throat, reminding me she exists.

She arches a single brow, her expression a perfect mix of smug amusement and pity. "You're in trouble, sweetheart."

Trouble? That's putting it mildly.

CHAPTER 19

Any reason you decided to interview Claudia without me?

"Terms" ring a bell? Like sharing the investigation?

Grams dragged me to the hair salon. Claudia just happened to be there. Figured I'd ask a few harmless questions.

How'd you even find out?

Melanie brought cookies to the station. Then announced, loudly, that poking the Wives is a terrible idea since they were all together that night.

LENNON

That's a cop-out if I've ever heard one. What's her deal, anyway? Why does she care if we interview the Wives—or the entire population of Cedar Cove? Isn't that literally your job?

JACK

. . .

LENNON

It's called an investigation, Jack.

JACK

Did you at least get anything?

LENNON

Same story as everyone else.

What if we're just chasing our tails? The killer could've skipped town weeks ago.

JACK

Don't quit on me, baby. We'll figure it out— step by step.

LENNON

"Baby" huh?

JACK

Been testing it out. You like?

LENNON

Hmm. Maybe.

JACK

Anyway, I've got a couple of the carnies at the station. Hoping one of them saw something—or can point us to someone who did.

LENNON

Can I tag along?

JACK

Only if you promise to go home with me
after.

LENNON

Promises, promises, Sheriff.

JACK

Don't break them. They're about the only
thing holding this town together.

CHAPTER 20

My body feels like it's been fed through a wood chipper, reassembled by someone who skimmed the manual, and then shoved directly into a marathon for good measure. Every muscle aches in ways that feel vaguely illegal, and as I watch the waves pound the shore with their usual indifference, a small, ridiculous thought crosses my mind: What if I just let go? Not in a dramatic "farewell cruel world" kind of way, but more like clocking out for an extended nap. A vacation from existence. Too bad life doesn't come with an out-of-office reply.

Not that logic helps. The pressure is still there, heavy and immovable, and not just in my legs or arms. My brain, my chest, my everything. I'm so tired it feels like my own existence is staging a mutiny. Add Jack and Reed into the mix, and it's a full-on civil war. Do I push them away? Pull them closer? Pretend they don't matter? It'd be nice to say my reasoning is noble—protection, self-sacrifice, some lofty nonsense—but no. It's just selfishness. I need them, though I can't quite articulate why.

Then there's Grams, who somehow weaponized her HGTV aspirations against me. The same woman who swore up and down that she "didn't need any help" is now treating me like a live-in contractor with no union rights. My body? Wrecked. My patience? On life support. And just when I thought I'd caught my breath, Blake called, practically lighting up the phone with his condescending rage about the work I'm allegedly "letting slip through the cracks." As if I haven't done everything short of interrogating the furniture back home to solve the case. Nothing's changed. The leads are still cold, and the only thing waiting for me when I get back is more paperwork.

Honestly, I'm holding everything together with duct tape and maybe half a prayer. On a good day. Grieving my parents, untangling Rhett's murders—it's like juggling flaming chainsaws while blindfolded. Guilt or purpose, or some unholy cocktail of the two, keep me tied to this investigation. It's not just a distraction—it's the only thing stopping me from unraveling completely. If I keep moving forward, maybe I will stay connected. To them. To the people I've lost.

I close my eyes and lean back, soaking up the last scraps of warmth from the sun. The November air gnaws at my skin, but I play pretend: Somewhere warmer, quieter. It works, briefly. The ache dulls, and for once, I remember there are things worth holding onto.

Like Grams. She's a full-blown firecracker, stubborn enough to argue with a brick wall, but these past two months? They've been a gift. Borrowed time. More than I'd ever get if I just stuck to our normal visits.

The salty air grounds me. For once, I'm almost still. Until the scrape of footsteps on rocks shatters it.

"Not sure if I should leave you to your daydreams or . . ."

That voice. Deep. Familiar. My eyes snap open, and I peek over my shoulder.

Reed.

God, he looks good—annoyingly good. He's standing there like he owns the shoreline, a black trucker hat pulled low with *Casco Bay Builders* stamped across the front. Construction boots crunch softly on the sand, his sleeves rolled just enough to flaunt the tattoos coiling up his forearms. Of course he has tattoos. My brain trips over itself, because apparently, I have a weakness for ink and forearms that moonlight as wrecking balls. Grams wasn't wrong—Reed's in shape. The man was sculpted out of granite by someone trying to win an art competition.

He catches me staring. Naturally. My face heats up, and I'm halfway to pretending I was looking at literally anything else when I notice his arms move—and that's when I see what he's holding.

A bottle of wine in one hand, a blanket in the other.

"What's this?" I arch a brow.

He doesn't bother answering, just flashes that boyish grin crafted to shatter me. A knot tightens in my chest, twisting low and deep, a vise crushing my heart.

What the hell, Lennon?

No clue. All I know is that he could pull a planet out of orbit, and I'm definitely not strong enough to fight it. I bite my lip and tilt my head, silently asking if he plans to stay. His grin widens, answering loud and clear.

Reed shakes out the blanket and spreads it on the sand. I push myself up to help, smoothing the corners because I need something to do with my hands. We both sit, facing the water, the evening tide curling and crashing in front of us. The silence stretches, heavy but not uncomfortable—like there's something unspoken between us, biding its time.

Eventually, I cast a glance sideways. "What are you doing over here?"

He doesn't answer right away. Instead, he nods toward the

Callahan house on the hill, his expression unreadable. "Demolition."

The word hangs in the silence, significant and final. That house, with all its memories and ghosts, is coming down. Along with the pieces of a life I've been clutching too tightly.

I swallow hard, willing the sting in my eyes to stay put. No tears—not here, not now. I just nod, hoping it says enough, and turn back to the waves, anchoring myself to their steady rhythm.

Beside me, Reed shifts, breaking the quiet with a soft pop —the wine bottle. There's a hiss of fizz, followed by a muttered, "Shit," as bubbles foam over the neck. I look over just in time to catch him tilting the bottle, lips sealing around the top to catch the overflow. He takes a long sip, then leans back with a smug chuckle.

"Crisis averted." He wipes his mouth with the back of his hand like he's just saved the day.

I snort softly, shaking my head, but a flutter runs through me, anyway. Damn him. He's sitting there, completely oblivious to the fact that I'm fighting the urge to stare at his mouth. My fingers brush over my own lips, as if that'll help. It doesn't. Memories creep in uninvited—the almost-kiss.

Naturally, Reed observes my stare. That grin reappearing. He holds the bottle out, arm making contact with mine.

I take it, mostly because holding something seems safer than continuing to spiral. The gold lettering on the label gleams against the dark glass, and my chest clenches.

Crimson Vale.

Of course. My favorite wine. The same one Rhett used to bring me back when everything was . . . well, whatever it was. Simpler. Or messier. Depends on the day.

"How'd you know?" My voice strains and I hate it.

Reed shrugs nonchalantly. "Didn't. It's all they had left at Sam's Grocery."

The local store. Figures. I let out a gradual breath and loosen my grip on the bottle, tension unspooling just enough to breathe. A coincidence. That's all it is. But the thought sticks, lodged in my brain.

I lift the bottle, the glass cool against my fingers. Reed's watching me, his expression a masterclass in unreadable intensity. His knee brushes mine—barely there, probably an accident—but my pulse goes into full-blown chaos, anyway.

He doesn't say a word, just sits there, his lips inches from where mine are about to be. The world suddenly feels one size too small. Screw it. I angle the bottle back, pretending my body isn't throwing up a dozen warning signs like a malfunctioning dashboard.

The wine hits my tongue—rich and familiar—but Reed's gaze turns it into something more complicated. He's daring me to keep it together, and I do. At least until Rhett barrels in, consuming my thoughts.

"Whoa, whoa, Len. Slow down."

Rhett grabbed the bottle from my hand, his grip strong but annoyingly careful, like I was made of glass or something. We're on the beach near his place, the salty breeze tousling his hair in that unfair way guys like him never notice. He was too busy flashing his easygoing smile—charming, yes, but with just enough concern to make it annoying.

I yanked the bottle back. He groaned, a deep, theatrical sound, and reached for it again. "I got this for us to sip, Len," he said, his mouth twitching at the corners like he was trying not to laugh.

And because I was me, I pushed the button. Smirking, I took another long swig, just to watch him roll his eyes.

"Sorry, Roo," I said around the neck of the bottle, "but you don't drink straight from a wine bottle to sip. That's what glasses are for."

He laughed, shaking his head, then lunged for the bottle again. I was faster, tucking it behind me.

"Look! A shark just jumped out of the water!" I shouted, pointing dramatically at the ocean.

Rhett actually looked. He whipped his head toward the waves so fast I'm impressed he didn't strain something. Perfect. I was on my feet and running before he caught on.

"Lennon, don't even think about it!" he yelled.

Too late. The sand shifted under my feet as I took off, laughing, the bottle tucked under my arm like I was an Olympic relay runner. Behind me, I heard him groan and then the telltale sound of pursuit.

The sunset turned everything gold, streaked with pink and orange, the wind whipping my hair into my face as I sprinted. Rhett's unrestrained laugh caught up to me, a laugh that stuck to you, even when the moment was gone.

I glanced back. He was barreling toward me, kicking up sand, his hazel eyes locked on mine like he was playing to win. God, he was handsome. His hair was a mess from the wind, his grin wide enough to split his face, and for a second, it was just the two of us.

The realization crashed into me, unexpected and all-consuming—I loved this boy.

Not that I ever said it.

Because a month later, Rhett was gone.

"Whatcha daydreaming about over there? I could see the entire narrative unfolding behind those beautiful eyes of yours."

I blink. Rhett's memory still clings to me. I don't answer Reed. Instead, I tip the bottle back and take a protracted defiant chug. The wine sears down my throat. Burns like hell. Not as much as the fire I'm attempting to drown, though.

"Whoa, whoa—slow your roll, Len." Reed's hand hovers in mid-air.

That nickname. *Len.*

My spine stiffens, and whatever heat I'd been holding quietly in my chest flashes into something sharper. I whirl on him, words spilling out like they've been waiting for their big debut.

"What's everyone's problem? Huh? Why does everyone think it's okay to call me Len?" The frustration claws its way out as I throw my hands up. "My name is *L-E-N-N-O-N.*" Each letter is its own personal attack.

Reed doesn't flinch. He tilts his head, staring at me with an infuriatingly blank expression, like he's debating whether I'm serious or just wine-drunk.

And then, of course, I hear it: My own words echoing back at me in the silence. It sounds ridiculous. The guilt sneaks in almost immediately, chewing away at my brief moment of righteous fury.

It's not his fault. He didn't know.

It's this place. These memories. This whole damn night.

Everything here seems to be a trap, designed to pull me under. To dig up the things I've been shoveling dirt over for years—the things I wanted, the things I lost. The things I'll never get back.

I exhale hard, shaky enough to notice. My limbs suddenly feel too long, too awkward, so I shift to sit cross-legged on the blanket, unsure what to do with myself.

Reed's hands land on my thighs. The air between us stills. Just like that, everything goes quiet, like someone hit the mute button on the universe. His grip is firm but careful, grounding me in a way I didn't know I needed.

And just as quickly, it ungrounds me. The heat of his palms seeps through the thin fabric of my shorts, and my brain takes the opportunity to malfunction entirely. He shifts, and in one smooth motion, he pulls my legs around his waist, like it's the most normal thing in the world.

If I weren't technically sitting, I'd be straddling him. The thought crashes into me, a runaway train of sensation, and heat courses through me—fierce, consuming, unyielding.

Reed, of course, looks perfectly calm. His face is maddeningly neutral. His gaze locks on mine, and suddenly the atmosphere is denser, loaded with something I don't have the words for. I should say something, anything, but my throat decides it's officially on strike.

Then, with zero regard for my unraveling, Reed picks up the wine bottle. He takes a leisurely sip, his Adam's apple bobbing as he swallows, every detail ridiculously magnified in my hyper-aware state.

He offers me the bottle, and I take it, my fingers barely brushing his. The contact lasts less than a second—enough to short-circuit my nervous system. I take a long drink, hoping alcohol might cancel out the electricity.

When I lower the bottle, I hesitate, unsure whether to hand it back or lob it into the ocean to break the tension. Before I decide, his hands slide down my legs, from my thighs to my calves, light as a feather. My entire body locks up, like someone just yanked the emergency brake. Not clear if I'm bracing for more or trying to resist gravity pulling me closer.

"How's the, uh . . . ?" I attempt, vaguely gesturing at the Callahan house. Not my finest segue, but Reed rolls with it. His attention shifts to the house, and his mouth curves into a weary smile—charming, but not adequate to cover the exhaustion bleeding through.

"Like shit," he admits, dragging a hand through his hair. "The Callahans are—"

"A lot," I interject.

That earns a quick flash of teeth. "Yeah. That's a nice way of putting it."

I laugh despite myself. He smiles too, but it flickers, dimming into something heavier. "The worst part?" His voice drops, leaning close enough that I catch the faint tang of wine on his breath. "I'm not even dealing with them directly. That's what my team's for. But today? I had to show up. And before I'm even through the door, there's Mr. Callahan, just—losing it. Completely coming apart at the seams. He doesn't want the job done."

It takes me a second to process that. And another second to realize his words hit harder than they should. My chest tightens, my pulse skips, and suddenly the bottle in my hand feels a lot heavier.

Mr. Callahan? Seriously? My brain stumbles over the idea. I'd always pictured Mrs. Callahan—the grieving mother, clinging to the house like it was her last lifeline to her son. The bricks, the creaky floorboards, the scuffed banister—every inch of it soaked in memories you'd need a crowbar to pry loose. She'd be the one to lose it. That tracked.

But no. It's him. Stoic, buttoned-up Mr. Callahan—the guy you'd think wouldn't flinch if the world ended mid-golf swing.

"Wow," I breathe, though it comes out thin.

Reed's focus shifts back to the Callahan house again, and mine follows. It looms, stiff and silent, like it's waiting for something—or someone. The curtains puff out lazily in the breeze, stretching through the open windows as if trying to escape. The sight sends a flicker of unease up my spine, and I inch closer to Reed. It's not even conscious—the way you sidle up to a fire on a cold night, not entirely sure if it'll warm you or burn you.

I'm gearing up to say something to break the weird spell the house has on us, when I feel it. The barest brush of Reed's fingertip against my ankle. It's nothing, really. But a whoosh of heat infuses in my veins, yanking my attention away from the house and planting it squarely on him.

The world doesn't spin or shift; it just . . . narrows. His touch is anchoring. My brain tries to protest—something about overthinking and consequences, but my body isn't interested. It's decided this is the only place I'm meant to be. Here. With Reed.

Reed catches my eye, and for a second, it's like he's asking a question. I don't know what the question is, or maybe I do, and I'm just stalling on the answer. Either way, my pulse is having a complete meltdown. I wonder if Reed can hear it. Or worse—if he feels this same strange pull.

Then he moves. Just slightly. His eyes lazily move from mine to my lips, lingering there. My breath catches, naturally. His hands find my waist, as if they've made this move a thousand times in his mind. Then they travel lower, sliding to my hips. Then even lower, fingers splaying over the curve of my ass like he's laying claim to the moment.

Before I know it, I'm straddling him. Seamless, natural—as if my body made an executive decision without consulting me first. His hands tighten on my hips while my brain churns out a list of poorly timed warnings: Jack. The Callahan house. The potential disaster waiting just outside this moment. It's a solid effort, but let's be honest—I'm not listening.

I lean in closer, deciding logic can take the night off. His chest rises and falls against me, shallow and erratic, as if he's barely keeping himself together. I don't know which of us closes the gap, but it disappears, and suddenly, there's nothing but him.

He brushes a loose strand of hair from my face, his fingers grazing my skin with maddening tenderness. They linger only long enough to make me forget how breathing works before trailing down the side of my neck. A shiver rolls through me—half pleasure, half nerves, and 100% inconvenient. My eyes close briefly, but I snap them open again because I'm not about to be that person. Still, I angle my head, because clearly, my body didn't get the memo.

His fingers find my cardigan, slipping it off with a gradual precision that feels way more dangerous than if he'd just yanked it. The fabric slides down my arms and lands on the blanket in a heap.

Reed leans in, his lips hovering over my collarbone, his breath warm against my skin. There's no time to think, let alone prepare, before his lips touch me. A quiet spark ignites, and my body reacts immediately, as if it has been waiting for this moment my whole life. My nipples tighten, my pulse flutters, and a low ache coils deep in my core. The soft moan that escapes my lips is unintentional, but there's no taking it back.

The world collapses to just this—no past, no future, only the raw, all-consuming intensity of now.

"God, Lennon." His fingers slide into my hair, tilting my head back until our foreheads touch. His breath fans against my lips, warm and uneven. "You have no idea how long I've waited for this."

He's right—I don't. I'm too busy trying to remember how breathing works. Every thought I've ever had has apparently packed up and left the building, leaving me alone with the liquid heat pooling low in my stomach. So I do the only logical thing left: I kiss him like the world's about to end, which, for all I know, it is.

Our mouths collide in a mess of desire and desperation. It's wild, uncoordinated, and completely ridiculous.

Reed's hands skim down my back, controlled and unhurried, and then suddenly—bam—I'm flat on the blanket beneath him. I brace myself, expecting unfiltered hunger in his eyes. But no. His gaze softens. Tender. He's looking straight into the cracks I've spent years covering up. It's unnerving, and my first instinct is to deflect—crack a joke, say something sarcastic, anything to dodge the weirdly intimate moment happening here.

"Lennon," he exhales, almost like he's afraid to say it out loud. "You're so damn beautiful."

Beautiful? The way he says it—like it's the first and last truth that's ever mattered—makes my heart skip. Or trip. Or just give up entirely.

His hand rises, fingers drifting toward my face. I can't. Not now. Not when I'm already unraveling in about twelve different ways. I catch his wrist before he gets there; the moment tightening around us like a noose. Too much. Too fast.

So, naturally, I do what any emotionally stable person would do: I shove his hat off and grab a fistful of his shirt, yanking him down like he's a lifeline. The second his weight settles on top of me, the air rushes out of my lungs in a way that's both deeply uncomfortable and weirdly addictive. I can't decide whether to scream or melt, but either way, I'm pretty sure I'm about to come completely undone.

CHAPTER 21

Reed

"What does it mean?" Lennon's gaze lingers on the tattoo on my forearm—a mask split clean in two. She's not asking for trivia. She's searching for something deeper. Truth, maybe.

We walk along the shoreline, our steps matching the hush of the waves. The beach is empty, the universe apparently giving us space for this moment. The air reeks of salt, and the breeze is cool, almost trying too hard to be cinematic. The moon, the water, her standing close enough that I can feel her warmth—it's perfect.

I steal a look at her, and a stupid smile creeps onto my face. This is what I wanted, isn't it? To have her here, in a moment pieced together from memories and wishes. She's real, and for once, she isn't slipping away. That thought terrifies me more than I'd like to admit.

Every glance, every excuse I made to cross her path; it all led to this. Fixing a fence that wasn't broken, checking a boiler that worked fine. Subtlety was never my strong suit.

I waited. Barely. She needed to feel it—the pull that's been tying me in knots since the first time our eyes met. I wanted her to want this, too. Now we're here, and the point of no return feels a lot closer than advertised. Not that I'm running. Yet.

Lennon's gaze pins me, like she's trying to X-ray whatever truth she thinks I'm hiding. I let her look, keeping my face as neutral as Switzerland, even as the gap between us narrows. Her stare lingers on the fractured mask inked into my skin. I glance down at it too, stalling. "Got it a long time ago," I admit.

Still no reaction. I up my shoulder in an exaggerated shrug. "It's a reminder. We all wear masks, right? The face we show the world, the one we keep hidden."

She doesn't blink. Doesn't flinch. Just watches. So I push on, because silence is worse. "The cracks happen when life doesn't go as planned. You break, you adapt, you move on. Eventually, you learn to live with the pieces."

"That's all it is," I say. Convincing? Probably not. Her eyes are laser-focused on me, like she's trying to decode the tattoo and uncover some hidden meaning buried in the ink.

I shift my attention to the water, letting the silence stretch. She's not getting more than I'm willing to give. Not tonight.

But Lennon? She's not the type to drop a thread once she's pulled it.

"Have you always wanted to be in construction?"

I let out a short laugh, relieved by the change in topic. "What's with all the investigating?" I nudge her shoulder, a smirk slipping through.

She shrugs, her eyes flickering from the tattoo back to my face. "I just don't know you that well."

"Don't know me?" I flash her a mock-serious look, my grin stretching wider. The easy charm slips back into place, comfortable as ever. "I'd say you know me pretty damn well by now."

She rolls her eyes and gives me a shove, but the laugh that

escapes her is warm. For a second, it's just us—two people walking by the shore, teasing and laughing, like nothing heavier exists. But quiet has a way of sneaking back in, heavier than before. It settles amongst us, and before I am able to steer us into safer territory, she speaks again, quieter this time.

"I guess we have that in common."

"What's that?"

"You knew what you wanted to do early on. So did I."

"Being a journalist?" I question, although we both know I'm not clueless.

Her eyes widen, and I have to fight off a grin at her surprise.

"Your Grams told me," I admit, smirking as her expression alters from startled to mildly irritated.

"Of course she did," Lennon mutters, shaking her head with the resigned air of someone who's been thoroughly outmaneuvered by Lillian Harrington before. There's no real bite to it, though—just the sort of weary acceptance that comes with being related to a professional busybody. Her lips twitch, and then it happens: *That* smile. The one that makes her whole face soften, like she's dropping her guard just for me.

Take a seat, Officer Mercer.

"She would love you fiercely"—Lennon's eyes spark with something half-teasing, half-serious—"but she loves her gossip just as much."

I laugh, because, well, she's not wrong. Lillian collects secrets the way a record collector hunts for lost gems—meticulous, relentless, always searching for the perfect addition. Odds are, she knows more about me than I do. But there's one thing I'm sure of: She doesn't know about this. About us. About how this girl beside me has always settled into my thoughts, a tune I can't help but hum.

How this was all a part of my plan.

I reach for Lennon's hand. Our fingers slot together like they were engineered for it. I'd braced myself for awkwardness tonight, especially after that heated moment. But when her thumb brushes against mine, the tension fizzles out.

I look over. Her curls bounce in the breeze, her blue eyes focused on the waves like the ocean is whispering state secrets only she's allowed to hear. My heart squeezes.

Is this what Rhett felt?

Did he ever get to see her like this—unguarded; armor left at the door? Did he earn those rare, fleeting smiles that feel tailor-made for you and no one else? Did he touch her the way I did, like he was trying to memorize the map of her skin before it vanished? Probably. He was her lover, after all. Before everything went to hell.

The thought lingers, sharp enough to sting. "Do you believe in coincidences?"

She stops mid-step and turns, fixing me with a stare so intense I half expect her to find my warranty information. Then, just as abruptly, she looks away and keeps walking. I follow. Of course I do.

"I mean," she admitted, her voice scarcely rising above the whisper of the wind, "I never did. Not until recently."

I give it a moment, then ask, "Because of Josie? Or . . . ?"

She nods, her pace slowing. "I mean, what are the odds that Josie was murdered . . . like my parents? Like Rhett?" She pauses, jaw tight. "They're linked. I know it. I feel it in my bones."

I don't say anything right away, letting her words hang there, heavy and unsteady. The connection she's making? It's like stacking kindling near an open flame—dangerous, yet impossible to ignore.

My gut tightens, but not for the reasons she might think. My own past lingers at the edges of my mind, a splinter lodged too deep to ignore. Growing up with my foster mom wasn't exactly "storybook." I didn't even know I was adopted until my teenage years and let's just say I didn't find out in the Hallmark way. She denied it at first—outright lied to my face—only to circle back a week later with, "Oh, by the way, yeah, you're adopted, but I have no clue who your parents were."

False. The woman knew. She just didn't want me digging, which, of course, only made me dig harder. Years later, I found out the truth. Why did she lie? Probably to save herself some grief. Or me. Or, let's be real, she just didn't feel like dealing with it.

I shove those thoughts down. Now is not the time for this.

Lennon's hand finds mine, grounding me. But then her next words give way. "And now . . . they're all g-gone."

When a single tear slips down her cheek, it feels like the burden of everything she's holding back might finally crack. But she doesn't. She's a master at keeping herself intact. Even now. Especially now.

I pull her closer, my heartbeat uneven. No one else gets to see this side of her. Not even Jack. Not anymore.

She hiccups softly, the sound fragile and barely there, and something in me twists hard. A fierce protectiveness swells up, raw and unfiltered. But lurking underneath is something darker. The plan.

The one I've spent years building—piece by piece, step by step—has led me here. To this moment.

Not exactly ideal timing, though. She's unraveling before me, tears falling in this quiet, determined way. And damn it, it twists something inside me I was pretty sure had rusted shut years ago. This wasn't the plan. Then again, plans tend to be overrated.

I've always been good at spotting the cracks in people, the little tells that give them away. Most aren't who they claim to be. Learned that early. But Lennon? She's something else. Or maybe just *everything*.

I reach out, wipe her tears with my thumb, my fingers brushing against her damp cheeks. She looks up at me, fragile and heartbreaking, her smile trying and failing to pull itself together. Before I even think about it, my hands are on her face, cradling her like she might shatter.

I kiss her. Just a light press, meant to reassure, nothing more. But Lennon has other ideas.

Her arms loop around my neck, pulling me in like gravity doesn't stand a chance against her. The kiss deepens—hungry, all-consuming. And suddenly, I get it. I *get* what Rhett saw in her, what Jacks sees. Hell, what anyone who's ever breathed in her orbit must feel. It's not a matter of resisting her. It's that you never had a choice.

Her fingers tug at my shirt, my hands sliding down her back as the air between us thrums with electricity, a storm on the verge of breaking. God, it'd be so easy—too easy—to lose myself in her again, right here on this beach. The rest of the world be damned.

I groan when she grinds her hips against me. She giggles, and God, that sound. Up close, it's a weapon. Cute, disarming, and far too effective.

"Sorry." She pulls back minimally, looking guilty. "Guess I got carried away."

Her cheeks flush pink, faint but unmistakable, even in the dim light. For a moment, she freezes, teetering between retreating and diving back in. I make the decision for her, closing the gap and brushing my lips against hers again.

"Get as carried away as you want," I murmur. "No complaints here, as long as it's with me."

She lets out a soft laugh, then swats at my chest like I've personally offended her, though it's all for show.

I laugh—a low, steady rumble—and that sends her into another fit of giggles.

"I like that," she says, settling against me. Her chin rests lightly on my chest, her cheeks still glowing, though now it's less embarrassment and more . . . comfort.

I raise a brow. "Like what?"

"Your laugh." She nudges my shoulder like I'm supposed to have known this all along.

My grin spreads wider. "Yeah? Me too." And I'm not even lying. When was the last time I laughed like this? Hell, when was the last time I laughed, period? Somehow, she's dragged it out of me, Lennon with her witty comebacks and way-too-soft look in her eyes. She's pulling me out of my own head without even trying.

We keep walking, her hand slipping easily into mine.

Eventually, we reach the rocks. *The place.* I knew we'd end up here; the thought has been sitting in the back of my mind all night, waiting. But I keep quiet. No need to rush—some things are better left unsaid.

Lennon drops my hand and drifts toward the shoreline, curiosity steering her like a boat with no anchor. She dips a toe in the water, then jerks it back, scrunching her nose in this adorable way.

I settle onto one of the bigger rocks and watch as the tide toys with her, pulling her in just enough to test her limits. She's part of the scenery in a way that feels almost deliberate. Meanwhile, my mind is elsewhere—underfoot, actually.

I peek at her, making sure she's distracted, then slide off my rock and head for the one at the edge of the water. Crouching low, I wait for the tide to retreat. And there they are—letters carved faint and worn but unmistakable.

R & L. Always and forever.

My pulse trips over itself. I don't move. Don't breathe. Those stupid letters sink their claws into me and hold tight.

Just as I start to wrap my head around it, she's there, suddenly right beside me.

Lennon kneels, her hand finding the carving with eerie precision. She traces the letters slowly, her fingers lingering like they're sacred.

Her name. Rhett's name.

The hit is brutal, knocking the breath from my lungs. Something dark knots in my stomach—sharp, bitter, ugly— but I don't move. I sit there, pressing my hands into the wet sand, holding myself steady, watching her face. The way she stares at the letters as if they're pulling her into a world where I don't exist. Maybe never did.

When she finally meets my eyes, her face is sad, but she speaks with measured calm. "How did you know this was here?"

"I didn't," I reply, way too fast. Smooth. Real smooth. I clear my throat and gesture vaguely at the rock I'd been sitting on. "I saw it from over there."

She stares at me, unblinking. I'm not sure if she buys it, but after a moment, she nods. The tide creeps in, splashing over the rock and drenching both of us, but she doesn't flinch. Her hand stays where it is, like moving it might erase the name forever.

"Rhett?" I ask, even though it's obvious.

She nods, barely. Her throat moves as she swallows hard, fighting to keep it together. It doesn't work. She's unraveling right in front of me.

"I know you probably don't want to hear this . . . " Her words crack, then dissolve into hiccups and soft, broken sobs.

Before I can overthink it, I pull her in. We collapse into the sand, and she folds into my body as if I'm the last thing keeping her upright. She trembles, grief pouring out in jagged, messy waves.

"But I miss him," she chokes out. "God, I miss him so

much. I didn't even realize . . . I didn't know I was still grieving him until I came back here."

Jealousy flickers—ugly, petty—but I push it down where it belongs. This isn't about me. My arms tighten around her, one hand tracing slow, clumsy circles on her back, trying to offer something that might feel like comfort.

Finally, I whisper, "Why's that?"

Her fingers dig into the wet sand. "I guess I never stopped grieving him. I just . . . buried it. But lately, it's harder to ignore. And with everything that's happening . . . " she trails off, her jaw tightening.

The silence between us is thick, heavier than the fog rolling off the water. I can almost see the wheels turning in her head, connecting dots no one wants connected.

I need to pull her back, even if just for a moment.

"Tell me about them." She blinks, startled, when my fingers brush a stray curl from her face. "Your parents," I clarify, leaning in to press a kiss to her forehead.

For a second, I think she's going to resist—throw up that patented wall she's so good at. But then it happens. She leans into me, her cheek resting against my chest, her breath warm against my collarbone. "They were amazing," she sighs. "The best thing about them? They never let me feel alone. Even when I was a total disaster. Stubborn, dramatic—you name it. They always made me feel . . . loved."

I nod, murmuring a quiet "yeah" when she peeks up. I know she's trying to tiptoe around my own personal carnival of childhood trauma, and I appreciate it. I do. But I don't let it show. I remain unfazed. Instead, I kiss her, as if it's the most natural thing in the world. "It's okay. Doesn't bother me."

That seems to unlock something. Her words come easier now, warm and unguarded. She talks about road trips, how her mom could make her laugh even when she wanted to throw something, and how her dad made her feel safer than steel doors and deadbolts ever could.

As she talks, there's this odd pull in my chest, like someone's cinching a thread tighter and tighter. It's not just her grief—it's how she wears it, stitched into every part of her now. "They were always there for me. Even when everything was falling apart. Especially then."

Her fingers find mine, anchoring herself to the present. "They sound like good people," I confess, because that's about as insightful as I can get right now.

"They were," she whispers, the words catching in her throat.

I give her hand a quick squeeze, trying to ground us both. And before I can think better of it, the words just tumble out. "What if you and Jack—" I say his name with all the enthusiasm of a root canal. "What if you don't find the killer?"

She doesn't recoil. Just shrugs. "Honestly? No idea. But every turn feels like we're getting closer. Maybe."

"How's that?" I ask, mostly out of morbid curiosity. Her lip twitches, like she's biting back something she can't—or won't—say.

She exhales slowly. "Let's just say . . . I've found some interesting artifacts. Things that are pointing us in the right direction."

"Artifacts?" I raise an eyebrow. "Like Indiana Jones artifacts, or the kind that won't hold up in court?"

Her lips curve into a faint smirk. "Let's just call them . . . hush-hush for now."

I stare down at her as her fingers fidget with her nails, like they've got a secret they're not ready to spill. I wait, giving her a chance to say more, but then she hits me with the last thing I expect.

"Jack, at one point, thought it was you."

She even lets out a sarcastic laugh, like this is all some

cosmic joke. "Can you believe that?" She glances up at me, shaking her head. "You?" she repeats, half to herself, mumbling something about how she knows it's not me but still found it . . . interesting.

Meanwhile, I stand there frozen, like someone pressed pause on my brain. Because if there's one thing about that accusation, it's that she's not wrong—it *is* interesting.

Why the hell would Jack think it's me?

CHAPTER 22

JACK

Want to go out tonight?

LENNON

. . .

Give me one good reason.

JACK

1. Me. Obviously.

2. Lobster. Fresh, not suspiciously frozen.

3. Margaritas, extra salt—don't act like I forgot.

4. Dancing. You know . . . that thing we do.

LENNON

Our "thing"? Really?

JACK

Don't overanalyze it. It's a night out, not a proposal.

Now get your sweet ass over here before I decide to eat all the lobster myself.

LENNON

Fine. I guess I'll save you from yourself.

CHAPTER 23

Go out with me.

Bold opener. Can't say I usually go out with strangers.

Where's the fun in life without a little mystery?

Don't worry. I always solve mysteries.

Ever the clever, beautiful journalist.

Flattery noted. Should I be impressed or concerned?

UNKNOWN NUMBER

Let's call it both. Just like how cute you looked when you won a Blueberry Pie eating contest.

LENNON

Wow. Stalker points for knowing how to use a library archive. Let me guess: Grams gave you my number?

UNKNOWN NUMBER

Love her. She's a gem.

So, one date? No strings. I'm leaving in a few months, and you'll crack the case soon anyway. Win-win.

LENNON

(Typing . . .)

UNKNOWN NUMBER

Don't make me get Grams involved again.

LENNON

You wouldn't dare.

CHAPTER 24

Oh, but Reed dared. Of course he did. The very next day, there he was—standing on my doorstep with a bouquet of flowers. Not just for me, mind you, but for Grams, too. He spun her some nonsense about wanting to wine and dine me. Grams? She was sold. I just stood there, shaking my head, half-smiling, while a familiar tightness crept up in my chest.

And now? Instead of working at the Callahan house, where drywall and sawdust are supposedly calling his name, he's here. With Grams. He's got her parked in the old chair under the oak tree, a blanket around her shoulders, a fire crackling nearby, and a cup of tea warming her hands. Sunlight's streaming through the branches like some kind of Hallmark movie set, and the two of them have been out there for hours, chatting away like old friends.

It's absurd, really. The way my heart aches when I picture someone else in that chair—Rhett. Would he have sat there, politely nodding while Grams rattled off pie recipes and detailed the antics of the neighbor's lazy-eyed cat? Absolutely. The man had the patience of a saint.

But Rhett is gone. And this man—the smooth-talking one currently sipping tea like he owns the air around him—is very much here. Worse, he's worming his way into my life, sneaky as a vine strangling an old fence. Grams is enchanted. Me? I'm . . . trying to fight it. Badly.

It's irritating, honestly. The way he commands a room, a conversation, or—against all logic—my attention. He's the sort of man who knows what he wants and doesn't bother asking for permission. That should make me bolt for the hills. And it does. Kind of.

Then there's Jack. Sweet, steady Jack. Sheriff Jack to everyone else. To me, just the man who makes everything feel a little lighter. No guessing, no games, no storms brewing on the horizon. Jack's the open book you read on a rainy day, one that promises a neat, happy ending.

Safe.

Predictable.

And yet, here I am, stuck between two men who might as well live on separate planets: One, steady as a rock; the other, a thunderstorm itching to make landfall. Naturally, it's the storm that keeps me awake at night.

"Lenny girl! You gonna stand there gawking at the grass like it's about to spill a secret, or are you gonna join us?" Grams calls out, laughter in her tone.

She's squinting at me through the kitchen window, arms crossed, moments away from banging on the glass. Next to her, Reed leans against the armchair, all casual confidence, watching me like he already knows what I'll do next.

I lift a finger to stall. Grams nods, unimpressed, while Reed—because he can't resist—throws in a wink. Naturally, my stomach flips, and the butterflies stage a full-on coup.

Then my laptop pings.

New email.

Subject: Jack Mercer isn't who he says he is . . .
Attachment: Photo.

The subject line is enough to stop me cold. I hesitate for a beat, long enough to consider walking away. But who am I kidding? I click.

The photo loads like it's being dragged through molasses. When it finally appears, the punch lands hard: Jack, shadows hiding half his face, handing a white envelope to someone I don't recognize. It's grainy, sure, but the exchange is clear enough to send a chill crawling up my spine.

The sender? Anonymous. No details, no explanations. Just silence where answers should be.

And then, the photo is gone. The email vanishes like it was never there, leaving my laptop black and silent. My pulse? It's not nearly as cooperative.

This is Jack. Jack Mercer, the sheriff. The man I've been trusting more and more to handle this case. The one slipping under my skin so easily it's feeling dangerous. He's supposed to be helping me solve this murder. And now this?

What am I even supposed to think? That he's the murderer? That I should start digging into *him*?

My gut twists as I stare at the screen, fingers twitching over the keyboard. I refresh the inbox. Nothing. The email's gone. My heart pounds like it's attempting to fill the silence.

I could just text him. Call him. Ask him about it outright. It's simple. Logical. But before I can work up the nerve—

"That woman sure loves her tea."

Reed's words float in from outside, so nonchalant, so perfectly Cedar Cove, that they snap me out of the spiral. I close the laptop, forcing myself to take a breath, even if it doesn't help much.

"Lennon?" His presence is suddenly behind me. "Hey. You okay?"

I don't answer. I can't. My thoughts are still running wild, and my body is stuck somewhere between panic and disbelief.

"Lennon," he repeats. "Look at me."

His hand brushes my arm, nudging me to turn on the barstool. Then his fingers are under my chin, tipping my face up so our eyes meet. He looks concerned—too concerned—but I can only hold his gaze for a second before it feels like my chest is collapsing in on itself. His hands shift to cradle my cheek, stable and too familiar. Such a familiar that makes you want to fall apart.

"Talk to me." His thumb brushes along my jaw. "You look like you've seen a ghost."

I almost laugh. The sound would've been hysterical if it made it past my throat.

I blink hard, striving to push back the burn in my eyes and focus. Jack, the envelope, the stranger—it's like trying to make a puzzle out of pieces that don't fit. None of it makes sense. Jack's meant to be the solid one. Dependable. Not . . . whatever that photo was. Whatever that photo *meant*.

"Lennon." Reed's brows pull together.

"I'm fine," I manage, though the lie scrapes its way out.

He doesn't look convinced. His hands drop slowly, but he keeps his eyes fixed on mine, searching for answers I'm not ready to give. Then, without a word, he leans in and presses a kiss to my forehead before pulling me into a hug. It's steady— safety itself—wrapping around me. But instead of comfort, all I feel is how much I don't deserve it.

"You sure?" He tilts his head, patience and quiet concern written all over him.

I slap on a weak smile. "Yeah. Totally fine."

I'm not, but admitting that isn't exactly on the agenda.

Reed's hand slides down to take mine, his grip reassuring. "Come on," he says, tugging me gently to my feet.

I let him lead the way, catching Grams' expression as he

lets her know we're heading out. She narrows her eyes like she can smell trouble, but then gives us a cheery, "Have fun!" I feel like a teenager being sent off to prom, except no one at prom is trying to not-cry over an incriminating email.

Reed opens the passenger door of his Tesla and waits for me to climb in before settling into the driver's seat. He doesn't say anything at first, just flips on the headlights and pulls us out onto the road. Then, halfway through adjusting the heat, his hand finds mine again, giving it a soft squeeze. His eyes stay on the windshield.

"You gonna tell me what's going on in that beautiful head of yours?"

I watch the streetlights smudge past, my gaze following the blur of oncoming cars. A red light catches us, and Reed turns, raising a brow in that insufferably patient way of his.

"Not really," I sigh.

He nods, lips pressing together like he's holding back. "Fair enough." After a beat, he grins. "Well, since this is our first date, prepare to have your socks knocked off."

A reluctant smile tugs at my lips. I shake my head, resisting the urge to roll my eyes. "Bold claim."

He smirks. "What can I say? I'm a bold guy."

CHAPTER 25

"This is officially the most fun I've had in ages," Reed chirps, his eyes shining. His smile has been relentless all afternoon—wide, easy, and entirely unfair. He's dressed like a proper Mainer in 20 degree weather: beanie, winter jacket, gloves. None of it stops a rogue drip of ice cream from sliding down his chin, which he wipes away with the back of his hand—still grinning, smug with the secret of happiness hidden in a waffle cone.

"Who eats ice cream in this weather?" I tease, turning to walk backward on the jetty. My boots scrape against frost-slick stone as I glance at him over my own cone.

"People who enjoy life," he shoots back without missing a beat. The light off the water catches his hazel eyes, turning them gold. He's still grinning—absolutely insufferable, as though he's completely aware.

The wind claws at us as it rips across the Atlantic, flinging salt spray over the rocks. The jetty stretches ahead like the crooked spine of some ancient creature, slick with frost and seaweed. Waves pound on either side, their roar drowning out the crunch of our footsteps. I tug my scarf higher, but it's useless—the brine clings to everything, sticking to my hair and skin like it's trying to claim me.

"This is your favorite spot?" Reed's voice rises above the wind.

"Yep." I shrug.

He glances out at the crescent-shaped cove ahead of us, dark and restless. The waves curl against the jagged shoreline, their white foam gnashing at the edges before retreating. Beyond the water, the lighthouse slouches slightly to one side, as if it gave up on posture years ago. The locals like to say the light still flickers through the fog now and then, though it hasn't been operational in forever. Yet, I know it does. I have been here before, memories in this exact spot. In this lighthouse.

"Remind me again why this was a good idea?" He raises an eyebrow, his breath clouding in the cold.

"Because I'm a genius," I deadpan, rolling my eyes.

"Bold claim." He winks.

My cheeks flush slightly, but his gaze drifts between the cove and the leaning lighthouse, his expression unreadable. The wind screeches between the crevices of the rocks, the world around us untamed. Like it's daring us to keep going.

We do.

"How's the, uh . . . case going?" he asks, casually, but his eyes are pointed as they flick toward me.

I take a bite of my ice cream. "Honestly? Not as good as I was expecting. But, well, disappointment is kind of my thing these days."

His gaze narrows. "Why's that?"

I sigh, buying myself a second by watching the waves crash against the rocks. "Let's just say it's complicated."

That answer doesn't satisfy him—of course it doesn't. Reed has an irritating way of making you feel like he's waiting for something *important* to fall out of your mouth. And for reasons I can't quite explain, I keep feeling like maybe I *want* it to.

Finally, I relent, letting the words tumble out. "I know one thing for sure: my parents' case, Rhett's case, and now Josie's case—they're connected. Same killer. Or killers."

He doesn't flinch, doesn't even blink. "You're certain?"

I nod, squaring my shoulders. "I don't just think so—I know so. I don't have hard evidence yet, but my gut's been right before, and it's screaming at me this time."

He takes another bite of his ice cream, smiling faintly, like he's trying not to be impressed. "So . . . you think the suspect's from Cedar Cove?"

The question stops me mid-step. It's the same one I've been circling for months. Are they hiding in plain sight? Or did they slip through my fingers while I was chasing shadows? Every lead, every suspect, every alibi—it's all too clean. Too perfect.

"I'm not sure," I offer, watching the uneven stones go by underfoot.

"But?" Reed prods.

I dart a glance his way. He still looks maddeningly casual, like we're just two normal people enjoying ice cream in freezing weather, not unraveling a nightmare. But the question sits heavy between us, heavier than the salt spray or the wind howling off the water.

"But something's off." I stop near the jetty. Cold seeps from the ice cream cone in my hand—a miniature glacier—but I grip it tighter, anyway. "If they're still here, they're either ridiculously careful, or they know exactly how to blend in. And if they're gone . . . " I let the words dangle. "Then I've got nothing. No leads. No idea where to start."

Reed doesn't answer right away. He just looks at me, then the lighthouse, then back again, like he's piecing something together—or maybe just trying to figure out why we're still out here freezing to death.

"You'll figure it out," he assures me. "You always do, right?"

The confidence in his words catches me off guard. It's so matter-of-fact. It's obvious to him that I'll pull this together, even if it feels impossible right now. And the weird thing is, for a split second, I actually believe him.

We stop in front of the lighthouse; the cove stretching behind us. The waves crash in steady rhythm, the only sound in the eerie quiet. Above us, the structure looms—crooked, weathered, and stubborn, like it's been standing here too long, bracing against every storm that's ever come its way.

Reed tosses our ice cream into the nearest trash can without a second thought, then turns back toward me. The movement's unassuming, but when he steps closer, my heart kicks up like it's trying to outrun me.

What is it about this man? I want to wrap up the way he makes me feel, bottle it, and save it for later—something to sip on when he's not around and the world feels too harsh again.

He brushes a stray curl from my face, his gloved fingers trailing down to rest against my cheek. His face is flushed from the cold, the tip of his nose a perfect match for a cartoon reindeer. The sight pulls a smile out of me. God, he looks ridiculous. Ridiculously adorable, of course.

For a second, something about him tugs at an old memory —Rhett, when we were teenagers. Back when life was somewhat lighter, and I hadn't yet learned the fine art of guarding myself like a fortress. But those days are long gone, and now Reed's looking at me with an exhilarating and terrifying intensity. My pulse spikes, and I can't tell if it's because of him or because he's yanking me into that same reckless feeling Rhett used to stir in me. That itch to jump, to let go, to be the wild, untethered version of myself I thought I'd buried.

"What's going on in that head of yours, pretty girl?" he murmurs. The nickname strikes true—simple, unexpected, and unfairly effective. Nobody's ever called me that before. I barely have time to process how much I like it before I'm already moving.

I grab Reed's hand, our fingers tangling together like they've done this a thousand times before, and tug him toward the lighthouse. The door groans as I push it open; the sound slicing through the stillness. Inside, it's darker than I expected —just enough light spilling in from the broken windows and the faint glow of the jetty.

The air shifts as we step inside. It's thick, almost oppressive, like the walls are holding their breath. Cold seeps in, but it's not just the chill. This place always had a pulse, like it's alive—or maybe that's just the weight of what I left here.

The past doesn't wait long to find me. It's already here, crouched in the corners, crawling into my chest. Reed's hand tightens around mine, a small anchor in the present, but the past? It's louder.

"Come on, Rocky. Don't be a chicken."

Rhett's words surface in my mind, clear as day, like he's still standing beside me. He had this gift—turning reckless impulses into something that felt meant to be.

"I'm not a chicken," I snapped back, though creeping into Cedar Cove's lighthouse in the middle of the night never made my list of life goals. It sounded like a distraction, though. A reckless, stupid, perfect distraction. Anything to drown out the sheriff's voice telling me the case went cold. Telling me it was time to "move on," like that was something I could just do.

Rhett didn't wait for me to overthink it. He grabbed my

hand and pulled me through the doorway, the heavy door thudding shut behind us. His fingers were laced with mine, and we were racing toward the spiraling staircase. Wind howled through the cracked windows, tangling his hair—and mine—with the same wild energy that always followed him.

"Lennon, what are we doing?" Reed's laugh bounces off the narrow staircase as we climb. That laugh—warm, easy, like something you could wrap around you on a cold day. Rhett used to laugh like that, too.

"We're almost there, Len," Rhett said, breathless, grinning like he had the whole world figured out. I laughed back, our breaths fogging in the freezing air, just as the top of the climb revealed itself.

Three massive windows stood open, letting the night rush in. The view stretched forever—waves rolling black and endless under the faintest shimmer of light.

"Wow," Reed muses, stepping behind me.

"Breathtaking?" I peek over my shoulder.

"Told you it'd be worth it," Rhett said, carrying that cocky edge I could never decide if I hated or loved. I bit back a grin, refusing to let him win. But then his hands found my waist, and for a moment, I forgot everything—time, place, my own name.

Except now it's Reed behind me, not Rhett. Rhett's gone. He's been gone for years.

So why does it feel like he's still standing right here?

The wind howls up the lighthouse, slamming the door downstairs with a crack that echoes through the hollow structure. A gust of cold air whips around me, cutting through my scarf and jacket like an icy knife. Or maybe it's not just the cold. Before I can unravel the thought, warm lips brush the back of my neck. Goosebumps ripple up my arms as Reed tugs my scarf down, pressing a kiss to the sensitive skin beneath.

"I can see why you'd want to escape here," he murmurs, smooth and soft against my ear.

But his words send me sliding backward.

"Can't you feel it, Len?" The question lingered between us, quiet but insistent. Rhett's chin rested on my shoulder, his brown eyes glinting in the fractured moonlight filtering through the lighthouse windows.

The breeze had howled around us that night too, rattling the metal stairs and slipping through the cracks in the walls, but Rhett's voice had a way of making it all seem quieter somehow.

"What?" I asked, though my heart was already hammering —a warning, even then.

"This," he said, throwing his arms wide as if he could claim the night for himself. The crumbling stone walls, the twisted spine of the staircase behind us, the roar of the unseen sea—it all felt heavier in his presence. "Being here. Away from everything. No curfews, no rules, no one watching. Just us and the night."

His breath hung in the silence, curling like smoke as he stepped closer. "Don't you feel it? That pull. Like you could just . . . disappear. Leave it all behind."

I glanced at the iron railing by the window—rusted, rattling whenever the wind shook it. If you leaned too hard, it'd probably give way. For half a second, I swore I could feel it: the drop, the weightlessness, the void yawning open beneath my feet.

"Maybe," I muttered, pulling my jacket tighter, as if that could still the slight tremor in my hands.

"You do," he said, sharper, with that reckless grin I could feel more than see. "You feel it. That tightness in your chest, like you've been holding your breath forever. The way the cold bites at you, and somehow you don't mind. Admit it—you like it. It's waking you up."

I bit my lip and looked toward the horizon instead. Out there, where the black sea blended into the blacker sky, there was no line, no edge, just endlessness.

Rhett exhaled, the sharpness fading from his voice. "It's like . . . " He paused, searching for the words. Softer, he said, "It's like standing on the edge of something. And knowing you could fall, or jump, or maybe even fly. And the best part? You don't care how it ends. You just want the rush."

His words curl around me, tempting, inescapable. My pulse betrays me, beating faster despite everything.

"I don't want to fall," I confess, the words fragile, unsteady.

Rhett exhaled a laugh edged with certainty. "You're already falling, Len. You just haven't figured it out yet."

And damn it, he's probably right. Falling is all I've been doing—first with Reed, then Jack, now this case, careening off the rails, a train with no brakes.

The past blurs as the cold stone presses against my back. Reed is standing there now, his eyes locked on mine, like an anchor I didn't realize I needed. And I do need him—need him to pull me out of this freefall Rhett keeps dragging me into, need him to make me forget the drop altogether.

I push off the wall, stepping closer to him, close enough that I'm on my toes. His eyes flash, and then he moves—no hesitation, no warning. His lips crash into mine, and the world tips over, a dizzying plunge.

But this time, I don't care. I don't want to stop the fall.

The kiss is hard and unrelenting, frantic in desperation. My hands knot into his jacket, pulling him closer, drinking in the heat that chases the cold from my skin. There's nothing soft about it—no second-guessing—just two people starving for something they didn't know they needed.

The wind roars outside, rattling the lighthouse so hard it feels like the whole thing might come apart at the seams. None of it matters. Not the cold, not the darkness pressing in—all of it fades under the heat of Reed's mouth, though somewhere in the back of my mind, Rhett lingers, uninvited and irritating as ever. Past and present blur until I can't tell who I'm running from or toward.

Reed's teeth graze my bottom lip, his tongue brushes mine. My skin hums, every nerve keyed into him.

"Lennon," he breathes against my lips, and for a split second, I think he's about to drop something profound—something life-altering.

But then he exhales, "We should head back to shore."

Practical. Sensible. Completely infuriating.

I nod, but my body has other plans. My lips find his again, and my hands decide they're smarter than my brain, sliding down the front of his jacket like they're on autopilot. My palm grazes the firm muscle of his thigh, and he groans, turning my bones to jelly.

His hand tightens on my hip, his fingers digging in just enough to send sparks shooting up my spine. His other hand tangles in my hair, and with a quick tug, he tilts my head back, leaving my lips free as his mouth moves lower. He kisses the curve of my neck, his tongue blazing a trail over my skin. My breath stutters as his teeth scrape just below my ear, leaving fire in their wake.

"Lennon," he repeats, but this time his voice is taut, teetering on the brink. "I don't think this is a good idea."

He sounds like he's trying to convince himself more than me. His grip stays firm—if anything, his hands wander lower, insistent and unapologetic, while his lips linger on my neck like he's determined to commit the whole area to memory.

Right then and there, I think he might stop. That reason or restraint might finally crawl out from under this train wreck of mutual chaos. It doesn't.

Because this isn't just want. It's need. Messy, inconvenient, skin-burning need that winds tight in my belly and won't shut up until it gets what it wants. Until the real world kicks in and ruins everything, I want more. More hands, more mouth, more of this, whatever it is.

He pins me onto the chilly stone wall, and the temperature difference ignites me. "Please," I whimper, though I have no idea what I'm asking for. Clarity? A shred of self-control?

Reed's face is so close I feel his breath against my lips. "Please what, Lennon?"

"Your hands," I manage, the words barely making it out. "I need your hands on me."

Something flashes in his eyes—desire, sure, but also the last shred of restraint holding on for dear life. Then it snaps.

He throws his gloves to the floor before running a hand with unhurried precision, brushing up my thigh under my skirt. My body arches into his touch instantly, like it's been waiting for this moment longer than I care to admit. Maybe it has.

When his fingers press against me, the rest of the world ceases to exist. The wind, the crashing waves, the faint scrape of reality in the background is replaced by the fire he's decided to start.

"Jesus, Lennon," he groans.

His hand moves higher, slipping beneath the thin barrier of my tights. When he finally finds that cluster of nerves, his touch is confident, relentless. One that ruins you for anyone—or anything—else.

My hips jerk on instinct, chasing the sensation, and his laugh rumbles low against me, dark and maddeningly smug. "Eager, huh?"

His hand slips under my thong, shoving it aside. Then he's inside me—one thick finger stretching me so thoroughly my head drops to his shoulder, breath coming in short, ragged bursts.

"You feel that?" His voice drips with a smirk he doesn't bother to hide.

Do I feel it? Yes, Rhett. I feel it. I feel everything.

"You're so wet," he states, like it's a personal victory. "Not that I'm surprised."

I choke on what could've been a laugh—or maybe a gasp—but it drowns somewhere during everything else he's doing to me. The world hums around us: the distant cry of the lighthouse, waves hissing as they batter the shore, muffled voices that feel miles away. His fingers work faster, deeper, each thrust dismantling pieces of me I thought were unshakable.

"I'm gonna . . . " The words spill out, wrecked and uneven, my breath snagging as everything winds tighter—so tight it feels like I might split apart. I'm seconds away, and I know it'll tear me to pieces when it hits.

"Do it," he growls, his free hand gripping my ass to pull me closer, his thumb brushing my clit with an almost careless precision that borders on cruel. "Come for me, Len."

The tension snaps, a rubber band giving way. My body bucks against his, shuddering as pleasure crashes over me. My nails dig into his shoulders, desperate for something solid while everything else unravels in one wild, all-consuming rush.

I clutch at him; he's the only thing keeping me grounded. Letting go isn't even an option.

For a moment, the world goes quiet. Just us, tangled

together, our hearts pounding like they're still trying to catch up with everything that just happened. His breath is hot and uneven against my neck, but I can feel the self-satisfaction radiating off him before he even speaks.

"Well," Reed finally drawls, "that's one hell of a way to end a date."

A snort escapes me—undignified, definitely not sexy, followed by a laugh I can't hold back. My head tips back against the cold stone wall, the chill biting into my skin, making me shiver, though it doesn't do much to dull the lingering, blissful haze still thrumming through me.

"Who says it has to be over?" I whisper.

CHAPTER 26

If sleeplessness were an Olympic event, I'd be the undisputed champion. My body's begging for a collapse, but my brain? It's doing laps like it's trying to break a world record. Team No Sleep, fueled by dubious levels of caffeine. Across the hall, Grams' snores rumble like a dying lawn mower—normally enough to send me scrambling for earplugs. Tonight, though, they're just background noise.

This should've been one of those nights where I pass out grinning like an idiot. What happened between Reed and me in the lighthouse? Unreal. The kind of thing romance novels oversell. When he said, "Bye, Len," on Grams' porch, his lips lingered on mine—soft, unspoken, full of something bigger than goodbye. That's the stuff you daydream about. I should be drooling on my pillow right now, blissfully unconscious. Instead, I'm here, glaring at the ceiling like it owes me rent money, tormented not by Reed's perfect hands but by that email.

Or more specifically, the email that has vanished into the ether.

Ridiculous. I'm a journalist. Solving mysteries is literally my job. Yet here I am, stuck on the case of The Disappearing Email while my laptop tries to bake my thighs. I've refreshed my inbox so many times that Gmail is probably plotting an intervention. But the hard truth is, there's only one person who might have answers.

Jack.

I glance at my phone. Midnight. Perfect. He's either saving lives or snoring louder than Grams. Either way, calling him now would make me *that person*—the one who drags you into their 3:00 a.m. anxiety spiral like it's a group activity.

I tell myself to leave it, to wait until morning. My hand has other plans. Before I know it, I'm swiping the screen and calling.

It rings. Once. Twice. My heart racing.

"Lennon?" Jack mumbles, thick with sleep and sluggish with confusion.

I wince. "Hey . . . Jack."

"Is something wrong?" There's a rustling sound, followed by a muffled thud. "Shit."

"No, no. You're fine. Sorry, it's late. I'll just—uh—call you tomorrow."

"It *is* tomorrow, Lennon."

I peek at the clock. Traitor. "Right. Technically."

He sighs, but there's no edge to it. "Why don't you just come over?"

My brain misfires. "Now?"

"Yes, now. You wouldn't have called if it wasn't important, right? Might as well just tell me in person." His voice carries an easy charm, impossible to turn down. "Besides, it's a good excuse to see you again."

I hesitate, my thoughts split between the warmth in his tone and that email still stuck in my head. Jack knows something—I'm sure of it. If I want answers, I'll have to go.

"Okay," I say.

I knock once, twice. Before I can go for a third, the door swings open.

Jack stands there. Shirtless.

Oh.

My.

God.

Low-slung shorts hang off his hips just right, and his chest is a masterpiece—toned muscle, smooth skin, and a faint sleep-warmed glow. His rumpled hair makes him look even better, like a walking ad for bad decisions.

"Are you coming in," he asks, leaning against the doorframe with a maddening grin, "or planning to stare all night?"

I clear my throat, forcing my eyes up to meet his. "I wasn't staring."

"Sure." His grin widens, as if he knows exactly how busted I am.

He steps aside, and I shuffle in, keeping my eyes firmly on the floor. But before I'm two steps inside, his hand closes around my wrist. He pulls me back, not hard, but enough to send my pulse skyrocketing.

My back is against the wall, and his mouth crashes into mine. It's deep, demanding—like he's chasing something, or proving a point. His body pins me there, solid and unyielding, shutting out the world. No emails. No hesitation. Just him.

I break away, pulse racing. "Hello, Jack." His eyes narrow, something unreadable flickering through them before he masks it with that carefully controlled expression.

"Hi, baby," he murmurs, stepping back just enough to let me breathe. His hand lingers against my neck before it drops away like an afterthought.

Without missing a beat, he drifts toward the kitchen. "Drink?" he offers over his shoulder.

I shake my head, watching him. He grabs a glass, fills it with water, then leans lazily against the counter, his movements smooth with efficiency. "Sit." He gestures toward a barstool. It's not a request. I stay where I am.

Jack arches a brow. "Have a good night?"

The way he says it suggests he already knows the answer, or thinks he does.

I shrug. "It was alright."

"Just alright?" His tone is light, teasing, but there's an edge there, coiled and ready.

"It was alright," I repeat, a little firmer.

Jack takes a slow sip of water, his eyes locked on mine over the rim of his glass. "Looked like more than 'alright' to me."

The air tightens, heavy with implication. My stomach twists, but I keep my expression blank. "What's that supposed to mean?"

He doesn't answer right away. Just sets his glass down with excruciating precision, the faint clink against the counter louder than it has any right to be.

Finally, he looks up, and for a split second, the mask slips. Beneath the polished charm, there's something darker.

"Lennon," he starts, all the playfulness stripped from his voice, "why don't you tell me why you're really here?"

I take a step closer, holding his stare. "Why don't you start by explaining what *that* was supposed to mean?"

Jack moves slowly now, a predator deciding whether to pounce. "I think you already know." The words aren't a suggestion; they're a dare.

Frustration rises hot in my chest. "If I knew, I wouldn't be asking," I shoot back.

His whole body tenses, shoulders tight, hands curling into

fists. "I saw you." The words burn, short and seething. "You. And him."

I freeze. My breath catches. *He saw us? Reed and me?*

No. That's not possible.

The guilt hits anyway, knotting my stomach. Not tonight. Please, not tonight.

Jack exhales hard. "Really, Lennon . . . how—" He stops, gaze falling. When his eyes finally find mine again, they're raw, like an open wound.

He paces, hands restless, dragging through his hair. "I shouldn't even care," he mutters, glaring at the floor like it holds the answers he doesn't. "We're not a thing. We've never been a thing. Right?" Bitterness bleeds into the words, but there's something unsteady beneath them, something he can't quite hide.

I open my mouth, but nothing comes out.

Jack lets out a short, hollow laugh. "So why the hell does it feel like this is ripping me apart?"

His words crash down like a collapsing ceiling—inescapable, crushing. Guilt coils tighter as I step closer, drawn by something restless and raw. His pain saturates the room, pressing in, more piercing than I expected. More piercing than I'm willing to admit.

And that alone should terrify me.

This is Jack. The man I nearly ran down with my SUV. The sheriff. The kind of person I've spent my life keeping out. I built my walls for a reason. But are they even standing anymore? Every time I rebuild, he's there, chipping away at the edges.

He wants in. And God help me, so do I.

But there's still one frayed thread between us, and when it snaps, what then? Chaos? Or worse—feelings.

Before I can second-guess, I reach for his hands. His fingers, rough and familiar, close around mine. When his eyes lock onto mine—really lock on—it's like missing the last step on a staircase. Gone is the smirking sheriff with his easy charm. What's left is raw, unguarded, fraying at the seams. Not quite angry. Just . . . hurt.

At what—or who—I can't tell.

He turns my wrists in his hands, careful but taut. My pulse stumbles, like it knows to run.

"Tell me, Len." The frustration is there, threaded through every syllable. His stare doesn't waver, sharp and searching. "Did he make you come?"

My brain slams the brakes and promptly bursts into flames. Did he just—?

Jack moves. One second, I'm standing; the next, my back collides with the kitchen island. The countertop bites into my spine—sharp, unrelenting—but that's not what steals my breath.

It's the heat. Low, insistent, pulsing. It unfurls in my stomach, spreads down my thighs, tightening them before I can stop it.

And just like that, the box where I shoved these feelings shatters into splinters.

What the hell, Lennon? You spent the night with another man. Now you're here, drawn to someone else like a magnet. Emotional stability? Not exactly your strong suit.

Is it really so unnatural to want two men so wildly different?

Jack—sunlight and simplicity, all warmth and ease.

Reed—the coming storm, destruction you can't resist because ruin has its own allure.

But there's no sunshine now, no soft breezes. Jack is fire— unyielding, all sharp angles and heat. He spins me, and my stomach meets the icy countertop. The chill stings, but not nearly as much as the furnace of him behind me. My hands splay against the surface, searching for balance. Useless—Jack is already there, pinning me, his breath scalding my ear. Every nerve sparks.

"Did he use his fingers?" Jack growls. "Or maybe his mouth?"

I can't breathe. My body locks, my mind blanks.

He shifts, the rigid press of him against me stealing what little coherence remains. I don't mean to push back, but my body doesn't wait for permission.

His hands skim down my waist, teasing—just light enough to torment, firm enough to make me jolt. The movement forces me harder into the island's edge.

"Did it feel good, baby?" The words smolder, dragging over my skin. "Did he do it the way you like?"

Before I can answer—not that I'd muster anything coherent—his hand slips beneath my joggers. My palms find the counter, searching for stability, but there's none to be had. This is freefall.

"Jack," I rasp, just as his fingers brush over my clit through the unremarkable cotton of my boy shorts—functional, unsexy, utterly irrelevant now.

His lips trace my neck, deliberate, incendiary. He radiates hunger, and I tip my head, offering more. The voice in my head whispers restraint, but desire shouts louder.

"Tell me, Lennon," he commands.

My pulse stutters, reason dissolving. I nod—breathless, burning.

"Jack." His name leaves me, stripped of hesitation, laid bare. I know what I want.

"I know, baby," he murmurs, a promise wrapped in possession. "Let me show you what it means to be touched by a real man."

I nod again—reckless, willing, lost. He moves my underwear aside, his fingers sliding through the slick heat waiting for him. A fractured moan spills from my lips, unbidden, undeniable.

"Fuck," he rasps, head tilting back, eyes dark with satisfaction. "I knew you'd be wet for me."

A thick finger presses inside, and for a fleeting second, guilt flares—sharp, accusing. Reed. Tonight. Two men, two sets of hands, two lines crossed without hesitation. I should feel something—remorse, shame, maybe even self-preservation. Instead, I surrender. I press into Jack like the world is unraveling, and maybe it is.

He moves in, chest flush against mine, his lips mapping a slow descent from my ear to my throat, then lower. He's charting a course only he intends to follow. His hand slides beneath my shirt, calloused fingers finding my breast. A firm squeeze, a sharp pinch, and a jolt tears through me, teetering on the edge of pleasure and pain.

I whimper. I beg. "More."

Jack chuckles, low and knowing. "Patience, baby. After all, you let another man touch you tonight."

Guilt, anger, and indignation ignite, colliding in my chest. He presses me flat against the counter, knocking the breath from my lungs. His fingers are relentless, and I cry out, my body wound tight, poised to snap.

"I think that calls for some punishment, don't you?"

Then—emptiness. His fingers withdraw, leaving me aching, only for his thumb to glide over my clit. My brain short-circuits. Thoughts? Gone.

"J-Jack," I stammer, grasping for words that won't come. Then he stops.

The absence is brutal. A whimper escapes me before he spins me around and yanks my joggers down like they've personally offended him. My shirt follows, stripped away with the same ruthless efficiency. Now I'm standing there in just my bra—exposed, breathless, pissed.

His hooded gaze drags over me—the kind of look that liquefies your spine and makes you forget you probably walked into the trap on purpose.

"Goddamn, Len," he mutters, rough enough to scrape. "You are so fucking beautiful."

And then he's on me. Fingers tangled in my hair, pulling me into a kiss that unravels everything. It's not gentle. Not sweet. It's a collision, a recalibration of reality.

I don't know how long we stay like this—his shorts hanging low, me barely clothed, clinging to each other. When he finally breaks away, both of us gasping, his eyes are wild, his breath ragged. I barely have time to recover before he lifts me effortlessly.

The cold countertop bites into my skin, a stark contrast to the fire curling through me. His hands skim my thighs, parting them, his gaze feral.

"Keep those legs open for me, Len," he purrs, like there's a chance in hell I'd disobey.

Then he stops. Lifts a finger. Measured. Intentional. Holding me right where he wants me.

Then—he walks out of the kitchen.

Good God, the man's dirty talk deserves its own award.

Months ago, I would've bet real money Jack didn't have this in him. Reed? Absolutely. Reed breathes this kind of energy. But Jack? Jack's the guy who apologizes to furniture.

And yet, my legs spread on the kitchen island, body wired to his every word, every move, like he's hacked directly into my nervous system.

When he returns, silver handcuffs dangling from his fingers, laughter spills out of me before I can stop it.

Jack doesn't blink. His gaze burns. The laugh dies in my throat, swallowed by something heavier, something that coils low in my stomach.

He steps behind me. "Trust me?"

It sounds like a question. It doesn't feel like one.

I nod, the space between us thick with something electric.

His hands skim my back, guiding me down until I'm flush against the countertop. Fingers trace up my arms, leaving sparks in their wake, before gathering my wrists behind me. A metallic click—cold, final.

The cuffs.

He secures the other end to the sink, and my pulse stutters. I've never done anything like this before, but the way Jack looks at me—intent, ravenous, like I'm his entire world—makes me want to give him everything.

His fingers hook into my panties. One swift motion—gone. Just gone. A sharp breath catches in my throat as heat unfurls between my thighs.

"Don't be shy," he murmurs. "That's it. Let those thighs fall open for me. Good girl."

Then—he winks.

Almost disarming. Almost. Right until his palm lands with a sharp slap against my pussy. A searing jolt, a mix of heat and sting, races through me like an electric current.

Jack chuckles, deep and smug, soaking in his own satisfaction. His fingers slide between my thighs. "God, Lennon," he murmurs against my skin, like he's savoring the moment. "From the moment I saw you standing in the street, all fire and fury, I knew you were different."

The words should be cliché. But paired with the wicked path of his fingers, they're lethal.

Without warning, he pinches my nipple. My spine bows, a gasp escaping as metal cuffs clink against the sink. Instinct drags me toward him, but the restraints hold me fast.

He leans in, lips barely skimming mine—a whisper of a kiss that sparks hot frustration.

I need my hands. Need to touch him, drag him closer—hell, pin him down if I have to.

"But it wasn't until our first date," he murmurs, lips grazing mine, "that I knew."

"Knew what?"

"That I wanted to taste just how fucking sweet you'd be."

The words barely land before his hands tighten on my thighs, spreading me wide with a confidence that borders on cocky. Then—utterly unbothered—he climbs onto the counter with me, pressing me into the unyielding surface.

His mouth traces a path from my neck to my collarbone, then lower, branding heat into my skin before crashing onto my lips. The kiss spins me off-center. I arch, desperate to erase the frustrating sliver of distance between us, but he leans back just enough to flash *that smirk*. The one with the dimple. The one that makes me want to kiss it—and slap it clean off his face.

I groan in protest, but the sound dies in my throat as his palm strikes my pussy again. Pleasure detonates through me.

Jack grins, then drops to his knees. His grip on my thighs is maddeningly firm, his control absolute. Our eyes lock, tension snapping tight between us—then his tongue drags through my slit, slow and devastating. Every thought I had? Gone.

"Jack—" His name shatters from my lips as my back bows, but his hand presses flat against my stomach, pinning me down. His mouth moves like he has all the time in the world, unraveling me with one agonizing flick at a time.

His fingers slide beneath my hips, angling me toward his mouth, his rhythm on my clit devastatingly precise. He plays me like he's mapped every nerve ending, relentless in his pursuit. My hips jerk, but Jack doesn't waver—he only drives me higher.

And then—he stops.

A low, satisfied chuckle rumbles from him. *Cruel.* "He

might've had you coming like that, Lennon. But I'll show you better."

He looms over me, shifting my hips as if arranging me to his liking, my wrists still bound against the sink. Cuffs bite into my skin. He plants my feet on the floor, pressing himself against me—heat and hardness, an unspoken promise. His lips graze behind my ear, then drift lower, tracing my neck.

The bra is next. He palms my breasts, squeezing just enough to steal my breath. I arch into him, a mess of nerve endings, dignity abandoned.

With effortless impatience, he shoves his shorts down. Instinct drags my gaze over my shoulder. *Jesus.* Hard, thick, and wholly unapologetic. He doesn't speak as he slides his cock through my wetness, dismantling my sanity inch by inch.

"Jack," I gasp, my voice splintering.

He brushes my hair aside, lips hovering over my ear in a dark whisper. "I'm clean."

I nod—too fast, too eager. "Same. Pill," I blurt, words colliding before my brain catches up.

That's all he needs. No hesitation, no preamble—just Jack sinking into me, stretching me open, wrecking me. It's almost obscene how good it feels, like he was made to dismantle me.

I arch back, craving more, but he stays maddeningly controlled, every intentional inch a reminder of who's in charge.

Jack chuckles, then cracks his palm against my ass—sharp, searing. My vision fractures like shattered glass. My body, ever treacherous, tightens around him.

"Remember this, Len," he murmurs.

He picks up the pace, each thrust a command, a claim. Pain and pleasure coil into one feverish pulse, the world narrowing to heat, friction, surrender. My legs tremble, seconds from collapse.

"What?" I gasp, barely forming the word.

"That—" he growls, driving deeper, "you always knew—" another thrust, harder, "I was the better man."

Before I can retort—or think—he's gone feral. A final snap of his hips, and my body detonates, pleasure slamming through me, blinding and merciless. I shatter. Jack follows with a groan, his body tensing, spilling into me, leaving me boneless, breathless—claimed.

CHAPTER 27

"You gonna tell me why you called me at midnight, then stormed in like you were on some kind of mission?" Jack's question comes through the dark.

We're tangled in his sheets, my body aching like it's survived an obstacle course designed by a sadist—kitchen counter, bed, shower. Even breathing feels like exertion.

Not that I'm complaining.

"Or are you waiting for me to go first?" he adds, his fingers are tracing lazy circles along my cheek. The tenderness is almost jarring, a stark contrast to the way he had me pinned hours ago.

For a moment, I let myself sink into the stillness. Our breathing syncs, slow and steady, like we've done this a hundred times before. It's almost too easy. Too familiar. I nearly forgot why I came here. Nearly.

Then his question breaks the silence. "How well do you know Reed?"

My eyes snap open. The fragile peace shatters. I push up

onto one elbow, studying him in the dim light. "Reed?" Jack doesn't flinch. His stare is weighted, unreadable—stone cold.

"And just to be clear, I'm not asking if you've slept with him."

I blink. Reed? Seriously? My fingers drift absently over Jack's chest as I bite back the urge to roll my eyes. "He's adopted. A contractor from Massachusetts. Runs his own business. Right now, he's working on the Callahan demolition project."

The silence stretches, thick and stifling, less like patience and more of a challenge.

"Why do you ask?"

Jack shrugs. "He's not who you think he is, Lennon."

A prickle of irritation creeps up my spine. "And what's that supposed to mean?"

He doesn't rush to answer. Just watches me, composed, like he's waiting to see if I'll flinch.

I don't.

"I was going to tell you sooner," he says, exhaling a slow, measured breath. "Last night, actually. After my shift. But you were . . . busy."

I cross my arms. "Yeah. I was busy."

His eyes flicker, narrowing just slightly before shifting to the side. Then back—sharp now, assessing, like he's deciding how much truth I can take.

"Just say it," I bite out.

He exhales hard, fists curling at his sides. Whatever this is, it's eating at him. "Do you remember when I said I was interviewing some of the carnies from the festival?"

I nod. I do. I was supposed to be there.

"Two of them—separate interviews—described the same guy." He drags a hand over his face, as if trying to wipe away whatever this is. "Sandy blond hair. Fit. Black beanie. Blue jacket. Gloves. Same details, no discrepancies."

My stomach knots as Reed's image flares in my mind—vivid, undeniable. But my face stays impassive. If Jack thinks I'll crack first, he's in for a long wait.

"So what? They saw the same guy at the festival." I flick a hand, dismissive. "Not exactly earth-shattering. Half the town owns a beanie."

Jack's jaw tightens. "Yeah. But they also said he wasn't from Cedar Cove." He pauses, his tone weighted. "These carnies work the festival every year. They know the locals. They recognize outsiders."

That makes me hesitate—just for a beat. *Outsider.* Someone who didn't belong.

"That still doesn't mean it was Reed." My arms fold tighter. "You've been fixated on him for weeks, Jack. Let it go."

He releases a terse breath, then, without another word, pushes off the bed and moves to the window. "You're not wrong. I've been digging." He stands there, a silhouette against the glass. Beyond him, the woods stretch into the void—vast, endless, swallowing the world whole. His back is rigid, tension humming in his shoulders.

I consider moving. Crossing the room. Saying something.

But I don't.

"You know all the murders happened on the same day?"

I nod, though he's not looking. He speaks lower. "It's Reed's birthday."

My breath catches. Jack's back goes rigid, like he's bracing for a blow—maybe from me, maybe from the universe itself.

"That means nothing." The words scrape out, thin and unconvincing. A wet match has more spark.

Jack turns, the dim hallway light etching sharp angles into his face. His gaze holds mine—unwavering, inscrutable, heavy with something I refuse to name.

"It's not a coincidence."

"It is." The denial fires out—quick, desperate, automatic. "It has to be."

He doesn't flinch. Doesn't blink. Just looks at me like he already knows I'm lying to myself.

Reed wouldn't—*couldn't*—be part of this. He's Reed. The one who makes me laugh when the world is collapsing. The one whose touch feels like home.

But three murders. Years apart. All on his birthday.

Of all the days.

We always said the date had to mean something to whoever's behind this.

I just never thought *whoever* might be him.

Jack moves. His footsteps carve through the silence. He stops at the foot of the bed, looming. His whole body is wound tight—fists clenched, veins ridging his forearms like fault lines. His jaw looks seconds from shattering under the pressure.

And yet, I stay still. No retort, no cutting remark. I don't tell him to breathe, to calm down, to ease off the True Detective routine.

He's wrong. He has to be. Reed isn't like that—can't be. But doubt creeps in anyway, slithering through the cracks. And Jack? He's not helping, pacing like he's both Sherlock Holmes and his own tragic case file.

"I believe in patterns." Jack starts pacing. "And something tells me this is all connected."

That certainty—so smug, so absolute—snaps my patience. My hands fly up. "You sure have a lot to say about someone you barely know. Someone who, surprise, might have secrets of his own."

His eyes lock on mine. "Secrets? What the fuck are you talking about, Lennon?"

My teeth clamp shut so hard it hurts. How does he not see it? How does he not realize everyone has secrets—especially him?

I look away, but he won't have it. His fingers find my chin, tilting my face back toward him. His stare is molten. "Speak." Not a request.

The words knot in my throat, tangled with doubt. My pulse hammers. Why is this so hard? Just say it. Tell him what I found in the email. Reed isn't—he's not—

Jack's hand trails from my chin to my throat, his thumb brushing against my pulse. Then his lips crash into mine, stealing the breath right out of me. The world tips sideways, heat surging through my veins. Suddenly, I'm not frozen anymore. I fold into him, a traitorous moan escaping.

"Is this what it takes to get the truth out of you?" Jack growls against my lips, his teeth grazing my lower lip.

For one reckless, intoxicating second, I want to let him win. To sink into his heat, his scent, the gravity of his need. To pretend none of it matters.

But it does.

I should stop. I have to stop.

Instead, my lips answer his. My fingers weave into his hair, pulling him closer, even as my mind screams—*Abort mission. Catastrophic mistake.* But logic is no match for the hunger, the aching urge to disappear into him, just for a moment.

And then he stops.

Jack pulls back, his forehead resting against mine, breath ragged. "Baby . . . just tell me. Please."

His voice cracks. For once—the guy who always has the answer before you even ask—looks lost. It's unsettling.

I exhale slowly. "I got an email yesterday."

Jack's brow furrows. "Okay . . . "

"It was about you."

That gets his attention. A beat of silence. Then: "What about me?"

I look away, my throat tight. This is the tipping point—

where everything either detonates or, against all odds, endures. My stomach knots, but I press on.

"There was a picture."

Jack doesn't move. Doesn't flinch. Just blinks, unnervingly still.

"You were outside. It was dark. You were handing another man a white envelope."

I pause, scanning his face for a flicker—guilt, recognition, anything. But he remains unreadable, the only betrayal a slight tension around his eyes.

"There was no sender," I add, gesturing vaguely, frustration threading through my tone. "No context. Just a cryptic email engineered to"—I twirl a finger near my temple—"send me spiraling."

"And you got this . . . when?"

"Yesterday," I admit, quieter now. Whatever resolve I have unravels beneath his indifference.

He steps back. The distance stings more than I want to acknowledge. The air shifts, colder without him, but the way he moves—restless, caged—keeps me rooted.

Jack turns to the window, dragging a hand through his hair. His whole body coils, bracing for impact. Or maybe trying to outrun it.

"I can explain that," he mutters.

I push off the bed, the icy floor jolting me back to reality as I cross the room. Jack doesn't turn. Doesn't acknowledge me. But tension radiates off him—clenched fists, rigid jaw, the fabric of his boxer briefs twisted in his grip.

"Jack."

He stays still. Just breathes. Slow. Measured.

"It was for Reed," he finally says, the words thick, reluctant, like they're being forced out.

I blink. "For Reed? What the hell does that mean?"

Jack pivots, his expression shadowed by exhaustion and

something harder to place. "I told you," he grits out. "He's not who he says he is."

A bitter laugh escapes me. "Oh, great. We're back to this again?"

His forehead tenses; a warning. For a moment, I think he's about to go off, but instead, he exhales—a slow, controlled release. Somehow, that's worse.

"Yes. We are." He steps closer, closing the space between us. "I'm a sheriff, Lennon. I don't get to play favorites. I don't get to look the other way when things don't add up."

"And what, exactly, doesn't add up?"

Jack shakes his head. "Reed's hiding something. Something bigger than you realize." His words drop to a hush. "I'm doing my job. That means looking into everyone in Cedar Cove. Everyone. Even the people you think you know."

I study him, searching for a crack in his resolve. Nothing. No hesitation, no slip. Is this Jack, the relentless sheriff? Or something else?

His fixation on Reed feels . . . personal.

"What aren't you telling me?"

Jack's jaw tightens, his hands flexing at his sides like he's torn between reaching for me and staying put. "I'm telling you everything I can."

"That's not the same as everything!" I yell.

The air between us tenses, thick with unspoken truths. I step closer, frustration bleeding through. "If you want me to believe you, stop hiding behind half-truths."

His gaze locks onto mine, unflinching. For a second, I think he might actually say something that matters. But then he swallows—hard—and whatever it was dies before it reaches daylight.

"I'm sorry, Lennon. I can't." The words feel hollow, yet his expression stays infuriatingly controlled. "You've always known I couldn't tell you everything. This case . . . it was always going to get bad. And now it's worse because you're—"

"I'm what?" Too late to take it back—my face burns.

Jack exhales sharply through his nose, his patience fraying. "Because you're involved with him."

Unbelievable. My hands shake as I scoop my clothes off the floor, the room shrinking around me. Jack's fingers graze my wrist. I yank away.

"Don't. I'm leaving."

"Why? Because I'm telling you the truth?"

"Because I'm saying what you won't."

I twirl around, my anger snapping into focus. "It's a *birthday*, Jack. Reed's *birthday.*"

"And your parents' murder," he shoots back.

The air locks up, his words hanging between us like the drop of a guillotine. Then he twists the blade.

"And Rhett's murder."

My jaw clenches so hard it's a miracle I don't crack a tooth. Still, I shove one arm into my shirt, fingers trembling, refusing to give him the satisfaction of stopping.

"Are you trying to hurt me, Jack?" I step closer, fists curling tight. "Or is this just how you work? Dragging up every dead person I've loved because you've run out of better ideas?"

His face softens, which makes me angrier. Those sad, regretful eyes might as well be knives. His hands drop to his sides, empty, like he's surrendering.

"Lennon, I'm—"

"No." I cut him off, raising my hand. "I don't want to hear it." I push past him toward the door. "We need time. Space. Something."

Anything to stop this spiral.

I've been neck-deep in the chaos they've dumped on me. The worst part? I can't even decide which one of them I'm angrier at. Jack, with his martyr complex, or Reed, with his whole mystery man from Massachusetts act. Honestly, it's impressive how efficiently they've derailed my life. My family's murder? The investigation? My sanity? All shoved aside for this.

I take a deep breath and force myself to look at Jack one last time. "I'm staying," I state. "But not for you. Not for Reed, either. I'm staying to figure out why Josie was killed. That's it. That's the only reason."

The lie burns going down, but I swallow it anyway.

Jack says nothing at first. His walls are back up, his face unreadable, but I've hit a nerve. He opens his mouth, but I'm already grabbing my bag and keys. He doesn't get the chance.

"Lennon." I freeze at the door. The way he says it, nagging on his breath, makes me pause.

I turn, peeking over my shoulder. He stands in the middle of his room, half-shadowed by the dim light from the hall, and for a moment, he just stares at me, as if he's weighing whether to say what's on his mind.

"Before you go," he finally says, "you should know something."

I cross my arms, impatient. "What?"

"Reed's not just from Massachusetts. He's from Maple Harbor."

The words don't hit me right away. *Maple Harbor.*

"And that night," he continues carefully, "when Rhett was killed . . . Reed was there."

My entire body goes cold.

"What?" I whisper.

Jack doesn't flinch, doesn't back down. His eyes meet mine, unrelenting. "He lied to you, Lennon. He's been lying to you this whole time."

I stare at him, the impact of his words settling in like lead in my chest.

But before I get to ask the million questions suddenly clawing at my throat—Jack steps closer.

"There's also something else you don't know. About Reed. About what really happened that night." He hesitates, then says, "If you're serious about the truth, Lennon, you need to stop trusting him."

I stand frozen, my legs rooted to the floor, my mind racing, but my heart is telling me one thing.

I don't know who to trust anymore.

CHAPTER 28

BENSON

Hey man, how's it going? How's Callahan
duty treating you?

REED

Not bad. Just demo work for now. That
house is a beast, though, feels like overkill
for two people. You ever been up there?

BENSON

Not much, but I helped out last week.
Something about fixing their security
system. That place is basically a museum
with a keypad.

REED

Security system, huh? Mrs. Callahan
worried someone's coming for her jewelry
box, or is she just paranoid about old
money problems?

BENSON

Could be either. Heard the cameras in the back and side were acting up, probably some relics from the Reagan administration.

REED

Figures. That house looks like it's barely hanging on. They still with the same security company, or actually upgrading this time?

BENSON

No upgrades. Just patching up the old system. Guess the mansion budget doesn't cover a Ring doorbell. But, hey, you didn't hear it from me. ;)

REED

LOL, secret's safe. The Callahans staying put for the holidays, or are they the "winter-in-the-Maldives" type?

BENSON

Mr. Callahan's heading out next week, some business thing. Why, you planning a hostile takeover of the estate?

REED

Haha, no. Just trying to avoid bumping into them while I'm working.

BENSON

Smart. Mrs. Callahan will still be there, though. She's busy planning one of those fancy Cedar Cove Wives events. You'll probably be fine as long as you steer clear of the catering trucks.

REED

Got it. Appreciate the intel.

BENSON

Anytime. Stay safe in the haunted mansion.

CHAPTER 29

Lennon

The night presses against the windows, thick and velvety. Outside, under the muted glow of those old-fashioned lantern-style streetlights, six women step out of sleek black cars. They look like they took a wrong turn off the set of *Bridgerton* and ended up in Cedar Cove. Corsets, sweeping skirts, glittering jewels—as if a Regency ball decided to crash the PTA meeting.

And, somehow, it all works.

The Wives of Cedar Cove are at it again.

"Ya gonna stand there gawkin' all night, or should I start chargin' admission?" Grams' question pierces my daze; her footsteps creaking softly on the living room floorboards as she shuffles up beside me. She looks at me, simultaneously amused and unimpressed, like this isn't the first time someone's brain short-circuited around these women.

I blink, still trying to process what I am seeing. "Who even owns clothes like that?"

Grams lets out a laugh, the kind that suggests she's seen it all and isn't planning to stop anytime soon.

Grams leans closer to the window, her breath briefly fogging the glass. "Ayuh," she says with a small shrug. "Your guess is as good as mine." Then she turns away, her slippers scuffing softly against the hardwood as she walks toward the dining room.

I assumed that was the end of it—just another weird event for the Wives of Cedar Cove—but she returns a minute later, something pinched between her fingers. Without a word, she plunks it into my lap. A single piece of thick cardstock embossed with gold foil.

"What's this?" I run my fingers over the cold, polished surface.

Grams folded her arms, her face drawn into an expression she usually saves for crossword puzzles with obscure clues. "Somethin' we got invited to." As if that clears up *anything*.

I skim the card. The looping script is so prim and perfect, like it time-traveled straight out of a Jane Austen novel. The embossed letters catch at my fingertips as I trace the words, trying to make them mean something.

"It's only for women," Grams adds, deadpan, as if that single fact answers all mysteries of the universe.

I arch an eyebrow. "So . . . what? A big dress-up party? A way to flash some cash and pretend it means something?" The sharpness in my tone is unexpected, even to me, but I let it stand. Extravagance is nothing new since I moved back.

Grams lifts a shoulder, still staring at the card like it might burst into flames if she glares hard enough. "Beats me."

I glance out the window again at the diamonds, the silk, the practiced elegance of it all. Something knots in my chest, anger simmering. "I mean, Mrs. Callahan's great and all," I mutter, half to myself, "but maybe she could pour all this effort into something . . . useful." My mind races. Why throw this kind of extravaganza when Reed's crew is getting ready to bulldoze the whole place?

The heat inside me bubbles over. I turn to Grams, throwing my hands up. "Do you realize what these women could actually do? The Wives of Cedar Cove—they've got money, power, connections. Instead of prancing around like they're auditioning for *Pride and Prejudice: The Musical,* they could do something. Raise real funds. Bring in real experts. Help figure out who killed Josie."

Grams gives me that long, measured look of hers, the one that always makes me feel like I either said something wise or ridiculous, and she is giving me time to decide which.

"They bring people in from all over for these things," I press on. "If they put even *half* this effort into hiring detectives, or forensic experts, or anyone who could actually solve this." I pause, swallowing hard, trying to shove the lump in my throat back where it came from. "Josie deserves better."

My parents deserved better.

Rhett deserved better.

This town deserved better.

But instead? Another gala. Another excuse to look the other way. Someone was murdered in Cedar Cove, and nobody wants to talk about it. Not really. It is easier to play dress-up and act like nothing has changed.

Grams shifts in her chair. "Ain't nobody sayin' you're wrong, Lenny girl." Her tone softens, almost thoughtful. "But you know these women. They like things the way they are."

I huff, crossing my arms. "Yeah, well, that's half the problem, isn't it?"

"Well"—she peers at me over the rim of her glasses—"why don't ya go tell her that?"

I blink. "Tell who what?"

She presses a hand to her chest, shaking with a chuckle that sounds far too pleased. "Ayuh, Lenny. March right over there and let Mrs. Callahan have it. Give her a taste of that Harrington fire. I know you've been itchin' for it."

She clicks on the TV, her eyes flicking to the screen like I no longer exist, though the slight twitch of her lips says otherwise. "Go on," she adds, waving a hand like she is shooing a cat. "It's in ya. I can see it. You've been sittin' on it too long, but it's there."

I laugh nervously, shaking my head. "Grams—"

"Don't 'Grams' me," she cut in, her smirk practically glowing with mischief. "You've been waitin' to tell that woman off ever since she threw that big fundraiser for the mayor's cat—or whatever foolishness that was. And don't you dare try tellin' me I'm wrong."

Grams isn't wrong. She rarely is. That alone makes me laugh harder, though the ache in my chest refuses to budge. She leans back in her chair, flipping through channels like she didn't just lob an emotional grenade into the middle of my evening.

The TV hums quietly in the background, but her words stick, loud and unshakable: "Go on, tell her."

Obviously, I'm going to tell her. Mrs. Callahan is Rhett's mom, for God's sake. And that ache—the one that sits somewhere between a heavy weight and a sharp jab—twists just thinking about it. She is tearing down their house. *His* house. Demolished. Like he'd never even been there.

I tell myself to let it go. It isn't my house. Mrs. Callahan doesn't owe me an explanation or a warning. She has every right to do what she wants with her property. But logic doesn't seem to care. The feeling—the restlessness crawling under my skin—refuses to let me sit still.

Grams emits a soft snore, her blanket sliding halfway off her shoulder. I cross the room and tuck it back around her, snug and careful, the same way she used to for me when I was little. She mutters something in her sleep, half a chuckle, and I find myself smiling despite everything.

And then, I am heading for the stairs. By the time I reach my room, my mind is made up.

If I am going to do this—and I can't believe I actually *am*—there is no way I am showing up empty-handed. I dig through my closet, yanking out the first thing that looks remotely Bridgerton-worthy. Because if you're going to show up on someone's doorstep to confront the mother of your dead first love, you might as well look like someone who could dominate a Regency-era social season with one perfectly timed insult.

This is a bad idea.

No, scratch that. This is a spectacularly bad idea. The nylons are riding up; the dress waistband is staging a full-scale rebellion against my ribs, and my boobs are about one quick inhale away from declaring their independence.

Before I can retreat and save myself from the humiliation, the door swings open so fast I actually flinch. And there she is—Mrs. Callahan. She blinks, surprised, though she buries it quickly behind her signature mask. Perfect posture, tight-lipped smile, not a hair out of place. Classic Mrs. Callahan.

"Lennon." Her voice could melt butter, but her eyes belong in a freezer aisle. "What a surprise. So happy you could join us."

Sure you are.

I force a smile, hoping it passes for sincere.

Josie. The case. The truth. That's why I'm here.

Even though Jack and I promised—swore—we'd tell each other everything. But this . . . this is mine to bear. I have to do it alone, no matter how much I miss him beside me. No matter how my heart aches, screaming that we should be doing this together.

I step inside. A wall of floral perfume slams into me—hydrangeas, thick and cloying. My lungs stutter, caught between the scent and the shock. This house isn't the one I remember. Not even from a few months ago.

The grand foyer has been transformed into the set of a period drama, complete with silk and lace draped from the ceiling like someone's Pinterest board exploded. Billowing waves of pastel ivory and pale blue frame the room.

I take a breath, though the dress squeezing my ribs makes that a challenge, and it hits me: *Who in their right mind would want to destroy a house like this?*

Even the chandelier—the same gaudy monstrosity I used to hate—suddenly looks like it belongs, its crystal drops winking in the soft glow of candlelight. Candelabras sit on every available surface, flames flickering like they're in on some secret. The marble floors gleam, reflecting golden light in a way that feels strangely alive. There's no trace of modernity, no harsh LEDs, no electric lamps humming in the corners. Just candles and shadows, moving like whispers across the walls.

The women gliding through the space match the setting perfectly. They're decked out in Regency gowns, empire waists hugging their figures, delicate embroidery catching the light. Gloves reach up to their elbows; pearls and diamonds drip from their necks. It's all so polished, so seamless, so utterly *extra*.

And then there's me. I catch my reflection in a mirror by the stairs. Big mistake. In the candlelight, I look like someone's overly ambitious craft project. My hair's piled so high it feels like it's defying physics, and the dress cinches my waist with the enthusiasm of a boa constrictor. My chest is shoved up so aggressively it's practically auditioning for attention. I'm not a guest—I'm a prop someone dragged out of storage for a theme party.

In the next room, the faint clink of glasses mingles with

the low hum of polite conversation. Mrs. Callahan glides toward me, her heels barely making a sound on the marble. "We're gathering in the parlor," she says.

The parlor is every bit as transformed as the rest of the house. Regency furniture is arranged with military precision—chairs with carved wooden legs forming a perfect semicircle around the fireplace. Candles flicker in ornate sconces, their warm glow bouncing off polished surfaces, while a string quartet recording plays softly in the background, as if the room needs even more ambiance.

The Wives of Cedar Cove are scattered across the space like props in a high-budget drama. Lace and silk drape over them, porcelain tea cups held in delicate hands that clearly haven't touched a dish sponge in years. Their smiles hover just shy of sincere, and their posture is the kind that could win awards. But their eyes? Cold, incisive, and assessing.

My skin prickles. It's impossible not to picture them silently cataloging my flaws or, worse, whispering about the fact that Jack and I have already interviewed most of them—and the rest are next on the list. Still, I keep my back straight, my chin up, and cling to my mantra like a lifeline: *Josie. The case. Justice. Answers.*

I might be the youngest person in the room, and this dress might be trying to suffocate me, but there's no turning back now. Mrs. Callahan gestures me further into the room with a smile so warm it might be convincing if her eyes didn't say something else entirely. I return the gesture with a polite grin stapled firmly in place and step inside.

Yep. Definitely a terrible idea.

"Champagne treating you okay?"

The question pierces through the chatter, landing squarely on me. My hand twitches, and I nearly fumble with my third glass. Yes, third. Don't start.

I turn, slowly, to face the woman. She's watching me, her gaze sliding lazily from my drink to my face, one brow arched like she's already filed me under possible disaster. I manage a polite Cedar Cove smile—equal parts charm and defense mechanism—and raise the glass for a sip.

Then it hits me. Not the champagne, unfortunately, but her eyes.

The breath stalls in my throat. She's the woman from the photo. Mr. Callahan's photo. The one where his arms were around her like he owned stock in her perfection.

Up close, she's even more intimidating. Flawless skin, hair spilling in glossy waves that probably required the GDP of a small country to achieve. Total Cedar Cove royalty. But those eyes—hazel, flecked with gold—those are the same.

Oh, I know those eyes.

They are beautiful, sure, but there's something unsettling about them, as if they're attempting to unearth a memory I can't pin down.

"Can I be honest with you?" She leans in, eyes shifting around the room.

I shrug, aiming for nonchalance even as my pulse hammers. "Honesty's risky, but I'll allow it."

A faint smirk tugs at her lips. "This"—she motions vaguely at the room—"is awful."

The snort escapes, a little too loud. "Not a fan of small talk?"

"Small talk?" She inclines her head, her expression amused and appalled. "Let's be real—it's gossip, dressed up in sequins."

I fight the urge to smile. "And the parties? Don't tell me

you're not here for the sparkling conversation and the hors d'oeuvres."

"You mean the weekly reenactment of 'Look How Rich We Are'? Yeah, no. Hard pass."

That gets me. A laugh slips out, unfiltered this time. Okay, I like her.

"The drinks, then?" I lift my glass and nod toward hers.

She clinks her champagne flute against mine. Finally, she smiles—really smiles—and it transforms her face to a degree that feels almost unfair. "The drinks," she remarks lightly. "The only redeeming factor."

I take a sip; the bubbles fizzing against my lips, and for the first time all night, the tension in my shoulders eases. I watch her out of the corner of my eye, trying to pin her down.

"What's that saying?" I ask, letting my tone dip into playful. "Champagne is like—"

"The perfect mask for misery," she interrupts, her hazel eyes glinting.

It catches me off guard. My smile falters, just for a second. There's something beneath her sarcasm—acute, intense, uncomfortably real.

I laugh again, but more forced now. "I was going to say something about luxury and bubbles, but . . . yeah, that works too."

"But it's true, isn't it? Everyone here wears a mask."

Her words strike somewhere deep, an unshakable verdict that drags me back to that night with Reed and his masked tattoo. Are they connected? No. No way.

A familiar voice slides into the moment. "Lennon, I see you've met Shannon."

Shannon.

Mrs. Callahan appears at my side, her smile pointed. Shannon's lips twitch—somewhere between a smirk and a shrug—

but she doesn't bother meeting Mrs. Callahan's eyes. The tension between them is impossible to miss.

I force a grin, trying to keep things light even in the prickly atmosphere. "Shannon was just saying how much she *adores* these kinds of events."

Shannon coughs, badly hiding a laugh, and I can't help but grin wider. Mrs. Callahan, on the other hand, doesn't flinch. Her attention fixated on me, unblinking and pointed, like she is reading some invisible fine print on my face.

The unease crawls up my spine and settles there, cold and unshakable.

"You're demolishing your house?" The words slip out.

Her eyes widen—barely a heartbeat—before her features reset to that polite, impenetrable mask she wears so well. The kind of composure you only get after years of tucking skeletons into closets and throwing away the key. "We are," she declares, her voice smooth but with just a trace of suspicion. "How did you hear about that?"

I dodge the question. "Why?"

Her stare darts to Shannon, then back to me, the silence between us turning dense and uncomfortable.

"It's just something Grant and I decided," she replies, as if trying to convince herself as much as me.

Sure. Grant decided this. Right after pigs learned to salsa.

I don't say it, but I don't need to. She is lying, and we both know it. Reed had already let it slip by the water—Grant hated the idea. This wasn't his decision. This was all hers.

Calling her out would've been satisfying, but ultimately pointless. Mrs. Callahan isn't the type to break under a little pressure, and I'm not about to start a war of wills in front of everyone. So instead, I nod, like her explanation makes perfect sense, while the truth twists in my gut.

But she isn't finished. Her breath tightens, her composure

slipping enough to reveal how much this matters to her. "I'll ask again, Lennon—how did you know?"

The question floats in the air, pressing against the walls like the room itself is holding its breath.

"I know the guy who owns the demolition company you're using."

Her stare hardens, icy and calculating. After a long pause, she gives a curt nod—more unsettling than any outright accusation.

"You know the owner of Casco Bay Builders?" Shannon cuts in, her eyes narrow, her tone crisp as a whip.

I nod, but before I can add anything, Mrs. Callahan turns on her with a look so frosty it might've knocked the room temperature down a few degrees. It isn't a warning. It is a full stop.

"How do *you* know the owner of Casco Bay Builders?" Mrs. Callahan clips out.

Shannon takes an infuriatingly slow taste of her drink, dragging the silence out like she is savoring it. When she finally answers, her tone is far too smooth. "Who doesn't know them? They're the best in Maple Harbor."

She smiles faintly, enigmatic as ever. "I have nothing but good things to say about Reed."

Jack was right about Reed and Maple Harbor. Fine. But the way Shannon said his name—like she knows him personally—itches under my skin. I keep my face neutral, no questions, no flinching, though the mystery is already gnawing at the edges of my brain. How well does Shannon know Reed? Do I even want to know? She doesn't seem inclined to explain. Instead, she takes another leisurely sip of her drink, like this is all background noise to her.

"Jett and I used them years ago," she says, as casually as if she is talking about a brand of toothpaste.

Years ago? My stomach twists. Reed made it sound like

Cedar Cove was some kind of untouched frontier, yet Shannon is talking like he—and his business—have been here long enough to leave footprints. Why leave that detail out? I don't have time to untangle it, though, because the universe decides I have had enough.

Melanie, *that* Melanie, steps forward, holding a microphone. Yes, a microphone. In the middle of someone's living room. Apparently, this gathering has now morphed into a budget-friendly awards show. I grab a drink off a passing tray and down it in one go, the burn in my throat easier to swallow than whatever fresh absurdity is about to unfold.

"We can't thank all of you enough for coming out tonight," Melanie's voice trembles like she is delivering a State of the Union instead of addressing a room full of tipsy acquaintances. Sure, Melanie. Deeply moved.

I'm not really listening, though. It isn't the speech that gets me—it is her smile. One dimple tucked neatly into her left cheek like punctuation.

I freeze mid-drink; the glass hovering just short of my lips.

The dimple hits me—familiar and unsettling all at once. And it isn't just the dimple. There is that itch of déjà vu I felt earlier, back when Shannon had started talking. It was like Jacks. Too much like Jacks.

My chest tightens, nerves firing off alarms for reasons my brain refuses to file a report on. Before I can sort out the mess, Melanie's composure fractures.

"Sorry," she mutters, swiping at her face. "I didn't think I'd get this emotional . . . " Her eyes shimmer, tears threatening to stage a full breakout.

Mrs. Callahan moves in with practiced precision. A napkin materializes in her hand like she pulled it from a secret dimension, but Melanie is already unraveling. Whatever composure she arrived with is circling the drain.

"It's just . . . this house . . . " Her gaze bounces around the room as though it might vanish if she looks away for too long. "There are so many memories here."

Her voice tugs at something inside me, but instead of sticking around to figure out what, I make the tactical decision to excuse myself. A well-timed trip to the restroom feels like the right call.

Setting my drink on a passing tray, I tug at the hem of my dress and slip out of the room.

The grand staircase looms ahead, its polished wood gleaming faintly under the chandelier's glow. My hand drifts to the railing, as though it has its own memory of this place. Muscle memory, or maybe just a stubborn habit.

It is as if I heard Rhett's laugh—loud, effortless, and just a little too big—echoing off the walls. We'd race up those stairs, each claiming a side, feet pounding as though the house itself dared us to leave it standing.

And there is a spot right outside Rhett's room. If you stand perfectly still, everything stops—the creaks, the draft— the whole house seems to hold its breath. For a second, it is like the world itself forgets to move.

I used to drift over to the Callahan house after the bad nights—the ones where I woke up drenched in sweat, haunted by dreams of my parents' empty faces. Most times, I didn't even bother knocking. I wasn't looking for company, just somewhere quiet to evaporate.

Except Rhett always found me. He had a knack for it, like some bloodhound for people on the verge of losing it. One night, I was standing there, fists clenched, determined not to cry, and there he was—leaning in the doorway, arms crossed, watching me come apart one piece at a time.

He didn't start with questions or clichés, just stood there. After a while, he stepped closer, quiet but steady. His presence was a safety net I didn't know I needed.

When he finally spoke, it was calm and deliberate, like he

was saying something I was supposed to believe, whether I wanted to or not.

> *"Rocky," he said, "whenever it feels like everything's falling apart, like you can't find your way . . . just remember this place."*
>
> *His hand rested lightly on the small of my back. "No matter what happens, you'll always have here. This house. Me. You're not alone, okay? Not as long as I'm breathing."*
>
> *I nodded back, leaning into him, letting his words settle in the hollow spaces.*

And now, here I am, outside his door, brushing my fingers against the wood—smooth, worn, and maddeningly symbolic, like it has been waiting for this moment of existential dread. For a second, I swear I can almost hear him—comforting but also teasing, throwing out "Rocky" as if it is a punchline to some joke only he got.

My breath catches. The sting builds behind my eyes, a slow burn that warns tears are coming. I close my eyes, swallowing hard, and push the door open.

Empty.

Of course it is empty. I knew that. I *knew.* But still . . . the emptiness hits like walking face-first into a freezer. The wall of posters we used to argue about? Gone. *"Rhett, you cannot hang a Slayer poster next to Bob Marley—it's a crime against aesthetics."* The crooked TV he swore was "level enough"? Vanished. Even the sign I'd made for him—"Future Pediatrician"—is gone, like it ran off to med school without him.

The whole room has been stripped clean. It isn't just empty. It is actively taunting me with how empty it is.

I want to break down into one of those ugly, snot-filled cries that leaves you questioning your life choices, but my body has other plans. Instead, I freeze, staring at the bags in the corner. Black trash bags, slumped over like they'd given up on life. My chest tightens. Why are they still here?

Downstairs, Melanie's voice floats up the stairs. Something about the street never being the same. Mrs. Callahan, of course, can't resist chiming in, stepping into the role of Grief Narrator. "She's right," Mrs. Callahan comments, saturated with the style of emotion you could buy in bulk at a discount store.

I drop to my knees, staying quiet, the floor cool against my skin. My hand hovers over the nearest bag. I shouldn't. I really shouldn't. But curiosity has a way of flipping off common sense.

"She's right." Mrs. Callahan repeats, "Nothing will be the same once my house is gone." She even adds a little hitch in her breath, the kind of detail that would make a second-rate drama coach proud. If she actually cared, though, she wouldn't be gutting the place. If she cared, Rhett's room wouldn't look like a crime scene.

I finally unknot the top of the first bag. Clothes. Not Rhett's—these belong to Mr. Callahan, judging by the collection of oversized polos. Disappointment sinks its claws into me. What if this is just a half-hearted pre-charity purge? A pile of old memories bagged up and ready to be forgotten?

I shove the thought aside and reach for the next bag.

Mrs. Callahan drones on, puffed up with self-importance. "And so," she announces, her tone unnervingly chipper, "here's to a new chapter for the Wives of Cedar Cove!"

New chapter?

I speed up, fingers working faster as her speech barrels toward its grand finale. I am on the last bag when she trills, "I can't wait to rebuild . . . and introduce The Crest!"

"To The Crest!" they chorus, perfectly synchronized, like they've been rehearsing in some PTA bunker.

What the hell is *The Crest*? My stomach twists, but it isn't just Mrs. Callahan's culty enthusiasm making me queasy.

It is what my fingers find.

A letter.

Not just any letter—a letter from Josie.

And it begins:

Dear Mr. and Mrs. Harrington.

CHAPTER 30

LENNON

What's "The Crest"?

JACK

Nice to hear from you too, Lennon.

LENNON

Jack . . .

JACK

Lennon . . .

LENNON

Just answer the question.

JACK

Should I know what that is?

LENNON

I don't know—should you?

JACK

Nope. Not a clue.

LENNON

Can you look into it? I would, but I don't exactly have access to . . . certain resources.

JACK

Fine. But you owe me.

LENNON

Name your price.

JACK

Come over this weekend.

LENNON

Probably not a good idea.

JACK

Please. I miss you. Just to talk—I'm sorry.

Promise I'll behave. Hands to myself. Scout's honor.

CHAPTER 31

Jack

"You've been here all day," Benson observes, his voice quiet yet insistent. His fingers sift through the disaster on my desk, nudging papers and receipts aside. His gaze lingers on the mess before shifting to me, expectant. He doesn't need to ask—I can feel the weight of his unspoken question pressing in the air: *What have you found?*

Not much. Welcome to the club, Benson.

Since Lennon texted me about "The Crest", I've been chasing shadows. Leads evaporate, theories crumble, and even my boss dismissed it as rich women flexing their egos. Cedar Cove's finest, swapping wine nights for a vanity project in marble and glass.

Still, it doesn't sit right. Why bulldoze a family home perched on the ocean—one steeped in history and memories —just to erect a monument to social climbing? It's . . . off.

And then there's Lillian. Lennon's grandmother would torch the whole place if she knew what was happening next door. She's hated those women for years—a special kind of grudge that comes with too many icy glares over shared property lines. The thought of them stepping any closer to her slice of peace? Yeah, that'd do it.

I let out a sigh, heavy enough to settle in my chest. "Yeah," I utter finally. "I'm heading out soon."

Benson studies me, like he's searching for a glimmer of hope, or maybe a miracle. "Any updates?" he asks.

"Nope. Same old dead ends." I shake my head.

But it's not just the dead ends. It's the way this case feels like every other one that dragged me to Cedar Cove in the first place. Messy, unfinished, leaving me with sleepless nights and the creeping sense I've missed something vital. The sort of cases that don't just haunt you—they move in, rearrange the furniture, and set up shop.

The chair groans under me as I lean back, staring out the window. My hands drift to the back of my neck, kneading at the knots that never seem to leave. "It's like solving a puzzle with half the pieces missing," I mutter. "Every lead fizzles out just when it feels like it's going somewhere. The deeper we dig, the messier it gets. None of it adds up."

Benson nods, but he doesn't stop watching me. "Any suspects?"

I huff out a bitter laugh. *Suspects.* I'm barely holding the pieces together—Lennon's parents, Rhett's case, and now this. It's like trying to outrun a storm you know is going to swallow you whole. And lately, that storm feels closer than ever, whispering doubts I've tried to ignore.

Lennon's face flashes in my mind, her eyes half a question, half a warning. She's pulling away. I sense it in every pause, every unspoken word. Especially after *that* night. The one I keep trying to bury, but it claws its way up. Raw, intense, the way I grabbed onto her like I was trying to win an invisible contest. And afterward . . . yeah, there was a shift. That look in her eyes, like she was reevaluating everything. Including me.

I mean, I get it. If the tables were turned—if I had been

close to someone who was a dead ringer for my first lover, personality quirks and all—I'd probably be questioning things too. Except Lennon isn't an idiot. She's a sharp journalist with a radar for bullshit, and I know she'll see through his act. At least, I *hope* she will.

"Not a single suspect. What's Dodger got to say to that?" Benson's question penetrates my focus. "Bet he wishes someone competent was on this case." He shrugs, as if that's supposed to soften the blow. "Might've actually gotten somewhere by now."

I don't miss the jab. Oh, I *could* fire back—something cutting enough to stick—but instead, I let my eyes roam over the chaos on the table: notes, reports, the parade of faces that have blurred together, and the dead-end leads we've been wading through for weeks. Still, no matter how hard I look, one name keeps bobbing to the surface. A name I can't ignore, no matter how much I'd like to.

"Just one," I finally admit.

Benson's eyebrows arch with the subtlety of a man expecting a front-row seat to a disaster. "Okay . . . " He drags the word out, leaning in. "Who?"

I hesitate, my gut twisting. Technically, Benson's on my team, but this feels . . . sticky.

"Mercer." His reply comes quick, his tone light enough to sound casual. "We're on the same side here."

Am I imagining that bite? Doubt it. This is Benson we're talking about. Sure, we grab beers and call it friendship, but the guy can't resist slipping in little digs—something about my job, my decisions, or the fact that he's from Cedar Cove and thinks it automatically makes him king of the department.

So, I let the name drop, just to see what happens. "Rem Prescott."

And oh, it works. Beautifully. Best thing about being a sheriff? Knowing how to read people like a damn open book

—even when the person is your deputy. Benson flinches, his jaw tightening. Then he jerks his head, way too fast, like he's trying to physically eject the idea from his skull.

He stiffens. "No way." A pause, then more forcefully: "No way it's Reed."

I stop cold. Narrow my eyes. Not just because the reaction is way too much, way too quick—but because *Reed*? How does Benson know Rem Prescott is Reed's real name? That detail's not in the standard updates.

Benson realizes he's overplayed his hand and tries to laugh it off, but the sound barely makes it past his throat. "Come on, Mercer. That guy wouldn't hurt a fly."

How would he know that?

I stand, measured and unhurried, keeping my eyes on the window. Main Street's dead, as usual—just shadows and a faint breeze pushing trash along the sidewalk. The clock ticks past 10:00 p.m.

"You know him?"

Benson hesitates, which is never a good sign. "Yeah, I know him. He's, uh . . . in town. Like you."

Believable enough, except it isn't. Benson couldn't sound more suspicious if he had a neon sign over his head blinking *LIAR*.

"Why do I feel like you're lying to me, Benson?" I say, but before I can finish the thought, I hear it—the faintest shuffle behind me.

My instincts scream.

My hand drifts toward my gun as I turn—

His gun. Pointed at me.

My brain stalls out. Benson. Gun. Me. None of this computes, but the icy knot in my stomach assures me it's all too real.

I raise my hands, palms out—casual, harmless. "Whoa. Benson, buddy. Let's not do anything . . . *permanent*."

His eyes are a mess—wide, wild, darting like he's seeing ghosts only he can name. The gun shakes in his hands so badly I'm afraid he'll fire out of sheer nervous energy.

This is Benson. The guy I've worked cases with; knocked back beers with. The man who once got way too passionate about defending pineapple on pizza at The Salty Slice. Now he's sweating, mumbling incoherently, and aiming a loaded weapon at me.

How did we get here?

His head snaps side to side, lips moving, rehearsing a script only he can hear. His eyes dart everywhere, desperate, like he's hoping a trapdoor might magically appear and swallow him whole.

"It wasn't Reed," he croaks. Then, softer, almost to himself: "It wasn't him."

I keep my face neutral, even as my gut twists. This isn't the guy who can destroy a burger the size of a hubcap and still make room for pie. The guy who lights up whenever he mentions his wife Jules. She is the center of his universe and he has said he is lucky she hasn't tossed him out of orbit.

"Okay." I keep my voice calm and controlled. Lies, both of them. "If it wasn't Reed, then who was it?"

His head shakes, slow and jerky. "I don't know. But if Dodger had handed me that title, I'd have it figured out by now."

I bite back a scathing reply, but then it clicks, all at once. My pulse drums in my ears. So that's what this is about.

"That should've been my job," Benson mutters, his jaw tight enough to crack. "My title. I worked my ass off for it." He huffs out a bitter laugh that has zero humor and a lot of venom.

"After the Harrington case . . . " He spits the name like it's poison, then kicks the chair next to him hard enough to send it skidding. "Fuck."

He's pacing now, edgy and restless, like the room's too small to contain whatever's eating him alive.

Out of the corner of my eye, Jeannie steps into view—our receptionist—clipboard in hand, probably here to let me know the night shift's clocking in. Just doing her job. Except she doesn't know. Doesn't *see*.

I don't shout. I don't move. My hands curl into fists as she comes closer, her brow furrowing at the scene in front of her. Then her eyes land on Benson and the gun in his hand. She stops cold, her hand flying to her mouth.

"No!" The word rips out of me. Her gaze snaps to mine, wide and startled.

Benson flinches, getting ready to turn toward her, and the gun follows like it's acting on instinct.

Ice floods my veins. I need his focus back on me. Right now.

"You worked the Harrington case?" I blurt. "And you didn't tell me because . . . ?"

Benson's attention shifts back to me, then to his pistol. He waves it around like a cocktail umbrella—casual as hell. All that nervous energy from earlier? Gone. Now he's cool, collected, and way too smooth for someone covering their tracks. "The case is cold. Nothing worth bringing up."

My brain slams on the brakes. Benson actually worked the Harrington case? He and Dodger both knew and said nothing? His name wasn't on a single scrap of paperwork. Not once. Is this why I got Rhett's case instead of him?

I keep my tone level. "So, you weren't assigned this case because of your history with similar ones?"

Benson shrugs. "Technically, I told Dodger I had it handled. But after the Harrington case, he wanted someone fresh, someone shiny," he mutters, scuffing his boot against the floor, "to see if they could crack it."

Translation: They didn't trust him to get it done. Great.

Now he's pissed because I have the case he wanted—and I'm chasing down a guy he's known and conveniently failed to mention.

Still, something about his tone won't let me drop it.

"How do you know Reed?" I press.

His jaw tightens, his grip on the gun keeping him anchored. For a moment, I believe he's about to tell me to shove off. Then, more quietly, he admits, "We grew up together. Same foster home. I know Reed. He wouldn't do something like this."

Same foster home?

The floor might as well drop out from under me. I pin him with a glare. "What the hell, Hale?" I take a step closer, arms crossed tight. "I've brought up Reed in, what, a dozen meetings? And it never occurred to you to mention you knew him? *Knew* him?"

Benson's head drops, shame spreading across his face. "I didn't think it mattered," he mutters.

Didn't matter? In this job, burying personal connections isn't just reckless—it's suicidal. My jaw tightens. "You should've told me! This isn't some casual oversight, Benson. It's about trust. It's about people's lives. If you've got ties to a suspect—"

"I don't!" he blurts, the words laced with panic. "I swear, Jack, I'm not involved! I didn't say anything because—"

"Because what?" I snap, cutting him off. My patience is in shreds, dangling by a thread. Everything I thought I knew is unraveling before my eyes.

The metal shakes in his hand. "I just . . . I didn't think . . ." He falters. "Reed's not involved."

"And how the hell do you know that?" My words slice through the room, sharp enough to sting. But underneath the anger, fear simmers—hot, choking, impossible to ignore. "How can you be so sure?"

He doesn't answer right away. His eyes drop to the floor. When he finally speaks, the words come out flat. Empty.

"It was me."

For a moment, I can't move, can't think—just stand there, reeling. The room tilts, and I have to remind myself to breathe.

Why would he say that? Why now? The question claws at my brain, but nothing makes sense. They grew up in the same foster home, sure, but that doesn't mean he owes Reed this. It doesn't mean he should . . .

My gaze snaps back to him. Too still. Too careful. But then it happens—his eyes dart away, just for a second. And when he speaks, his voice stumbles, a fracture in his perfect control.

He's lying.

But I can't call him on it. Not now. Not with the gun clutched in his grasp as though it were about to make the decisions.

I swallow hard, forcing my tone into something composed. "Okay, Benson. Just . . . tell me what happened. We'll figure it out."

My hands remain raised, palms open. Every muscle in my body is itching to grab my gun, but one wrong move and we'll be redecorating this room in arterial red. And not just mine.

"Tell me everything," I demand. He shakes his head. Of course he does. Benson's hiding something, but there's no time to untangle whatever web of lies he's caught in. My eyes scan him. His wild stare has a strange intensity, almost soft, like he actually cares about Reed. Or Rem. Or whoever the hell he's pretending to be today.

Jeannie's pinned against the far wall, one hand clamped over her mouth. Fuck.

The gun in Benson's hand wavers enough to make my chest feel like it's in a vise. His knuckles are bone-white, his breathing's shot to hell, and his eyes are broadcasting a big, flashing *Detour: Do Not Enter Mental Stability.* We've got seconds before this whole thing implodes.

"Benson," I force my words to stay calm even though I feel about as stable as a blown fuse. "Look at me. Just me."

His stare connects to mine, then back to the gun. Sweat trickles down his temple. He's circling the drain, and we're all circling it with him.

Jeannie stifles a whimper. Benson's head whips toward her like a dog catching a scent, and my stomach free falls.

"Benson!" I snap, louder this time. His head jerks toward me, startled. "Eyes on me. Not her. Me. You don't want to do this."

I take a careful step forward, hands raised. "Come on. Put it down. We'll work it out, okay? I promise."

His grip shifts, tightening, loosening, like he's testing the trigger for answers. Behind him, Jeannie looks ready to faint.

"Benson," I try again, quieter now. His breath hitches. There it is—the trace of something human in his eyes, fragile and uncertain. For a moment, he really sees it: the firearm in his hand, the sheer panic on Jeannie's face.

"He didn't do it." A shaky breath. "He . . . he came here to help the Callahans. That's all."

"Exactly. You're right." Another step forward, slow and deliberate. "He didn't do anything. And it's not too late. You can end this, Benson. Just put the gun down. Please."

The barrel trembles in his hand, and for a second, I think he might actually lower it. His grip slackens. His breathing steadies.

And then it all crumbles—panic to guilt, guilt to fear, fear to full-blown disaster. My gut twists. He's gone.

The doors explode open with a bang that could wake the dead, or at least make them reconsider staying that way. Uniforms flood the room, barking orders, weapons drawn.

Benson jolts like a puppet on a short string. The barrel jerks wildly, his finger twitching on the trigger.

There's no time to yell, no time to think. I lunge, slamming into him just as the gun goes off.

The shot cracks through the air. Jeanie screams, and Benson hits the floor beneath me, the gun skittering across the tiles.

The room erupts into chaos, but my world narrows to a single, fiery point just below my ribs. Pain flares, hot and searing. My legs give out, and the tiles rush up to meet me, their chill doing absolutely nothing to douse the blaze under my skin.

Someone's shouting—Jeannie, maybe? My coworkers? Everything sounds muffled, like I'm trapped in a fish tank. I press my hand to my side and feel something warm and slick.

Benson's still squirming beneath me, but my grip's slipping, and every twitch sends a spike of pain severe enough to make me see stars. I grit my teeth and hold on. Letting go isn't an option; someone else might not walk out of this room.

The shouting grows louder. Heavy boots stomp toward me, and then hands grab my shoulders, yanking me off Benson. The sudden shift sends a fresh wave of molten agony ripping through my side. I gasp, the edges of my vision swimming.

The last thing I catch before the darkness takes over is Jeannie's face, pale and frozen, her mouth forming my name in a scream I can't quite hear anymore.

CHAPTER 32

"Don't worry, Grams. I won't be long. Save me some tea," I say into the phone, forcing a calm tone I don't feel. My tires crunch to a stop outside Jack's house.

Two days ago, Grams came into my room—moving as fast as her knees would let her—breathless and wide-eyed. *"Jack was shot," she panted, the words tumbling out in a rush.*

My heart didn't just sink, it shattered. The thought of Jack, the man who'd barreled into my life like he belonged there, suddenly gone? I couldn't imagine it. And in that split second of blinding panic, something else clawed its way to the surface—raw and undeniable. I cared about him. More than I'd let myself believe. More than I wanted to.

Grams' voice echoes in my head, soft but unwavering: *"Honey, those tears? They're happy tears. To let someone fully into that big heart of yours? Oh, Lenny girl, what a beautiful thing that is."*

Beautiful? Maybe once. Before I knew better. Before love became synonymous with loss.

I squeeze my eyes shut, but it doesn't stop the memories

from gutting me open. Rhett's body. The hollow space my parents left behind. The way I swore, with every shattered piece of me, that love was a fluke—something rare and fleeting, never meant to come back around.

And yet, here it is, unraveling me from the inside out, waiting for me to say the words. To be brave enough to hand over the last scraps of my heart.

But then, two days ago, everything changed. That letter. The missing piece. The kind of thing you don't announce unless you're trying to set the world on fire. No, this had to go through Jack. He's the professional, the one with the authority, and the one who actually knows what to do with evidence that could close a case.

Naturally, my timing was terrible. Just as I was ready to talk to him, the Benson fiasco happened: a gun, a meltdown, and the station plunged into chaos. So, I waited. Patiently. Okay, not so patiently. Nervously. Freaking out, if we're being honest. Why Benson? Why pull a gun on Jack? Even Grams didn't have an answer, and if *she* doesn't know, no one does.

Jack's been lying low since it happened. Healing, as his doctor, his boss, and even Grams insisted. But it's been 48 hours. That's reasonable, right? How long is a girl supposed to wait before telling the guy who infuriates her, makes her laugh, and occasionally makes her want to shout that she's falling for him and, more importantly, that I found the key. Josie's letter isn't just some tear-stained confessional—it's a straight-up admission of murder.

I kill the engine, kick the car door open, and step into the cold. Slamming the door shut behind me, I march up the walkway, pointedly ignoring the nagging little voice whispering, *This is a terrible idea.*

The last time I was here, I told Jack we were nothing—just partners, just a case, just business. Lies, all of it.

I stop at the door, my hand hovering inches from the

wood. My pulse thrums in my throat. What if he's still angry? Then I remind myself: This case. I have the answer. This isn't about the past, this is about justice. A prickle of unease crawls up my neck. Someone's behind me.

"He's not home."

That voice. I turn, already bracing myself, and find Sawyer standing there, all smug smirk and unsettling proximity.

"Do you know where he went?" I ask, keeping my tone calm—because someone has to.

Sawyer shrugs like he couldn't care less, which is probably true. "Said something about Maple Harbor Hospital."

Maple Harbor Hospital. My stomach tightens. Jack just got out of *another* hospital. Most people might consider, I don't know, *resting* after that. Not Jack, apparently.

What really catches my attention is the location. Maple Harbor is over an hour away. What could he possibly be doing there? If anyone knows, it's Sawyer.

"Why is he there? Shouldn't he be resting?"

Sawyer just stares at me, then zips his lips with a smug little gesture, like he's auditioning for mime school. What is that even supposed to mean? But fine. I don't have the patience to unpack his cryptic nonsense right now.

Instead, I focus on the real question eating at me. Narrowing my eyes, I step closer, suspicion coiling tight in my chest. "Did you know about Benson?"

This time, I'm not backing down. I make sure to close the distance so he can't tower over me like some brooding gargoyle.

Sawyer's mouth shifts—just a twitch, more condescension than curiosity. "You're the journalist, aren't you?" He barely inflects, like he already knows the answer. "You tell me."

Just a deflection—classic. And honestly, that tells me more than if he'd actually bothered to confess.

He moves closer. Too close. His presence is heavy, pressing into my skin, and I flinch.

He mutters a curse under his breath. Then, just as quickly, he steps back and pivots like he decided I'm no longer worth his time.

And that's when I snap.

"Tell me!" The words tear out of me, harsh and louder than intended, but I'm past caring.

Sawyer freezes mid-step, sighs—a long, theatrical sound that manages to make *me* feel like the problem—and turns back around. His hands lift in mock surrender. "You want me to say it?"

His laugh comes low and bitter. He runs his fingers through his hair, tugging hard. He's seconds from unraveling. When he finally looks at me again, his eyes are pure venom.

"Fine," he spits. "I never liked you. Not from the start."

He steps closer, slow and controlled, hostility radiating off him in waves. "I told Jack he could do better."

Another step. His breath cuts through the cold night, close enough to feel, but I hold my ground.

"I told him digging into this case was a mistake," he continues. And then he's right there, inches from my face. "And I told him you were involved with Reed."

His words hit like a sudden blow, but I lock my knees and refuse to flinch.

"You knew exactly what you were doing to Jack," he growls. "And don't even try to pretend Reed didn't matter."

He slams his foot on the pavement, the crack of his boot echoing in the chill. His breath billows out in a puff of white, vanishing almost as quickly as his patience.

"FUCK!" The word rips out of him, jagged and unfiltered. "Do you even get it? Jack could've *died.*"

A pressure builds in my chest, but I keep my face

composed. Crying in front of Sawyer would only make this whole mess even more unbearable.

"I warned him not to take that case." Sawyer shakes his head. "Nothing good came out of those investigations. Josie's wasn't any different, but Jack? Jack couldn't leave it alone. Then you two got tangled up with those . . . *Wives of Cedar Cove.*" He spits the name like it's a bad taste he can't quite swallow. "Interviewing them one by one . . . that's when I told him to stop."

I want to ask why. Why stop in the middle of an investigation? Why them? But the words stick somewhere behind my ribs.

Sawyer's eyes pin me in place. "My mom was a part of that group. Did you know that? Did you dig that up in your little investigation?"

My mouth tries to do something—drop open, close, form a syllable—but it just . . . hangs there, useless. His mom? Jack had mentioned his parents were from Cedar once, but this? Was she in that photo? The Wives never claimed whose kids were whose, and we didn't push. Maybe we should have.

"Yeah. Thought so." Sawyer kicks at the frosted driveway, scattering shards of ice like a man trying to break something just for the satisfaction. "Those women—Mrs. Callahan— they have secrets worse than anything you could dream up. My mom knew that better than anyone. When my dad shipped out for the military and she followed him, that was her escape route."

He keeps kicking at the ground, his boot scuffing against the ice like it personally offended him. "Best thing that ever happened to us, if you ask me. I was just a kid when it all went down, but even then, I knew something wasn't right. Felt like the whole damn world was haunted back then. And now . . ." He exhales sharply, his breath fogging up in the cold. "Now it's like all of it's come back. Some things need to stay buried.

Dug up, sure, but then put back where you found them. And left the hell alone."

"I know," I manage, though it feels like my throat might give out. "That's why I'm still here."

Sawyer laughs, humorless. "Here? For what? To say you're sorry? Fix it all with some half-assed apology? What's next—group therapy?"

He drags a hand through his hair, his eyes narrowing with something hotter than anger. Anger's there, yeah, but there's something else underneath it. Something raw.

"He told me, Lennon." His chest rises hard, unsteady. "Jack told me what you said. And for all his goddamn bravado, all that 'too strong to feel' crap—it was a lie. You fucking shattered him."

Guilt churns low in my stomach. I can barely look at him. Sawyer's scary when he's like this, but isn't this what people do when they care? Protect, defend, rage on someone's behalf? Hell, I'd do the same for Maggie.

"I know." The words burst out of me. "I know, okay? It's not like I planned any of this—Jack, Benson, the case, Reed—none of it. I didn't want it to go this way. But it did."

He doesn't blink.

"Could you just . . . cut me some slack? I'm here, aren't I? Trying to figure this out. That's why I came."

As much as I want to scream in his face that I discovered the piece to put all this away, I keep my lips shut. Last thing he needs is to hear that, let alone giving him another excuse to tell me—again—to stay away from Jack and this case.

For a second, nothing happens. Just silence, thick and stretched so tight I half expect it to snap. Then his demeanor shifts—not by much, but enough. The anger doesn't disappear, but it ebbs, like it's too tired to stick around. What's left looks worn out. Frayed.

Sawyer exhales, long and slow, like he's swallowing something bitter. "I didn't know about Benson. We were tight. Buddies. I thought he had our backs."

For once, Sawyer doesn't look invincible. He doesn't look angry or dangerous, either. Just tired. Burned out. Betrayed. Somehow, that's worse.

"Guess we can't always trust the people we care about."

He turns before I'm able to respond, the door clicking shut behind him—not a slam, not dramatic. Just quiet. Final. And that hits harder than any shouting ever could.

I know exactly who he's talking about. I just wish he'd given me the chance to explain—him, or Jack.

CHAPTER 33

Another day. Another 24 hours of not losing my mind at Grams' place. A personal record, really. Do you know how hard it is to keep it all together? Spoiler: It's impossible.

Jack's silence isn't just quiet anymore—it's a freaking event. No calls. No texts. Not even a pity "K" in response to the message barrage I sent. I've officially become that person, the one who stares at his house from a parked car like an undercover detective. Except there's no movement, no mystery —just me, looking desperate.

Grams caught me mid-backslide this morning. Keys in hand, halfway through rehearsing an excuse to "accidentally" swing by Jack's place. She stopped me cold with that signature no-nonsense glare only grandmothers and overworked TSA agents can pull off. Said something about a snowstorm coming, like bad weather; her way of saving me from my own poor decisions.

I should tell her about Josie's letter, let her know what's eating me alive. But I won't. I already know how it'll go: She'll demand we drive it straight to the station, full speed ahead, no questions asked. And while I'd love her enthusiasm, this isn't her case—it's Jack's. And I need *him*. Problem is, while I'm stuck here, camped out on Grams' living room floor with a bombshell of information, Jack's off the radar. It's like the universe hit "pause" just to mess with me.

Until it didn't.

Because the next thing I know, there's Reed. Strolling into Callahans' house like nothing's happened.

I can't hold back any longer. I'm finished—finished waiting, finished second-guessing. This ends here and now.

CHAPTER 34

My heart's pounding as I shove the letter into my back pocket, cutting across the Callahans' yard. So much for patience. I tried—really.

The evening air stings. A couple of workers linger by the sheds, finishing up for the night. I scan the faces, doing my best not to look as unhinged as I feel. He's here. I know it. I saw him.

I stop outside the Callahans' kitchen, my chest tightening like my ribs are trying to crush my heart for sport. My phone buzzes in my pocket. Jack's name flashes on the screen.

Days of silence. And *now* he calls?

I think about answering. My thumb hovers over the green button, half hoping it might fix something. But no. I hit decline.

This isn't about Jack anymore.

It's about my parents.

About Josie.

About Rhett.

And—yeah—it's about me, too.

I slip my phone back into my jeans, and the breeze strikes me out of nowhere—cool, salty, like it knows exactly what I don't want to think about. I look up. And there he is.

Sandy blond hair, wind-tousled as usual.

Hazel-brown eyes that could drag you under without you even noticing.

That voice. Low and commanding, it wrapped around my thoughts, refusing to fade.

Time doesn't stop. It just trips over itself, wheezing long enough to knock the air out of my lungs.

For a second, I'm not here—I'm there. Back then. Back with him.

"Rocky, let's go!"

Rhett's voice carried the chaos of summer storms—loud, untamed, and electrifying. Barefoot in the doorway, ocean sprawled behind him, he grinned like a boy who never learned to take life seriously.

"Come on!" he yelled, his eyes hooking mine. That look—wild, maddening, unmistakable: Follow me.

And then he was grabbing my hands. His grip was warm, alive; insistent. Before I could think, we're moving. Through the doors. Across the deck. Like the universe might collapse if we stopped.

"Follow me, Len."

That name—hits me so damn hard that I'm suddenly running. The cold sand bites at my feet, the wind slaps my hair into my face, and snowflakes dance in the sky. It's chaos, but I don't care. I never cared. Not about the cold. Not about the breeze.

It's him.

The man who strolls into your life like a hurricane and leaves you wondering why you ever thought you were safe.

The man who unraveled me with less effort than it takes to breathe.

The man who knows every corner of you—the messy ones, the secret ones, the ones you pretend don't exist.

The man who makes you feel like you're flying and free-falling all at once, never bothering to warn you which it'll be.

The man who makes you believe he's your first great love —right up until you realize he's just a fever dream with good timing.

CHAPTER 35

Reed

She pulls her hands from mine, and the warmth vanishes like a flame snuffed out. What's left isn't just an ache—it's a void. She's pulling away.

Heat floods my veins, a simmering fury clawing its way to the surface. Not after everything. Not after years of careful planning, every step measured and precise. I'm no amateur stumbling in the dark.

The last time I held her, it was perfect. Just us under the stars, waves lapping at the shore, the world stripped down to that one perfect moment. She fit perfectly in my arms. It was inevitable. I had her. I had everything.

And now? The universe plays its cruel game. Perfection is always a trap, isn't it? Just when the stars align, there's always some bastard waiting to step out of the shadows and take it all away.

Screw the universe. Screw the bastard in the shadows, too.

Lennon is mine. She always has been—just like she was Rhett's before me. He always got everything first: the perfect family, the perfect house, the perfect love. He always won. But he's gone now. And I'm here. I was here first. It's my turn.

And Jack? Off chasing ghosts while the Callahan house crumbles around him. Her grams' fall? That was no coincidence. They all fucking deserve what's coming—every last one of them.

"Lennon, what's wrong?"

Stay calm. Stay steady. Don't let it show. My pulse, though? A wildfire, setting every nerve alight.

I take a stride forward, closing the distance between us. She steps back.

And just like that, the wildfire dies. Turns to ice.

Her words tremble. *Break.* "Why didn't you tell me?" I hear everything in them—the hurt, the betrayal, the weight of what comes next.

"Tell you what?"

She laughs, a brittle, hollow sound. Snowflakes cling to her hair and lashes, catching the light in what might've once been beautiful. Not now. Not with that bitterness slicing through the moment like broken glass.

"You're good." Her lips curve into something razor-edged. "I'll give you that."

I tilt my head, the picture of composure. Detached. Controlled. Never give anything away. "Tell you what, Lennon?"

"That Shannon Stiller is your mother?"

The words strike like a well-aimed dart—precise, smug, and all too familiar.

Of course. Jack.

Lennon gasps, spinning toward him. Her eyes flash, betraying that split-second instinct to run to him, to cling to him like some kind of lifeline. But she doesn't.

Smart move, Rocky.

Jack takes a step closer, his infuriating stillness practically radiating off him.

Oh, piss off.

This guy. Always sniffing around, wagging his tail, like the world's most persistent stray. He's the reason Lennon's looking at me like I'm a stranger, the reason everything's unraveling. And now, here he is, rolling in like some dollar-store knight in shining armor.

Yeah, no. Not happening.

Jack has no clue what it took to get here. What I've done. What I've scraped together out of nothing.

We might've been molded from the same dirt, but we're not the same species. He's soft. I'm not.

I step forward, boots sinking into the sand, fists curling like they've been waiting for this moment.

Jack lifts his hands, palms up. "I'm not here to cause trouble."

I cock my head, sizing him up. "You sure about that?" Another step. Slow. Deliberate. "Because I call bullshit." The sand crunches under my boots, loud enough to scrape at my nerves. "You've been sticking your nose where it doesn't belong, Jack."

His eyes lock onto mine, serene and unflinching.

The wind picks up, flinging snow into wild spirals—like the weather thinks it's part of the drama. Cute, but unnecessary. There's already enough tension in the air to cut with a dull spoon.

We stand there, a crooked triangle of fury, regret, and too much knotted history to untangle.

Lennon folds her arms against the cold, her shoulders trembling just enough to tempt me to move closer. I don't. I need to play this out right. Go accordingly and most importantly, because I love her.

More than Jack ever could.

More than Rhett ever did.

She's mine. Always has been. Even if her first mistake was thinking my little brother was worth her time.

Or is it little brother's?

CHAPTER 36

Lennon

What even is my life?

Jack knows Shannon was Reed's mom. Shannon—like *Wives of Cedar Cove* Shannon. Does he know about Mr. Callahan? About Rhett's dad? About . . . everything else?

My chest tightens, and for a split second, I think about the letter in my back pocket. It wasn't just the affairs she wrote about, though that would've been bad enough. It was the murders. One in particular.

It didn't take long for it all to click after that. The inexplicable pull toward Reed. That "meant to be" chemistry I had practically written sonnets about. Turns out, it wasn't magic. Wasn't fate. It was . . . biology.

I want to crawl out of my skin. Every moment I've ever spent with Reed replays in vivid detail, perfect in the worst way. He wasn't too good to be true. He was just too good at lying.

Before I can stop myself, the words are out: "Tell me something, Reed."

He flinches. Barely, but I catch it. His eyes soften,

reminding me of the way he used to make me forget every-thing. Yeah, well, not anymore.

"Tell me something real," I say, louder this time. The words scrape up my throat like rusted nails. "Just once." I shake my head, the weight of it all pressing down. "If you knew it was fake—everything—then why? Why me? Why my parents? Rhett?"

"Len . . ." His voice tiptoes around me, like I might shatter. Rhett used to do that, too. Back when I let myself believe it meant comfort.

Funny thing about comfort—it never lasts.

The snow's coming down harder now, sticking to my hair, sliding icy streaks down my neck like nature's way of saying *buck up*. Except it doesn't sting as much as everything else. I'm hollowed out, unraveling thread by thread, and honestly, I'm not sure there's enough left to fix. My vision blurs, though whether it's from tears or the cold, it doesn't make a difference.

The truth isn't just harsh—it's surgical. Precise. Cruel.

I reach for the letter in my back pocket, and the moment I move, I see it: Reed's face drains white, his eyes narrow to slits, and he looks at me like he's calculating all the ways this could go sideways. Guilty people always do.

I know it was him. Of course, it was him. Those black bags at the Callahan house didn't move themselves, and Reed sure didn't have a problem coming and going from their place as their contractor. Although, the Callahans never seeing Reed really shows how clever this man truly is.

I can feel Jack staring at me, yet I keep my focus on Reed —or should I say, "Rem?"

His brow shoots up, surprise breaking through his usual smugness. Clever bastard. Should've thought twice before messing with someone whose bloodline runs deep with investigative journalists. Turns out, he wasn't as good at covering his tracks as he thought.

"Yeah, that's what I thought." I click my tongue. "Care to explain this?" I wave the letter in the air, snowflakes dusting its edges. Not that I'm worried—pictures were taken, and the file's already sitting cozy at the police station. First rule of journalism: Keep the evidence safe. Especially when it ties back to my parents' murder. And Rhett's.

Reed, or Rem, whatever he's calling himself these days, shrugs. "What's it look like? A piece of paper."

I laugh. Not a chuckle. A full-on laugh. It's so loud I catch Jack shifting uncomfortably in my peripheral vision. "A piece of paper? Really?" I take a step forward, not too close, but close enough to knock Reed off balance. "Don't be stupid, Reed. Or maybe I should call you Rem? Which one do you prefer?"

He doesn't answer, just stands there, stiff as a board. Typical. I've dealt with guys like him before—always so composed until they're not. The mask never holds. It always cracks. And when it does? Game over.

"Were you planning on telling me?" I demand. "What was the plan, huh? We'd live in some happy fairytale? I'd fall head over heels for you. We'd get a white picket fence and two kids?" I snort, loud and unapologetic. "Funny thing is, for about five seconds, I thought we had something. That you made me feel—what's the word—*special*?" I hold the letter up above me. "But no, it wasn't love. It was revenge."

I turn away, unable to look at him any longer. The man doesn't even flinch, doesn't look remotely guilty. Figures. When I spin back around, I step closer, daring him to move. "This letter doesn't spell out your grand plan, not exactly, but it tells me enough."

He moves his head—fast, frantic.

I clench my fists. Breathe. "How could you kill them all?"

He still doesn't answer. Probably still thinks he's the victim here. What was the plan? Come in, charm everyone, and destroy the people who had the life he wanted?

"You don't understand!" he roars, loud enough to make me flinch. He starts pacing like a caged animal before turning sharply in my direction. Jack steps forward, but Reed holds out a hand, and I shake my head at Jack. *I'm fine.*

I have Josie's letter—damning and ironclad—to put this guy away for life. But there's a part of me, a reckless, curious part, that needs to hear it from his mouth. Those lips. God, those lips. The ones I kissed. The ones that made my heart think it was auditioning for Cirque du Soleil.

"They took my fucking *life*!" His chest heaves, the pressure of years pressing down on each breath. "My life started with an affair," he spits out, each syllable like a knife. "An affair they buried by shipping my mom off to have me like I was some goddamn inconvenience. Cedar Cove's golden family couldn't let their bastard ruin the view."

He laughs, splintered and jagged.

"So she left me," he continues, "And the foster nurse? Didn't give a shit. Just shoved me around like a broken toy nobody wanted." His tone turns bitter. "I had nothing. No parents. No family. Not even one goddamn friend. Nobody cared about me. Not once."

Reed paces again, slow and uneven, snow falling gently around him as if mocking the storm rolling off his shoulders. His eyes are wild, haunted by memories that even a river of blood couldn't drown.

"And Rhett?" He hurls the name, his lip curling. "Rhett got everything. The girl. A family. A future. A place to belong." His knuckles tighten around the gun, the tendons in his hand standing out like pale wires. "And me? I got nothing. Not even a chance."

"What does this have to do with me? My parents never knew you?"

"Oh, but they did." Reed nods toward the letter. "Your dear old mother—she figured it out. Found out I was adopted, that I came from an affair. It's why she never got into that precious little wives' circle of hers. Guess she dug a little too deep." His laugh sharpens, brittle as ice. "A journalist with a nose for secrets? Yeah, that wasn't going to work for me."

He steps closer, his shadow stretching long and dark. "And I couldn't have that, now could I, *Rocky*?"

My breath stutters, my pulse hammering in my ears. He knows Rhett's nickname. How? When?

He doesn't stop. Keeps moving like this is just another stroll in the snow. Meanwhile, my mind spirals, snagging on the nickname, the scope of his plan, and the horrifying realization: My parents died because they were just doing their job.

"Lennon. Hey." Jack's boots crunch closer. His warmth reaches me before his touch. "Focus on me, baby. Just focus, okay?"

I barely register his words before I hear it.

Click.

The world halts. Ice floods my veins, rooting me to the spot.

Reed has a gun.

Jack freezes mid-step, his hands lifting, palms out. "Easy," he says, but I can hear the shakiness to it.

My breath stumbles as fear crashes over me in waves. Run. Scream. Do something. But I can't move. My body's locked, my brain's splintered, and panic digs in like a knife. Relentless.

"You didn't let me finish," Reed snaps. "Now, where was I?" He taps the gun against his chin. "Ah, yes. Your mother. Sure, she figured out the affair—but it wasn't until *years* later that I kept digging, kept planning, kept uncovering."

He pauses, his lips twisting into a grin that doesn't reach

his eyes. "Like how Josie couldn't be alive if she knew about Rhett's murder, right? Yeah, I probably could've handled that one better." He shrugs. "But you already knew that, didn't you? It's all in that damn letter."

My heart stutters as he draws near. Then he stops abruptly, tilting his head as if savoring a punchline only he can hear. "Oh, and I found something else, too . . . "

He swings the gun toward Jack.

Jack's mask of calm falters, just for a second, and the panic in his eyes wrenches something deep in my chest.

"Why don't we put the gun down, hmm?" My words hushed, coaxing. My pulse thunders in my ears, but I keep my tone composed, my movements slow. "We don't need that, do we? We can figure this out. Just you and me."

Jack's presence is a quiet weight at my back. I give the smallest shake of my head. *Stay back. Don't make this worse.*

Reed's hands tremble, the gun wobbling like it's suddenly too heavy for him. Slowly, it dips, the barrel pointing uselessly at the sand by my feet. His fingers stay hooked around the grip, but his hold is slipping.

Good. Keep it there.

"Jacky-boy," Reed purrs, tilting his head. "Did you ever tell them about Mommy and Daddy?"

Jack's jaw tightens, his shoulders locking up.

Reed whips his attention to me, his eyes bright with something unhinged. "Go on, Jack," he croons, sing-song and syrupy with mockery. "Tell her."

Jack doesn't move. Doesn't speak. The silence stretches thin and tight.

Reed's knuckles go white around the gun. "Tell her that you and me, Jack—we share a father."

CHAPTER 37

Jack

He's lying. No way do I share blood with this man.

This man, who pulls strings like the world's his own twisted puppet show.

A manipulator. A murderer.

Oh, he thinks he's clever. Thinks I don't see the cracks forming. Sure, I don't have a smoking gun yet—no file stamped CONFIDENTIAL—but his web of lies is unraveling, one thread at a time. And Lennon? She's standing directly in the midst of it.

Exactly where I told her not to be. Weeks ago, I begged her to step off this runaway train. She didn't. And now?

Now it's too late.

"M-Mr. Callahan—" Lennon chokes on the rest, barely pushing out, "is your dad?" Her shoulders jolt, and then the tears come, fast and unstoppable.

My hands curl into fists. God, I want to pull her out of this mess. Hold her, shield her, fix it. But Reed's standing there. Watching. Smirking.

"Lennon, look at me," I murmur.

She doesn't. Just shakes her head, biting her lip so hard I'm half-convinced she's about to draw blood.

I step toward her—slowly, carefully.

And then I feel it.

Cold, hard metal slamming into my chest, knocking the air from my lungs.

"DON'T!" Lennon's scream pierces through the chaos.

Reed doesn't. He just smiles. Like a man who knows the game is already his.

"He's lying, Lennon."

Reed cocks his head, calm as a coiled viper. The gun doesn't waver. "Lying? Me? Why would I bother?"

The barrel digs harder into my chest, my pulse spiking into full-blown panic. In less than a week, I've faced two guns and a battered body—but I didn't stop then, and I'm damn sure not stopping now. Apparently, neither is he.

Reed, ever the showman, steps back. Casual, like this is all just a minor chore on his to-do list. He holsters the gun with an almost bored precision, then twirls it.

Snow clings to the barrel as he paces, boots grinding against the sand. "You know," he says, almost conversational, "I've been waiting for this moment for a long time."

Reed stops, letting the silence stretch just long enough. "I thought about keeping it simple. Just walking in, dropping the truth like a bomb, and watching everyone scramble through the wreckage." His grin splits wide, all teeth. "But where's the fun in that?"

His eyes lock onto mine, stripped of smirks or flair. What's left is raw—splintered and bitter.

"They deserved this. Every single one of them. For what they did to me. For what Rhett never had to suffer."

I don't bother answering. What's the point? The air's too heavy to carry words. This isn't a man falling apart; this is a man who's spent years knitting his pain into something bulletproof.

Reed studies me, his expression flickering, and for the first time, I see it: He's not just furious—he's hollow. There's an ache in his eyes that doesn't go away; you carry until it becomes the only thing that feels real.

"They never told you, did they?" His tone shifts, softening like a lull before a punch. "What she did. What your mother Melanie did."

Melanie? My mother? The woman who always remembers my favorite desserts? Who makes a point of asking about my job like she actually cares?

"Shannon had me first." Reed doesn't blink. "They sent her away to Maple Harbor, made sure no one here ever knew. And when it was over, she left me at the hospital. Just walked away. Didn't even look back. And then? She came home. Built a new life, like I was never part of the old one."

The words hit hard, but I know this train wreck doesn't start—or stop—with Shannon. Mrs. Callahan's fingerprints are all over it. That woman doesn't so much as sneeze without an agenda. Her husband's affair with Shannon? Just the first domino. Now she's bulldozing the Callahan estate, erasing history, like it's an embarrassing typo in her perfect life story.

And Melanie? She's been around me for years. Smiling. Chatting. Playing friendly, like she's got nothing to hide. Turns out she's my mother. *My actual biological mother.* The woman I've been chasing for years has been right here the whole time, acting like I'm just some random man in Cedar Cove. My chest tightens, a mix of anger and disbelief. I don't know what stings worse: The betrayal or the fact that she was so damn good at it.

Lennon's sobs start up again, and my chest splinters apart with every sound.

"You have to believe me, Lennon. I didn't know," I say,

quieter now, as if speaking softly might make this less painful. "You knew I only took Rhett's case because I was looking for my birth parents."

She moves her head—frantic, desperate.

Before she can say anything, Reed steps forward, gun raised, smirk fixed in place like he's practiced it in the mirror. Probably has.

"Touching little heart-to-heart," he drawls, "but I'm kind of on the clock here, and closure's not really my style."

So what? That's his endgame? He's here to shut me up, one way or another.

The words tumble out. "You gonna kill me?"

He shrugs. "Can't say it hasn't crossed my mind. Wasn't exactly a struggle with our other brother."

Behind me, Lennon lets out a gasp, followed by another sob that cracks me in half. I peek back at her. She's pale; lips trembling, tears streaking through the wet mess of snow melting on her cheeks. She's gripping her arms like sheer willpower might keep her from breaking apart.

"Lennon, breathe," I say. "In and out, baby."

She rocks in place, sucking in shallow breaths like life itself might give up on her. And honestly? Looking at her, it's hard not to feel like the whole world might be caving in.

Reed's smirk doesn't budge. Bastard.

"Fuck this," I mutter, stepping into the barrel like I've got nothing to lose. His eyebrows twitch—caught off guard—but he's a second too slow.

Lennon slams into me, arms locked tight around my waist. We collapse on the sand in a heap, the chill biting into my back, but all I feel is her trembling.

"It's okay, Lennon," I murmur, rubbing lazy circles on her back. "You're good. I've got you."

Her fingers twist into my jacket, clinging as if it's her last lifeline. Bit by bit, her breathing evens out, the sobs shrinking to little gasps. I brush some snow from her hair, the ice melting against my palm.

But the second she's steady, my attention snaps back to Reed. The anger surges, burning through the cold.

"What's the plan, Reed?" I ask. "Kill us all and call it a day? That's your big move? Does it fix anything? Rewrite the ending?"

His glare sharpens, but there's a crack in it now. A trace of something—hesitation, doubt.

"Benson?" I toss out his name like a lifeline, though I'm pretty sure it'll sink.

He snorts, "That fool? Benson doesn't know half of it. Doesn't have a clue what I've done. What I've been building for years." He grins, crooked and mean. "And the best part? He'd still do whatever I asked. Just like you will. Isn't that right, Jack?"

My teeth ache from how hard I'm clenching them, but I swallow the retort clawing its way up my throat. One wrong word and this goes sideways fast.

I shift, pulling Lennon closer, wrapping her up, and Reed's already swinging. She doesn't need to see this—or hear it.

"What do you want?" I grind the words out.

Reed tilts his head, tapping the barrel of the gun against his chin like. "What do I want?" he yells. "I want the life I *deserved*. But since that's not happening, I'll settle for watching the people who made my life hell get what they've earned."

Lennon goes rigid for a second, then crumples. Her sobs tear out of her, raw and relentless.

"It's okay," I murmur into her ear, holding her tighter. "I'm here. I've got you." Her tears soak through my shirt, and it kills me that this—*this*—is all I can do.

I snap my glare back to Reed. "You think killing us is going to fix this?" I say, dragging his attention back to me. "You think it'll balance the scales? You've spent your whole life running from what they did to you. Don't let them win by turning you into exactly what they wanted you to believe you were—nothing."

In a flash, something cracks in him. His hand trembles, the gun slipping just enough to make me want to believe. But it's not enough. He's still dangling over the edge, too stubborn—or too far gone—to grab hold.

"You said Rhett had everything," I press, leaning into that tiny crack like my life depends on it. "But he didn't. He was hiding, just like you were. Maybe worse."

Reed's face twists, his rage curling like smoke—but there's something else now. Doubt. It's slipping. I just have to keep tugging.

"This isn't on Rhett," I state the fact. "He didn't even know you existed. You blame him because it's easier than facing the truth. But killing him? Killing us? That won't fix anything. It won't undo what they did to you or to me. It'll just leave you exactly where you've always been—alone."

His body trembles, caught between holding it together and falling apart. For a second, I think I've reached him, that *just maybe* he'll lower the gun.

His eyes harden, and a bitter smile creeps across his face, one that knows it's already lost but refuses to go down alone. "You really think this ends with me walking away?"

The gun swings toward Lennon.

The shot splits the air.

"NO!" I lunge without thinking, instinct yanking me forward.

The world detonates.

I slam into Reed, my shoulder driving into his chest like I'm trying to break through stone. The gun fires again, followed by Lennon's scream—raw and fractured.

We hit the ground hard, snow exploding around us. Reed's fists are on me in an instant, a blur of knuckles and fury. I barely register the blows. My brain is stuck, looping the same word on repeat: Lennon. Lennon. Lennon. Is she okay? Is she still breathing?

We roll through the snow, the cold clawing at my skin. But none of that matters—my world narrows down to the gun. I grab Reed's wrist and twist hard enough to make something snap. He yelps, his grip loosening enough for me to snatch the weapon and hurl it into the snow, where it disappears.

Reed bucks underneath me, but I slam his shoulders into the sand and pin him there. We're both wheezing like broken accordions, white puffs of breath fogging the frigid air.

"Stop," I bark, adrenaline making my voice shake. "It's over, Reed. Game over. Take a bow."

And, shockingly, he does. He just lies there, staring up at the snow swirling down like some kind of poetic cosmic joke, chest heaving. For a moment, all I can hear is the wind howling. Then I catch it—Lennon. She's coughing, gasping. *Alive.*

Relief hits me so hard I almost fall over. When I turn around, she's on her knees a few feet away, clutching her chest and wheezing. No blood. No bullet hole. Still breathing.

The bullet missed.

Thank God.

In the distance, sirens start wailing. Shadows are moving closer—coworkers, my boss, the whole backup crew.

Help is finally here.

EPILOGUE

Lennon

RECKONING DAY
ONE YEAR LATER

"Baby, you almost ready?" Jack calls out from the bedroom—our bedroom now.

"Almost!" I call back, eyeing myself in the mirror one last time. White bodysuit, black pants, black jacket, pearl earrings, black heels. Tasteful. Professional. Deadly, if necessary. The only thing that really pops is Mom's blue beret pinned in my hair. She'd want to be part of this day—though she'd probably have opinions about the outfit.

Reckoning Day.

Justice never tasted so sweet. The relief? Overwhelming, like finally exhaling after holding your breath for a year. Hard to believe it's almost over. I shut my eyes and take a long, slow breath, trying to keep my pulse steady. Last night, sleep was a lost cause until Jack decided to . . . *help.* Thoroughly. Even then, I still woke up early, restless and wide-eyed, so I buried myself in working on a new case.

Nothing says "closure" like diving into the next battle. But this battle? It was nothing like the ones I'm used to. Not the missing persons, the gruesome murders, or the twisted mysteries I typically thrive on. No, this was personal. Too personal.

Over the past year, I've learned more about myself than I ever wanted to. Turns out, my obsession with solving other people's tragedies wasn't entirely altruistic—it was my way of stitching up my own wounds. Screwed up, sure, but it worked. Sort of. Until Cedar Cove happened.

That town forced me to face everything I'd been running from: grief, guilt, and maybe the scariest thing of all—love. When Rem was arrested and the dust started to settle, Jack and I needed time. Time to process the insanity of it all: Jack uncovering the truth about his birth parents, me learning that the man who killed my parents—and Rhett—was someone I'd once been drawn to. Benson got arrested for teaming up with a murderer and, oh yeah, shooting Jack. The Crest didn't exist because Mrs. Callahan had been busy orchestrating cover-ups, bribing people like Shannon and Melanie to stay quiet, which got her booted from the Wives of Cedar Cove.

Yeah. Layer upon layer of messed up.

I grieved. I healed. I took care of Grams. Finally convincing her to try a residence home. She didn't hate it, but I couldn't leave her there. Not after everything. So, once we sold her house, I moved her out and back in with me. Well, technically, with *us*. After convincing Maggie I was truly okay after the whole ordeal, Jack and I bought a house together— our own little slice of Cedar Cove. Coming back felt like picking up right where we left off, as if no time had passed. And Jack? He was worth the risk, even if trusting someone with my whole heart had felt impossible at first. Losing the people I loved most without warning had left scars, but when

I let Jack in, really let him in, I knew. This man was it. My forever.

And yes, I may have "accidentally" almost run him over with my SUV when I came back into town. Again. In true Jack fashion, he just laughed and picked me up like some scene out of a Hallmark movie—snow falling, the whole town clapping. Swoon-worthy and ridiculous, but I loved every second of it.

"What's my beautiful girl thinking about, hmm?" His hands slide around my waist, palms warm and steady against my stomach.

Butterflies. Always butterflies with him.

I don't answer right away. Just being close to him, with his arms around me, feels like stepping into a warm bath after a storm. Jack rests his chin on my head, then presses a soft kiss there.

"You know I'll be there with you, right?" he murmurs.

I hum a quiet "mhm," and I feel him smile against my hair. When I finally look up, I meet those impossibly blue eyes of his. They could make any woman's heart stutter but, for me, they feel like home.

And those arms of his? They're safety. Strength. Love.

"Len," he told me, "these arms? They'll always protect you."

He meant it, too. When my world had crumbled and I didn't know how to piece myself back together, Jack didn't rush me. He just waited, patient and steady, until I was ready.

Now, those same arms pull me tighter, anchoring me. He squeezes my hand before turning me to face him, tilting my chin up with a finger. "Let's get you some closure."

I nod, swallowing down the emotions bubbling to the surface. Later. I can deal with those later. Jack leans in, brushing his lips against mine—a kiss that starts gentle but deepens in the way only Jack can. Because if there's one thing I'm still learning about this man, it's that he's a master of balance. He can go from an old-school gentleman, opening doors and using words like *darlin'*, to the guy who pins me against the shower wall to remind me exactly how good he is with his hands.

This kiss? Somewhere in between. Enough to leave me breathless, but not enough to ruin my makeup. Not yet, anyway.

He takes my hand, leading me into the kitchen. Our house isn't huge—it doesn't need to be. It's just the right size for the three of us. Honestly, I was surprised Jack was okay with Grams moving in, but then again, it's Jack.

"How was your meeting with . . . " I trail off, letting him fill in the blank.

"It was . . . " He hesitates, then nods. "It'll take time, but I think we're getting somewhere. I've got a good feeling."

I smile because I know how much this means to him. These cautious meetups with his birth mother, Melanie, are a big step. At first, we were both in shock, but Melanie? She's sweet. She's been quietly loving Jack from a distance for years —always bringing cookies or desserts to the station, trying to connect in her own way. It's more than I can say for Mr. Callahan, who Jack has no interest in building a relationship with. I can't blame him. Still, it's wild to think that Rhett, Rem, and Jack all share the same father.

Sometimes I wonder if that's why I was drawn to them in different ways—shared DNA and all—but it's not. Jack is who he is. Just like Rhett was. Just like Rem . . . Well. Rem is another story.

I give Jack another kiss, just as Grams joins us. Then, together, we pile into Jack's Explorer and head for the courthouse. Closure is waiting.

For someone who's only been inside a courthouse once—when my grandma got custody of me after my parents were murdered—it still manages to claw under my skin in the same eerie way. The feeling settles in my bones and sends goosebumps crawling across my arms, like the building knows what it's seen and isn't about to let me forget.

"Just a couple of hours, then we're outta here," Jack states, his hand pressing lightly on my lower back. It's meant to reassure me, but mostly it just reminds me I'm here. One of the police officers gestures for us to follow, leading us to the room where the trial will take place.

When Rem was arrested that night on the beach, we'd been warned it could take months—or even a year—before the court made a decision. I'd been furious at first, but I understood. Justice is slow, especially when it involves taking down someone as carefully corrupt as him. After all, we'd waited years just to uncover the truth. What was a little longer?

Still, a shiver runs through me at the thought of last year. Rem, Reed, Rhett—whatever version of him I'd let myself believe in. I'd wanted him to be something good so badly that I'd stitched together pieces of old memories, pretending the man I was seeing was someone else entirely. But in the end, the mask slipped, and all I was left with was the reality of who he really was. And it wasn't magical. It wasn't even close.

"Right this way." The police officer leads us to the elevator. We cram in, and a few seconds later, we're stepping off on the third floor, trailing after him in silence. Even Grams keeps up with our pace, which is saying something. She's not exactly spry these days, though her weekly senior fitness class has helped with the limp she's had since . . . well, the one Rem so cleverly inflicted.

My heels click against the polished floor as we walk, the sound echoing faintly in the open space. The courthouse is massive—four stories tall, with grand wooden staircases and iron railings that circle around the floors. If you look down from the top, you can see the whole place, like some elaborate ant farm filled with lawyers, cops, and people who wish they were anywhere else.

"Just a moment. I'll let you know when to come in," the officer says, stopping us outside a pair of heavy doors.

Jack gives him a quick nod and immediately checks his phone. He's still technically on call, even though we're hours from home, here in the only courthouse close enough to handle this mess. Massachusetts isn't exactly convenient, but it's where Rem's been serving his time.

"Breathe, Lenny girl," Grams murmurs, squeezing my hand.

I do, but it doesn't help much. The moment the double doors creak open, I feel it—a breeze, soft and cool. My hair shifts slightly, and for a moment, it's almost cinematic.

Then I see him.

My stomach drops. This is the man who whispered every perfect lie I wanted to believe, the man I trusted with parts of myself I didn't even know how to share. The same man who murdered my parents, Rhett, and Josie in cold blood.

He's thinner now—too thin, with shoulders that seem angular, and dull, lifeless eyes that stare at nothing. His hair is longer, brushing past his shoulders, and the handcuffs around his wrists clink faintly as he moves. For one fleeting moment, I almost feel sorry for him. But the anger burns that away quickly—hot, raw, and impossible to ignore.

Angry. Hurt. Embarrassed.

That's how he makes me feel, all at once. And yet, the room still manages to spin around him, like he's the center of the universe.

"The more you let him see you like this, the more he's going to feed on it, baby," Jack whispers, his breath warm against my ear.

He's right, of course. That's exactly the type of man Rem is. He thrives on cracks in the armor. Knowing that doesn't make it any easier, though.

Jack's hand slides around my waist, grounding me. I close my eyes for a moment, letting myself lean into the quiet strength he offers. These arms have always been my shelter, and I know they'll keep me from falling apart today, no matter what.

We start moving, Jack steering us forward with a gentle pressure, and I force my eyes to stay anywhere but on Reed. Instead, I take in the courtroom; the room is designed to feel both oppressive and underwhelming. Stiff wooden benches line the gallery, polished to a shine that probably took more effort than they were worth. Overhead, fluorescent lights buzz faintly, casting their unforgiving glare over every scratch, smudge, and regret the place has soaked up over the years.

At the front of the room, the judge's bench looms on a raised platform. The jury box sits empty to the left. The walls are painted a shade of off-white.

There's a smell, too—cleaning solution, fighting a losing battle against something metallic and vaguely sour. If dread had a scent, this would be it: Equal parts bleach and bad decisions.

Jack's hand tightens at my waist as we reach the defense table. I sit, the chair scraping against the floor with all the grace of nails on a chalkboard.

The noise ricochets in the silence, and in an instant, it feels like the whole room inhales. Just a few feet away sits Rem. The man who broke so much. I don't look at him. I won't.

The courtroom's tension shifts as the door to the judge's chambers opens. Judge Masters appears, robe billowing slightly in a way that suggests he's given some thought to his entrances. He takes his seat behind the massive bench, moving like a captain taking the helm of a very doomed ship. His face reveals nothing.

"All rise," the bailiff announces, and the room complies with the awkward creaks and shuffles of people who are collectively unsure whether they're standing out of respect or sheer fear. Jack brushes my elbow as if I need the reminder, but I'm already on my feet, moving on autopilot.

Judge Masters nods, and we all sit, the thunk of bodies hitting wooden benches oddly synchronized. The trial begins. The charges are read—four counts of first-degree murder. Each word lands with precision, clean and clinical. My parents. My best friend. The anchors of my life, now reduced to legalese.

Reed sits at the defense table, cool as stone. The suit he's wearing probably costs more than my car, but somehow it just makes him look like a well-dressed monster. If there's an award for Most Punchable Face, he'd be giving an acceptance speech right now. Beside me, Jack tenses. He's good at hiding his emotions—just not from me. Not here.

"Mr. Rensen," Judge Masters says, addressing Rem's lawyer, a man with slicked-back hair and a smile so cutting it could double as a weapon. "You may proceed with your opening statement."

Jack's hand brushes mine—a quiet reminder to breathe. On my other side, Grams sits ramrod straight, gripping her purse like it's the only thing keeping her tethered to the ground. For a woman who once threatened to ground me for slouching at the dinner table, she looks seconds away from launching herself across the courtroom. Honestly, I wouldn't stop her.

Rem's lawyer starts droning, spinning a tragic tale about his client—a misunderstood man, cruelly swept up in unfortunate circumstances. I grit my teeth. Each word scrapes against me like sandpaper, and every glance at Rem's blank demeanor stokes a fire I can't let show.

The prosecution rises at last. The district attorney—a woman with cheekbones sharp enough to open cans—strides forward and gets to work. Her tone is measured and precise. Bit by bit, she dismantles the defense's excuses, cutting through the nonsense with surgical efficiency.

Then come the witnesses.

Grams takes the stand first. She holds herself together, but I hear the tremor beneath her words. She talks about the grief, about how losing them tore everything apart. The whole courtroom is hanging on her testimony, but I can't look at her. If I do, I might break, too.

When it's my turn, the room closes in and stretches out at the same time. Cavernous and suffocating. The jury watches, waiting. Judging. Reed watches too, but I don't give him the satisfaction of meeting his gaze. Instead, I focus on the DA's questions, keeping my answers measured and composed, even as the memories claw at the edges of my mind. My parents. My best friend. Their faces, their laughter, all frozen in amber.

I talk because I have to. Because it's all I can do for them now.

When I finally step down, my legs feel like rubber. Jack's hand finds mine as soon as I sit.

The trial barrels forward. The judge listens, his face carved from stone, though you can almost hear the wheels turning behind those tired eyes. The jury files out to deliberate, and the room falls into an uneasy silence. Everyone seems to be holding their breath, waiting for the world to tilt one way or the other.

And then they're back. Too soon and not soon enough.

The verdict is read: Four counts of first-degree murder. Guilty.

My breath rushes out. After all this time, the weight eases, just enough for me to breathe again. Jack squeezes my hand, and when I look at him, his eyes soften.

Beside me, Grams makes a sound that's somewhere between a sob and a sigh, like she can't decide if she's heart-broken or relieved. She dabs her eyes with a tissue, but her spine stays upright. Nothing's breaking her today.

Rem is led away in handcuffs. His indifferent mask cracks for just a second as the weight of reality hits him. I don't watch him go with triumph, just a quiet, steady satisfaction. Finally, the past isn't mine alone to carry.

Jack leans in, his breath warm against my ear. "It's over."

I nod. It's not, of course. Not really. But for now—for this fleeting moment—it's enough.

We shuffle out of the courtroom, Jack grabbing my hand as we pass through the heavy courthouse doors. Every step feels lighter.

Grams wipes at her tears and emits a quick exhale. "Well. That was something, wasn't it?"

I tug her into my side and kiss the top of her head. "You can say that again, Grams."

She hugs me, then disappears into the crowd, spotting someone she knows. It buys Jack and me a few quiet moments as we step out into the winter air.

Snow drifts down. The cold bites, but it's bearable. For once, the sight of the snow doesn't stir memories of that night with Rem. I can still enjoy this. I just have to remind myself where I am now, and who I'm with.

Jack moves closer, standing below me on the courthouse steps. He looks up and grins, the real, dimpled grin that always gets me.

"There she is," he says, brushing his thumb over my cheek.

I smile back. He steps up, closing the space between us until we're chest to chest.

"It's me and you against the world now, baby."

I bite my lip to keep from teasing him, but I catch the flicker of nerves in his eyes. He's serious, and for once, I don't feel the need to undercut it.

"Tell me something, Lennon," he whispers.

I take a deep breath, the words I've been holding onto for weeks rising to the surface. I step up another stair so we're eye level, then grab his hand and guide it to my stomach.

His brows furrow, his eyes darting between my face and where his hand rests. "Well, I love you," I say with a grin.

He snorts. "I know that, baby."

"I just like saying it," I tease. Then I add, quieter, "It's not just the two of us against the world anymore."

His eyes widen, and for a second, he stares at me, unblinking. Then his expression softens. "Wait. Are you serious?"

I laugh, shaky and nervous, but nod. His hand stays on my belly, and he lets out a whoop before picking me up and spinning me.

"Jack! Put me down!"

He stops abruptly, setting me back on the step like I'm made of glass. His face shifts to full-blown panic. "Shit. Did I just hurt it?"

I take his hand and press it back to my stomach. "Jack, it's the size of a seed. You're fine. No need to be gentle—yet."

Relief floods his face, quickly replaced by his signature smirk.

I laugh. "You sure about this?"

Jack nods so fast it's a miracle his head doesn't pop off. "Lennon, if you'd told me the day you nearly ran me over with your SUV to put a baby in you, I would've. No questions asked."

I shake my head, but he's not wrong. Honestly, I probably would've said yes, too.

"I'm so damn excited. You have no idea." His hand rubs slow circles over my stomach, his eyes dropping to it before locking back on mine. "I love you, Lennon Harrington," he whispers. His hand lingers on my still-flat stomach, resting there gently, afraid to press too hard. "And I'm going to love this little one just as much. Promise."

A lump rises in my throat, but I manage to swallow it down. Fear? Uncertainty? Gone. All I feel is warmth, and the unshakable belief that somehow, we'll figure it out.

Wherever life takes us, whatever comes next . . . we've got this. *Together.*

SCAN HERE
FOR ALL THINGS
ROMANCE!

For the readers who enjoy their fictional
men like their drinks - spicy!

@authorcharlicotner

ACKNOWLEDGMENTS

First off—big, squishy virtual hugs for picking up this book!

Writing my very first romantic suspense novel has been an absolute rollercoaster (the fun kind, with just the right amount of screaming), but the fact that you're here reading it? That's the real thrill.

To my amazing family—thank you for your endless support and for keeping me caffeinated. To my kiddos, your laughter (and, let's be real, your well-timed interruptions) remind me why I do this. And to my other half—you're the real-life romance hero who puts up with my late-night writing sprees, wild plot rants, and general bookish chaos. You deserve all the gold stars (and maybe a nap).

A massive shoutout to my editor, Chelsea, at Represent Publishing—you've taken my beautiful mess and turned it into something truly special. Your patience, encouragement, and magical editing skills mean the world to me.

And to everyone who's been part of this journey—whether you cheered me on, kept me sane, or simply believed in this dream—you're officially my favorite.

Much love and infinite gratitude,
Charli Cotner

www.ingramcontent.com/pod-product-compliance
Lightning Source LLC
Chambersburg PA
CBHW030117310726
48970CB00004B/1303